The Unquiet Gods

By the same author

The Lion's Claw
(*the first Guy Greville novel*)
The *Titanic* and the *Californian*
An Agony of Collisions
The Sea is a Magic Carpet
Aim Straight
(*a biography of*
Admiral Sir Percy Scott)
Broke and the *Shannon*
(*a biography of*
Admiral Sir Philip Broke)
The Battleship Era
Guns at Sea
(*a history of naval gunnery*
and gun tactics)
The Great Naval Race – Anglo-German naval rivalry 1900–1914
Nelson's War
Tide of Empires – Decisive naval campaigns
in the rise of the West. Vol. I: 1481–1654

Peter Padfield

THE UNQUIET GODS

HUTCHINSON
London Melbourne Sydney Auckland Johannesburg

Hutchinson & Co. (Publishers) Ltd
An imprint of the Hutchinson Publishing Group
3 Fitzroy Square, London W1P 6JD

Hutchinson Group (Australia) Pty Ltd
30–32 Cremorne Street, Richmond South, Victoria 3121
PO Box 151, Broadway, New South Wales 2007

Hutchinson Group (NZ) Ltd
32–34 View Road, PO Box 40–086, Glenfield, Auckland 10

Hutchinson Group (SA) (Pty) Ltd
PO Box 337, Bergvlei 2012, South Africa

First published 1980

British Library Cataloguing in Publication Data

Padfield, Peter
The unquiet gods.
I. Title
823′ .9′1F PR6066.A27/

ISBN 0 09 141040 1

Set in Linotron Times
Printed and bound in Great Britain by
REDWOOD BURN LIMITED
Trowbridge & Esher

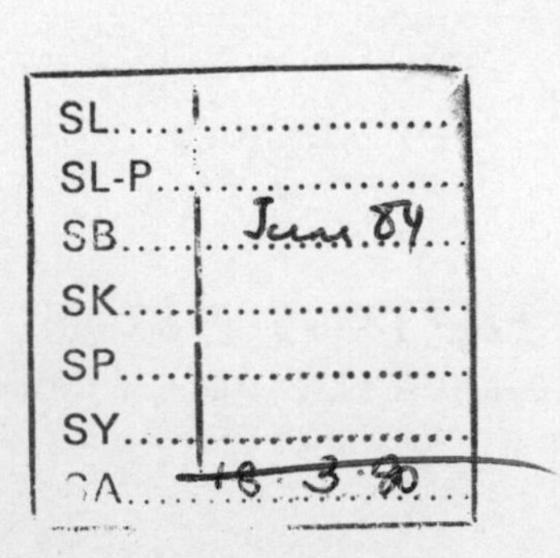

The Unquiet Gods

1

A waft of frangipani overlaying the bazaar smells recalled Guy from the timeless Indian evening. He experienced a wave of displeasure; he would soon be there.

The *ghari* creaked like an old boat and jerked from side to side, the rumble and judder of the wheels transmitting through the frame and hard, stuffed seat to his own frame. It was an agreeable sensation. He would have been happy for the journey to continue for a long while. Free of responsibility, free from shipboard routine, away from the faces that had become more familiar to him than his own, slipped from his character as first lieutenant, he was an empty vessel afloat on the warm Bombay night. But the fragrance impinged, reminding him of his destination; it was drifting from the compounds of the great houses and bungalows on Malabar Hill, and he could see their lights glimmering through foliage, winking off as shrubs or branches intervened, on and off again. One set belonged to his uncle's house. He felt the upward trend of the road and the slower, straining motion of the *ghari*.

He knew the hill well. As a midshipman he had walked it often enough to his uncle's to save a few rupees, walked up and usually staggered down afterwards blown out with such meals – he had sicked the first one up in the shadow of the bushes in the drive of a wealthy Parsee. The drive had become a private landmark; as he jogged past it now, he felt a sensation of sharp hunger, inseparable from his time as a 'snotty', mixed with an image of eclairs, ices, cream, fizz, luscious tropical fruits, greed, self-disgust.

The *ghari* swayed round a left-hand bend and he turned his head to see the panorama of Back Bay opening below; the familiar horseshoe curve of the shoreline to Colaba Point was picked out in lights, whose reflections wrinkled towards him across the dark water, and another image rose: Fran in a white evening gown. It was less distinct in detail but more painful.

He had touched her hand on just such a night while looking out over the bay to Colaba. He had succeeded in detaching her briefly from the others, the first time he had managed it, and not until the last night before sailing. He had written her adoring letters by every mail, receiving one rather cool and non-committal reply which he had read a thousand times before the ship returned to Bombay and he had asked eagerly after her.

'Fran – she got married, y'know – ' He had forgotten the name, a four-thousand-a-year man twice her age. An echo of the pang assailed him as he looked over the magical spread of lights on the water.

He wondered what outwardly demure, secretly calculating young spins his uncle and aunt had arranged for him this evening. They did their best: undoubtedly a splendid table and a fair selection of pulchritude would be provided – all that a fellow could wish. Yet the game had staled since his midshipman days. He neither wished for a lasting attachment which would divert his thoughts and energies from the service, nor could he afford to marry – and nor would he wish the lonely life of a sailor's wife on anyone he really cared for. It could only be a social game now. He needed more in the brief periods of freedom ashore.

The *ghari*-wallah shouted and turned the horse's nose into his uncle's drive. The wide lawn before the house was spread with light and shadow from the lower verandah, and he heard the hum of talk – the controlled hum of English voices floating strangely over the background noises of temple bells and tomtoms from the city, dinning cicadas, the harsh, high bark of a jackal from somewhere far away, and from above the quiet metallic rustling of palm fronds moving in the breeze. He felt a stab of dissatisfaction.

'My dear boy!' His uncle grasped him on both arms.

He grinned at the warmth of the greeting. 'Uncle Jack!'

'Hang it! Where was it this time? The Gulf!' He half turned towards his wife, retaining a grip on Guy's right arm. 'Looks uncommonly well for a fella that's bin up the Gulf – ' He jerked his head round to look at Guy again with keen eyes. 'You've some tall tales this time, I'll be bound.'

'Some rather hot ones – ' he started.

The old man let out a benevolent roar and propelled him

back towards his aunt, whom he kissed without affection; they exchanged routine greetings, she with her polite but empty smile and maddeningly even voice until, stiff-backed formalities over, she led him as he knew she would to his partner for the evening and, with the nearest to a meaningful look that she could manage, began introductions.

Her name was Miss Case. She was pretty in a straightforward, brown-eyed way without any striking features, but with the freshness of youth; he guessed that she had not been out long. Her father, also in the group, was a cavalry colonel; they usually were. Uncle Jack was wealthy beyond the dreams of his own father, and ran the Indian affairs of the great United Trading Company, but he was no more than a box-wallah to the military, and his aunt, feeling it deeply, lavished all her attention on soldiers, virtually shunning his colleagues or anyone tainted with trade. The cavalry, who considered themselves a cut above everyone, were of course her favourites.

'You are to take Miss Case in to dinner,' she finished. 'Your seats are on the left.'

Guy bowed his head.

As his aunt smiled her way to another group, he looked down at Miss Case with a cordiality he was far from feeling, asking if she had been out for long.

'About eight hours,' she replied quickly, her eyes lighting in anticipation of interest.

Her father found the response amusing. 'Don't know her yet ourselves!' The others in the group laughed.

Someone asked her how things were in England, which led to exchanges on the weather and comparisons between the winter 'at home', and the 'cold weather' in Bombay, from thence to mutual acquaintance. Anglo-India was a relatively small community for the right people and everyone knew several of the names that were bandied about with increasing verve around the circle, or if they didn't know them personally had heard of them from others; and it was a jolly, elevated group of people, inspired by certainty of their membership one with another that smiled and nodded and parted to look for their assigned partners after the butler announced dinner.

The Noah's ark procession formed in almost military style – which was not surprising – and moved slowly in an aura of meaningless pleasantries, and on Guy's part keen anticipation of the meal ahead, along the carpeted verandah. He heard the shriek of a bird outside, and imagined the freedom of the night.

Two uniformed, brass-bound chuprassies were standing guard on either side of the entrance to the dining-room; as always his aunt was overdoing it. Their dark-browed faces were impassive. He wondered what they thought of the ritual; probably it never crossed their minds to question it – any more than the guests would. It was the law and custom of the white sahibs – that was sufficient. It was also rather grand: the ladies were elegantly turned out, more consciously up-to-date than the Europe whose fashions they studied in the illustrated papers, their brilliant colours and shimmering jewellery contrasting perfectly with the stiff black and white of their escorts.

Just ahead of Guy in the procession were two well-built fellows almost as tall as himself. The one immediately ahead had a bull neck and powerful shoulders swelling the immaculate cut of his cloth. For all his restlessness Guy felt a surge of pride and kinship. He was of the master race, whose rule of this huge, strange continent was assured by the strength and gallantry represented here tonight; with such splendid men and women the Empire was guaranteed; its beneficent, civilizing influence would spread wider yet and wider – the feeling was spiritual in its intensity. He was part of a fellowship much greater than himself.

'I declare,' Miss Case looked up softly from his arm, 'their uniforms are rather splendid.'

He glanced at the chuprassies, whom they had almost reached, and smiled down at her. 'Aunt Ernest loves uniforms.' The remark would be lost on her.

'Aunt?' Her brows rose.

He was puzzled for a moment, then realized. 'You thought they were my people? Lord!' He leant closer, 'We haven't this much tin.'

'What's money?' she retorted quickly with a defiant toss of her head.

He warmed to her. 'Miss Case!' in mock astonishment. 'I believe you really have only just arrived.'

They entered the dining-room, and he steered her to the left of the long table, agleam with silver and glass, with great bowls of exotic flowers spaced down its length. Uncle Jack was standing by the head, eyes alert to detect anyone who had trouble finding their place, behind him the Goanese butler, Fernandez, resplendent as always in white and gold. His acolytes, only slightly less splendidly arrayed, were spaced around the room waiting for his command. The tablecloth was crackling white. Each setting had a name card and a painted menu standing beside crested Venetian glass.

Guy's companion exclaimed under her breath. He smiled at the schoolgirl idiom; she really wasn't a bad sort at all. He ushered her to her chair, feeling a waft of scented air as the great central punkah swung away. Certainly there were far worse ways of spending an evening; he'd experienced a number of them over the past months in the Persian Gulf.

After grace, soup plates were passed deftly and remarkably quickly under Fernandez's inexorable glance. Guy picked up his spoon, catching a quick glimpse of himself miniaturized and upside-down in the deep shine; his eyes were cold grey against the tan of his face; even at that size his nose appeared distinctly powerful. Did he really look so stern and distant?

His companion was wrinkling her nostrils at the delightful aroma. 'I do love turtle.'

Her animation was attractive; he thought he liked her a lot in a thoroughly brotherly way. Her defiant snap, 'What's money?' had reminded him of his favourite sister, Helen. It was exactly what she would have said. 'Now tell me,' he started briskly, 'what adventures did you have on the way out?'

'Well – ' she looked up at him as if pretending she had much to hide, but couldn't restrain a smile as his gaze rested on her quizzically. 'Let me see – nothing very much happened before Malta – oh, I didn't see very much of the Bay.'

'Bad crossing?'

'I don't suppose you would have thought so – '

'I'm always sick,' he said confidentially.

'But how can you bear it?'

'Not every time. It's when we're pitchforked into a big sea straight after a spell ashore that I really suffer. It doesn't last long.'

'What ship are you in now?'

'The *Dulcinea* – a little corvette – built about the time of the ark!' He stopped as he saw her eyes light in some kind of recognition, her soup spoon halfway to her lips.

'The Earl of Saxmundham,' she said with a provocative gleam.

'Old Sax!' He grinned delightedly. 'You know the Old Man?'

She sipped her soup. 'He has a reputation as something of a diehard for sails hasn't he?' She had decided to be mysterious.

He nodded. 'He don't like steam much.'

'Do you like him?'

He fixed her with a mock-stern stare. 'When you have answered my question, I shall answer yours.'

'Very well then – ' she looked at him as if to judge the effect her remark would have, 'I heard about him from your new first lieutenant. He came out in the *Peninsula* with us – ' she paused at his expression.

He gazed without seeing her, stunned by the suddenness of it. He had known they would send someone out: old Sax had told him that neither the commander-in-chief nor their lordships would authorize the promotion he had given him on Smallpiece's death. He was far too young and there were too many lieutenants with years of service kicking about on half pay. But it had been so long ago, so long since the affair at Witu when poor old Smallpiece had been brought in with arrows sticking out of him like porcupine quills. There had been so many cruises since then, and sea and desert and heat and belligerent sheiks, it was almost a distant memory. He had grown accustomed to being first lieutenant; the ship's company had grown accustomed to him.

She was staring at him.

He attempted a smile. 'What is he like?'

'Oh dear – I thought – really you looked – well, how can I possibly – he was so entirely different you see from anyone I have ever met – '

He wasn't really listening, but an image of someone entirely different from anyone she could have met formed amidst the whirling chaos of his mind – shambling like an ape, like old Smallpiece.

' – such a queer, nice man, and he was awfully good to me – but some of the other passengers – '

Another Smallpiece – undoubtedly somewhat alarming to the other passengers with his uncouth nautical language, but good to a fresh young spin on her first time out.

She had stopped talking as the soup plates were cleared away. An elderly man opposite was launching into a story evidently intended for the section of the table as a whole and, as she looked across at him, Guy too transferred his attention, thankful for the respite to collect his thoughts.

A low voice addressing him from the left made him turn his head. He had noticed her as they were taking their places, liking what he saw. She was older than he, in her middle thirties perhaps, with grey eyes and a self-contained look, a somewhat lean face in repose, and finely formed; now that she had turned her attention on him, half smiling with a low, beautifully precise, but very natural, voice he found her extraordinarily attractive. The evening held a new excitement.

'I've been longing to get a word in edgeways,' she was saying, smiling, 'my chance has come with the fish.'

He smiled.

'I noticed your nose, you see, my husband was at one time devoted to bumps and features and really you have such a very – significant nose I know he would have loved to pronounce – ' She spoke quickly and he noticed her fingers moving on the handle of her knife in an agitated way. 'I do hope I do not cause offence, but I feel we waste so much time talking of things which can have no interest for anyone, do you not?'

He smiled; a kindred spirit. 'My sentiments exactly.'

'Oh, good!' She seemed genuinely pleased. He noticed that when she smiled her mouth was slightly out of symmetry, the left side rather less mobile than the right, a charming imperfection which added in some strange way to the air of nervousness produced by her moving fingers. He received a clear impression she was strung very tight.

'But my nose can have no interest for anyone,' he said, 'except myself.'

'In itself. But as an example of the manner in which our characters are displayed in our features it is probably quite fascinating – do you not think so?'

'If it were true.'

'Then let me tell you,' she examined his face for a moment. 'No, it would be far too flattering to you, and not at all frivolous enough for the dinner table. Tell me an amusing story.'

He laughed outright. 'The Russian, the Frenchman and the Englishman?'

'I believe I have heard it.'

'Then I shall ask you a riddle.'

'No, I shall ask you one.' Her hand went to her lap and like a conjuror she produced a long white glove. 'Twenty buttons. Can you imagine? Doing them all up – why should we wear the beastly things in this beastly climate, or anywhere else for that matter?'

For the first time he noticed the hint of shadowed skin beneath her eyes cunningly concealed. She leant closer, her lips parting as if they were not quite under control. 'Do you know, I really believe we are all quite mad. It's India – we should never be here – ' She stopped in mid-sentence and deliberately turned back to her plate. Her partner seized the opportunity to reclaim her; a moment afterwards she looked down with a little gurgle of laughter and tucked the glove away somewhere.

Guy turned to Miss Case. Her brown eyes had an amused expression. He remembered the new first lieutenant, but did not want to think about him, and indicated his plate. 'What d'you say?'

'Quite delicious.'

'There can be no two opinions about Aunt Ernest's cook!' He felt almost proprietorial as he told her how popular he had been in his gun-room days when there was the prospect of several of them being invited up to Malabar Hill.

As the champagne and claret were brought round, he stole a glance at his neighbour on the left, hoping to catch her eye again, but she was engaged in conversation with her companion. Soon afterwards raconteurs took the attention of the table; the time for *tête-à-tête* had passed.

'Very quiet, m'boy!' his uncle boomed down the table after Aunt Ernest had collected eyes and the ladies had sailed off. 'Bowled out by Mrs Vaneyke, I'll be bound.' There was a roar of laughter. 'I told Ernest it was a risk, sitting you next to her; devil of a risk, I said, the boy's only just back from the Gulf.' Another roar greeted the sally.

'I'm glad *you* took the risk,' he replied, turning the laughter.

'Ah, if I were your age – ' he left the sentence unfinished, and his expression became serious. 'Any news of the *Curlew*?'

Guy realized the question was addressed to him. 'I've not heard any,' he replied. 'Why?'

His uncle's brows rose. 'You've not heard?'

'No.'

'I'm surprised you fellas haven't been sent out to look for her. Surely they *must* have told you? She's missing'. Bin missin' six months or more.'

'Good Lord!' Guy heard the port decanter arriving by him and stretched to take it. There had been something, he remembered now, the agent at Bushire had mentioned it, but almost *en passant* – no suggestion of anything serious. 'What do they think?' he asked.

'Don't believe they know what to make of it. Vaneyke's not the sort – hang it! He's strictly Queen's Regulations.'

The connection clicked in Guy's mind. He looked up quickly. 'Mrs Vaneyke?'

His uncle nodded. 'You have it. She carries it off well, I'll say that.'

'Plucky woman,' Colonel Case put in authoritatively.

'Everyone's rallying round magnificently,' said the elderly raconteur opposite, 'but what can one do, I mean to say – '

'Any reports of a hurricane?' Guy asked.

His uncle cut the end of a cigar carefully. 'Not a thing. I tell you, it's a complete mystery. Just disappeared into the blue.'

There was silence as they contemplated one of Her Majesty's sloops and a full complement of men disappearing into the blue. His uncle, evidently feeling guilty at having plunged them into thought, cut into it heartily, 'But you should be telling *us* about naval affairs, hang it!'

'I confess you've floored me tonight,' Guy replied. 'To tell the truth, I feel as if I'd strayed into the Naval Intelligence Division. I discovered earlier that my replacement as first lieutenant has arrived in Bombay.' He looked at Colonel Case. 'Your charming daughter, sir.'

The colonel's eyes widened, then he chuckled. 'You don't say so! The little minx. Had it from the first lord himself I dare say.' He looked up the table for applause.

'I gather she travelled out with the fellow.'

'Ah! It must be true.'

'No time to lose.' His uncle leaned over the table and jabbed his cigar towards him. 'Up steam and away! Before the fella finds where you're berthed.'

'The owner's up country,' Guy replied. 'I fancy he might have something to say if he came back and found us gone. He don't much care for steam in any event!'

There was a round of laughter; the Earl of Saxmundham's aversion to engines and engineers was well known even amongst the military.

'On *shikari*?'

'He took his guns,' Guy nodded.

Colonel Case addressed the table. 'You heard about the tiger at Khandala Station?'

A chorus of eager comment greeted him.

'He was in full possession of the down platform for the best part of the afternoon,' the colonel went on, looking at Guy. 'The station-master barricaded himself in and sent a telegram.' He imitated a native accent, 'Very large tiger jumping about platform. Men will not work. Please arrange.'

A roar of laughter greeted the story, which led to tales of the hunt and shooting, until at length reluctantly, they rose to join the ladies.

The whist tables were laid out in the drawing room. Guy felt bound to sit with Miss Case, although he hoped that chance would bring him to Mrs Vaneyke's table before the night was out, and he found himself looking over towards her frequently. It was absurd. In all probability he would never see her again after this evening. Yet the more he reminded himself of it, the more important it became to resume their brief and enigmatic acquaintance. She was different; of course she was tense, and now he knew why, but he wondered if that explained everything. She could hardly blame India for the disappearance of her husband's ship. Perhaps the constant worry of not knowing had driven her to irrational convictions and a dislike of the country itself. Yet her eyes gave no hint of imbalance. She was a contradiction; her eyes were steady while her lips and fingers moved involuntarily; she professed no use for convention, yet dressed in the height of fashion – twenty-button gloves! She sounded at one moment like one of the earnest 'new women', at the next she was provocatively frivolous. Her husband was the devil knew where, yet she had turned the full glow of her attention upon him. Evidently she had a reputation, that was clear enough from Uncle Jack's remarks – they had been in questionable taste, he thought.

He looked across again to where she sat, fanning herself gently with her cards; her lips, he suspected, quivered for a moment, but otherwise she was perfectly poised, seemingly without a care in the world. Had she seen him glancing at her too often for fractionally too long?

She could have no interest in him. Her behaviour would be the same towards all men; it came of the compulsion attractive women felt to prove to themselves they were irresistible. She would collect slaves as he collected butterflies, but without his scientific curiosity. Perhaps she did have some curiosity; she had found his nose interesting.

After the first rubber, which he and Miss Case won, they moved to the next table, where they found her father and Aunt Ernest. The move was in the right direction, towards Mrs Vaneyke, but as she was rising evidently about to move on too, no ground was gained. He tried again to convince himself that it made no difference – a few more minutes near her, a few conventional remarks about the hands played, he would be no nearer a place in her real life, her very real anxieties.

He tried to give full attention to the run of the cards, but found himself losing track of trumps, let alone the other suits, and he played by instinct, navigating through a fog, and only aware of the siren light outside the circle. It did not seem to matter: the pack was with him. Aces and court cards fell over themselves to take their place in his hands; he had only to place them on the table one after another. Miss Case laughed happily, but as the points mounted she stole increasingly frequent glances at her father, who had become ominously silent and was taking deep draughts of brandy and soda.

Suddenly she was there, standing, resting her hand lightly on Aunt Ernest's shoulder, with that slightly asymmetric smile and low voice, 'I mustn't interrupt your game. Really!' as his aunt looked up. 'It has been *the* most wonderful evening, but – please!' and as his aunt rose. 'I must go, I shall be perfectly all right. I have asked Fernandez to send for a *ghari*. You must go on with your game.' She motioned Guy and the colonel to resume their seats, then touched her forehead lightly. 'I have not been sleeping well.'

'My dear—' Aunt Ernest rallied quickly to distress. 'You should have told me. You must go home.'

'I do not want to cause a fuss.'

'Nonsense.' His aunt looked round at him, then quickly thinking better of it turned to the colonel.

'Allow me – ' Colonel Case said promptly. 'We should be delighted to take you home on our way.'

'I wouldn't think of it,' she replied firmly. 'I insist, Colonel, that you sit down and finish your game.'

Guy said, 'We have finished. And it would be an honour if I might escort you, Mrs Vaneyke.'

His aunt's smile thinned momentarily, and she looked at the colonel, who turned to Guy, brows lifting.

'I have to be on watch at midnight,' he lied. 'I shall have to leave soon in any event.'

'In harbour?' the colonel muttered disbelievingly.

Mrs Vaneyke closed her eyes momentarily and touched her head again; his aunt put an arm around her shoulder and together they moved towards the doorway.

The colonel grunted, 'She don't want to make a fuss, by George!'

Guy bowed to Miss Case, 'I have enjoyed meeting you. I hope I may see you again before we leave Bombay.'

She smiled. 'Please remember me to Mr D'Arcy-Green. Your new first lieutenant,' she explained.

'Of course.' He turned to the colonel, who was rootling around in his pocket for money. 'I insist we call it even, sir. My luck was bound to turn.'

The colonel hurrumphed, and looked at his score card; they had not finished the game, but it was clear that once they did so the rubber would be over, and he would owe several rupees. 'Very well,' he said after a moment, letting the money jingle back into his pocket. 'Very sportin'. Another time then.'

'I hope so, sir. Good night.'

The colonel lifted his glass and, half turning as he left, muttered, 'Your luck *has* turned young fella!' His eyes gleamed above his puce-veined nose and trim, greying moustache.

Guy made his apologies and farewells to Uncle Jack, and after making a general bow strode to the doorway and out to the verandah. Mrs Vaneyke was half lying in one of the long

Bombay chairs with his aunt fanning her with a cushion, and Fernandez shouting at a peon to fetch a punkah.

'Is there anything I can do?' he asked.

'Do please go back to your game,' Mrs Vaneyke said weakly. 'This is really too stupid. Ernestine, you must send him away.'

The final words were barely audible, and his aunt took him aside and said anxiously, 'I think perhaps you ought to call at Dr Armstrong's on your way. The *ghari*-wallah will know the house.'

He nodded and, taking the cushion from her, started waving it up and down over the motionless form on the chair; he was soon joined by the peon with a fan. Mosquitoes buzzed in, attacking his neck and even his moving wrists.

After what seemed a long while they heard the sound of hooves from the roadway, and soon afterwards a *ghari* swung into sight around the shrubs at the end of the drive, a peon running in front gesticulating. Mrs Vaneyke was helped to her feet and down the steps, and he handed her up into the carriage while Aunt Ernest gave the driver instructions in a low voice. Then he jumped in and sat down in the far corner. Aunt Ernest slapped the horse's flank. They were off.

'Thank you again Aunt Ernest,' he called. 'A capital evening – even by your standards.'

'We shall see you again before you sail?'

'Of course.'

They were away, bowling down the drive towards the darkness of the road and the great spread of stars above the palms. He could scarcely believe it. There she was, with her white gloves and her slim gown that changed colours with the lights, and the diamonds at her throat. She was draped picturesquely over the corner of the seat with her legs stretched out and her arm jogging off her lap to the cushion as they swung into the road. Her eyes were closed. Was it his imagination, or was she sliding slowly down and off the seat? Surely she hadn't fainted, and she could scarcely be asleep. Yet undoubtedly she was slipping.

'Mrs Vaneyke – '

There was no reply, but he saw her shoulders trembling.

'Mrs Vaneyke!'

She was either sobbing or laughing, but at least she had stopped her slide. He leant nearer and looked into her face.

Her eyes were open. She was looking up at him, shaking with merriment.

'Mr Greville!' she said at last.

He sat back in his corner. 'I assume you have recovered.'

She eased herself up. 'I knew I could count on the Navy!' She smiled. 'You did very well to cut out the gallant colonel. That would have been tiresome.'

He gazed at her silently, wondering how she could be so frivolous.

Apparently reading his thoughts, she said, 'D'you know my husband is also in the Navy, Mr Greville?'

He nodded.

'They call him "Ivan the Terrible".'

He smiled, hoping the darkness would conceal it. 'Everyone has a nickname.'

'What is yours?'

'I haven't reached that level yet. I'm plain "Number One" to most – ' a shadow passed across his mind. 'Tomorrow I shall be even plainer "Guns".'

'A gunnery specialist?'

He nodded.

'You must be clever.'

'Extraordinarily.'

'I thought you were.'

He smiled at the tone of her voice.

'My husband is extraordinarily clever too. But really, it's rather awful what they call him.'

'It's a compliment. There's nothing the jacks admire more than a terrible man.'

'They call me the terrible Mrs Vaneyke.'

He laughed. 'Who do?'

'*They* do,' she gestured with her arm as if to take in the whole of Bombay. 'D'you suppose that is a compliment?'

'Very likely.'

'I think you are wrong.'

'I am seldom wrong,' he smiled.

'On this occasion I think you are.'

He bowed his head.

'Wrong,' she added decisively.

They jogged in silence for some minutes. The wailing sing-songs of India came from the city. On the right the lights of

Colaba were still visible. Back Bay shone under a half moon. The evening could not have been more perfect, his partner could not have been more fascinating, but he found himself growing increasingly exasperated. She should have been anxious, even in despair. He would be happy to be her knight, to comfort and reassure her the *Curlew* was bound to return; ships of the Royal Navy did not disappear without trace; her husband had probably made some large diversion to an out-of-the-way corner of the ocean where there were no telegraph stations – chasing slavers perhaps, or lying in wait for gun-runners. The engines might have broken down; if he were to leeward of the monsoon he might spend weeks beating back to civilization.

Again she seemed to read his thoughts. 'You disapprove of me.'

'Why should I?'

'That is not an answer. Where is this idiot taking us?'

'To Dr Armstrong's.'

She started up. 'Kindly tell him I wish to go home!'

'Are you sure? Would it not be wise – '

'You *clever* men!' She sounded suddenly tired. 'Please – take me home.'

'Very well.' He leaned forward and shouted to the driver, '*Ne mungta Dokitor Armistrong*.'

The Indian turned and grinned. 'Ah, Dokitor Sahib – goin' mos' speedily kiweek – '

'*Ne mungta Dokitor Sahib!*'

The grin fell away.

'*Memsahib koti jow!*' he shouted. 'Cumballah Hill!'

'*Memsahib koti!*' The grin appeared, wider than before. '*Atcha, Sahib!* Oh, goin' mos' speedily!'

Guy turned. 'I fancy his English is on a par with my Hindustani.'

She made no response.

After a moment she said, 'Do you have doubts, Mr Greville?'

'Frequently.'

'Yes. You have imagination, have you not?'

'Now and again.'

'Please don't laugh. My husband has imagination.' She stared ahead. 'He is also a very thorough man. I'm afraid that the two do not mix. It is difficult to be thorough if you have doubts, and you can hardly help having doubts if you have imagination.' She looked at him as though she were asking.

'Very thorough doubts, I dare say.'

It was supposed to be light-hearted, but he thought before the words were out that it was not the thing to say. She took it seriously, leaning forward with more animation than she had displayed since she had been in the *ghari*. 'But that is quite right. His doubts are extraordinarily thorough.' She gazed at him.

He wondered what kind of doubts, but, before he could say anything, she went on, 'He is extremely clever, you see, and extremely imaginative. Worst of all, he is extremely thorough – that is his trouble.'

He thought he detected a shriller note entering her voice, controlled but only just. She was appealing to him for help, but he was out of his depth. And how should he, a lieutenant, quiz a senior officer's wife about her husband's doubts?

'They say I married him for his money and his position,' she went on more quietly, 'of course they do. Perhaps they are right. But I married him for more than that. I knew he would go far. I wanted him to go far. I married him for what he *would* do, not for what he was – certainly not for what he had. A fool could have had that.' She stopped and gazed at him again.

The trees and shrubs on either hand gave way to shanty dwellings and the discordant music was suddenly closer. White bundles at the side of the road stirred briefly to life at their approach, and several naked boys ran up alongside with their palms outstretched for pice. He felt for his winnings at the first table and tossed out several annas, one after another, listening to the boys shout and scramble behind. A smell of buffalo and dung and spices, bad drains, warm dust, assailed his nostrils.

'Do you know East Anglia?' she asked.

'Not really.'

'Why should you? I remember so well the first time I visited Bickley Hall. In the autumn. The elms and sycamores were turning, and the paths were carpeted with brown and gold leaves. The bricks of the old house glowed in the sunshine.' She turned. 'Bickley has been in the Vaneyke family for nearly three hundred years – It was afternoon. The sun was thin. There was an autumn nip in the air. Robbie came out to meet us with his brother, Harry. They had just been round the estate, their faces were so red and fresh-looking. Robbie was at the Admiralty then. He did very little work, he said, but that wasn't like him at all. Well, he got away to Bickley nearly every weekend. He was wearing a Norfolk jacket and his boots were muddy. He was inclined to stoutness even then, and he looked such a thorough John Bull! The next day he took me for a ride with him; I think it was really to show me all the gadgets he had invented. They were everywhere. There were gates you could open without leaving the trap, automatic feeding machines for the poultry, there was scarcely anything he had not thought about and then designed some machine to make life easier – he had even made an elastic contraption to fit over the cashier's fingers at the local bank, to help him count out the notes. Can you imagine?' She turned to him again. 'You have never sailed with my husband?'

'No.'

'All his ships are like that. That is how he first crossed swords with the Admiralty. There is so much tradition. It is like a dead weight. Do you feel that?'

He thought of Saxmundham, of his excellence as a sailing ship seaman and the practical uselessness for all war purposes of the skills in which he was training his officers and men, brilliant though it all was. 'Absolutely' he replied.

'Robbie has no tact. He has imagination, but no tact. He is clever and so arrogant! He *cannot* see things from anyone else's viewpoint.' Her shoulders jerked involuntarily. 'He is very tiresome. Have you tried arguing with an Admiral?'

'Lord!' He laughed.

'Robbie has. And he always wins arguments. That is his trouble really.'

'With Admirals?'

'That is why he is out here', her tone rose, 'and why I am out here. That is why he is still waiting to be made up to captain. He is very near the top of the list, there are only passed-over men above him now.' Her arm tensed on the seat between them. 'I despise them all. They are afraid of imagination. Brains they can cope with but, if you have imagination besides, you are a pariah!' She spat the words out. Then her expression changed; her lips lifted in the curiously imperfect smile. 'You must not let them suspect you, Mr Greville!'

'I believe I have succeeded so far.'

'Yes, you will. You are more flexible. Robbie is an oak – ' she paused, examining him.

'An alder?' he suggested.

'A fir. A Russian fir that has grown up with *lots* of space – straight and tall as a mast. You will make your way. You have imagination and energy. Robbie is a stubborn old English oak.'

'An oak with imagination.'

'That is his trouble.' She looked out as the *ghari* slowed. 'We are nearly there.' She leant forward and called instructions to the *ghari*-wallah in what sounded like fluent Hindustani, then turned back to him. 'I have so enjoyed talking with you, Mr Greville. It was so good of you to see me home.'

'It has made my evening,' he said and, hearing the conventional ring, added, 'you *know* it.'

She smiled, changing chameleon-like into her previous character. 'At all events your reputation is made now.'

'Driving with the terrible Mrs Vaneyke!'

'It is dangerous.'

'Exceedingly!' He meant it.

The road was bordered by bushes and trees again as it had been at Malabar, and as they turned into her drive there was the same heavy scent of tropical shrubs. The roof of the bungalow was white in the moonlight, details of the leaves and flowers and twining tendrils of plants climbing the lattice around the verandah were picked out in the same sharp, cold light. There was no sign of life, but a dog started barking from somewhere near at hand, taken up by others, near and far until there was a chorus answering each other. A native voice began shouting shrilly.

'How queer it all is,' she said. 'I believe, you know, I shall never become used to it.'

He jumped down and handed her out. She leant very close as she stepped down, then quickly rose on her toes and kissed him on the cheek, a brush of her lips, a perfume.

'There!' she smiled and turned towards the steps up to the front entrance.

He followed so that he could rouse the servants for her, but she stopped him. 'I do not want to be bothered with anyone. Besides, they'll all be drunk and sleeping it off by now. Much better to leave them.'

'As you wish.' He hesitated. 'I hope I may see you again before we sail.'

She studied him for a moment. 'I have decided to pay a call on the commander-in-chief, so perhaps there will be no time – '

'You're going to Trinco?' His heart leapt.

'I must let the Admiral know about Robbie.' Her eyes looked tired suddenly.

'But so are we – when we come out of dock!'

She smiled. 'What a very small world it is! Well then – until we meet – in Ceylon. Good night, Mr Greville. I am so grateful.'

He waited until she had reached the top of the steps and turned and waved once before he strode back to the *ghari*, elated by her confidences. It was not until he was on the road back to the city, and reliving her farewell, with its promise of a future meeting at Trincomalee that he began to wonder what she had meant about the Admiral. Surely the Admiral would let *her* know – or tell her what he didn't know. What could she tell him? Undoubtedly she knew the *Curlew* was missing, it was the talk of Bombay and had been implicit in the attitude to her that evening – and her own attitude of bravely concealed distress. He smiled. Undoubtedly she knew. Yet she had giggled at her ruse in escaping from the house and, when she had talked to him of her husband, her anxiety had been about his character and career, not his whereabouts. Her use of the present tense had been unequivocal. It had been as if her concern was with what he was doing, not where he might be.

The *ghari* was very empty without her.

2

Guy was not surprised at the length of the defaulters' parade. From what he'd heard already that morning, Grant Road had enjoyed an unusually lively night. They looked a sorry bunch; one or two were scarcely able to hold themselves upright. He imagined how Saxmundham would dispose of them with a few scornful phrases, ending inevitably in an allusion to the disgrace they had brought on the *Dulcinea* – *their* ship. He wondered if any would attempt to take advantage of the Old Man's absence. They should know him by now – but always before his authority had been buttressed by Saxmundham's gigantic shadow. He tucked his telescope deliberately under his arm and faced them.

The first half-dozen were easily dealt with, leave-breakers who accepted a week's 'blacklist' with philosophic resignation, but the next man, Davis, was hostile. Guy knew him well as a gun captain, a smart fellow with a ready Welsh tongue who had licked his crew into first rate shape, and was inclined, given the opportunity, to do the same for his officers. He had evidently been in a rough-house: his left eye was closed and bulging yellow and blue, and his upper lip grossly swollen. His right eye was bloodshot and belligerent as the master-at-arms read out the charges – offering violence to the ship's police, swearing at them and resisting arrest.

'What have you to say, Davis?'

'I never did –'

'Sir!' The master-at-arms barked.

Davis's swollen lip drooped officiously. 'Sir!'

Guy's blood rose. He snapped, 'Call the first witness!'

The first was the master-at-arms himself; he described how he had proceeded with a party to Grant Road after reports of a disturbance caused by the ship's company at a drinking saloon. He had seen a *ghari* being driven fast down the road and had recognized Davis driving it. He had shouted at him to stop, but

Davis had sworn at him and continued on down the road at speed. Another *ghari* coming up behind was being driven by another member of the crew, Halliman – next in the defaulters' queue, Guy saw. The master-at-arms party had succeeded in bringing him to a halt, but shortly afterwards Davis was seen bearing down upon them from the other direction, standing up in his equipage, shouting, 'Charge!' and using insulting language, aiming to run them down. Some of the party had scattered, Halliman's horse had shied and run away, causing a collision between the two which broke off the port-side front wheel of Davis's *ghari*, throwing both him and Halliman to the ground. The story was confirmed by the next witnesses, two ship's corporals.

'Do you still deny it, Davis?'

'Yes, sir.'

'Where are your witnesses?'

Davis half turned to indicate the men behind him in the line. Guy sensed trouble. There were five of them, including Halliman. 'What are the charges against the other men, MAA?'

'Sir! The same charges sir! Halliman was driving the second *ghari*. Smith, Mann, Hobbs and Ricardi was inside it, sir.'

He turned to Davis. 'And these are your witnesses?'

'They got a right to speak, same as the jaundy 'ere –'

'Silence!' Guy yelled.

Davis's swollen lips moved wordlessly.

'I shall decide who has the right to speak.'

A hush had descended over the ship. Even the bluejackets at cutlass drill nearby seemed momentarily stilled. Guy noticed a figure appearing through the entrance port on the other side of the deck; he had curled blonde hair, check suiting with an exaggerated cut-away coat, a large yellow and blue cravat; behind him came a coolie with a wooden packing case. Concentrating on a way to outflank the direct conflict of testimony he foresaw, a part of Guy's mind registered surprise at the appearance of such exaggerated elegance aboard.

'Davis and Halliman were driving, MAA. Where were the *ghari*-wallas?'

'Runnin' be'ind, sir.' The master-at-arms added, 'Screamin' like banshee, sir!'

Guy turned back to Davis. 'What have you to say to that?'

The man cocked his head to the side in a quick way he had.

'We 'ired 'em,'

'Sir!' the master-at-arms shrieked.

'Sir!' Davis yelped in a passable imitation.

Guy saw Halliman's lips twitch. Controlling himself with an effort, he said, 'You stole the *ghari* Davis –'

'No, sir –'

'You stole the *ghari* from its owner, drove it recklessly without thought or consideration and wrecked it in collision with your partner in crime.'

'We was 'urryin' to the bunder, sir, so's not to miss the barge – it were an accident.'

'An accident caused by your thoughtless behaviour. You realize, Davis, you represented not only your ship last night – not only the *Dulcinea*' – he paused – 'but you represented the Empire.' He gazed at them each in turn. 'You were the representatives of our dominion over this country.' He waved his free arm to indicate the vastness of the charge. 'The Viceroy in his palace, you – Davis and Halliman – in Grant Road. What can the natives expect from you two? To be cheated, their means of livelihood stolen and wrecked, their persons insulted?'

Davis stared at him, his thick lips turned down in a sneer; suddenly he tossed his head and projected a spurt of tobacco-stained spittle expertly into the scupper.

Guy felt the blood pounding at his temples again. He waited, motionless until he could be certain he would have full control of his voice. Davis's bloodshot eye widened. The silence closed in, shutting the two of them off from the others.

Guy turned to the master-at-arms, and heard himself saying very quietly, 'Place them on the captain's list – to await his return in the cells. And Davis' – he swung on the shocked gun-captain – 'I shall have the carpenter make up a new wheel for the *ghari* and you shall be escorted ashore to present it to the *ghari*-wallah in person with suitable expressions of apology. You will have time between now and then to compose a speech. If it proves unsuitable to the occasion you shall find yourself spending a good deal of your watch below on the quarter-deck. Thank you, MAA.'

He returned the salute crisply, and strode off, sickened. Images rose to mind of his own behaviour as a midshipman – of a donkey race through the bazaar, scattering stalls and produce without thought for the feelings of the poor devils, the stuff of whose livelihoods lay broken or crushed on the road; he remembered his great friend Ablewhite, 'the gorilla', holding a terrified punkah-wallah suspended over the edge of a top storey verandah with one hand because the wretch failed to pull the cord in time to the National Anthem. Here were Davis and his companions, many of whom had been cooped up in the ship for more than three months, kicking over the traces and enjoying more or less innocent fun at the expense of a couple of rascally *ghari*-wallahs who were undoubtedly used to jack and his ways ashore, and letting fly at the unloved ship's police in their brief exultation of freedom – they had far more excuse than his own class. Yet he had thought fit to lecture them on responsibility! And, when Davis had reacted in the only way he knew, kicked them down to the cells –

'I say –'

The elegant visitor was standing in his path with his hand outstretched, an amused expression on his face. His eyes were prominent green below sandy brows, his nose thickish and flattened, his mouth decidedly heavy; the chief impression, though, was of the crisp and beautifully curving brim of his hat, the brilliant azure and yellow of his cravat, held by a pearl pin, and a vast expanse of white pique shirt-front. The officer of the day, Geoffrey Stainton, was hovering, but the visitor gave him no chance at introductions.

'A first-rate show!' His voice was as affected as his turnout. '*Bravo* I'd say!'

Stainton tried to say something, but the visitor cut in, 'D'Arcy-Green.' He thrust his hand out, 'Reginald D'Arcy-Green. Pleased!'

Guy felt the rings on the man's fingers as he took the hand and introduced himself. The name was familiar; he tried to think where he had heard it, as the newcomer went on, 'First lieutenant. I dare say you've been informed?'

He experienced the same sharp stab of dismay he had felt when Miss Case had broken the news the previous evening. D'Arcy-Green seemed unaware; his attention had wandered towards the hammock nettings at the side, his eyes travelling slowly along the line of the bulwarks towards the fo'c's'le.

'By Jove!' he exclaimed suddenly. 'How old *is* she?'

The tone put Guy on the defensive. 'She'll outsail any ship

on this station.'

'*Sail*. Of course! Tell me – the owner's up-country, they say?'

Guy nodded.

D'Arcy-Green waved his be-ringed right hand towards the open engine-room skylights and the base of the yellow funnel visible beyond the awning. 'Does he ever? I'm told he don't.'

Guy was disarmed by the confidential air; he smiled. 'Not much.'

'Capital!'

Stainton arched his brows and grimaced at Guy before making off quietly towards the accommodation ladder, while D'Arcy-Green headed back for the entrance port, then turned beckoning to Guy to follow, putting an arm across his shoulder as he caught up. 'I say it's providence – hanged if it ain't!' He held up his gloved left hand and unbent the fingers one after the other, 'First, my aunt, bless her, kicks the bucket, leaves me some of her tin – second, they send me here as number one – third, the owner's a sailing man. Well! What d'you say?'

Guy had no idea what he meant, but undoubtedly beneath the affected front, D'Arcy had an engagingly frank manner. 'The Lord moves in mysterious ways,' he replied.

'You *have* it!'

They reached the entrance port, where there were several packing cases. D'Arcy slapped the largest with the glove he held and addressed the quartermaster, 'Let's have the lid of this fellow awf.'

The quartermaster tore his gaze from the yellow and blue cravat, and looked at Guy, who nodded.

D'Arcy-Green waved his glove towards the other cases. 'I spent yesterday in the bazaar. Heaven knows where my portmanteau is – or my shirts for that matter. If the P & O have their way they'll end up in Hong Kong. You never saw such bobbery at Ballard Pier.' He started imitating a *babu*, 'This very ticklish business, sahib; many, many passengers wanting baggage, damn customs always saying, "What is this case? What is that case?" But we have hopes, sahib, be patient.' He ended an excellent imitation, 'I was not!'

Guy laughed. 'We can fire a shot across the *Peninsular*'s bows if she tries to sail.'

The new first lieutenant started back with exaggerated alarm. 'Guns! My dear fellow –' he shook his head. 'No smoke, no coal, *assuredly* no gunpowder. Look here,' he glanced quickly round at the quartermaster, who was prizing up the lid of the case, and said in a stage whisper, 'This old tub's my ticket for promotion, don't you see?'

Guy had seen it some seconds earlier. The connection between D'Arcy's previously incomprehensible three proofs of providence became clear. They were in for a housemaiding cruise – paintwork, brightwork, brasswork, burnishing – with no smuts to besmirch the spanking decks. The windfall from his late aunt would allow D'Arcy to purchase sufficient enamel and gold leaf to turn the old corvette into a peacock for the Admiral's inspection. He wondered how Saxmundham would take it, how indeed he would take to the peacock, D'Arcy-Green.

'Then I shall have time to catch up with my reading,' Guy smiled.

D'Arcy's brows rose for a moment. 'Bless us, you must be the gunnery jack! My dear old fellow' – he glanced along the deck at the stubby 64-pounders – 'quite the reverse. You'll be surprised what can be done with these pretty fellows.' His expression became speculative. 'Museum pieces undoubtedly – capital! A touch of fantasy – restrained colour – what d'you say? I'd appreciate your views.' Then, noticing that the quartermaster was waiting with the lid off the packing case, he motioned him to lift out the contents. 'Handsomely now! She'll cost a few rupees to replace – hanged if she won't!'

Carefully the quartermaster drew out two carved wooden hands followed by the arms and the rest of a large intricately decorated figure of a Hindu deity – very evidently female. She was in a seated position with eight bent arms radiating from her torso, each grasping an object of some kind. Her expression was ferocious and in the centre of her forehead was a single vertical eye. Parvati in one of her guises, he thought, perhaps Kāli, the black.

'Ain't she splendid?' D'Arcy breathed.

'Splendid!' he agreed. The carving was exquisite.

'She's yours.'

He looked round quickly. There was no trace of humour in the very open green eyes. 'Saint Barbara,' D'Arcy explained, evidently disappointed with Guy's reaction, 'the patron saint of you gunnery fellows, ain't she?'

Guy looked at the goddess again, and back to the new first lieutenant's face. The thing was absurd, yet he was evidently serious – more than that, enthusiastic. He studied the figure. 'It's uncommonly fine workmanship.'

'It?' D'Arcy interrupted. '*She*, my dear fellow, *she*. But ain't she just the absolute cheese? Quartermaster!'

The quartermaster peered over the sensuous fingers of the carving. 'Very 'andsome, sir.' His tone was flat.

D'Arcy stared at him. 'Put her away.' He turned to Guy accusingly, 'I thought a gunnery man would appreciate her.' His eyes were hurt. Beneath the studied exterior, extraordinarily, he was vulnerable.

'I'm delighted,' Guy said. 'I'm certain the gunner will also be delighted.' He thought of the gunner's grim and powder-scarred face, and imagined his biting comments.

'Well then?'

'To tell the truth, I don't recollect Saint Barbara having quite so many limbs.'

'Great heavens, Greville!' D'Arcy glanced towards the quartermaster's bent figure, and turned to move away from the entrance port, taking Guy's arm as he did so. 'It won't take a second to hack a few arms awf. What else displeases you?'

'Since you ask me –'

'Imagination' D'Arcy cut in. 'That's all you need, Greville, hanged if it ain't!' He stopped suddenly as if indicating the subject closed until Guy was able to take a more constructive view. 'When d'you like me to take over? What about nine o'clock tomorrow mornin'? And by the by' – he thrust his hand into an inside pocket. 'you may like to peruse my chitty.'

As Guy took the Admiralty headed paper and read the few lines signed by the secretary, his disappointment surfaced again, sharpened by prickings of apprehension he had begun to feel as D'Arcy talked. It was impossible to imagine Saxmundham taking to such affectation. And D'Arcy, for his part, was so ingenuous; his hurt at the rejection of Saint Barbara would be as nothing to the shock when the Old Man rejected him and his grand schemes.

'Pukka?' D'Arcy's green eyes were very prominent.

Guy handed the letter back, fighting down rebellious thoughts. 'I'll have my man move my traps.' He motioned towards the companionway.

They were met at the foot of the steps by the old paymaster, about to come up. He looked at Guy over his *pince-nez*; his lined face wore a more than usually worried expression.

'Bad news, Pay?'

'I fear so.' He looked at D'Arcy, his gaze lingering a shade longer than necessary before turning back to Guy. 'There is a communication from the Admiralty –'

'Bravo! They've remembered us.'

'They have particularly remembered you, Number One. They are sending out a Mr D'Arcy-Green –'

Guy gestured towards the new first lieutenant. 'Allow me –'

The paymaster's eyes grew larger behind his glasses.

D'Arcy thrust out his hand. The rings flashed in the light from the companion. The paymaster grasped it, temporarily lost for words.

After a moment he said, 'There is also a confidential letter' – he looked from one to the other – 'from the commander-in-chief.'

D'Arcy's eyes were wandering appraisingly over the gun-room flat. 'If you feel it should be read before nine o'clock tomorrow I suggest you let Greville have it.'

Guy slit the envelope with his finger and extracted the letter; it had an embossed ship's crest at the top and was headed, HMS *Sovereign*, Trincomalee.

Sir,

1) The *Curlew*, Commander Vaneyke, has not been heard from since sailing from Muscat in May. All Her Majesty's ships on the station and the ships of the Royal Indian Marine are requested to seek out information as to her whereabouts from whatever sources may seem to offer prospects of gaining intelligence. Masters of dhows and local craft, and fishermen are particularly recommended. It is surprising how observant many of these men are, and no opportunity should be passed up of sending an officer accompanied by an interpreter, if available, to examine any craft met with in the normal course of cruising. Reports of sightings of one of Her Majesty's vessels, even if of doubtful veracity or accountable by the presence of another vessel known to be in the area, should be followed up and full enquiry made.

2) After leaving the dockyard, you are to proceed to Trincomalee, calling on your way at the principal islands of the Laccadive and Maldive groups and making enquiry of the islanders. To our

knowledge, none of Her Majesty's vessels on this station has been in the islands for several months, and should you hear of one you are to spare no exertions in gaining a knowledge of her proceedings and if possible her identity. You are to follow up any indications of her subsequent movements, reporting your course of action as soon as it may be convenient, but not making a detour to a telegraph or mailing station if by so doing you lessen your chances of discovering the missing vessel.

It was signed: E. R. Bousfield, Vice Admiral, Commander-in-Chief.

Guy handed the letter to D'Arcy. The paymaster, who had evidently been examining his face while he was reading, dropped his eyes, then looked up again with a studied blank expression, and said, 'The captain can be reached in a case of urgency.'

'That will not be necessary.'

The watery eyes moved to D'Arcy.

Guy relented. 'What d'you know of Vaneyke, Pay?' The old man was a walking encyclopedia of service lore and personalities.

His expression sharpened immediately. 'The *Curlew*? Yes, I heard it yesterday while ashore – she has been discovered?'

Guy shook his head.

'Ah,' he paused and, as Guy said nothing, went on, 'no, I never did meet Vaneyke. Of course, one heard. He was at one time very confidently expected to reach the top – oh, the very highest posts.'

'He *was*?'

The old man's brows lifted, 'Oh yes. But it was the bottle.'

It was Guy's turn to look surprised.

'An extremely violent man,' the paymaster went on, 'when in drink you understand. It wouldn't surprise me greatly if that turned out to be the cause of the trouble on this occasion.'

'There you have it,' D'Arcy interrupted, waving the letter towards the paymaster. 'Ivan the Terrible! But where are we going to find the terrible fellow?' He handed the paper to Guy, slapping it with his glove as he did so. 'Providence again. It follows me, hanged if it don't! A few weeks in the islands on our way – made to order. You'll not recognize her, Greville, by the time we make Trinco – no more shall the Admiral.'

Guy was stung by the implications. 'Dodging about among the reefs. We'll need to raise steam you know.'

D'Arcy's gaze sharpened for a moment, then he laughed and put a hand on Guy's shoulder. 'My dear old fellow, he *don't*! You told me so yourself.' He looked for confirmation to the paymaster.

The old man rubbed the side of his nose, looking from one to the other with a slightly puzzled expression. 'There was one occasion –'

D'Arcy turned to Guy, 'I'm not saying she ain't in absolutely tip-top condition – I could see that the minute I set foot aboard.' He started moving towards the open entrance to the ward-room, leaving the paymaster in mid-sentence. 'But I say what I mean, and what she lacks my dear old fellow, is *art*.' He repeated the word slowly to ensure that Guy understood. 'No blame attaching to you. Positively you have no cause to take offence – but I'm cursed, Greville, with an artistic fibre. I can no more restrain myself than I can fly. Besides' – he dropped his voice confidentially – '*promotion*! It's now or never. I'm not exactly just "out" you know!'

Guy's annoyance vanished, replaced once more by apprehension. How could he warn the fellow about Saxmundham? Above everything the Old Man detested pretence. And if he were warned what could he do? From his bleached, curled locks to his patent boots and spats, from the pitched extravagance of his vowels to the wave of his glove, he was a pretence that had crystallized into something as real as whatever it had replaced. It would take as much for him to turn into Saxmundham's idea of the thoroughgoing naval officer as for his servant to transform himself into a gentleman.

They entered the ward-room, and he caught sight of a pair of boots up on the arms of one of the leather chairs, and the long form of Heighurst, lieutenant of marines, stretched between them and another chair drawn up by it. He was reading an old copy of *The Graphic*; there was a picture of Gladstone in the House of Commons on the front. As he heard them Heighurst dropped the magazine to his chest and stared up with an unnaturally dull expression, sharpening at the sight of D'Arcy. He brought his hand up to smooth the end of his moustache.

Guy started introductions. D'Arcy took over in his usual fashion, while Heighurst swung his legs to the deck and stood, facing him. 'I'm delighted you've arrived.' Guy looked at him sharply, and the marine returned the glance with his flat pale green eyes as he continued, 'Poor old "Guns" here – dreadfully overworked.'

'Overworked be damned!' Guy said, annoyed.

D'Arcy turned to him, his supercilious expression vanishing as it did when his interest was engaged. He looked concerned.

Heighurst broke the short silence. 'D'you know, these Japanese fellows 'ave become ashamed of their oriental looks. They've taken to 'avin' their eyelids nicked – it makes 'em the proper shape.'

Guy glanced at *The Graphic* on the chair. 'No one would accuse you of overwork.'

'One keeps abreast. I mean, if we was to meet one of these fellows,' he looked at D'Arcy, 'they might seem just like you or me.'

'I trust not.' D'Arcy said with a trace of self-deprecating humour.

'I remember,' Heighurst continued after the briefest of pauses, 'I went aboard one of their Nipponian cruisers in Singapore some while back – a smarter little tub you never saw in your life, taut as a bottle. We were most taken by their gunnery jack, a strapping fellow, six feet if he was an inch!' He leant forward and lowered his tone. 'On making discreet enquiries we discovered his secret – roast beef!' He held up a hand at their expressions, 'And not without the trimmin's either.'

'Were his eyelids nicked?'

'It did not appear so. Nor could the poor chap disguise their colour. Splendid fellow, nevertheless. Seemed to know everythin' there was to know about Kipling. It put us at something of a disadvantage.'

D'Arcy appeared not to be listening; he turned suddenly to Guy. 'Take a few days awf, Greville – directly we're in dock. What d'you say?'

Guy stared at Heighurst, not troubling to conceal his annoyance, but beginning to wonder if the man had not been right; perhaps he did need 'a few days awf'. Perhaps it was the heat building up, or more probably D'Arcy himself with his schemes for transforming the ship – *his* ship now, damn him – and the trouble that he could see ahead. A few days off was exactly what he needed, or a few weeks. He realized suddenly that he had lost all interest in the *Dulcinea*; he wished only to be away from her and allow D'Arcy his fancies and Saxmundham his sailing evolutions – forget them and damn them all! He would go ashore with Heighurst. Heighurst was one of the best fellows he had sailed with; he hardly knew him better now than when they had first met, but he knew his worth and his steadiness. He never changed. The searing heat of the Persian Gulf had failed to shake his confounded off-hand manner. His eyes, like his blood, were cool, green ice. As he looked they returned his glance with the merest hint of conspiracy.

He turned back to D'Arcy. 'I'll let you know tomorrow morning – one minute past nine.'

'Capital!' D'Arcy's thick lips lifted.

Guy sensed that he was relieved; no doubt he would find it easier if his predecessor were out of the way at the start.

Heighurst turned to pick up *The Graphic*, murmuring something about a spot of shooting in the hills.

Uncle Jack was a different person on his own. There was none of the striving for effect and jollying people along that marked his party performances; he was good-humoured and genuinely interested, even anxious to listen. He seemed to take to Heighurst at once, laughing at his laconic drolleries. Aunt Ernest was evidently impressed with the marine too, and not simply because he came into her category of 'Army'; his mixture of precise formality and deftness of phrase made instant appeal to the opposite sex.

'And how long shall you be staying?' she smiled.

Guy said, 'We had thought – that is, Heighurst likes to shoot things.'

'And you like to catch things,' Uncle Jack cut in. 'Yes, by Jove!' He turned to Heighurst. 'Have you seen the butterfly collection?'

Heighurst lifted a brow. 'I did hear something –'

Aunt Ernest laughed, 'Of course, you must have heard all about it. I think sometimes Guy cares for little else. But do come and sit down.'

'Yes, sit you down.' Uncle Jack motioned them towards the long, cane-bottomed chairs in the verandah. 'What d'you say, not too early for a peg and a cheroot' Without waiting for a reply, he turned and called, 'Boy!' Aunt Ernest smiled as if they were being very wicked, and excused herself, and the old man came and sank into a chair beside them. There was a moment of quiet. The evening enclosed them. The noises from the city seemed far away; the breeze, delightfully scented from the flowers twined about the verandah trellis reminded him of Mrs Vaneyke.

Perhaps it reminded his uncle too, for he turned and said, 'I'm glad to see you back again, by Jove! I have to confess, we rather wondered' – there was a gleam in his dark eyes – 'after the manner in which you left us on the last occasion.'

Guy remembered her sliding off the seat in the *ghari* and laughing. 'The way you speak of her, she might be a witch.'

'Hang it!' The old man slapped the flat teak arm of the chair. 'Ain't she! If I were your age –' He turned to Heighurst and said confidentially, 'Did he mention her?'

'Not a word.'

'Ah! That's deserving of remark, wouldn't you say so?' He stopped as a servant appeared on noiseless feet. 'First things first. Brandy and soda?' They nodded and he gave the man instructions, adding something afterwards in Hindustani.

'I've told him to fetch Anthony for you,' he went on as the servant departed. 'A first rate boy. He'll see to you. I'll stake my life on it. Now' – he sank back with a grunt – 'have you anywhere in particular in mind?'

'Has the tiger been seen again?' Guy asked.

'At Khandala? By Jove!' He looked at them in turn. 'Why not? Only four hours by train. Grand country.'

Guy looked at Heighurst. 'D'you fancy a tiger?'

'Is that the very best you can do?'

They laughed.

'Khandala it is then.' Uncle Jack said decisively. 'Your Aunt Ernest can work out the *bunderbuss*,' he turned to Heighurst, 'your programme. She knows the times of all the trains – an extraordinary woman. And Anthony will find you a *shikari* if one's to be had. To tell the truth, I've not heard of that tiger since you were here.' He turned to Guy then, at the approach of a small Indian with a white coat and bare feet, said, 'Speak of the devil!'

The man salaamed to them each in turn. His eyes were wide

apart and intelligent, his expression eager.

'Anthony,' Uncle Jack said, 'this is Lieutenant Greville, and' – turning – 'Lieutenant Heighurst. They are going up to Khandala for a spot of shooting.'

Anthony's face split in a wide smile. 'Oh, tiger, sahib, most awfully big tiger, many gentlemen going.'

'I dare say, Anthony – you will look after these two gentlemen. The dak bungalow will be best.' He turned to Guy, 'There is an hotel, but it's the most frightful pot-house. You'll be better off in the bungalow. At all events, Anthony knows the ropes.'

'Oh, yes, sahib, I am most exceedingly happy –'

'Good. They will be taking my new rifle, Anthony, the Ariel, and a twelve-bore.' He turned to Guy. 'I prefer a twelve-bore firing a bullet. It's as true as a rifle at sixty to eighty yards, and a good deal lighter to carry.'

'That's very good of you.'

'Nonsense! I'm stuck down here. I'd much rather they were used.' He turned back to Anthony. 'You'd better rub the guns down with paraffin oil tonight, and don't forget plenty of vaseline. And take a picnic basket for the train – and my tiffin bag.' He looked round at Guy. 'A canvas bag I invented for rough shooting. You'll find it has everything you need – compartments for sandwich cases, several knives, bottle compartments, corkscrew – I think you'll find it answers well enough for a night shoot. Both kitted out?'

They nodded.

As the butler appeared with glasses and a silver cigar box on a tray Anthony took the opportunity for voluble protestations of happiness at seeing to the wants of the two lieutenant sahibs. Uncle Jack cut him short, and he salaamed and left, still smiling.

'A first rate fella, but he'd stand there jawing all night if you let him.'

Heighurst placed a brandy glass on the arm of his chair and leant to take a cigar from the box. 'Not a man-eater, by any chance?'

'Good Lord, no! There'd be the most frightful to-do if he were. No, he's just an old fella that fancied the shelter the station afforded one afternoon. I don't hold out much hope to tell the truth. As Anthony said, a number of sportsmen have been out looking for him.' He took a gulp of brandy. 'But Khandala's a pleasant spot – set you up no end. There's an interesting cave temple not far away – you should go and see it – originally Buddhist, now Hindu.' A new tone came into his voice. 'Vaneyke used to go there. He was pally with a Brahman, told us about it one night at dinner – fearfully metaphysical!' He glanced at them in turn. 'Did you know him?'

They shook their heads and he went on, 'I shouldn't say so, perhaps, but it's my opinion he wasn't quite – At all events latterly he was distinctly queer. Difficult to put a finger on it.'

'Drink?' Guy asked.

'No, no, he never touched it.'

'I'll be damned! I heard it was the bottle more or less put an end to his prospects.'

'That may be so. Never knew him before he came out here. But he'd mended his ways by then, I'd stake my life on it. Never touched a drop. What's more he never ate flesh, did you know that?'

'A vegetarian?'

'Absolutely. And a strict one. It caused your Aunt Ernest a headache or two I can tell you. They came up here several times when the old *Curlew* was in Bombay. As you know your aunt has a fondness for the service –' There was a funny look in his eye, as if asking sympathy for his wife's social hunting. 'Dhal curry and nuts, good Lord! But he looked strong enough – a big fella.' He shook his head. 'He really was a loose kind of fish.'

'You're talking as though he were dead and gone, Uncle Jack.'

'Of course, the *Curlew*'s bound to turn up somewhere. '

There was a thoughtful silence. Guy's mind returned to the *ghari* ride with Mrs Vaneyke, the quick little jump she had given as he bent to hand her from the *ghari* at the end, the perfume as her lips touched for a second. She would have left for Ceylon by now. He wondered where she was. What could she hope to accomplish? What could she tell the Admiral about 'Robbie'? He pictured her anxious look as she said it, grey eyes turning their full attention on him at dinner, 'I've been longing to get a word in edgeways.'

'I never knew whether he was joking,' Uncle Jack's voice broke into his thoughts. 'I rather fancy he wasn't. He would not take meat, he said, because he didn't like the thought of possibly eating his old grandmother.'

'Reincarnation,' Guy said.

'You have it.'

'The Brahman!'

'Hang it!' The old man turned to Heighurst. 'I see he's not slowed down.'

'He's left me behind,' the marine replied.

'I had a start,' Guy said.

'His father,' Uncle Jack explained, 'my brother as it happens, not content with the Church into which he was ordained, meddles in oriental religions.'

'Hardly meddles.'

'I knew him before you, young fella!'

Guy smiled. 'You should see him now.'

'Very much the country parson, I don't doubt it. But when he was your age my boy – you're very like him, did I tell you that before? He was never satisfied with anything anyone told him, no more than you are. He had the brains in the family, no question about it.' He pulled at his cigar and stared reflectively into the night as if wondering at the very different roles life had cast them in.

Guy looked at Heighurst. 'Hindus believe in reincarnation. It's the central thing you might say – like our Trinity.'

'As mutton?'

'As anything living. They make no distinction. The form you take in your next incarnation depends on what you do in this life, whether you move up or down the scale.'

Heighurst breathed out smoke, watching it rise. 'It don't make much sense. Take a good Hindu, moving up every time – that's correct?'

'Every deed has its effect, yes.'

'Very well. He comes to the top as a Hindu, then where does he go on to?' He leant forward and tapped ash off his cigar. 'He becomes an Englishman don't he?'

Uncle Jack put his head back and roared.

'Of course he do,' the marine went on. 'Then what does he learn?' His brow lifted ironically.

'It's a neat way out,' Uncle Jack said, still chuckling. 'I always thought it a most fearfully tiring prospect, travelling on and on for ever.'

'Being good,' Guy said.

'Hang it!' he snorted. 'That's the deuce of it!'

Guy felt a vague sense of disappointment. He would have enjoyed a philosophic discussion. Yet with Heighurst that was impossible. He was not unintelligent; he was sharp as a rapier when it came to any practical problems, and he had just put his finger unerringly on the great conflict between eastern and western belief – a conflict that raised endlessly fascinating questions. Yet in the very act he had reduced it to the level of his own cynicism. It would be interesting when they reached Khandala to visit the temple and talk with the Brahman. He would take Heighurst there and force him to participate, damn him! Of course it would be no use. The man had a polished shell which deflected the shafts of the outside world as effectively as it concealed his own thoughts and emotions. Nevertheless, it would be interesting to talk to the Brahman, and perhaps find out more about Vaneyke. It was scarcely possible that the man really accepted reincarnation – that would imply a rejection of the Christian Church. An image flashed into his mind of Mrs Vaneyke next to him at the dinner table. He saw the shadowed skin beneath her eyes, felt the tension and heard her precise accents 'It's India – we should never be here.'

He turned to his uncle. 'You think Vaneyke was serious?'

The old man gazed at him. 'Had you ever met the fella – Oh, yes, I fancy he was serious enough. But you know what it is with these clever fellas – you can never tell if they mean it or if it's done to tease.'

'He is a vegetarian.'

'Indeed he is.' His uncle looked at him intently. 'I fancy you're right. If you're driving at what I think you are.'

The old man stared out into the night. Guy saw a single bright star through a gap in the leafy trellis. He moved his head slightly and it disappeared, back again and it was there, tauntingly out of context.

'He was a terrible fella at the dinner table,' Uncle Jack went on. 'He took a positive delight in taking the opposite view.' He laughed. 'I wondered your aunt went on inviting him. Nervous as a cat, she was – each time. He broke all the rules, you see. And one couldn't argue with the fella – even if one wished to, and heaven knows it wasn't the place. He simply would not allow anyone else a view – or a brain in their head come to that.

He got away with it somehow. One had to like him, I suppose. Hang it, he was – *pukka* – always himself.' He chuckled. 'He was something of a catch as a matter of fact. Ivan the Terrible!'

'And the terrible Mrs Vaneyke!'

The old man laughed. 'I fancy you may know more about her.'

'She was talking of *him* most of the time.'

'Yes, yes, I dare say.' His expression had become serious. 'You may think I'm speaking after the event, but I fancy he changed. I noticed it on the last two occasions he came up here. I can't put a finger on it, he always was a queer fish, but he seemed not so much queer as different – as if he'd somehow left us.'

'Left you?'

'It's the only way I can put it.' He seemed to search for words. 'As if he were no longer any part of us,' he gestured with his arm, 'out here.'

'You cannot believe he has left literally – sailed off?'

'I hardly know what to believe my boy.' He shrugged. 'It was my impression – one develops a nose for that sort of thing out here.'

He was interrupted as Aunt Ernest appeared and announced that a cold supper had been laid out in the dining-room; his manner changed immediately.

'Well, enough of that!' He turned to Heighurst. 'To business!'

'I've heard about your table, sir,' Heighurst replied crisply. 'To tell the truth,' he swung his legs to the floor and rose easily, 'the shootin's just an excuse.'

Uncle Jack roared and clapped a hand on his shoulder. 'Any friend of Guy's –'

'Yes, indeed.' Aunt Ernest smiled with more warmth than Guy had often seen her display.

As they entered the house Uncle Jack turned back to him and said quietly, 'I should not have said so much.'

'I'm glad you did.'

'You understand – '

'I'll keep it under my hat. And you can rely on Heighurst.'

'It pays to know your man.' His brows lifted over a meaning look.

The conversation had not been as casual as it had seemed.

'Thank you, Uncle Jack,' he said.

'There's more to this than meets the eye. If you find him, my boy – take care.'

Guy wondered if the *shikari* could have been mistaken. After examining the scuffled ground about the kill, and the tail marks the big cat had made before leaping, he had pronounced it a panther – an unusually bold and powerful one since it had attacked a buffalo – but certainly a panther, and had promised its return that night. It was disappointing after their hopes for a tiger. Apparently the tiger had left the area though.

He scanned the darkening trees beyond the path across which the buffalo lay, its neck twisted unnaturally in death, flies clustering about the bulging eyes. A tiger would have been worthwhile. He imagined Saxmundham's face had they returned with a prime head and skin. A panther hardly merited sitting up all night. Heighurst would not agree of course. For himself he would rather have a day's cricket. His eyes and wrists were starved of the weight of the willow, the sweet thump of the ball, timed and middled. He would have given a lot to have played against the Parsees, and he would have done so if the *Dulcinea* had arrived a few days earlier; his reputation as a forcing bat had followed him out to India – somewhat enlarged on the way! The Parsees had won, as they always did. It would have been a challenge.

This waiting game was a poor substitute. They might spend hours numbed or cramped, keeping still and silent inside the circle of bush the *shikari* had fashioned into a hide for a brief thrill of danger if the beast appeared; as it had been agreed that Heighurst would have the first shot, he might not even fire.

He felt the marine nudge his arm, and looking to the right he saw several dingy pariah dogs just out of the trees, sniffing the dusk. Cautiously they moved along the path towards the dead buffalo, the leaders swinging their heads sideways from time to time as if to reassure themselves they were not alone, increasing their pace as they neared the carcass. Soon they had reached it and were ripping at the belly and hindquarters with excited yelps and grunts, dipping and jerking their teeth sideways, muzzles spotting with blood. One backed out with straining legs pulling at something, and others jumped in snarling to take it. He averted his gaze from the disgusting sight.

He heard the temple bells from Khandala ringing to drive away the spirits, and nearer and high to his right a hammering noise like an exaggerated woodpecker. The branches which he had been able to distinguish only a few moments ago were merging into the darkness of the trees beyond. The sky still had a pale band in the west, but night was rushing in and strange, disjointed noises were starting in every direction. Something else was changing; the snuffling, nuzzling sound of the pariah pack had ceased and they were moving off as rapidly as they had come. He felt Heighurst stiffen beside him and heard the click of his safety catch drawn back, a faint, urgent whisper from the *shikari* to his left, Anthony drawing in his breath. He strained his eyes across the clearing which the path afforded. There was nothing to be seen. Whatever the pack had sniffed was either some way off or using the scattered cover skilfully. He moved his head slowly, scanning to the left. The darkness seemed to close by the second. He felt his arms tingling and resisted an urge to swing his gun with his eyes.

Then they heard it – a distant snorting something like a horse only rougher.

'He coming!' the *shikari* whispered.

The snorting ceased; there were warning calls and small noises about them as if every creature in the vicinity were aware of the killer's approach and far away to the left in the direction of the great rock known as Wellington's Nose a colony of birds seemed to be shrieking, 'Did y'do it? Did y'do it?' Something pale flew from the trees just ahead, gliding silently off and merging into the night. Still there was nothing to be seen near the path. He wondered if the cat would circle the area before moving in. If so it must get wind of them. He could feel the faint breeze against his right cheek. He wished it were a tiger hunt; they would have built a proper *machan* up in a tree. Down here on the ground in this hurriedly extemporized hide, the cat had only to sneak up and spring from the side or the rear to be amongst them. Its night senses were so much better than their own. It was said that a panther turned man-eater was a far more dangerous proposition than a man-eating tiger.

A shadow moved near the edge of the path some twenty yards away. He stared. The movement continued, and a shiver passed down his neck and spine. It was a longer shape than he had expected, heading slowly in towards the path from the left; he could imagine but not see the deliberate drawing up of one leg after another, belly scraping the ground, tail flicking, eyes fixed on the dead beast, ears cocked for the slightest noise. He found himself wanting to draw in more breath, and controlled it lest the animal hear the sound. He didn't look to see if Heighurst had spotted it; he was certain they all had; he could feel the silence about him.

By now it was quite dark, and even as the cat moved closer it was impossible to distinguish much more than the stealthy movements it made. It reached the hindquarters of the carcass and seemed to sniff or lick the flesh. He wondered if Heighurst would risk a shot; there was no detail to aim for and the stiff back legs of the buffalo were raised across part of the target. It would be a fortunate shot indeed if it reached a vital spot. Heighurst evidently thought so too for he did nothing. After a minute or so Guy realized the cat was moving away. It had raised itself to its full height, and he saw it for a moment in outline, a long beast with a deep chest and powerful quarters, then it was gone, a light patch on its tail flicking away into the darkness. He found himself letting out a long-drawn breath.

They waited for a minute or so in silence. The *shikari* whispered, 'All right sahib, coming back later.'

'A fair size,' Heighurst breathed.

'Splendid,' Guy agreed. His legs were aching, and he eased himself by degrees into a new position, hoping they would not have to wait too long for the next appearance. The mosquitoes had found his range and were biting even up his arms beneath his shirt; some insect had managed to work its way through his socks and was gorging on his calf. He tried to squash it with his other leg, cracking a branch as he did so. It was an overrated pastime.

He thought of the brandy in Uncle Jack's tiffin bag, and whispered to the *shikari*, 'Is the coast clear?'

'Coas', sahib?'

'May I move?'

'Oh yes sahib. He coming back. Maybe one hour, maybe two –' Guy imagined the shrug and sideways motion of his head.

He turned to Heighurst, 'Not too early for a peg?'

'Do you think I should've had a shot?'

'I'm glad you didn't.'

He felt the marine moving, and heard him unscrew the top of the bottle, a gentle plash of liquid against tin, and reached across to take the mug.

'Unpleasant-looking brute,' Heighurst said as he slid the bottle back into the canvas.

The neat brandy flared down Guy's throat. He realized that the animal and bird sounds were normal again; they were reassuring. He took another gulp, his mind beginning to wander back over the day – the tonga ride along the Poona road past the ramshackle, thatched shelters that served the villagers as homes, men in loose white dhotis with what looked like towels wrapped around their heads, hanging down at the back and another towel around their neck, women slapping dhobi against boulders by the sides of the numerous tanks, others washing pans or filling chatties from the same water, and on the road oxen, with heavy brass ornaments swinging from their foreheads and thick wooden yokes depressing their necks, drawing carts on which their scrawny drivers sat chanting without tune or rhythm.

They had left the tongas after five or six miles and walked up to the cave. The air had been like crystal; despite the heat it had been an exhilarating climb.

It was cool in the temple, and very dark at first after the glare outside. He had been struck as always by the contradiction between the simplicity, even asceticism of the Brahman priests and the voluptuous carvings. A thin woman in a red sari had been walking round and round, silently round and round under the arched wooden roof, touching the caste mark on her forehead at every circuit; her withdrawn expression provided another contrast with the naked sensuality of the idols.

He had asked one of the priests if she were doing penance.

'How do I know what is in her heart?'

Encouraged by his excellent English and benign expression, he had asked him if he knew the Brahman whom Vaneyke had visited.

He had smiled and said that it was possibly himself.

'He is a friend of mine,' Guy lied.

'And now you are looking for him.'

'How do you know that?'

The priest had paused for a long time, so long that he had wondered if he were going to speak again. 'He was troubled,' he said at last. 'His mind was troubled with questions. I told him that no man can answer these questions. It is only through belief that they cease to trouble.'

'What questions?'

The priest had looked at him, and he had the impression from the shrewd gaze that his lie had been unmasked; no friend of Vaneyke's would need to enquire.

'The questions all men ask.'

He had searched back through the conversation on Uncle Jack's verandah. Vaneyke had taken a 'positive delight in the opposite view' and 'one couldn't argue with the fella – he simply would not allow anyone a view.' Here he was, though, questioning the Brahman. He had not said quite that; he had said Vaneyke's mind was troubled with questions. Disputing the Brahman's own beliefs?

Seeing carvings of elephants in stately procession along the wall beyond he had remembered suddenly that this had once been a Buddhist temple. Buddhists and Hindus shared the same belief in reincarnation, based on the immutable forces of *dharma* bearing life on through its continuous transmigrations, the impersonal agents of the universal order. Consequently they set the same value on all life, animal or human. Where the Buddhists differed radically from the Brahmans was in their denial of a first cause of the universal order.

'He cannot believe in one God,' he had ventured.

'With him, it is not belief or doubt, for him everything is reason. There is nothing that will not yield before his reason.'

'The Creator cannot yield to reason.'

'For him there is no Creator, no Creation.'

'No beginning and no end. This is the question that troubles him.'

'I do not believe it troubles him any longer. When he came to say goodbye, he had resolved the question.'

'He said goodbye?'

'Yes.' There was an inscrutable expression in the priest's eyes.

'And did he mention where he was going?'

A smile lit the round face. 'That is a question that will surely yield to reason.'

They had been interrupted by a little boy running to the Brahman, who had lifted him to his arm and introduced him as his son. The boy had stared with appealing, dark eyes, then turned to say something to his father. 'It is a simple question he asks,' the priest smiled. 'He wishes to know if you can make a paper boat like the other Englishman.'

As they were about to leave the temple the priest had come up to him. 'There is something that may help you. You have heard of the Jains – I think you are better informed about our beliefs than many – they had a saying about the ladies you know. They likened them to lamps burning along the path to hell.'

'How very true!' Heighurst had said.

Guy puzzled again over the inference. His first thought had been that Vaneyke had perhaps become entangled with a woman who had induced him to leave his wife. But that didn't lead far. Then he had wondered if the Brahman had meant Mrs Vaneyke. Certainly she had acquired a reputation in Bombay; she was exceedingly attractive and had probably led many a fellow some way along the path to the everlasting flames – it was difficult to conceive of a more alluring lamp. Perhaps her behaviour while he was away at sea had provoked his search for reasons?

As he groped for a solution he realized that all he had heard about Vaneyke held the inference that it was some change in the man himself rather than an outside cause or accident that lay behind his disappearance. His wife had set off to tell the commander-in-chief something about him – what? Uncle Jack sensed the man had already 'left them'; now the Brahman had guessed Guy was looking for him and implied that he knew where he had gone: 'That is a question that will surely yield to reason.'

Reason – Buddhism – the two went together. Could it be that he had gone to the great stronghold of the clergy of reason, to Ceylon?

Mrs Vaneyke had set off for Ceylon because the commander-in-chief was at Trinco. But why should she travel in person when she could write or cable easily enough? What could she have to say that could not be set down on paper? He had a strong feeling that he was close to the answer, but tantalizingly could not find the question. Why, after all, if Vaneyke had sailed for Ceylon, should he disappear? It would be difficult with the naval base at Trinco on one side and the great commercial port of Colombo on the other side of that not-very-large island to conceal a man of war and her complement. Why on earth should anyone wish to?

He felt a nudge and wondered if he had dozed off, he had such a vivid impression of saffron-robed monks against luxurious Sinhalese forest, and a high conical mountain above, which he recognized as Adam's Peak, on the topmost point of which the Buddha had left one of his footprints.

The scene had changed since the panther's visit. The moon had risen and painted a fairyland of stiff spear grass and silver leaves and branches over a patchwork of darkness; the legs of the buffalo were raised like old grey posts, and the twin barrels of his express shone with a cold lustre. They were pointing up at an angle; his left hand had dropped away into the bush, and as he withdrew it cautiously he felt the skin scraped and torn. It was strangely quiet all around. He stared into the forest beyond the path and saw why, stopping still with his hand among the branches, his heart thumping like a steam piston. The panther was sitting, blending into the shapes of moonlight beneath the thinning trees some fifty yards off. Its head was round like a domestic cat's, its expression similarly deeply serious, its eyes glowed unwinking. He was struck by its size. From this distance its chest and shoulders appeared as broad almost as a small ox at a prize show, its legs as thick as trunks. The minutes passed. The panther continued to sit in silence, occasionally moving its head, arrogantly surveying its domain. Guy could hear Heighurst's breathing, long and steady, and in the distance, sometimes near, sometimes far, the weird native chanting and drumming. Somewhere in the direction of Khandala a donkey brayed, and after it several dogs started barking. They seemed a long way away. He began to wonder how much longer he could hold his unnatural position, but he had to. A movement, even the flash of light on the gun barrels might alarm the beast and they would not see it again – the long discomfort and bug bites would be wasted.

How long it was he couldn't tell – twenty minutes, half an hour. Just as he thought he would never be able to straighten his legs from their cramped position, and his arm must drop, the beast rose and growled; the sound was startling in its menace. It stood for a minute or so reverberating with the low warning, then turned and moved away and became lost in the trees, although they heard it still.

Guy eased his position quietly and took a grip of his gun. The beast could not have got wind of them, but its behaviour was uncommonly cautious as if it had sensed their presence. He wondered if they would see it again.

Heighurst evidently had the same thoughts, for he said, 'He seems to know we're here.'

The *shikari* whispered, 'Coming back later, sahib –'

Guy wondered if he said the same thing every time. He pulled out his watch and manoeuvred it to catch the moonlight, surprised when he saw that it was not yet nine o'clock. It felt like midnight. It was the change of air, no doubt, and their scramble up to the cave temple that afternoon. He must not allow himself to drop off again. He thought of the extraordinarily sharp image he had had on coming to and wondered what Vaneyke could be doing in Ceylon. Taking himself up to the Temple of the Tooth to dispute with the Buddhist priests! But how and why should he contrive the disappearance of a ship and her whole complement?

Something touched his shoulder, claw-like and sharp. An image of the panther seized him and he froze, every sense sharpened in horror. He realized it was a steady pressure, much too light for the cat, and began to turn his head cautiously; something knocked against his ear and he felt a draught and saw a spread of white feathers as a large bird rose, as startled as himself.

He had scarcely recovered when the growling started again in the distance. He eased his finger over the trigger of the express and tried to make himself comfortable while there was time. The growling drew steadily nearer, allowing him to estimate the position of the beast, so that he was able to pick up the movement in the darkness under the trees at comparatively long range. It came on without pause or attempt at concealment this time, still sending out the reverberating warnings, moving with a beautiful rippling rhythm, the spots on its sleek coat interchanging with shadows from the moonlight. He recoiled from the thought of killing such a perfect creature.

It reached the buffalo and sank down, ceasing the growling and evidently about to start its meal, but then rose suddenly, and making a detour around the head of the dead animal started towards the bush in which they were concealed. Guy felt the trigger pressure under his finger and wondered how long Heighurst would leave it. His own position was slightly better for a shot to the heart as he could see something of the left side of the beast. Heighurst would be looking almost straight into its eyes.

The twelve-bore went off deafeningly close. The air filled with the roar of the beast. It seemed to sag for a split second, then hurl itself into the air towards the hide. Guy had an image of snarling teeth and eyes shining as he brought his rifle up instinctively, firing one barrel on the swing. There was a crash of undergrowth behind to the right and he glimpsed another bounding motion like a dappled wave rolling away. Then there was silence. He felt his legs trembling.

They waited a long time. The silence continued. Heighurst turned to the *shikari* and said softly, 'Coming back later?'

It was a relief to smile.

'Oh, no, sahib! Not coming back. Finish! Most certainly finding him in morning – going little way quick, quick, quick – pht!' He made a gesture to indicate the beast expiring.

Guy hoped it would be quick. He wondered where his shot had gone. No doubt, if the *shikari* were correct they would find out in the morning. He rose, stumbling a little as his leg refused to untwist itself. The others rose too and stretched, then they started working their way cautiously out of the bush. He felt an absurd remorse; it had been such a superb animal; it seemed a tremendous waste. He heard the high bark of a jackal. The moonlight was cold and hostile.

3

The *Dulcinea* was out of dock by the time their week's leave was up. Guy wondered how he would find D'Arcy and what changes he had made. He was glad to see the familiar shape of the little ship as they sailed towards her in the whaler, but was seized with a recurrent empty feeling at his lost position. Since his time as first lieutenant had ended he realized how much it had agreed with him, how hollow it would all seem now.

'He's wasted no time,' Heighurst said, gazing towards the ship.

A sound of hammering struck clearly over the water; whole strakes of the stern had already been laid bare of paint, and there were stages over the side along the length of her on which the hands were sitting, chipping or scraping away. Guy saw that a spring had been led to the cable to swing that side away from the sun which was becoming fierce. The masts, yards and funnels had already received the treatment; they shone a brilliant yellow. The top of the slim funnel had been picked out in a band of black, and Saxmundham's racing green separated by the thinnest strip of white. The yard-arms were white with gilt tips, and the upper five feet or so of the t'gallant masts were white surmounted by shimmering golden orbs, flashing shafts of sun as the ship moved on the water. Above the main was the representation of a figure, also gilt; it appeared to be a man holding a long pole. He realized it was a lance. Don Quixote! Keeping an eye on his *Dulcinea*. A touch of fancy indeed! But all in all she looked a picture above the partly stripped hull. The boats dancing at the booms were also sparkling white with bands of Saxmundham's green around their gunwales.

'I hope, for his sake, we have a fair passage,' he replied.

'I foresee storms when the owner returns.'

Guy thought of his earlier apprehensions. Somehow in the morning light, with the wind driving ranks of waves before their boat, and the corvette looking as pretty as a yacht against the green slopes of the further shore, they seemed exaggerated. D'Arcy was keen. Saxmundham would like that. As for his manner, after a week or so it would scarcely be remarked. And D'Arcy's use of the Saxmundham colours was sure to please the old man – besides he was really an engaging character beneath it all. It would be a shock at the start nonetheless. He thought of the rings flashing on D'Arcy's fingers, and smiled.

'It may prove interesting.'

'Decidedly.'

He was about to say that he thought D'Arcy was tough and would be no easy meat for Saxmundham, but he thought they ought not to be discussing him while the midshipman and hands might hear. Instead, he said, 'I dare say Old Sax's temper will depend on the size of his bag.'

'I trust rather larger than ours.'

Guy had an image of the leopard springing over the hide in the moonlight, the picture of power and harmony in motion, and wondered again what had become of the splendid beast. They had not found its carcass the next morning, and even the offer of a reward to the villagers had failed to produce a sign of it. It was difficult to imagine missing at the range at which they had fired, and the bullet from Heighurst's twelve-bore should have stopped an elephant. He hoped it had not dragged itself away to die slowly. If that were the case it was odd the *shikari* should have lost the trail of blood. He wondered as he had many times whether an unconscious aversion to killing such a noble animal might have interfered with his aim. He had had a perfect angle under the left shoulder at six yards or so, and he remembered the sights on target as he swung; he had pressed the trigger instinctively – had he instinctively hesitated? And why only one barrel? He heard the beast's roar of rage and saw the flying coat of spots. They would never know.

He turned to the midshipman, Aimes, at the tiller, and nodded towards the ship. 'We shan't recognize her soon.'

The lad grinned. 'Wait till you get aboard, sir.'

He raised his brows.

'It's pandemonium!' Aimes's expression suggested that it was an interesting kind of pandemonium. 'The bo'sun's in two minds whether to laugh or cry. You never saw so much gold leaf. He keeps it in the spirit room and issues it each morning like soap. The old chief's taken to his bunk.' The words tumbled out eagerly. 'The yarn is he's bribed him to use the black gang.'

'Steady! Who's bribed whom?'

'Dolly – D'Arcy-Green, sir.'

'*Lieutenant* D'Arcy Green.'

'Yes, sir, Lieutenant D'Arcy Green has bribed the chief with crates of whisky – so it's said. He's using the firemen on deck at all events, and the chief's not been seen this week.' He grinned delightedly.

Guy looked at Heighurst. 'We appear to have missed the fun.'

'You haven't missed it, sir, it's just beginning. The captain's been recalled.'

'Recalled!'

'Yes, sir, you haven't heard? The most frightful *burra* stink. They're using the "cat" – in the *Curlew*, sir – and there's a number one, full-scale search on for her.'

'The "*cat*"!'

'Headlines in the papers, and the Admiral's off his head.'

'Steady on, Aimes. Headlines?'

'In the London papers, sir. Captain Bligh sails again – all that sort of rot.'

'Why the London papers?'

'One of the subs wrote home. His people got in touch with the Admiralty.' Aimes raised both arms to indicate a considerable explosion. '*Boom*!'

'The cat's not been used these twenty years,' Heighurst said with more interest than was his wont.

Guy cut in, 'If the fellow wrote home, they must know where he wrote from.'

Aimes's expression cooled, and he thought for a moment. 'She may have sailed since then, sir?'

'No doubt.' The search area would be narrowed considerably though.

'It's the Laccadives and Maldives, sir, where we have to look. At least that's what's on the tapis.'

'I see.' Their destination had not changed. Either it was not known where the letter had been posted – which seemed inconceivable – or the *Curlew* had been in or near the islands. He thought of his conclusions about Ceylon; both groups were near enough. He wondered if the islanders were also Buddhists. Buddhism hardly squared with the 'cat' though. He had been on the wrong track. He thought of Mrs Vaneyke and tried to imagine her feelings when she heard.

'Is the captain aboard yet?' Heighurst asked.

'No, sir, but he's expected later today.'

'We shall be sailing then.'

'In the morning – if the captain arrives.' Aimes grinned. 'It's pandemonium, sir.'

'Seems to suit you at all events.' Guy said. He couldn't free his mind of Mrs Vaneyke and what she must be feeling, and how he was going to miss seeing her again if the search in the islands delayed them long. It might even lead them elsewhere. 'Come on!' he said roughly, indicating the tiller. 'I'll take her.'

Aimes handed over with a slightly startled expression, and moved forward.

Heighurst lifted a brow. 'They believe in a floggin' every now and then, these Buddhists of yours.'

'Only marines,' Guy snapped, remembering the enthusiasm with which he had told Heighurst of his guess about Vaneyke, and feeling foolish.

'My guess is the fellow's a Hindu,' Heighurst went on. 'One of these fakirs. You've seen them to be sure. Sleep on nails and whip themselves within an inch of their lives. Bless us! Vaneyke's just givin' his merry men a few pointers. Afterwards they'll be able to manage it for themselves.'

'I don't suppose they find it so diverting.'

'Religion ain't.'

'There are more things in heaven and earth, Horatio – '

He tried to think what it was Heighurst had said a moment ago that had made a connection of some kind. It had gone though.

They were closing the ship; it was time to point away under the stern. He cautioned the hand on the sheet and pulled the tiller up. The whaler heeled as she came round. The men on the overside stages looked down briefly as they passed, and he saw that some were shouting remarks to their neighbours above the din of the hammers – about his return perhaps. They would anticipate some coolness between him and the new man! Perhaps they were simply remarking on the return of the officers preparatory to sailing on the search for the *Curlew*. He remembered Davis and the other men he had sent to the cells, and felt a stir of guilt. They would have been baked down there all this time – and driven mad with the hammering.

The sail sagged and shook as the bulk of the ship shielded it from the wind, and the next moment a back eddy took it from the other side. The boat rocked. He leaned inboard and nodded to the sailor standing by at the halliard; the canvas flagged as it dropped. Aimes helped to gather it in. Guy brought the boat's head sliding along the gangway, and at the last moment gave the tiller a little push; the stern swung in, touching with the barest shiver. It was a satisfying feeling.

Stainton was standing inside the entrance port as they reached the top of the gangway and raised their hats to the quarter-deck. He had the same sort of lively, anticipatory expression as Aimes. The new regime seemed to agree with people despite the shattering noise on deck. Aimes's description fitted the scene – pandemonium!

'Successful trip?' Stainton asked.

'Extremely,' he replied.

'Fattened up the bugs no end,' Heighurst said. His eyes were hard. 'But then, of course, one of 'em might have been my late lamented aunt.'

Stainton's round face looked puzzled for a moment. 'Ah, well – we sail in the morning. Fresh fields and coral atols new!'

'Is the fellow really usin' the "cat"?' Heighurst asked.

'So we've heard.'

'How often?'

'No one seems to know. It's most probably one of these stories cooked up by the papers – you know what they are. That, at all events, is what our hero believes.' He nodded up the deck to where Guy saw D'Arcy standing, hands behind his straight back, by the carpenter's bench. 'Not, mark you, that he thinks of much outside art. But hist! methinks he doth approach. I must away – ' He swept his hand in a bow. 'Good gentle sirs, farewell!'

'I'll see thee more, sweet pilot.'

'I doubt it not.' Stainton strode off towards the other side, skirting the groups of hands and the paraphernalia they were working on, which littered the deck like a dockyard scene. Tarpaulins or old sails covered nearly every inch of planking and much of the interior of the ship seemed to have been dismantled and deposited on them. Men were kneeling or squatting at work with files, brushes, paint, polish, palms and needles, or splicing fancy designs in new white rope. The sheep pens and hen coops had all been moved forward to clear a wider space; in their place were four huge watertight doors from the main deck with a horde of firemen beavering over them with files, like fiddlers from the infernal regions, sweat running in continuous trickles down their pale faces. Others nearby were burnishing ring-bolts and stanchions. The ship's pet white geese, the 'heavenly twins', waddled between them all with a bewildered manner, giving vent every now and again to a passable imitation of the racket, and leaving droppings on the canvas. Beyond, on the inside of the bulwarks, squares had been scribed in triple lines, and he saw two hands with cutting-in brushes painting carefully in green between them.

He heard D'Arcy approach, and looked round to greet him. The prominent eyes were alight with eagerness and pleasure. 'My dear old chap!' He nodded to Heighurst. 'My dear fellow!'

His uniform, if it could be called such, was as extravagant as the suit in which he had first appeared. There was a similar cutaway sweep to the blue jacket displaying the same white pique shirt-front beneath a huge black silk cravat held with the pearl-headed pin. His white cuffs extended an inch below the sleeves, with prominent pearl links; his gloves were spotless. His trousers were white duck flared at the foot and so tight at the knee it seemed he had to stride as stiffly as a cavalry officer. His blonde curls burst out from beneath his cap, jammed down at the front as if to give more play to the luxuriant growth at the back of his head.

Heighurst's expression was a picture of restraint. 'Smacking it about somewhat,' he said.

'You think so?' D'Arcy's thick lips parted in a smile. 'Of course, it don't look much yet.'

'I'd not say that.'

D'Arcy looked pleased. 'A harmony in green, yellow and gold. What d'you say? No other colours – except white. Green, white, yellow and gold.' He raised his hand to indicate the far bulwark. 'A line of white panelling outlined in green with a fine gold band, gun ports the same, gun carriages painted white, picked out in green, green bolts, trucks and slides, gold pins, cascabels and' – a thought struck him – '"Guns" – my dear chap, you simply must see her! Come!' He beckoned and started striding forward.

They followed between a line of ABs standing braiding fancy lanyards, and marines painting six-inch shell with bands of green and yellow. He shuddered, wondering what Saxmundham would make of that.

Forward of the funnel casing and bridge pillars on the port side the sailmaker's gang squatted, stitching away at little pieces of canvas which looked like nightcaps. D'Arcy turned and nodded at them. 'Covers for the ring-bolts. The dew.' he added.

On the starboard side the carpenter and his mates were fashioning gratings of various shapes and sizes, several rather nicely curved. D'Arcy paid no attention to them, but strode up to a quartermaster working with great concentration with his back to them. Guy saw he was painting the Hindu image that D'Arcy had displayed so proudly on his first arrival. She looked different now. Most of her arms had been cut off to leave the regulation two, demurely folded below her navel; her headdress had also been shorn, in its place a carved crown of laurel leaves, painted green. A carved wooden scroll had been placed across her open knees, hiding some of the exotic decoration of her short skirt, but it could not conceal the equally exotic designs on the leggings protruding beneath, nor the semi-circles of beads across her bare midriff and plump breasts. It was the scroll that the quartermaster was touching up with green. He turned his head as he became aware of their presence.

D'Arcy leant and peered at his work. 'A-one,' he said after a moment. 'Distinctly excellent, Hopson.' He straightened and looked at Guy. 'What d'you say? You don't recognize her? Ain't she just – '

Guy looked at the goddess's face, rendered fiercer by attempts to remove all traces of the vertical eye in her forehead, for the marks remaining appeared as an angry frown. He turned to Heighurst. 'Saint Barbara.'

'Of course,' he replied. 'I would have known her anywhere.'

'Hang it!' D'Arcy said, unable to contain himself. 'I say she's the cream cheese!' A momentary shadow passed across his face. 'The gunner lacks imagination. Wait till he sees her in place.' He pointed to a pedestal that had been fixed to the fo'c's'le bulkhead, and was receiving a finishing coat of white paint. 'She shall be the focus of the deck, Greville, all eyes drawn towards her.' He made a drawing motion with his arms and body. 'An arrangement of form and colour you understand? What d'you say?'

Guy wanted to warn him about Saxmundham, but it was not the time. 'I say she'll be an inspiration.'

'So do I, hang it! So do I!'

Heighurst's gaze returned to the carving. 'What is the flesh colour to be, Number One?' He eyed the breasts, rounded out like balloons.

D'Arcy looked down. 'Her langtries, my dear fellow. Exquisite are they not? White. White for purity,' – he leant towards the marine – 'picked out in gold where you blow 'em up from.'

The quartermaster grinned.

'I dare say you'll enjoy that,' Heighurst said to him.

'That is the secret,' D'Arcy came in enthusiastically. He nodded to the quartermaster to continue his work, and turned to walk back down the deck. 'They do enjoy it. This is their home – it's what we like to forget. Drills are all very fine, but first of all what the ordinary jack wants – what you or I want, hang it – is pleasant, harmonious *artistic* surroundings. Now I'll guarantee absolutely that when this scheme is complete, when the jacks can come up on deck of an evening an' contemplate the beautiful effects they have wrought,' he turned, waving a glove in emphasis, '*they* have wrought, when that time comes, my dear fellow, I'll guarantee you a smaller blacklist. It might even come to the point we can pay off the ship's police!' He gazed at them each in turn with bulging eyes.

'They might not like it,' Heighurst said. 'The jacks, d'you see? No one to blind at.'

'My dear fellow, you've hit the absolute nail. They shan't feel the need, don't you see?'

Guy said, 'The difficulty is – if you'll allow me – we've been with Old Sax a goodish time now.' He looked at Heighurst.

'He cannot surprise us much,' the marine agreed.

'He don't like change,' Guy went on very deliberately, 'not all at once. It's my advice you don't show him your hand too quick. He'll come aboard this afternoon expecting to sail in the morning.' He looked meaningfully at the miscellaneous activity about the deck. 'It's my idea he'll not be interested in much else.'

D'Arcy had stopped by the entrance port with a disappointed expression.

Guy pressed on. 'Take Saint Barbara. You have already placed Don Quixote at the main – '

D'Arcy's expression brightened. 'What d'you say? The armourer cut him out from a picture.'

'First class!' Guy replied. 'Absolutely A-one. I'm positive the Old Man will think so too. So it's my advice you allow him to get used to him – the Don – before you spring Saint Barbara.'

'*She* is the focus,' D'Arcy said as though explaining a point to an uncomprehending child. 'Hang it, Greville, I can no more leave her out than Adam might have forgot a fireplace.'

'I had an idea it was a fig leaf,' Heighurst murmured.

D'Arcy glanced at him without comprehension, and quickly back to Guy. 'What is it you're saying, Greville – the owner's goin' to object because I'm disbursin' a good deal of my tin on this old bucket?'

'I'm only sayin' he cannot abide change. At all events not sudden change.'

'We shall see.'

'Well – ' Guy looked at Heighurst and shrugged.

D'Arcy seemed to remember that they had just returned from a week ashore. 'You had a good trip?' He put an arm on Guy's shoulder.

'I enjoyed it. Thank you. I fear we didn't butcher enough livestock to satisfy my chum here.'

'He fell asleep!' Heighurst retorted. 'The biggest cat you ever saw in your life sittin' there, and the poor fellow can think of nothin' better to do than put his head down and snore.'

Guy sensed him feeling his way towards some grotesque elaboration of the shoot for the mess that night and, nodding to them, turned and made for the companion.

Arriving below, he was surprised to find his servant in his cabin and his uniform whites laid out on the bunk. The man straightened and turned as he entered, his long face lightening briefly. There was a strong smell of polish despite the open port. He was thankful it was not the side the hands were chipping, even so the noise was distinctly unpleasant.

'Not enjoyin' yourself on deck, Basset?'

He could never quite get used to the marine; he had the feeling that the man stood on his dignity a good deal, as if he resented doing duty as an officer's servant. Probably he did; he had a strong, intelligent face with dark, arched brows and reflective dark eyes, and some of his remarks gave evidence of more than a smattering of reading. He was known by a variety of names on the mess-deck, all making play with his serious countenance or the hound suggested by his surname, but Guy always felt it would be an intrusion for him to use any of them; the man could not very well return the compliment.

'The new jimmy said you'd be back this morning, sir.'

Guy's brows rose. So D'Arcy had some time for other matters.

'Seeing as how he turned you out of your cabin – ' Basset went on.

'Ah! Guilty conscience!' It was good of D'Arcy. 'He's makin' a few changes,' he said, fishing for the lower deck view.

Basset's look told him he knew the purpose of the remark exactly; he seemed to weigh up the answer, which might, of course, be a delicate one.

'He's shaking down, sir.'

'It appears to me, Basset, he is shaking *up*!'

The marine grinned. 'That's a way of putting it, sir, he is an' no mistake. He's shook up a few too. The gunner's properly shook up. Says he's not goin' to serve with no heathen idolator – "'eathen hidolerator", he calls him.'

'But it's all for his benefit.'

'That's what he tries to tell him, but he says that's no Christian saint that he'd ever look up to but a diabolical black hidol carved by hidolerators.'

''eathen ones!' Guy grinned, thinking of old Jason's shot-blasted face. 'Not "the right 'n proper manner" of furnishin' the gun deck, I dare say.'

Basset smiled at his imitation. They were really getting along better than ever before; D'Arcy seemed to be acting as a catalyst in all sorts of directions.

The marine sensed the change in their formal relationship; his expression lengthened and he nodded towards the bag and gun that one of the hands had fetched up from the boat.

'There'll be some dhobi, I expect, sir.'

'Yes, open it up, Basset, you'll find a good deal of blood – mostly mine after the bugs had extracted it.' They exchanged places in the small space between the washstand and the wardrobe, and he started taking off his jacket and tie. 'To tell the truth I'm looking forward to a good night's sleep. These shootin' fellows have a queer way of enjoyin' themselves, you know.'

'They've nothing better to do, sir.'

He caught the resentful tone he had heard before on occasions.

'How's that, Basset?'

The marine looked up from the open bag. 'It's a question of ownership of the land, sir.'

Guy's brows rose. He slipped off his tie and started unbuttoning his shirt. The marine bent again to rummage for the soiled clothing. Guy watched him for a moment.

'Well?' he prompted at last.

Basset looked up. 'Ownership of the land, sir.' His tone implied that no further explanation were necessary.

'I really haven't the least idea of what you're drivin' at.'

The marine looked surprised. 'You being an educated man, sir – ' He didn't seem to know how to continue but, as Guy stared at him, 'Well, sir, the way I see it, ownership of the land is at the bottom of everything. Those who can't get at the land – call them for argument's sake the proletarians – '

The use of the word 'proletarians' crystallized a suspicion that was forming in Guy's mind. 'Are you a socialist, Basset?'

The marine's mouth froze over his last utterance, and his expression sharpened as if realizing he had revealed more than he meant. 'No, sir,' he replied after a moment. 'You asked me, and I was trying to give you an answer.'

Guy continued to gaze at him.

He straightened with the clothes in his arms. 'I'll take these away, sir.'

'Good. Thank you, Basset.' He placed his foot on the chair seat and bent to unfasten his laces as the marine left. The fellow evidently read more than was good for him. Political stuff. It would be interesting to find out more.

Guy felt the heat pressing down through the sunlit tarpaulin above; there was scarcely a breath of wind to disperse it. The bo'sun's pipe shrilled, signalling the close approach of the captain's gig. He glanced up the deck, cleared now of the extraordinary paraphernalia of the morning, and presenting a sweet sweep of white planking, interrupted only by the guns and the arcs of the brass racers cut into the teak. Perhaps his words had had some effect. But no doubt D'Arcy would have had the mess cleared up in any case. There was little now that the Old Man could take exception to; the grand transformation was still in its infancy, the guns still black and business-like, the panelling effect on the bulwarks still only a quarter of the way along one side, the shot and shell, admittedly colourful in their racks around the hatch coamings and skylight casings, were scarcely revolutionary. If Saxmundham had not taken objection to the fancies up aloft which he must have seen on his way out to the ship, there was little inboard to shock him – except Saint Barbara. She had been fixed up on her pedestal ready for the finishing touches of paint and gilding. But there was no reason why he should spot her if he walked aft.

The decks were silent, the few hands visible frozen in their positions as the second series of rising and falling shrills heralded the Old Man's footsteps on the gangway. Guy could see a small area of glaring water through the entrance port. It became partly obscured by the figure of the surgeon, who had come up first from the boat and now stood aside to allow Saxmundham through before him. The great man appeared a moment later, his huge figure blocking out the remaining area of sunlit water. The marine guard crashed to the present, bugles blared. Saxmundham raised his felt hat to the quarterdeck. The red ring etched around his forehead dividing the pale area beneath his hair from the weathered, vein-chased skin of the rest of his face seemed intensified by the heat; beads of sweat rolled down across it to his tangled brows, and others meandering further disappeared in the great, tawny growth of beard which obscured his lower face and spread over the lapels of his shooting jacket. The blue eyes were alight with zest though; behind him the surgeon also looked in excellent spirits. Thank the Lord! Sport had been good!

'Greville!' The familiar roar. 'On my life!'

Guy could not restrain an upward twist of his lips as he pulled his hand down from the salute. 'Sir!'

Saxmundham stood where he was, raising both hands a little way, palms uppermost. 'Charming!' He turned to the surgeon.

'Indeed.' the surgeon nodded. 'Most pleasin'.' His glance moved to D'Arcy, and travelled up and down his figure.

Saxmundham scarcely seemed to notice him though; he came straight towards Guy and grasped his arm. 'I'd like to see Bousfield's face when he sees her!' and, in a lower tone, 'Cost you a pretty penny, my boy?'

Guy was about to explain and introduce D'Arcy but Saxmundham had caught sight of the green panelling on the bulwark, and was following it with his eyes up the deck, taking in the multi-coloured shot and shell in the racks.

'Bless my soul!'

It was not clear whether he approved. Guy waited, stealing a glance at D'Arcy, whose face had become a picture of satisfaction.

'Bless my soul!' Saxmundham repeated, bringing a hand up to stroke his beard.

'My successor – ' Guy started.

Saxmundham started striding forward. 'Show me what you intend.'

Guy fell in with him, turning and shrugging to D'Arcy as he went. Evidently the recall cable had contained nothing about the change-over; there was no reason, of course, why it should have done. But surely it must have been apparent from D'Arcy's position in the reception committee.

He tried again. 'The Admiralty have sent out a new man, sir, to take over as first lieutenant – as you said they would do.'

'All ready for sailin' are we?'

'I believe so, sir.'

The blue eyes glinted. 'No reason why the fellow should catch us up then. On my life!' He chuckled, turning as if to invite Guy to share the joke. 'We'll make certain he don't. Hang it, if they've left it this long!' His brows drew down. 'I shan't have it, Greville.'

'He's here, sir.'

'On board?' Saxmundham stopped abruptly. 'That fellow in the fancy outfit? I was about to ask you about him, Greville.' He started forward again slowly, his great head lowered in thought, then stopped and turned to face him. The beard was jutting, the blue eyes hard. 'Where's the fellow now?'

Guy looked back down the deck. 'Waiting.'

'We must cut round the other side – no, I shall cut round the other side. Do you go back and engage him, Greville. Allow me time to reach my quarters, then come in – directly.'

'Aye, aye, sir.'

'And don't look so down, my boy! We'll cook up something, depend on it!' There was a zestful light of conspiracy in his eye as he swung off and around the forward end of the bridge stanchions.

Guy wondered if he would notice Saint Barbara. He turned and made his way back to where D'Arcy and the other officers stood grouped by the entrance port.

D'Arcy's blond brows were raised quizzically. 'What does he say?'

'I'm not sure,' he replied, disliking the game he was forced to play.

'Don't he like it?'

Guy smiled. 'It?'

D'Arcy gazed without humour. 'He seemed pleased enough when he came aboard.'

'I'm positive he was.' He saw Saxmundham striding aft on the other side.

D'Arcy saw him too, and stared for a moment before turning back to Guy.

'I've explained the position,' Guy said.

'In that case – ' D'Arcy's expression was harder than Guy had seen it yet and, without bothering to finish the sentence, he turned to follow the captain.

'Don't go now!' Guy said holding out his arm. 'He wishes to see me – some arrangements for his trophies ashore. That is all that concerns him at present.'

D'Arcy stared. Guy looked at the other officers, watching silently. There was nothing to be said. He made his way aft.

The marine sentry outside Saxmundham's door came to attention, an expectant look on his face. 'The captain said you was to go straight in, sir.'

He knocked once and opened the door.

'I'll not have it, Greville!' The Old Man was standing bareheaded, the ring around his forehead an angry red, his eyes belligerent.

Guy paused, prepared from long experience, but uncertain

how to deal with the mood.

'How did the fellow get here?'

'P & O, sir. He arrived a week ago.'

'Bin here a week!' The tone was accusing. 'What've you done about it?'

Guy's brows rose. 'I handed over – '

'You handed over!' Saxmundham's voice rose and he lifted a fist as if about to thump a rostrum. 'Who told you to hand over, sir? I left *you* in command. On my life, I never thought to come back and find – someone else. Who told you, sir?'

'He has a letter, sir – '

'Letter, be hanged!'

'I dare say I should have cabled you, sir – '

'I dare say.' Saxmundham swung and paced a couple of steps each way before coming to a halt before Guy again. His expression was cooler. 'What's to be done?'

Guy gave himself time, 'That is the question, sir.'

Saxmundham remained very still, staring at him. 'Since it was you handed over, Greville, it's up to you to find the answer. That's fair ain't it?'

Guy knew it was thoroughly unfair. It was not the time to say so. 'In the first place,' he started, 'we might assume that I handed over acting command of the ship in your absence. Something for which I had no authority,' he added.

'I'm glad you agree.'

'Since you have now resumed command on board, his acting command ceases, and – with respect, sir – the matter of his takin' over as first lieutenant lies in your hands.' He avoided mentioning the Admiralty letter, knowing it would have the effect of a red rag.

Saxmundham started chuckling. 'So you wash your hands of the affair? I should have known it! Bless my soul! You young cub!'

Guy hastened to use the change of mood, before Saxmundham could say something irreversible about D'Arcy and himself. 'I have been ashore for the past week, sir, gathering intelligence on Commander Vaneyke.'

The blue eyes widened.

Guy saw the course he must pursue. 'My enquiries led me to a Hindu temple above Khandala.'

'You don't say so!'

'I spoke with a Brahman whom Commander Vaneyke had been in the habit of visiting. It was my impression – it is my impression still – that Vaneyke has renounced the Christian Church.'

'Renounced the Church!' Saxmundham looked startled.

'I believe so, sir.'

'Chosen the devil!' The great chest heaved with laughter. 'It would not surprise me. He always was a deuce too clever.'

'Not the devil, sir. I believe he has chosen the Buddha.'

The blue eyes regarded him for a moment. 'There are some, Greville – I may say I do not count myself amongst them – who regard you yourself as more than a shade clever.'

Guy smiled. 'I have to deny it, sir.'

'On this occasion I have to accept your denial. For don't it strike you as curious, Greville, that a fella turned Buddhist should start floggin' his ship's company?'

'We only have newspaper reports, sir.'

The Old Man rubbed his beard. 'They ain't in the habit of reportin' that sort of thing, not without they have some evidence.'

'I've been into this matter of Commander Vaneyke most thoroughly, sir – I've spoken with his wife – '

'The deuce you have! You young rascal!'

'And several people who knew him in Bombay, besides the Brahman I mentioned. It's my opinion he has turned from the Christian faith to one of the eastern religions – I believe it to be Buddhism.' He pressed on. 'I also believe the disappearance of the *Curlew* is in some way – and I confess I have no inkling in what way – connected with this change of faith.'

'My boy,' Saxmundham cut in, 'If the fellow has turned as you say he has – bless my soul! – it stands to reason he don't want to be found. It's clean contrary to the Articles of War!'

'Yes, sir.'

'On my life!'

'If I may make a proposal, sir – '

'Fella on the quarter-deck in a yellow robe. Can you see it, Greville?'

'No, sir,' Guy admitted.

'No more can I, my boy. And not with a "cat-o'-nine-tails". You've never seen a man flogged, Greville?'

'I've seen a caning, sir, in the *Britannia*.'

'Boys' work. The cat's for men, Greville.'

Guy thought of the tales he had heard of men lashed, spreadeagle to the gratings, a leather thong thrust between their teeth to chew on as the bo'sun's mates took turns to lay on the multiple strokes, the bloodied, butchered backs –

'I've witnessed its employment on a number of occasions,' the Old Man went on. 'You've not heard of "Bully" Bates?'

'No, sir.'

'A good many years before your time. He was my commander in the old *Aeschylus*. There was nothin' he enjoyed more than a good floggin'. The cat for the men and the masthead for the boys was his motto. And his downfall. He went too far on one occasion. Chose the wrong fella – a sea lawyer by the name of Johnson – a nasty piece of work, I remember his fox-face well, but on this occasion I fancy he did the right thing. Smuggled himself ashore and bared his back all the way down Fleet Street! That was the end of "Bully" Bates – and not before time. I dare say their lordships remember that episode.'

'Meat and drink to the Liberals, sir.'

'Indeed it will be, my boy.'

'Damn the service in the eyes of the public, then reduce the estimates.'

Saxmundham took a turn towards the chintz-covered settee along the outer bulkhead and sat down. 'That is why we have to find the damn-fool. Chop-chop!'

'If I may make a proposal, sir,' Guy tried again, 'if I am correct about his, Vaneyke's, change of faith, he may well have gone to Ceylon.'

'No question of it, m'boy.' He wagged a finger. '*If* you are correct.'

'One interestin' circumstance, sir – his wife has gone to Trinco to visit the Admiral.'

'The devil she has!'

'I had the decided impression she was under strain when I talked with her, and it was not on account of the *Curlew*'s disappearance – not directly – she never so much as mentioned the ship. I believe she was worried about something she knew of her husband.'

'She has every reason to be – if the fella's taken the yellow robe!' Saxmundham started chuckling.

'Exactly! And why should she travel to Ceylon in person?'

Guy took a considered leap. 'I believe she may know she will find her husband there.'

Saxmundham's brows rose in surprise before the amused gleam returned. 'I fancy I can sniff out your games, my boy! There's usually a reason for what you have to say.' He stared up, challenging with his eyes.

Guy assumed a puzzled expression.

'On my life!' the Old Man roared suddenly. 'Out with it then! You young dog! You wish to follow her!' He jabbed a heavy forefinger in the air. 'As my intelligence officer, as you once were, you wish to interview her at Trinky, leavin' me with that swell – what's 'is name? – for first lieutenant!' The great beard jutted, its fuzzy outline haloed in red where the light from the ports caught it.

'I was not – '

'Yes, sir, you were, sir. That's what this whole flapdoodle rigmarole's bin about, sir! D'Arcy-Green – that's his name ain't it?' Saxmundham's expression changed to one of distaste, and rising he began pacing in short turns from one side of the cabin to the other. 'That's a fella that's renounced the Christian Church!' He stopped opposite Guy again and glared at him. 'Stickin' idols on the foredeck!'

'Saint Barbara, sir.'

Saxmundham started chuckling. 'Barin' her langtries for the jacks! I dare say it might amuse your gunnery fellas, but it's a departure, Greville, you have to acknowledge it. She's wearin' long pants, as I recall.'

'He had to make the best of what he could purchase, sir. He is most anxious the ship should make a good impression on the Admiral.'

'Lookin' for promotion is he?' A shadow passed across the blue eyes. 'The poor fella!' Guy wondered if he were thinking, perhaps of Smallpiece – Smallpiece with his broken leg and prickly heat and dogged determination, brought in like a pincushion from the native darts and arrows.

'You shall have your way,' Saxmundham said abruptly. 'You'll wish to go overland. I'll fog out a letter for the Admiral.' He frowned. 'I would not do this for many officers, Greville.' He turned to pace away. 'It's madness. But you have been correct on a number of former occasions,' and swinging round abruptly as if he had made up his mind, 'I always had my suspicions of Vaneyke. He never was content with the accepted thing. He made his reputation on it. I knew him well. You wouldn't have been given odds against him makin' First Lord then – he was marked out for the top. And I'll say it, he stuck out a mile for intellect and thoroughness – in his own estimate too mind you – '

He was interrupted by a knock on the door. A frown creased his forehead. 'Come!'

Guy's heart sank as he saw D'Arcy; he had the letter in his hand. He looked quickly back to the Old Man; the blue eyes were hard.

'I trust I'm not intrudin', sir,' D'Arcy started, his high vowel sounds made more extraordinary by the preceding growl from Saxmundham. 'There are a number of matters requirin' decision before we sail.'

Saxmundham's glance moved up from the rings glittering on his fingers to his face, remaining there.

D'Arcy stepped forward with the Admiralty letter held out. 'D'Arcy-Green, sir. I have been appointed first lieutenant – '

Saxmundham took the letter and, without removing his eyes from D'Arcy's, tore it deliberately in two pieces, and handed them back. 'Thank you, Mr D'Arcy-Green.'

D'Arcy's expression froze, his eyes very prominent as he stood holding the two halves of the letter out before him.

Saxmundham broke the silence. 'I have no cause to request a new first lieutenant.'

D'Arcy made no reply, but continued to hold Saxmundham's gaze, his heavy lips tightened, a muscle twitching at the side of his jaw.

Saxmundham went on after a moment, 'I dare say you are accommodated on board? Until such time as I can communicate with the Admiral, please consider yourself supernumerary. I'm obliged, sir.'

D'Arcy shot a glance at Guy. The shock had turned to anger. Guy was confirmed in what he had sensed before; beneath the foppish front D'Arcy was a tough character, and probably a capable one.

He put the torn halves of the letter very deliberately in an inside pocket of his extraordinary jacket, and swung and left the cabin without a word.

Saxmundham looked at Guy; his eyes were as belligerent as

at the start of the interview. 'I'll not have it!'

The die was cast.

'You will resume your duties as first lieutenant,' Saxmundham went on in a low tone. 'Ready for sailin' at first light?'

'Aye, aye, sir!'

'Send the pilot in – and the chief!' As Guy turned and stepped to the door, he added, 'We may need his infernal engines if we're to find the *Curlew* first.'

Guy knew that was far from the real reason; he thought of all the money and enthusiasm D'Arcy had lavished on the paint and gilding, and was filled with a sense of foreboding.

3

The heavenly twins waddled up the slope of the deck, necks thrust out, giving notice that the ship was under way again; they had been doing it for half an hour or so, the chumps. Hens fluttered their wings against the wire of the coops or jerked their heads with watchful eyes as Guy walked aft. It was good to feel the little ship alive again underfoot. There was promise in the early morning air.

He turned on impulse and made his way forward again to the bridge ladder, steadying himself with both hands on the rails as the bow lifted to the swell; she was feeling the open sea now. He climbed up. Sunlight darted off the dimpled backs of rollers gliding away ahead; flying fish skittered in long curves, skimming the surface flecked with streaks from the breaking crests of waves. Already the air felt cleaner and somehow brisker. The lightship lay off the bow, its red sides heaving, darts of sun flashing from the great reflecting glass; they would soon be up to it. Astern the Prongs Lighthouse stood up bold white with a band of red before the clustered barracks of Colaba, and beyond them the green, wooded slopes of Malabar Hill with the houses and bungalows interspersed charmingly amongst the trees.

He wondered if he would meet her again in Trinco – whenever they reached Trinco! The Lord only knew where the hunt might take them, or for how long. 'You have heard of the Jains – they had a saying about the ladies, you know – they likened them to lamps burning along the path to hell!' He smiled.

Turning inboard to walk across to the port side, he caught sight of Saxmundham and Stainton together inside the little chart-house, and changed his mind. It was too late. He saw the great face raised from whatever it was they were poring over, and heard the roar, 'Greville!'

A chart embracing both the Laccadive and Maldive groups of atols and reefs was spread out on the table before the two with a worn copy of *Imray's Indian Ocean Guide* open on top of it, the pages flicking back, one after another, to a more familiar section.

Saxmundham's good humour had returned; his eyes were glinting. 'The islanders were Buddhists at one time.'

Guy declined to be drawn. 'Where d'you propose calling first, sir?'

Saxmundham looked down at the chart. 'The dhows sailed across on the monsoons,' then up again at Guy, his beard jutting aggressively. 'Now – there is no God but Allah. And Mahomet is His prophet. D'you fancy Vaneyke as an evangelist, Greville?'

Guy grinned. 'I dare say the *Curlew*'s Nordenfelts would procure a number of conversions. What puzzles me, sir – the Admiralty must know where the letter was posted. Would that not be the place to begin the hunt?'

'Letter – ? I've heard of no letter.'

'About the "cat" – from the *Curlew*.'

'There was no letter from the *Curlew*. As I understand it, the only letter was from an officer in her chummy ship. ' His brow crinkled.

'The *Cormorant*, sir,' Stainton prompted.

'I fancy it was the *Cormorant*. The two ships were together for a time in Muscat, where I gather the officers of the *Cormorant* learnt of the flogging from an officer of the *Curlew*. I understand they were concerned about what they heard – in no small measure I dare say. But naturally it was not their affair. It was not until the story got about that the *Curlew* had not been seen for some months that one of the subs wrote to his people – I imagine mentioning what he heard on that occasion. How the Admiralty and Fleet Street became involved – ' He shrugged, and waved his hand across the chart. 'So here we are.'

'She might be anywhere.'

'Where would *you* go, Greville?'

'If I were Vaneyke?'

'Where would you *not* go?'

'I'd not go back to the Gulf!' Guy laughed.

'Precisely.' Saxmundham thumped his great palm over a group of atolls on the chart. 'He'll be here somewhere – depend on it.'

Stainton said, 'Rather as the *Bounty* made for Pitcairn?'

Saxmundham nodded. 'The garden of Eden. I own I look forward to this little outin' myself.' He leant over the chart. 'I propose makin' a start here – at Cherbaniani' He pointed to a pear-shaped reef at the northern extreme of the Laccadive group. 'No permanent residents, but fishermen resort to the place in great numbers – so *Imray* informs us. They'll be able to tell us a thing or two, I'll be bound. What's more my boy' – the blue eyes were alight – 'the place is stiff with turtle. What d'you say to that?'

'I say we should start there, sir.'

'Yes, that's what the pilot says.' He took Guy's arm and steered him out of the chart-house door, glancing aloft at the set of the fore t'gallants and topsails as he followed. 'She's enjoyin' it. On my life!' He stood for a moment, scanning the stress lines from the clews of the flat, sunlit canvas. 'At the rate we're goin' we'll make the reefs between eleven and midnight tomorrow.'

Guy looked round sharply into his face.

The great chest shook with subterranean chuckles. 'I've no intention of doin' so. They're live coral, m'boy – come straight up from the bottom like a wall – no warning whatever except you keep your eyes and ears open.' He paced to the starboard rail, staring keenly at the lightship, now sliding rapidly astern, two hands waving at them from her red sides, and raised his cap courteously in response. 'No, the reason I mention it is we shall have some little time to lose on the way.' He turned with a meaning look, gazing at him for a moment, then swung a contemptuous gesture towards the racks below filled with multi-coloured shot. 'We can employ it most profitably by throwin' 'em overboard.'

'Over the side?'

'Great heavens, Greville! Through the cursed guns!'

'Target practice.'

Saxmundham grunted, and a speculative look came into his eyes. 'I intend our swell is given a job of work to do.'

Guy began to understand the meaning of the looks and pregnant pauses he'd been subjected to: the intention was to make D'Arcy gunnery officer, directly responsible for firing off the shells he had painted with such care – rubbing his nose in his artistry before the whole ship's company. He had seen this trait in Saxmundham before – not cruelty for its own sake, so much as intense dislike unrestrained by any appreciation of the other's feelings.

'Since you've changed positions with the beggar, he cannot object to takin' on your job,' and, coming up with a pleased expression now that his secret was out, Saxmundham grasped Guy on the arm, sure that he must appreciate the grand joke. 'It'll give him an interest – aside from his curlin' tongs.'

'The gunner would never agree to it, sir.'

The blue eyes clouded with surprise, changing rapidly to disbelief, then anger. 'The *gunner*!'

'He is convinced that Lieutenant D'Arcy-Green is a heathen – an idolater.'

Saxmundham stared.

'I believe it would be impossible for the two to work together.' Seeing the anger momentarily dispersed by thought, Guy pressed on, 'I am convinced that such an arrangement would lead to trouble. I know Jenkins, sir.'

'He has a point!'

There was a moment of silence, then Saxmundham turned abruptly away to the forward rail, gripping it with both hands, staring ahead. Guy waited, aware of Stainton following the drama from inside the chart-house.

As suddenly as he had swung away, Saxmundham turned back. 'Jason is right. The idol must be ditched.'

'D'Arcy purchased it, sir.'

'He set it up in my ship,' Saxmundham's voice rose again dangerously. 'Our ship. It is ours, I *will* have it overboard!' He thumped the air with his fist. 'Are you sayin' I shall not have it overboard?'

'I doubt it would make any difference, sir. If you or we had it thrown overboard, I'm certain it would only serve to confirm Jason in his idea of the first – of D'Arcy, sir.'

'Very well, D'Arcy must pitch it over himself.' The beard jutted triumphantly.

Guy made no reply. Saxmundham glared.

'There is another reason, sir.'

'You usually have another reason.'

'D'Arcy's rather too keen on files and emery paper – in my opinion, sir – and, were he to be allowed his head with the guns, I believe a good deal of damage might result. The modern sights are tremendously delicate, and the firing tubes – ' He stopped, aware that the Old Man's attention had transferred to someone coming up the bridge ladder behind. Turning, he saw D'Arcy himself his cap thrust forward at a more than usually extravagant angle, the sun glinting on piled blonde curls behind. He was climbing with an awkward roll induced by the tightness of his white flannels at the knees; his face was pink and cheerful as he looked up and caught sight of them.

Reaching the top, he saluted. Saxmundham returned the salute briefly, glancing at Guy, then back to D'Arcy again, running his eyes down the cut-away blue jacket to the spotless flannels flaring over white canvas shoes, and up again by way of the pique shirt-front and yellow cravat to the heavy face.

'Are you aware, sir, of the uniform regulations?'

The green eyes held steady. 'I understood I had been relieved of my position, sir. I had not heard that passengers in HM ships were required to wear uniform.'

'Supernumerary! Supernumerary, sir!'

D'Arcy shook his head slightly as if to clear it after the roar, but remained silent.

Saxmundham glared at him. 'Have the quartermaster fetch a bucket, Greville. I feel sick.' As if unable to contain himself he strode to the ladder and went down it, grunting ominously.

D'Arcy turned to Guy, his pale brows raised in a look of mixed incredulity and triumph. 'Uniform maketh man! It's difficult to understand a fellow like that – at all events, I find it so.' He strolled to the rail and turned, lounging back with his elbows resting on it.

'These squalls blow up fast – ' Guy started.

'Don't think I'm concerned, ' D'Arcy cut in, his eyes hardening. He reached inside his jacket and pulled out the torn Admiralty letter – it had been stuck together, Guy saw – and waved it languidly. 'I'm glad you were a witness to this transaction. And since you evidently enjoy his favour, as they say, I doubt your veracity will be called in question when the Admiral asks you for your account.' He smiled, replacing the letter. 'So, my dear old fellow, I intend seein' to it that you and I and our meat-eatin' friend,' he jerked his head aft, 'come to no harm *en route*.'

'I'm obliged,' Guy smiled. He was not certain of the implication, but had to admire D'Arcy's assurance.

D'Arcy picked himself up from the rail and took a stiff pace towards him. 'I may not be the most popular fellow in the after cabin, but you, my dear old chum' – his tone dropped – 'have a number of enemies forward. Among the foretopmen to be precise.'

Guy's mind flashed to Davis and his companions.

'I see you know what I mean – the "Viceroys of Grant Road" as they now call themselves, with some pride. A select little band.'

'Rot!'

D'Arcy's tone became crisper. 'Not rot to them, my dear. It was beastly hot while you were away. I did my best for the poor devils with a windsail, but a windsail's not much use when there's no wind. It became necessary to call the surgeon on one occasion.'

'What are you driving at?'

D'Arcy clapped a hand on his arm. 'There's nothin' annoys the jacks so much as an injustice.'

'They thoroughly deserved their punishment.'

'You failed to listen to their side of the story y'see. And after, you betook yourself to the cool air of the hills – there to live on honey and consort with the fair daughters of the Raj as officers are supposed to – notwithstanding, the officers can be seen goin' down the gangway with guns and comin' back with dead meat! Meanwhile the jacks are left to stink in the cells. That, my dear fellow, is how I imagine it appears to them.'

Guy found they were pacing together across the bridge. 'I can see that.' He was cursed with the ability to see things from almost any angle; it was no good; it had been absolutely necessary to come down on Davis from a tremendous height. As for taking the days off, that had as much to do with Davis as with the man in the moon. 'They come up before the owner this morning,' he said sharply. 'I've discussed the whole matter with him. I believe he intends releasing them on the grounds they have received sufficient punishment already.'

'It will confirm them in their opinion, I'd hazard – '

They turned at the rail and found Stainton approaching, his round face bright with enquiry. 'Anyone gone for the bucket?'

Seeing the man's heavy shoulders and portly figure, it came to Guy that his uniform would probably fit D'Arcy; it would need taking in perhaps, but one of the jewing firms aboard would manage it easily enough. He stopped and looked from one to the other; they were about the same height.

He turned to D'Arcy. 'What d'you say to trying on the pilot's jacket for size?'

D'Arcy's eyes widened and he stared for a moment at Stainton's prosaic and somewhat rumpled regulation white tunic, then back to Guy, his pale brows lifting. '*Et tu Brute*!'

'I know old Sax,' Guy said angrily. 'These moods mean nothing – isn't that so pilot? They come and go but, if you persist in flaunting yourself' – he waved a hand across D'Arcy's expanse of shirt front and loose cravat – 'he'll gain a fixed idea – you'll never shake him then.'

D'Arcy's eyes were bulging with mock-astonishment, his thick lips lifting at the corners.

Guy turned away. 'I'm for breakfast.'

Stainton was looking at D'Arcy, his good-natured face unusually serious. 'It's absolutely right; once old Sax gets an idea fixed in his head – Listen, I'd be happy to lend you some whites.' He too stopped at D'Arcy's expression and his tone changed. 'Well, think on't good, gentle sir,' and he turned with Guy.

They started down the ladder; D'Arcy stood watching. His affected voice followed them down.

'What a blessing to be able to turn to art and poetry! I simply do not understand how people *exist* who have no resources of this nature.'

Guy couldn't restrain a smile.

'And Greville – ' D'Arcy went on.

Guy looked back from the ladder. D'Arcy was waving the Admiralty letter again.

'I fancy you're forgettin' who it was fired the first shot.' The green eyes were cold, the lips and full jaw very firm.

'I fancy *you* forget we are five thousand miles from Whitehall.'

'Bound for Trinco though.'

'You know as well as I do, it might take weeks. In the meantime – '

'In the meantime I've been stripped of my position' – D'Arcy smiled suddenly and his tone lightened – 'so my dear old chum, I intend enjoyin' myself – hanged if I don't!'

Guy felt sorry for him – alone in his exquisite rig, his marvellous former enthusiasm shrunk to simple defiance of an authority he had no hope of challenging, his hopes of promotion vanishing by the minute. Even in the unlikely event of the Admiral supporting his complaint it would not stand to his credit that he was unable to rub along with a captain as outstanding in so many respects as the Earl of Saxmundham. By comparison with Sax's influence and fortune D'Arcy had nothing – save the windfall from his late aunt. He smiled, shaking his head as he turned and followed Stainton down.

The navigating officer looked back with raised brows.

'An obstinate fellow.'

'It's worse than I feared.'

The promise of the morning had gone; ahead loomed a heightening clash between D'Arcy and Saxmundham which neither would conclude and from which the only results could be ill temper and moods affecting the whole atmosphere of the ship. There was something else too, hanging like a thunder cloud in the background; he remembered Davis.

A group of the watch on deck were hardening in a fore brace as they strode past; he glanced into their faces, wondering if he would detect any sign that his unpopularity had spread from Davis and his companions in crime. The men were intent on their work. But would they not under normal circumstance have given some sign of recognition? As the rope was belayed, two of them trotted aft past him, disturbing the heavenly twins who were busy stealing chicken feed through a torn wire mesh; the geese flapped away stupidly across their path, stretching their necks with token hisses of anger. One of the men swore violently and let fly with his bare foot. Guy wondered if the extreme reaction were directed solely at the geese.

He recognized two of Davis's division, Hales and Bowen, at the wheel and, instead of turning down the companionway with Stainton, carried on, greeting the quartermaster beside them.

'No need for steam today, Smithson.'

The man grinned broadly. It was a standing joke. 'No sir!'

He looked into the starboard binnacle, then up at the set of the t'gallants.

Smithson said expectantly, 'He'll be gittin' some more on her presently?'

'Too easy for you is it?' Guy nodded at the wheel.

Smithson grinned again. 'Aye.'

'No such luck. We've time to lose – or else make the reefs in the dark.'

The quartermaster nodded sagely. 'Larnin' caution is he.'

Guy smiled, glancing at the faces of Hales and Bowen. They were set, apparently concentrating on the wheel.

'D'you remember sir,' Smithson went on, 'goin' up to Lamu through them reefs?' He sucked in through his teeth.

Guy recalled the night: Saxmundham had seemed to con her through with some extra sense he alone possessed, amongst dangers that could be heard close on either side, but seldom seen.

'The old chief buffer, sir, you knowed he packed his bags – that's the truth – they was all stowed and piled under the ladder ready for when we was piped into the boats.'

Guy laughed, and turned to Hales. 'You were on the lookout that night, Hales.'

The man looked up, surprised and evidently pleased the fact had been marked. 'I was that.'

Thank the Lord! He was smiling in his black beard, his eyes candid and friendly. 'Not much to see was there?'

'I 'eard plenty though.' Hales grimaced. 'Gawd *knows* 'ow we missed 'em.'

'That's the answer,' Guy said. 'God knows!'

The men grinned.

'Helm up,' Smithson said, 'easy!'

They leant to the great spokes; the gear creaked. At least they had nothing against him. He could read them like the open books most of them were; if they had a grudge he would have seen it in their eyes and their manner. He nodded at Smithson and, seeing the officer of the watch – the young fifth, Hardy-Penfold – approaching, took a pace to meet him and exchanged a few words before going below.

He found Basset in his cabin, one knee on the bunk as he worked at the brass of the port with a cloth; there was a strong smell of Globe polish in the close air. Had it been Duff, his dear old 'Figgy', he could have asked him about disaffection amongst the foretopmen, and he would have been given a truthful answer – not the whole truth, but sufficient.

'Morning, sir!' Basset had removed his knee from the bunk and was facing him, his dark eyes expressionless.

'It is indeed, Basset!'

'Will you be taking your tub later, sir?'

'I'll have a bite first. I'll pass the word.'

'Aye, aye, sir.'

He must make a determined effort some time to break this constraining formality with its background potential of resentment; it was absurd – they'd been together for more than eighteen months. He didn't feel up to it now though – it was not the moment. He turned to the washstand, poured some water into the basin and picked the soap from its dish.

As he washed he sensed that Basset was unusually silent even for him, and turning saw him standing looking at him uncertainly. He returned his gaze.

'Will the captain be releasing the prisoners, sir?' The words tumbled out as if they had been damned up.

Guy's brows rose. 'How can I know what the captain will decide?'

Basset's expression closed in.

He had said the wrong thing, or expressed it too forcefully. He smiled. 'Why do you ask?'

Basset hesitated. 'There's talk on the mess-deck.'

No doubt there was; there would be a great deal of talk about other matters too – D'Arcy's demotion for one, and the dusky maidens of the Laccadives, even Vaneyke and the *Curlew*. Why should Basset select this particular topic? Why was he looking so uncomfortable?

'In favour of their release?' he asked sharply.

'I don't know as anyone's taking sides, sir.'

There was something very strange about Basset's look, as if he wished to say something, but didn't quite know how to express it, or whether he should.

'Basset, is there something I should know?'

'No, sir. As you said, sir, we'll have to wait and see what the captain decides.'

Guy gazed at him for a moment; he was still fishing. 'Well' – he turned back to the basin – 'strictly between you and me and this bar of soap, you understand – '

'Yes, sir.'

'It's my guess – my *guess* – that Old Sax will most probably decide they've served their term.'

Basset did not reply. Guy looked round and found that he

was up on the bunk again, about to continue his polishing.

The conversation was closed. What on earth had it been about? He rinsed his hands and dried them. There was really only one explanation. Basset was not telling him something he thought he ought perhaps to know because it would cut across the code of the lower deck if he did so, and give away something or someone that should not be given away to an officer. Obviously it had to do with Davis and his companions. Yet they could scarcely have got up to any mischief in the cells, and the questions had been about the probability of their release. Whatever it was it must be contingent on their release. Probably Davis had threatened retribution for his week of hell. It tallied with what D'Arcy had said. Basset, too, had been warning him.

He stepped to the door and pulled the curtain aside, looking back as he was about to leave.

'Thank you, Basset.'

The man turned with his hand on the port. 'I reckon the heat sent him up the pole, sir.'

'Davis?'

'Yes, sir.'

'I shall bear it in mind, Basset.'

He thought he detected a flicker of relief in the dark eyes as he let the curtain fall back.

It seemed to Guy only a moment after his head touched the pillow that he was being reawakened by the bugle sounding 'man and arm ship'; he rose through throbbing layers of darkness and rolled his legs to the deck. He should have guessed Saxmundham would spring a surprise night quarters – working off some of his mood and losing some of the time he needed to lose on passage. He had been given a hint that morning, or was it yesterday? He flicked the light switch, glancing at the time as he let slip the loose lungi he wore in place of pyjamas and pulled his drawers on hurriedly. Saxmundham would be on deck with his gold hunter in his palm, staring at the moving second hand. He pulled up his trousers, buttoning them hurriedly and grabbed at his tunic over the back of the chair while pushing his feet into his shoes. The bugle died away; sounds of movement, bangs and hoarse voices, bare feet on the deck, the baa-aahing of sheep and cries of fowl took over. He bent to tie his laces. The ship was heeling further – the wind must have gone round. He straightened, snatched his cap from the hook and pushed out through the curtain. There were sounds from the cabins round about, and lights, but the ward-room was still empty. He dashed for the door.

The gun-room flat was alive with half-naked midshipmen tricing up their hammocks or shifting into trousers as he strode through to the companion ladder; the atmosphere was none too fresh. He doubled up, feeling a welcome draught of cooler air.

Saxmundham was on the quarter-deck by the wheel, as Guy had known he would be. He was clad in white flannels and velvet smoking jacket with a dark muffler scarcely visible beneath his beard; he held his hunter in characteristic position at waist level in his left palm; his eyes were shadowed from the light striking up from the binnacle, highlighting his left cheek above a tangle of whisker, and brightening the fierce line of his brow. Men, no doubt from the watch on deck, were already starting to loose the guns, others running past to their stations, one pulling a jumper over his head, some hitching their trousers up. Forward the ladders were rattling under a stampede of bare feet. Saxmundham stood, apparently oblivious to the rush and noise, glancing from the compass card to the face of his watch, and up briefly to the phantom shapes of the t'gallants against the stars way above. Stainton was the other side of the wheel with the midshipman of the watch, Bowles.

A frantic fluttering and clucking was issuing from the hen coops; the hens were being dragged from the bulwarks at the run towards the engine-room skylights, there to be lashed against the sheep pens, whose anguished occupants circled and bleated as if they too were parties to the evolution, being timed by old Sax's hunter. From below decks the oaths of the bo'sun's mates urging on the laggards reached a crescendo of brutality. Nearly all the hands would be up by now, every gun position was a centre of frenzied activity; already the breeches of the Armstrongs had been thrown open and shell passed; at the 64-pounders the hands grunted on the tackles and the stubby monsters slewed from the ports. Midshipmen hovered by the working groups. Lieutenant Phillips, who had taken over Guy's duties as gunnery officer, strode rapidly aft, gazing keenly at each crew as he passed.

Guy intercepted him. 'I have an idea he intends a full-scale night firing.'

Phillips looked startled. 'Target practice?'

'I fear so.' Guy indicated the shell in the racks. 'He don't like 'em. I'd have some hands rig a target.'

Phillips hurried away forward again.

Guy stepped across to the other side. The confused movement was beginning to dissolve in more or less still lines of men between the guns, answering to their numbers and presenting equipment. As he watched, the smartest crews began loading; soon all were opening the cartridge cases and handling rammers. It was a thoroughly creditable performance after the recent break in routine. Shell were passed and one after another the lines of side-tackle men heaved the pieces outboard; gun captains hooked on their firing lanyards and, stepping back to the extent of the line, raised a hand above their head. The tackle men between each piece stood quite still, leaning to the heel; midshipmen reported to the lieutenants of the quarters. A strange silence fell over the deck. Guy wondered what had happened to Phillips. Walking back across the deck, he caught sight of his white cap cover amidst a group about a 64-pounder by the bridge stanchions; there was evidently something wrong. He strode forward, realizing as he went that this was number eight – Davis's gun.

Phillips turned as he came up. 'The eye on the firing tube's snapped off and the tube's jammed in the vent.'

Guy nodded. 'Report all guns ready except number eight.'

As Phillips hurried off Guy motioned one of the hands who was holding a lantern to move it over the gun and, stepping over the tackle, jumped up on the slide to take a closer look at the vent, feeling as he did so a warning tingle at the back of his neck – Davis's gun. The metal gleamed where the eye had broken off – remarkably cleanly. He bent his head closer but only succeeded in shutting out the light. It would have to be examined in the morning. In the meantime it looked as though the tube would have to stay where it was; it appeared to have been jammed hard in; there was scarcely anything left to grasp above the metal of the gun. The detonating mechanism inside would be intact; it would be dangerous to touch, let alone withdraw it until the powder had been ignited somehow. He turned and jumped off the slide.

'Davis!'

'Sir!' The man's eyes glinted from rings of shadows cast by the lantern.

'How did this occur?'

'I don't know, sir.' The consonants were thicker than usual.

'Hold the lamp up.' Guy said, and took a step towards him.

The man's eyes glowed fiercely; his face appeared to have shrunk since he had seen him last; sharp lines down his cheeks were etched in the swaying light. There was a faint smell of spirits, but he couldn't be certain whether this came from Davis or from others round about – or indeed from all of them. He might have expected them to purchase grog from the usual sources to celebrate their release – no doubt they'd been sleeping it off when roused by the bugle. He looked round the circle of faces, wondering how many were in a fit state for duty.

As he turned he caught sight of a figure crouched on the funnel casing half hidden behind a ventilator cowl. He stared in disbelief, and beckoned him out. The man uncoiled hesitantly, then jumped down to the deck, amid grunts of suppressed laughter from the men round about. Guy saw it was an ordinary seaman, Smith, known as Dick on account of unfortunate eruptions of acne all over his face. He wore a jumper, but below he was quite naked. He stood clasping his hands across his front.

'A fine figure of a man!' Guy said. The dammed up laughter broke around him.

'I suggest you get below and complete your dress.'

''e's triced his pants up in 'is 'ammick,' one of the men said to another outburst.

'Crusher sent 'im up,' from another voice.

'Can't speak up for yourself, Smith?' Guy said. 'Off with you, then!'

'They'll 'ave 'im, sir.'

Guy stared at the speaker as Smith turned uncertainly towards the ladderway.

'Sir – ' Guy recognized the voice of Fisher, the Old Man's 'doggie' behind him, and swung round. 'Captain's compliments sir – would you inform him what is the hold-up, sir.'

'Is that what he said?'

The lad grinned.

Guy put a hand on his shoulder. 'Tell him number eight gun is out of action. I'll report directly.'

'Aye aye, sir!' The lad scampered away.

Guy turned to speak to Davis but he wasn't there. He called his name and, following the direction of eyes, swung round towards the muzzle of the piece. Davis was by the bulwark; for some reason he had taken the lantern.

'*Davis*!' he roared, alarmed at the look on his face; the man was glaring, or so it seemed in the flaring light; there were points of brightness at the centre of each pupil. After waiting quite motionless for a moment, he ambled slowly back towards Guy.

Guy had the feeling a crisis had passed.

'Line the hands up inboard,' he snapped. 'No one so much as to look at that gun again tonight, Davis, or I'll have you up before the owner before you can blink.'

'I'd expect that – sir.' Davis's mouth drooped cynically.

Guy controlled his voice. 'If you haven't blown yourself to kingdom come.'

The dark eyes stared back.

'I assume she's loaded?'

'Of course – sir.'

'Line 'em up then!'

As Davis shouted out his instructions, and the hands moved away from the gun, Guy turned and strode back towards the wheel.

Saxmundham looked up at him from the face of the hunter, still resting in his left palm.

'Number eight gun is effectively spiked, sir. I've instructed the crew to stand clear.'

'Twelve minutes, twenty-three seconds.'

'The other guns have been ready some time, sir.'

Saxmundham stared at him in silence. At last he growled, 'See if you can manage a night firin' better.'

'Sir!' Guy snapped a salute and swung round on Phillips nearby. 'Guns! Have a target prepared for laying out!'

Phillips had started up the deck almost before he completed the sentence.

'Greville!'

He turned.

Saxmundham was gazing down at the hunter again. 'Where

is the supernumerary?'

'I'm not sure, sir.'

'Still at his *toilette*? Oblige me by sendin' the beggar up!'

'Aye, aye, sir! Guy moved across and told the midshipman of the watch to see if D'Arcy were in his cabin, and if not to find him and ask him to step up on deck. Then he went forward and shouted at the bridge, 'Searchlights there! On the beam!'

A moment afterwards the night was pierced by two brilliant bands of light, one each side. Thank the Lord! They wavered, then settled on swathes of sea some five hundred yards out from the ship. Through the nearest gunport Guy saw breaking crests of wavelets sparkling against a pale, undulating surface.

He began to calculate how long it might take to fire off all the shell in the racks, but seeing activity at the break of the fo'c's'le – evidently the party preparing the target – started forward. Davis's crew were silent as he passed them, backed up against the funnel casing. He couldn't see Smith, and told one of the hands off to go down and find out what had happened.

'Bein' chased round the deck, sir, I reckon.'

It was an entertaining picture.

'Below there – ' Guy recognized D'Arcy's tortured vowels and looked up quickly.

D'Arcy was leaning over the bridge rail, clad so far as he could make out in his usual rig with an enveloping muffler in place of a cravat. 'I tried to tell the silly bugger, if he required the loan of a well-made pair of – you know what – but he hopped awf like a rabbit.'

Guy laughed. 'I dare say you terrified the poor fellow.' He nodded aft. 'The owner would like a word.'

'That's where you're quite wrong. He'd cheerfully fire me awf with the rest.' D'Arcy waved a glove at the shells in the racks. 'In lieu of which he means to see that I witness this charade. Do me a favour, old chum, back me up when I tell him the supernumerary's action station is up here. I gather he don't care for it much.'

'Done! But I suggest you get aft – he's timing your appearance.'

'Do he take his dinner cooked – or raw?'

There was a growl of laughter from the gun's crew.

'*Silence*.' Guy swung on the men. 'And you – Hobbs' – he turned on the hand he had sent after Smith – 'jump to it!'

Hobbs made off quickly. Guy continued towards the fo'c's'le, where he made out Phillips and the bo'sun side by side, bending over the floats of the target; its small masts and rectangle of canvas between shone palely above their bent backs. They straightened as they heard his footsteps.

'She's ready to go,' Phillips said.

'Capital!'

The bo'sun leant closer in a confiding way he had. 'It's Mr D'Arcy-Green, sir – he's the Jonah – '

Guy turned away.

The old sailor grabbed his arm. 'You'll 'ave to make 'im see, sir. 'e can't wear them rings and yaller ties, not with Old Sax.' He fell in beside as Guy made his way back to report the target ready. 'I bin with Old Sax a fair spell, sir.'

'So have I Bose.'

'There's good stuff in 'im – Mr D'Arcy-Green, sir – an' Sax, 'e's main cliver at spottin' the right stuff in a man, sir, I seed 'im bring on a poor scrap of a sub you an' me wouldn't 've looked at twice – an' make a proper sailor out of 'im.'

'Why don't *you* try your hand?'

''E'd niver listen to me, sir.'

'Nor to me, I fear. I tried yesterday. He told me to "bugger awf".'

The bo'sun grunted.

Guy tapped him encouragingly on the shoulder. 'See what you can do. It's worth a try.' He left him and strode up to Saxmundham. 'Target ready, sir.'

The Old Man opened his lungs. 'Hands abou-out ship!' Satisfied with the response, he turned to the quartermaster. 'Ease the helm down!'

Guy pushed the stores indent forms to the top of his desk and sat back. It was late; after the previous night on deck at target practice, he badly needed sleep – yet he felt too oppressed. It was more than tiredness.

He looked at the photograph of his sisters sitting at the stern of a skiff on the river; as always Helen claimed his attention, leaning towards the camera, smiling, her hair loose as she liked it. How many times had he studied the picture and regained some sanity in the heat of the Gulf? He knew every detail, every ripple in the water caught in that instant of sunlight at Godalming, England; tea and scones and apple pie at The Boathouse with its low cracked beams and enclosing smell of flour and pasties.

He found he had drawn a sheet of ship's headed paper from the pigeon-hole and charged his pen.

Dearest Trojan,

This is turning out the most beastly trip. Old Sax, you know how much I looked up to him in the past, I think now I'm beginning to loathe him –

He stared at what he had written, then took the sheet and tore it across, then again and again before he dropped the small pieces in the waste basket.

Dearest Trojan,

You will have read in the papers of our new Captain Bligh, well we're after him and hot on his scent! We're bound for the Laccadive Islands and expect to make the first reef where the local fishermen are said to foregather tomorrow morning early. We spent most of last night steering the wrong way so we shouldn't make it in the dark. During the course of it we pumped every one of the shell on deck overboard – I should say at a target of which we made a thorough mess eventually. The real reason for the sport was an unnatural dislike Old Sax has taken to a new lieutenant who was sent out from home to take over from me. Sax took this as trespassing on his authority! And he refused to let him take over – *after* I had handed over to him I may say! And the whole affair is the most frightful mess. It made me wonder whether I was right in handing over in the first place. But when you see the Admiralty crest and the signature of such a nabob as the secretary to the LC you don't ask questions. Old Sax is a law unto himself. He tore the holy writ before our very eyes without so much as a "Bless my soul" to ward off spirits. Now he's conducting a campaign of furious hate against D'Arcy – that's the new man – and D'Arcy, poor fellow, is reacting with furious *indifference*, and dire threats about how the Admiral will deal with Old Sax when we get to Trinco where we're bound after the islands. He, that is D'Arcy, haunts the bridge because he knows Sax loathes the place, and parades up and down in the most aesthetic cravats you ever saw, flashing the rings on his fingers whenever he sees the Old Man, and singing a weird song he's made up to the tune of 'The Man who broke the Bank at Monte Carlo'; 'As I walk the bridge of *Dulcinea*, with an independent ear, you can 'ear the jacks declar, 'e must be a millionear' etc. etc. It would all be tremendously funny if it weren't so sad. As the old bo'sun said to me last night D'Arcy's got plenty of the right stuff in 'im, but he's just got up Old Sax's nostrils with his fancy airs, and now neither of them will back down, and I'm in the middle, the discipline of the ship is suffering, and goodness knows how it will end.

He read what he had written and, wondering if it sounded a shade frantic, re-charged his pen.

The worst part of it is that I like both of them a lot, and you know how I've always looked up tremendously to Old Sax, it's a disappointment to watch him behaving like a child. Don't that sound patronizing? And from *me* you'll say! – The curse of it is no one can *tell* him.

He smiled at the picture conjured up. 'Sir, with respect, I have to inform you – for the good of the officers and ship's company – ' The picture dissolved in Saxmundham's ice-blue gaze. He had felt that overpowering disapproval once before when he had had the temerity to question his judgement.

He read the letter through again, feeling better now that it was down in pen and ink – yet there was another hanging cloud, one that he could not write about except in the most general terms; it was altogether too alarming.

He thought back, as he had a hundred times over the affair at number eight gun. Davis and the others had been drinking – that was understandable, and it was simply unfortunate that they should have been subjected to night quarters on the very night of their release. Yet Davis had not been so drunk as to be unaware of what he was doing. He had been very well aware: there had been hate in his sunken eyes. And whether or not the top of the firing tube had been deliberately damaged, the tube itself could scarcely have been jammed in the gun without intent and prior doctoring.

In the morning light loose gunpowder had been discovered on deck by the muzzle of the piece and in the rifling grooves down the bore – a trail of explosive leading to the charge within. It was theoretically possible that the cartridge had been torn accidentally after being taken out of its case for there had been no powder inside the case – but he had never known it happen. In any case it could scarcely have escaped the notice of the loading numbers. Yet nothing had been said.

Had it been a deliberate plot to injure him? 'Injure' was euphemistic; he would have been lucky to escape with his life if the powder trail had been ignited while he was peering over the damaged tube – he would have lost an eye at the least, and been mangled as the piece recoiled. Yet it was difficult to see how Davis could have calculated that he, not Phillips or the officer of the quarters or the armourer, would examine and perhaps attempt to remove the tube. Not so difficult perhaps; it was evident that he, as the gunnery specialist, would have been called at some stage. Assuming this, how could Davis have lit the trail without drawing attention to himself, or without blowing *himself* up? The fearful dangers of the loose powder train scarcely bore thinking about.

In his frenzy for vengeance, perhaps Davis had been careless of his own safety. In that case why had he *not* lit the train? The opportunity had been there. Perhaps he had appeared too suddenly; it would have been difficult for the man to work around from the breech to the muzzle without drawing attention to himself – and with the scene so well lit. Perhaps whoever it was called for the lantern had saved his life.

He had a vivid image of Davis with the lantern by the bulwarks afterwards, and remembered his impression that a crisis of some kind had passed. The man must have been standing right on top of the loose powder at that moment.

How many of the gun's crew had been involved? All had denied any knowledge – 'an accident, sir. One or two 'ad a drop too many.'

It had been no accident, but whether it was a conspiracy or the work of one vengeful maniac was unclear. Equally unclear was the best response. If he marched the whole crew up before Saxmundham it would be further proof for the malcontents of his unnatural vindictiveness towards anyone connected with Davis. If he singled out Davis, that would be worse. He would never be able to prove *intent*.

He would strip Davis of his privileges, hold another enquiry with witnesses from nearby guns' crews. It would not remove the disturbing thought that a man, or men, aboard were prepared to go to such extremes. He had been warned. He couldn't say a word to Trojan.

How is father? I liked your description of him lighting carbolic smoke balls all down the aisle to ward off the dreaded influenza. Do write, Trojan – you have no notion what a tonic it is to hear the simplest everyday *ordinary* things in such an asylum as this ship has become.

He jammed the pen down on the desk and rose with a feeling of despair. The remedy was not working. He went out through the darkened wardroom and into the gun-room flat, assailed by snoring and the usual close atmosphere, and quickly up on deck.

After a while the darkness and the hiss of water along the side and the ever present stars began to clear his mind.

5

Stainton had wedged himself in the angle of the starboard bridge rail, binoculars to his eyes. Guy watched him move them slowly forward, slowly back again; he made his way up the ladder to join him.

The ocean stretched away benignly under a clear sky. The swell advancing from the starboard quarter lifted the shadows of the sails as the *Dulcinea* dipped to meet it. Some way below, a long, greenish shape slid rapidly towards the bows, surfacing in the lazy curve of the displacement wave and arcing with erect dorsal, dark and glistening over the reflections beneath the cathead.

Guy searched the distance ahead. There was a hollow feeling behind his eyes, and he was aware of his lower lids, but as so often after periods of missed sleep his faculties seemed heightened. As he scanned what appeared to be endless, empty sea, disappointment too was sharp.

'Curious, pilot. No fishermen.'

There was a pause. 'Ramadan I expect.'

'Perhaps they've lost their way.'

Stainton lowered his glasses and examined him. 'Oh, ye of little faith!' He turned and leant nonchalantly against the rail. 'Navigation, number one – unlike some other specializations I hesitate to mention – is something of an exact science. You may ask,' he shrugged, 'naturally you will ask – if that is the case why does the poor fellow hang over the end of the bridge rail pulling his eyes out of their sockets when he might be snug below in the most perfect confidence – feet up and nose in a three-year-old copy of the *Sportin' and Dramatic* –'

'Jolly weather for fishing.'

'For all I know,' Stainton pressed on, 'the fishermen may not have studied their *Imray's* recently. They may not have the least idea they're expected.' He paused as they heard someone coming up the ladder, and turned to look.

The surgeon appeared, his pink face wearing its usual happy expression, as it would Guy felt sure if he were diagnosing an outbreak of cholera.

'If I might have a word' – he looked at Guy with the absurdly innocent china-blue eyes – 'in confidence.'

'Of course.' Guy straightened from the rail, turning briefly to Stainton, 'I wish you luck!'

'A plague on your fishermen!'

Directly they were out of earshot the surgeon said, 'Davis is unfit for duty. I am keeping him in the sick-bay.'

Guy looked at him, wondering why it should be a matter for confidences.

The surgeon gazed back. 'Since the discussion in the ward-room –' There was a meaning gleam in his eye.

'About the accident?'

'If such it was. Yes – in the light of that discussion I thought it would interest you to hear the nature of Davis's injuries.'

'Injuries?'

The surgeon stopped and faced him. 'The man has received a very thorough flogging.'

Guy stared.

'Within an inch of his life. I've not witnessed the like before. It's not pretty.' He might have been discussing the bouquet of the ward-room port.

'The hands have done this?' It was a rhetorical question. He'd known a case of this form of mess-deck punishment before, in his first ship as a midshipman. An ordinary seaman had been found with property stolen from his messmates. He had been lashed spread-eagle across two hammocks over a chest and given four dozen with a hammock clew made up of twenty-two separate lines. He had not seen the result, but the affair had caused a small sensation in the gun-room. He thought the practice had been stamped out. 'D'you know why? Did he say anything?'

'He was in no condition to say much. Of course I made enquiry –' He shrugged.

Guy started again towards the port rails. 'You mentioned the affair at the gun. You believe – ?'

'It seems a possible explanation – it occurred on the evening immediately following.' He shrugged. 'Who can say?'

'If that was deliberate.' Of course he knew it had been.

They came to the bridge end and he gazed out, seeing the faces of the gun's crew glowing in lantern light. 'It was risking every man jack.' He turned. 'And not only his own crew.'

The surgeon nodded. 'You know best about that. I shall have to report it to Sax of course.'

'Of course.'

'I thought I should warn you first.'

'Thank you.'

They started back again. 'You think I brought this on?' Guy asked.

The surgeon grasped his arm. 'Davis? It doesn't seem to have affected the others in quite the same way.' He smiled as his father smiled to greet the faithful after matins.

'No.'

A light baritone sounded behind them. 'Dame Fortune smiled upon me as she'd never done before.'

D'Arcy stood at the top of the ladder as if making a grand entrance at the Lyceum. 'What a perfect surprise!' He came stiffly towards them, eyes bulging with pleasure. 'It's usually so damned quiet up here. Now there are three' – he caught sight of Stainton at the other side – '*four* of us. And I've such lots of money I'm a gent – yes, I've such lots of money I'm a gent – d'you fancy our pilot looks anxious?'

Guy's annoyance at the interruption faded in the glow of D'Arcy's ingenuous good humour. 'I should ask him.'

'I shall, I've bin thinkin', Greville, what d'you say to a banyan party on the reef?' He took Guy's arm. 'It's what the jacks need you see. They're fairly done up. I've noticed it since I came off duties. It's showin'. They need to recreate. What d'you say Sawbones?' He looked at the surgeon and, without waiting for a reply, 'I say there's nothin' like a picnic to put 'em to rights.'

They were interrupted by a cry from the fore crosstrees, 'Breakers ahead!' and immediately afterwards a shout of triumph from the end of the bridge. Stainton was standing quite still, glasses raised, looking forward.

They made towards him. He turned, a pleased expression on his face, and as they came up handed his binoculars to Guy. 'Sorry about the fishermen!'

Steadying himself against the rail, Guy scanned the sea ahead. At first he could see nothing but the ocean rolling towards the horizon, then something bright caught his attention and, holding the glasses on it, he made out at intervals between the swell a flashing line; it might have been breaking waves or sand, or almost anything reflective. As he examined it he heard Saxmundham calling up from the deck.

'It's the reef, sir,' Stainton replied. 'Eight miles – perhaps more – fine on the starboard bow.'

'Two hours,' the Old Man said, as if to himself.

Guy lowered the glasses.

Saxmundham called up again. 'Any fishermen?'

'Not a sign of them, sir.'

'You certain it's Cherbaniani?'

'Nothing else it could be, sir.' Stainton paused, looking at Guy brightly for a moment, then down again. 'It's possible, sir, the fishermen may not have consulted their *Imray's*.'

Guy glanced at his face, amused to see a shadow of apprehension crossing it.

Saxmundham stared up for a moment. 'I trust the turtles have done so, pilot.'

'Yes, sir.' Stainton grinned with relief.

Saxmundham started aft; they heard his footsteps down the deck. 'D'you understand from that he means to pay a call in any case?'

The surgeon smiled. 'Make no doubt of it. When he's satisfied as to the quality of the turtle meat he'll proceed – and not a moment earlier.'

'Hang it,' D'Arcy said. 'I'm inclined to agree with him.'

They laughed.

'It's a good anchorage,' Stainton said. 'If he were to press on, well she's not exactly expressin' – I'd say he was right to anchor. Either that or raise steam.'

'Right or not,' the surgeon said, making for the ladder. 'He will – you may depend on it.' He waved cheerily.

Stainton started for the chart-house, warbling to himself, 'Beau-ootiful soup – sou-oop of the evening –'

D'Arcy turned eagerly to Guy. 'Remember what I say – a picnic party, hauling the seine – I'm your man!'

Guy wondered if he detected a hint of desperation. 'I'll ask Sax.'

D'Arcy beamed. 'You're an excellent fellow, Greville.'

'I fancy a run ashore myself.' He thought of the look on

Davis's face under the lantern, and imagined the wiry fellow struggling as they seized and lashed him across the hammocks on the mess-deck, shivering at an image of his teeth biting into the gag as the blows cut across his back – and again and again unmercifully.

'You have no idea,' D'Arcy was saying, 'the voyage out in the *Peninsular* was a model of tedium – but put yourself in my position here.'

'I can imagine,' Guy said, finding it impossible to think how one of the smartest gun captains aboard should have been brought so suddenly to this and wondering again where his own responsibility lay.

'I doubt that. No,' D'Arcy leant back against the rail, 'there's nothin' brings a man down like lack of occupation.' His eyes were unnaturally dull. 'We may fancy we'd enjoy the life of ease – and the bullion to go with it – but when it comes down to it, Greville, no, it takes the heart out of a fellow to feel he's no use to man nor beast. He begins to think, d'you see, that's an uncommonly dismal occupation, don't you know, and it don't get a man far – to put a fine point on it, it don't get him anywhere.'

'I'll see what I can do,' Guy said, starting to go.

D'Arcy's pale brows rose. '*Do,* my dear fellow?'

'You're right. You must have some occupation.'

D'Arcy's gaze had hardened. 'It's not occupation I require, Greville.'

Guy gazed at him.

'The fellows that sweep the streets have occupation.'

'D'you want his blood?' Guy snapped.

'At first,' D'Arcy seemed to ponder, 'yes – but that's not what it is, Greville. You don't understand – no more could I have understood a little while back.'

Guy looked at him from the top of the ladder, irritation surfacing. 'It's in your hands. Lord – Take off your rings, borrow Stainton's uniform, play another role – one *he* might understand.'

'Knock under?'

'If you like.'

D'Arcy stood from the rail. 'He's taken my position, torn up my appointment, blasted my shells overboard – he'll have Saint Barbara next – *banished* me up here.'

'He's not banished you.'

'Now you wish me to give him *myself*!' His eyes bulged with emotion. 'Kiss the deck should I when he passes?'

Guy said quietly, 'It's affecting the whole ship.'

'I have nothing to give. It's in *his* hands. He started it. *He* may finish it – not I!'

Guy looked at his set face. There was nothing he could say. He started down the ladder, at the bottom turning back for a moment.

D'Arcy stood at the top, grasping both side rails, a jaunty smile back on his face. 'I am constant as the northern star.'

Guy started aft, annoyed as much by his own impotence to affect the situation as by D'Arcy's attitude. He saw the men at quarters cleaning the guns and his mind turned to Davis, searching their faces for an outward sign of what they had done on the mess-deck during the night. They? Some of them – which were the leaders? which the unthinking herd? – had humiliated a man, one of their number, savagely broken him for transgressing their code. They looked the same as before. There was no discernible difference; their beefy, bronzed, square, bearded faces were intent on their tasks. After he had passed he knew their concentration would lapse into the usual easy banter – brightened today by expectation of a break in routine – a banyan party if Old Sax decreed it. His thoughts returned to D'Arcy, striding stiffly across the bridge, singing his spirits up.

It was a curious sensation to be sailing in deep water through which you could peer and discern below the brilliant upper translucence only the darkness of unfathomable distances, and to look up and see less than a cable to starboard a beach of white sand glistening in the sun, and a lagoon beyond like a bathing pool in different shades of calm green, and nothing else – nothing at all in the wide ocean. There was a sense of fantasy about it. They should not be sailing so close to sand; a beach should mark the edge of land; it should shelve decently, not rise from nowhere and end in nothing save a shallow bowl surrounded by deep blue moving rollers.

The proximity of the sand made it appear as if they were moving fast but, even with every possible sail set, they were making no more than four knots. It would take almost an hour to reach the southern end of the reef and round up to the anchorage. Guy looked aft to where Saxmundham stood in his usual position by the wheel. He had been right in the decision to anchor. He would have been more right, perhaps, to call for steam – and yet they might need the coal later.

'There's a passage into the lagoon, sir.' The bo'sun was beside him gazing abeam.

'None too deep by the looks of it.'

'Deep enough for the launch, sir.'

Guy looked round. 'You too, Bose!'

The old sailor frowned. 'It's what the hands need.'

Guy looked across at the lagoon, so serene and inviting on the surface, and he remembered the delights of picnics and seining parties, and wondered whether it was lack of sleep or the tensions within the ship that made him doubt if he would ever find the same simple delights again.

After a moment of silence, the bo'sun prompted, 'There's a few doin' a toot, sir.'

Guy looked at him. 'What would you say might justify them taking the law into their own hands, Bose?'

The veined old eyes evaded his gaze as the man pretended not to understand.

'Don't come the old soldier,' Guy said sharply.

The bo'sun's lips made a hard line beneath the criss-cross marked, pouchy cheeks.

'Stealing from a messmate?'

The gaze met his blankly.

'Threatening life?'

An element of doubt had crept into the eyes. So that *was* it! Davis's fanaticism had been his crime; he had placed the limbs and lives of his entire gun's crew at terrible risk; they had wrought their own terrible retribution.

'Well?' he went on sharply.

The bo'sun scratched the white stubble above his ears. 'Supposin' a man wouldn' git 'is proper punishment aft –'

'*Proper* punishment!'

'There were some as thought it wrong to do away with the cat.'

Guy tried to think what crimes had been punishable by flogging – desertion, drunkenness, fighting, insubordination, violence against a superior –

Looking at the old sailor he realized he would get nothing more from him, but he had learned enough.

'I'll see what I can do,' he said.

Saxmundham and the surgeon went away in a cutter soon after they had anchored, returning in mid-afternoon with the bottom boards alive with turtles, their flippers waving clumsily as the boat rocked alongside, lugubrious heads suggesting they had prepared themselves, poor creatures, for the end – indeed had never expected anything better from life.

Saxmundham's eyes glowed as he stepped through the entrance port and raised his felt hat to the quarter-deck. 'What d'you say Greville?'

'A capital bag, sir!'

The Old Man raised his arms, displaying the sleeves of his tweed jacket soaked well above the elbows. 'On my life!' He looked round at his sporting companion.

'I thought you were lost on a number of occasions,' the surgeon smiled.

Saxmundham chuckled hugely. Guy waited while they exchanged comments on the hunt like boys after a house match, then seeing his opportunity asked permission for the hands to go ashore that evening to haul the seine net.

'Of course they shall!' Saxmundham replied. 'On my life!' He started aft and Guy fell in beside him. 'We'll be off at first light,' and frowning, 'I don't like it. Wind's dropped away entirely.' He raised his head. 'It don't smell right.'

'The glass is high, sir.'

'I'm pleased to hear it. All the same' – he waved a hand towards the lagoon – 'deserted. Don't that strike you as queer, Greville? There's fish of every description – the water's stiff with 'em. These fellows – hang it, they must know there's some weather on the way or they'd be here.' He looked round, puzzled. 'And there's another thing, there's a sauce bottle on the beach – Harvey's.'

Guy searched for the connection.

'Don't that suggest anythin' to you?'

'Harvey's. A British ship?'

Saxmundham grunted and looked around for the surgeon,

about to go down the companionway. 'That bottle, James –'

The surgeon looked up. 'Indeed!' He turned to Guy. 'Harvey's sauce, if you please.'

'Clean,' Saxmundham prompted, 'uncommonly clean.'

'Clean as a whistle,' the surgeon nodded.

The Old Man turned triumphantly to Guy. 'That's our contribution, m'boy. Now, do you go off, see what you make of it!'

As he went in to his quarters Guy stepped across to Hardy-Penfold, pacing the deck, and asked him to have the whaler piped; afterwards he made his way up to the bridge to tell D'Arcy he might make preparations for a seining party.

'You're a good fellow, Greville. I shan't forget it.'

Guy went down on deck as the call sounded for the whaler's crew then below to the ward-room. Heighurst opened an eye from the depths of a chair.

'What d'you say to a run ashore?' Guy asked.

The other eye opened. 'Bathin' party?'

'Why not?'

Heighurst raised himself on his elbows. 'I've bin hearin' about your chum, Davis.' And, as Guy's gaze sharpened, 'Basset, as a matter of fact. Not usually the most talkative fellow –'

'Basset!'

'From the way he came out with it, I gathered I was to pass it on. But it don't surprise you –'

'Did he say why they did it?'

'No, he didn't care to explain.' Heighurst rose and went across to his cabin door. 'It *was* mixed bathin' you mentioned?' He paused, one brow raised. 'No! Fishermen turned up?'

Guy moved away, shaking his head. 'I'll tell you in the boat.'

It was a long haul along the reef to the channel into the lagoon and the fitful breeze was little help; the sails flapped lifelessly; for the most part the journey was made under oars, and by the time Aimes pushed the tiller across to turn the bows towards the entrance the sun was low in the west, directly in his face. He raised a hand to shield his eyes as he peered forward against the glare off the water.

The swell became steeper as they approached, sucking at the coral and leaving whirlpools in the channel. Looking back along the line of disturbed sea and the bare, intermittent ridges of the reef they had passed, Guy saw that several boats had put out from the ship and were heading in their track, oars flashing rhythmically.

Heighurst followed his gaze drawling in a fair imitation of D'Arcy. 'The seinin' party's away then.'

Aimes said, 'There'll be a few more bottles on the beach by the time they've finished.'

'Enough of your sauce my lad!'

The live coral was suddenly very close beneath them, standing up in fantastic knobs and convoluted branches, falling away into grottoes through which curiously shaped and coloured fish darted – a brilliant fairy scene which never failed to delight with its freshness and fantasy, however many times Guy saw it.

The crew drew strength from the knowledge that they were near the end of the long haul, and leant back to the stroke. The thwarts creaked, eddies from the oar blades swirled astern. The coral bottom rose, and the dark caves between upstanding clumps gave way to sand, rippled with light from the waves of their progress.

Aimes called out, 'Oars!' and shortly afterwards ordered the bowmen over the side to haul her up the beach. Guy looked at the men, damp with sweat, shoulders heaving, and told the midshipman to give them a ten minute 'spell' before joining the search.

'It's not only bottles we're looking for,' he explained. Anything which might have come from a British ship.'

A voice from forward said, 'The *Curlew*, sir?'

'I doubt we'll come across anything with her name on it – but yes, if it's British and recent it could be from the *Curlew*.'

'We may find the ship's cat, sir!'

There was a shout of laughter. Guy looked at their faces, wondering how they could joke about it after what had happened to Davis; he realized that was why they had. The laughter was much too loud.

'If you do,' he replied, 'I'd see if it can swim,' and they roared again. The bo'sun had been right: they needed a run ashore.

He jumped out, landing in shallow water, and walked up to the dry sand of the beach.

'You know,' Guy said to Heighurst when they were out of earshot of the boat, walking slowly between the high tide mark and the edge of the lapping lagoon, 'it's curious, this business with Davis.'

Heighurst looked at him sharply, 'Puts one in mind of the *Curlew*.'

Guy nodded.

'It may not be Vaneyke after all,' the marine went on, 'but the jolly jacks takin' matters into their own hands.'

'Taking the ship too?'

He had been thinking on these lines since the surgeon had told him about Davis that morning. Yet it hardly fitted with the ideas he had formed in Bombay, nor with Mrs Vaneyke's departure for Ceylon – at all events not with *his* interpretation of her departure.

'That looks like it!' Heighurst was gazing up the beach above the high water mark.

Glass flashed in the sun. All around and down to the water's edge the sand was imprinted with tracks as if Saxmundham and the whole of the cutter's crew had been up to have a look, and as they approached it became evident that the shining thing was the Harvey's sauce bottle. The label had been washed off, but the familiar size and shape were sufficient indication. It lay in the scuffled sand in the middle of nowhere, indisputably British.

'I'll hand it to old Sax,' Heighurst said, 'He knows a sauce bottle when he sees one.'

They gazed down at it. A small drift of sand darkened the lower inside, and there were grains adhering to the thread for the top, which was missing; otherwise it looked as pristine as the day it had been manufactured.

Guy knelt and picked it up. 'No water inside, no top' – he looked around – 'no top nearby. *Ergo,* it didn't drift here. It was dropped.' He looked up. 'Yet it's absolutely clean.'

Heighurst brought a hand up to the end of his moustache. 'In my experience the last of the sauce remains in the bottle – *ergo,* if it didn't drift, it was washed out.' He raised one brow. 'Or the fellow that dropped it had the devil of a long tongue.'

Guy smiled. 'If it was washed out, it was used for something else.'

Comprehension dawned for both at the same instant. Guy put the bottle to his nose and sniffed, then handed it to the marine, who did the same, shaking his head as he lowered it. Guy took it from him, shook the sand from inside into his palm and raised that to his nose; it smelt of heat and sea shore. There was, however, a minute wedge of it left in the very bottom which would not move however much he hit the bottle.

'If we could get a sniff at that –'

They looked around for something long and thin yet stout enough to scrape the sand out, but there were only dried branches of seaweed and shells.

'Break it,' Heighurst said.

There was nothing heavy enough, so they walked back towards the whaler. Aimes and the crew had just left and were walking towards them in a line abreast spread from the water's edge to just above the debris of the high tide line, searching the sand before their feet. As they closed, Guy asked the nearest man for his knife, then laying the bottle on its side in the sand struck it sharply with the handle. The glass starred and a crack spread. He hammered it again harder, several times, before a piece of the side disintegrated, leaving a jagged hole through which he could insert the knife blade. Carefully he scraped the congealed sand out on the point, carefully withdrew it and raised it to his nostrils. There was a metallic aura from the blade, but also he was sure a faint whiff of spirits. He wondered if he had imagined it, for when he put it to his nose again the smell had faded and there was only metal and hot, fishy sand.

He held the knife out before the sailor from whom he had borrowed it. 'What d'you make of it, Lowe?'

The man bent and sniffed as he had done, his expression changing from doubt to a sudden beam of delight. 'That's rum, sir!'

'That was my impression.' Guy turned to Heighurst. 'That clinches it – a British man of war' – he looked at Lowe again – 'unless secreting and selling the grog ration is also practised in merchant ships.'

'No, sir,' one of the other sailors piped up, 'that they don't, I been on the Aberdeen clippers, sir –' realizing that he had almost admitted the illegal custom of hoarding grog, he stopped suddenly. There was a shout of laughter.

'Thank you,' Guy said mock solemnly, and turned again to Heighurst. 'A British man of war – a picnic, a seining party perhaps – a few sauce bottles full of teetotallers' grog taken along?'

'It fits the bill,' Heighurst nodded.

'And not long ago, or we shouldn't smell it.'

'It don't tell us where she's gone, though.'

'It narrows the field.' He felt elated. 'We're warm, I'm certain of it.' He looked at the men. 'See what else you can find. There's not much daylight left. Cover as much ground as you can. Afterwards –' he stared at them coldly – 'you may assist with the seine.'

There was a roar of approval, and the men dispersed, grinning; forming a line abreast again, they started moving slowly away, searching the sand before them.

'Anything at all!' Guy called out then turning to Heighurst. 'I promised you a swim.'

The marine's brows rose suspiciously.

'They would have thrown most of the bottles in the water,' Guy went on. 'I'm surprised we've found this fellow.' He bent and picked the splintered bottle from the sand, placed the shivers of glass inside and, holding it carefully by the neck, swung it in a bowling action out into the lagoon. It arced, flashing in the low sun, and splashed down out of sight. 'Somewhere out there,' he added.

Heighurst watched, his silence more expressive than words.

Guy smiled broadly. 'We're on the scent – great heavens!' He began unbuttoning his tunic.

'Go boy! Find 'im!'

Guy removed his tunic and swung it hard at the marine, who took a quick step back. He folded it carefully and laid it in the sand, pulled off his vest and wet spine pad, and bent to untie his soaking shoe laces. When he looked up he saw that Heighurst was doing the same.

The water in the shallows was almost hot. A shoal of small fish with wavy, greenish markings spread away before them and crabs sidled off stirring up small clouds of sand. Ahead the sky was suffusing with sunset; a golden orange path flared towards them over the placid surface.

'We had better come in before D'Arcy and his merry men arrive,' Heighurst said.

Guy laughed, imagining D'Arcy's popping green eyes if the two of them were hauled in the seine.

The sand shelved very gradually, and they had to wade through the shallows for a long time, making detours around coral outcrops or upstanding fronds of crimson weed concealing who knew what poisonous spines or giant shells waiting to close on the unwary foot. They were conscious of teeming life about them, feeling sudden startling movements beneath their feet, but catching only fleeting glimpses of the fantastic creatures they were disturbing as they concentrated on finding a clear path ahead.

As soon as it became deep enough to swim, they fell forward into the water and floated on with lazy movements; it was like a bathe in a warm spring; there was no shock, only a delicious suspension of effort. Guy felt the tensions of the voyage, even the excitement of the recent deductions flowing away from him like the patterns of light seen on the crystalline sand below, spreading and changing shape until they were gone. The splendid idea of searching for some further sign of the British ship – if such it had been – faded; the odds against finding anything in so wide an area without any guide save the possible range of a man's throw seemed laughable. Heighurst had been right. It struck him suddenly that perhaps this calm state induced in him by the water and the tranquil warmth of late afternoon was Heighurst's normal condition!

He rolled over on his back to put the question, but when he looked, the surface of the lagoon was empty. He felt a stab of alarm. There was a disturbance behind, and he turned quickly.

Heighurst was rising, dripping hair streaked down his forehead, one hand high clutching a dark bottle. Seeing Guy staring, he flung it towards him.

Guy stretched a hand up and caught it.

The marine's eyes glinted as he gasped in breath. 'Murrees pale ale!' It was intended as an excitable Indian accent. 'Most awfully empty, sah'b, one tremendously dead marine' – he held out an open palm – 'oh, ticklish work, sah'b –'

'Oh, dear, dear me!' Guy interrupted in similar vein, waving his head from side to side, 'where my damn trouser gone this time –'

'Oh but I am wantin' shirrt off sah'b's back –'

They were interrupted by a commotion some distance to their right; a large area of the surface of the lagoon boiled with movement, a silvery shape leapt from the outskirts, touched for a moment with pink from the sky, and after it several others jumped from different parts of the maelstrom; they looked exceedingly large fish for such shallow water.

'Dinner time!' Heighurst said. There was a different note in his voice.

'They'll not want to be disturbed'. Guy turned towards the beach.

'No.' Heighurst turned quickly with him. 'Correct to retire.'

Guy clutched the bottle as he ploughed overarm to the shallows, feeling a tingling in his feet as if he were being pursued, then rose and pushed towards the beach, raising spray either side. There was little warmth left in the sinking sun on his back, and before he left the water he was feeling distinctly chilly. The masts of D'Arcy's flotilla were close now, and as he looked up at them briefly from his course between coral and weed, he saw that the leading boat was moving through the channel into the lagoon.

By the time all the boats had pulled in and discharged their crowded benches, the red in the western sky had been overtaken by midnight blue with just a pale band above the horizon to mark roughly where the sun had disappeared to brighten another day. Soon even that had given way to rushing night, and the stars had become brilliant; they struck back from the smooth black surface of the lagoon as from a polished mirror. The air hung still and mild.

Only D'Arcy's hordes disturbed the grandeur; they were everywhere on the beach, pale figures moving, whooping or calling out to one another, some dragging dry seaweed fronds or driftwood from the ocean side towards a pile of debris being prepared for a fire by the side of the lagoon, some tumbling, laughing or wrestling like children released from school – indeed many of these were midshipmen – bringing to the lonely reef the bustle and vulgarity of a London river outing.

There was a crackle of flames and, looking towards the firewood pile, Guy saw D'Arcy crouched with a spent lucifer match in his hand, staring at the results of his handiwork; orange light flickered over his chunky features, his thick lips were parted, his eyes protruberant, and in profile he looked much as Guy imagined an anarchist dynamiter might look after planting a bomb under a pillar of government. His rig belied the idea; he wore what appeared to be a striped cricket club blazer and white shirt open at the neck above the usual tight flannels, flaring out at the foot.

Satisfied with the fire, he rose and, waving his arms, yelled to the men to hurry with the driftwood and man the launch. His excitement was infectious; the figures dragging objects quickened their pace, cheering; others ran, some stumbling to their knees in the sand, shouting and laughing. In a short time the crew of the launch were at the oars and a noisy contingent around the stern was pushing her out. As the craft floated and the crew leant into the stroke, others tailed on to the ropes from the seine net as it was paid out over the stern. She went straight from the beach at a fair speed sending ripples widening over the lagoon, gently rocking the stars. Then she slowed as hands in the stern sheets began paying out the bulky net itself with its cork floats at the top and lead weights beneath. D'Arcy hopped up the beach, his arms waving like a mad conductor, directing some men to the lines from the net, others to another group some distance down the beach where he expected the launch to come in, others to light burning torches from the fire and stand at the water's edge to attract the fish, others to fetch yet more fuel.

'He don't like to be forgotten,' Heighurst said.

'Obstinate brute,' Guy replied, thinking of their argument on the bridge.

Heighurst looked at him for a moment evidently reading his mind. 'It don't do you any harm.'

'How's it going to end? Old Sax is a devil.'

'The trouble with you – ' Heighurst started, then changed tack. 'Reason don't serve, you know. It's all very fine for mathematics and riddles of that kind, but it don't serve between people.' He sank down and sat in the sand, legs drawn up. 'I was taught that young. It's been my pleasure to observe the truth of it ever since.'

Guy forgot D'Arcy and Saxmundham for a moment in this startling revelation of Heighurst as philosopher, and sank back beside him. 'That's a subject I don't remember at school.'

'My dear fellow, that's what I'm tellin' you. You are, without doubt, the most reasonable fellow I ever came across.' He raised an eyebrow. 'It don't do. Really it don't do!'

Guy smiled. 'I feel like Alice.'

'Ah! You've been taught like Alice. The world's reasonable, people are reasonable' – his voice had an unusually hard edge; abruptly he reverted to normal – 'the male half at all events.'

Then, catching sight of D'Arcy, now down on his knees blowing furiously into the fire which had dulled under a weight of seaweed, he nodded towards him, tut-tutting.

A long way beyond the launch had almost merged into the darkness of the lagoon, but it was evident from the pale shapes of the crew and the ripples from the oars that she had turned and was pulling parallel to the beach, the net tumbling from her stern like ghostly gauze. The groups on the beach watched, their former exuberance stilled in anticipation of delight to come – or did they too have an inkling of the grand scope of the scene and their own incongruity?

He lay back and gazed up at the stars, noticing with some mechanical part of his brain the constellation of Pegasus very bright above, but thinking of Heighurst – almost letting down his guard!

'You wouldn't make a Buddhist,' he said.

'Reasonable are they?'

'Uncompromisingly. The clergy of reason.' He looked round. 'On the other hand I suppose you might. They reason away our God or anyone else's god for that matter as pure theory.' He rested his head on his hands again. 'It always appears to me that whatever form He may take those stars arrived up there somehow or other. To deny a Creator – at all events to deny Creation seems more unreasonable than to invent one. If that is what we've done.' The words sounded banal; his feelings were too profound for expression.

Heighurst was silent for a while. 'I fear we have,' he said at last. 'Another thing I was taught at a tender age.'

Guy rolled on his side, grinning. 'Where was this school?'

Heighurst stared out into the night. 'In hell I believe.' He looked round, his eyes as dark as the sky. 'The head was High Church. He taught me some useful lessons about *his* God. He was seldom content unless he drew blood.'

Guy resumed his position on his back, gazing up.

'I prayed,' Heighurst went on. 'It had no effect. I wrote to my people – they were in the Punjab – beggin' them to take me away and put me somewhere else. My mother replied. She would write to my Aunt Mary – I stayed with her – and ask her to look into my situation. My father wrote tellin' me to bear up. A canin' never did a fella any harm. He was knocked over by a bullet on the frontier. My mother remarried out there without ever comin' home.' He paused for a long while. 'Then I realized the God I prayed to wasn't up there at all – or if He was He didn't care much for me.'

Guy thought of his own father's faith and robust goodness, and his own doubts surfacing about the time he went to the *Britannia,* but they had been intellectual doubts –

'I've not seen her to this day. I've no notion where she is.'

'You two!' D'Arcy's voice sounded close and eager. 'The fun's about to start.'

'Good Lord!' Heighurst assumed surprise. 'What are you goin' to do next?'

D'Arcy laughed then, hearing a cheer from the water, turned and started back rapidly towards the edge of the sand, waving his striped arm for them to follow.

Guy sat up. The launch had completed its last leg, and was being pulled up to the beach by D'Arcy's second group of men, who were noisily hauling in the line from the end of the net. Soon it was taut, and the serious business began. Both groups spread themselves along their lines and used their weight to heave the net in between them, swaying and grunting a chorus in time. It was not long before the lines had given way to the floats and hemp mesh, and signs of movement and phosphorescence appearing in the water between the two groups indicated a catch; the swaying chorus increased in pace. Guy and Heighurst rose and ran down to lend their weight.

As more and more of the net was hauled out and flaked down on the sand, and the area of water enclosed by the floats, which jigged and dipped like live things, grew smaller, the movements under the surface increased to frenzy. The area began to boil with incandescent foam and leaping, twisting shapes of fish. D'Arcy tore off his blazer and with a cry like a dhervish, flung it away up the beach and charged into the water, throwing himself bodily on a monster that had become stranded in the shallows. Others rushed in with him, plunging their arms after the frenzied fish, slipping, falling, wrestling in spray, colliding, laughing, swearing, shouting in an orgy of savage release. Guy saw Heighurst stride in and, calmly choosing his prey, stalk but lose it; choosing another, Heighurst dived and struggled, drawn over on his knees before an explosion of silvery energy.

Guy started in to join him, when he heard an urgent voice at his side. The bo'sun was staring up with a frozen look.

'This way, sir,' he rasped.

The abruptness of his manner, and the attitudes of the men standing in the shallows looking down at a part of the net which had just been hauled in, suggested an accident. There was something caught in the net. It looked horribly human – yet it was far too small for a man. The sailors grouped around it parted as he splashed up. It was like a quarter of beef, hacked and gouged, but at one end was a single arm; it was the arm that was caught in the mesh of the net.

He turned and shouted for a light, then bent over the grisly object. The head had gone, and the other arm and half the shoulder, leaving a smash of bone and strangely bloodless tendon and skin. At the other end, where the waist should have been, there was nothing. Mercifully the water concealed that part. It was the severed chest and right arm of what had been a man.

He stood, feeling sick, waiting for the light. Behind him the sounds of the party in the water had almost ceased; only the fish still threshed the water. The men spoke in low tones, jostling nearer to catch a glimpse.

'We'd better haul it out,' he said to the bo'sun. Ought he, perhaps, to have said 'him'? He gestured to the hands nearby to tail on the net.

The thing surged towards the beach, arm out ahead, like some ghastly swimmer making a final, desperate effort to escape whatever had torn it limb from limb.

Guy followed it out, then took the blazing torch to examine it. The arm was almost straight, the fingers clasped tightly. Intricate dull blue tattoo marks chased sinuously up the muscles to the elbow, showing starkly against the bleached, yellowed flesh – an anchor, a heart, scrolls, 'mother', did it say?

There was a discolouration at the lower end. He bent closer and moved the net away; diffused green-grey marks encircled the pale wrist.

He moved the torch up the arm again to the back, hearing as he did so the sound of breath drawn in sharply. What he had taken for dark mottling was the same greyish discolouration in weals and blotches spread over practically the whole surface of the flesh, which was torn and broken as if scraped by a giant grater. The silence around him was tangible.

D'Arcy pushed his way through to his side. His curls were wet and flattened, his shirt and trousers clinging to his body. His eyes bulged as he looked down at the sight.

'I seen it afore –' the bo'sun said slowly. 'It weren't like that I never seen it, not like that.'

'The cat?' Guy asked.

'Thieves' cat. With knots – see?' the old sailor pointed.

'Poor devil.' Guy heard his voice crack.

The noise of the fish splashing and smacking the water behind seemed very loud in the silence near him.

'We'd better make a note of identifying marks,' he said, bending and moving the torch over the arm – wondering what mother would wish for this identity.

6

Images of the severed chest and arm returned to Guy at odd moments throughout the next day like sudden waves of nausea, diverting him momentarily from whatever he was doing. It had been worst in the early morning on the fo'c's'le as he watched the links of the cable ascending slowly from the limpid water. The hands had been subdued. Few words had been passed and they had been necessary. It had been the same throughout the day. A mood such as he had not witnessed before gripped every man, displaying itself in a hardness of the eye and firmness of lip and an absence of inconsequential chaff and rudery about the decks. Even the fearsome threats of the bo'sun's mates seemed to lack conviction.

Saxmundham had strode the deck for a full quarter of an hour in the morning with the chief engineer bobbing beside him on his short legs, trying to keep pace; it had never happened before, yet no one remarked on it. All day the smoke from the funnel came straight aft depositing a pattern of soot on the tarpaulin stretched over the quarter-deck and causing singed patches and holes from live embers which, in normal circumstances, would have raised the Old Man to boiling point. He scarcely seemed to notice; his only comment was to send down to ensure that the chief was making all the steam the boilers were capable of. When a group of firemen appeared on deck straight from the stokeholes in their grimy working gear to gasp some air into their lungs no one ran them down to wash and shift; the temperature below was said to be 120 degrees.

It seemed scarcely less on deck. The only breeze was from the ship's own progress; the sky was cloudless; beneath the dark-spotted tarpaulin the air was like the inside of a glass-house smelling of melting tar, hot teak and burning iron. The *Dulcinea* throbbed unnaturally, lifting to the following swell, leaning to an ominous hint of longer rollers across the trend, and corkscrewing down again. Saxmundham's nose had been correct.

The approaching storm matched Guy's mood; the prospect of it merged with the recurrent images from the seine net until the two were inseparably linked – natural violence and human violence plucking at strings of violence within him below his conscious feelings.

He pulled out his unfinished letter to Helen.

Thursday. There has been a development in our search. Yesterday we found a part of the body of a sailor who had been flogged – such marks, Trojan, I cannot get them from my mind. He had been tattooed on the arm with the usual devices so we knew he was British. No one doubts he came from the *Curlew*, poor fellow. There wasn't much of him left, I suppose the sharks had the rest, but previous to our finding him we found a bottle which smelt of rum, and a beer bottle from a brewery which has been set up out here to supply the garrisons, and which has proved popular with our ships out of Bombay, so all in all it seems we must have stumbled on the *Curlew*'s tracks.

It's a queer business. I have the distinct impression we are meant to find the *Curlew*, and that I have some part to play. Everything appears to confirm it. Why should I have been placed next to Mrs Vaneyke at dinner that night in Bombay? Why indeed should she have been invited just the night I went? Why should D'Arcy have practically sent me off the ship, giving me the opportunity to meet the Brahman? And there's another thing – while none of this business seems to make any sense at present I *know* I have the answer although it's locked up just out of reach. You know the feeling. People say things which unlock it for a moment, I reach in and it's gone. But I know it's there though. Then last night, just before we found the part of a man I told you about, I was talking to Heighurst – he actually treated me to some remarks about himself – his schooldays! He was fearfully badly treated by a master who took a delight in beatings, and he lost his belief. I happened to be looking up at thousand upon thousand of the brightest stars you ever saw and I *knew* he was wrong. It wasn't – as I told him – because *someone* must have arranged them up there and us down here, it was rather when you hear music sometimes and it plays *inside you*. There's no *reason* for it, and no *reason* why I should feel like that looking up at the stars, yet it happens, and to my mind this is *proof* there are things inside us beyond our reason. To brush this aside as being of no practical use, as Buddhists do, seems to me to be dodging the question. Anyway, no sooner had we indulged ourselves in philosophy – and I may say I never was so surprised at Heighurst – than we find *proof of evil* hauled up in the seine. It confirmed all that I had been thinking, for the existence of evil must mean the existence of its opposite. Here's the proof of *that* theorem! Every man jack aboard recognized evil, I'm certain of it, for there's an absolutely different mood in the ship today, you can see it in their faces. Yesterday the *Curlew* was a subject for debate or jokes, today there's only grim determination. Old Sax about sums it up. He's standing up there under the most tremendous shower of sparks and soot you ever saw without blinking an eyelid – and hobnobbing with the chief, who can't believe his luck! And D'Arcy's wearing a black tie in place of a cravat! And no pin! You see what this means, there's something in most of us that can't abide evil – *ergo* there's something *outside* reason that stands up for good. What's that if it's not *proof* of God – however we clothe Him – working through us?

He paused, feeling better at having put his jumbled impressions into some kind of pattern, yet disturbed suddenly by the logic. He was applying reason to what he had defined as beyond reason. As always, the arguments were circular.

Poor Helen! Philosophy at breakfast! He started a new paragraph.

You'll think this a most indigestible letter. At all events you have an opportunity to be mysterious when father asks if it's a book I've written you. Tell him we're reasoning our way to the *Curlew*, for I keep remembering the Brahman. Enough of that – I shall be required on deck soon. The swell's up and there's a wind now for the first time today, the jacks are thumping about overhead getting some canvas on her. They'll be taking it off soon, as I know we're in for something – I *long* for it! At present we're on our way through the reefs towards an island called Kalpeni where there are a few villages, to question the fishermen there, but I fancy we'll soon be steering out into the ocean. Even Old Sax won't relish dirty weather among the reefs! I hope to . . .

He reached out to hold the ink as the ship gave a lurch. From all around came sounds of sliding and falling objects; he saw a drawer beneath his bunk halfway out and, as the deck came more or less level again, he quickly screwed the top on the bottle and put the sheets of the letter away in a pigeon-hole.

Water had worked beneath his oilskin collar and down his chest. The night, the wind, the deck, the very air streamed water unleashed from the sky or driven from the sea in a flat haze above the hammock nettings. His lips were full of salt one moment, lashed fresh the next. His mind reeled with noise, his body ached with the effort of remaining more or less in the same position, jammed against the fo'c's'le bulkhead.

He had forgotten in all the hot weather cruising the brute power of a cyclone. Nor, he thought, had he been so near the centre of one before. Unable to follow the rule for avoiding it because of the reefs, they had steamed almost due east for open water while the wind, steadying on the beam, increased in strength almost by the minute, and the bottom had fallen out of the barometer. Now it was impossible to tell whether the wind was rising or not – it had gone beyond the point of analysis; it was naked energy, raising the ocean and splitting it off in solid slabs which hurtled through the night, exploding against the ship's side; masts, yards, funnel, boats, shining briefly in the glimmer from the open fo'c's'le door as they smoked away. The *Dulcinea*, bare of all save two minute storm trisails, drove up the sides of invisible ridges and fell into valleys, hitting the floor with thunderous blows and double concussions which reverberated up through the frames and beams.

He had looked forward to release in violence; now all he could think of was coming through it. There was an image at the back of his mind of Saxmundham in oilskins and sou'wester, a line around him fast to the starboard binnacle, legs braced apart, head raised slightly as if scenting out his opponent, great beard streaming water haloed in the light from the compass, a prophet exalted; it was a more potent image even than the fury outside the walls of the ship. He didn't doubt their survival so much as wonder how it would be accomplished.

Suddenly the sky was lit – yellow main mast and yards, yellow-banded funnel, white bridge rails and boats and pieces of shattered boat and twisted davits gleamed through the chaos, and as suddenly it was dark again. The discharge had been very close, but he didn't hear the thunder; he was hit from above by solid water. He fell, locking his arms about the lifeline he had been holding, and felt himself being hurled headlong, legs dragging as if surfing out of control. The sea was everywhere inside his clothes and boots, foaming about his head, now bare, and up his nostrils, down his neck, strong salt in his mouth. As the wave receded, he drew breath and struggled to get his knees under him, but the deck was falling the other way and he could do nothing but cling to the lifeline and let it swing him across on his side. His legs struck something hard, and at the same instant the ship jolted, then jolted again as if she had fallen on a submerged reef and been struck by a wall of water immediately afterwards. A tremendous crash and scream of tearing metal sounded from somewhere very close, above the howl of the storm, but he didn't know which way up or round he was, and couldn't think where it came from. Another wave enveloped him, pressing him to the deck, pulling at his oilskins and boots, rushing about his ears with a noise like a cataract; he clung to his only security and felt himself going again like a runaway coach. This time he was brought up with his legs sliding round in a free arc. Anger at his impotence welled up; he unlocked his arms and clawed at the line with his hands, heaving and jerking into a crouch.

The deck was steadier, and for an instant almost level. Another flash of lightning lit it, and he saw with a shock that he was almost under the bridge; another five feet and he would have hit the supporting pillar to which the lifeline was made fast. In front of him were the round, canvas-covered bases of the two ventilators forward of the bridge and, just beyond them where it should never have been, a 64-pounder sliding along the side of the stokehole hatch, its tackles and breeching hanging in disorder – a snub black bull on the loose.

Darkness shut out the sight as he heard the thunder, but another flash almost immediately revealed the gun gathering momentum forward as the bow plunged again. He tried to lean down the incline but the forces tearing him from the line defied gravity, and he had to heave himself towards the fo'c's'le as if he were climbing, hearing the gun thud against steel somewhere the other side. Then the bow started to rise and he was actually climbing, but the deck was slipping away to starboard, and he could do nothing but hold on. Another torrent, vaguely luminescent as it passed the open fo'c's'le, foamed across the deck, and with it the gun, stubby barrel pointing incredibly skywards; it somersaulted towards him over the fore hatch, passing eighteen inches away almost before he had time to recognize the danger. He heard it crash into the starboard bulwark, then he lost all grip with his feet; the deck had become vertical. At the top of the crest she was lying over on her beam ends. The pressure tearing at his cheeks and oilskins had gone and in the comparative calm he heard the sea swirling around the starboard guns a few feet below and saw salt patterns in the glow of light from the fo'c's'le. The bow started falling; the deck hung, then eased back, shuddering, almost to the horizontal, and the sea inside the bulwarks flooded forward like a tidal wave; if the rogue gun were with it he knew it was the end; his legs were swept from under him by the water, and he could do nothing but cling to the line, his back tingling in anticipation of the blow.

It never came and, as the level of the water over the deck dropped, and the ship held miraculously steady in the trough, he waded and heaved himself along the line to the fo'c's'le entrance, noticing St Barbara's dark eyes on him, and envying her calm detachment. The hands were crouched inside with their arms around riding bitts, the legs of the armourer's bench, or gripping sideframes, water tumbling about their legs; they stared up as if he were the old man of the sea come to claim them. He looked for the bo'sun and found him not three feet away in the angle made by the bulkhead of the seaman's heads, gazing at him with his watery old eyes.

'*Gun* . . .' he yelled, '*broken* . . . *loose* . . .'

The words echoed from the deckhead. Thought began to return; they would need a net or a collision mat to damp the gun's antics before they could secure it in these conditions Another thought struck him: '*seine* – ?'

The bo'sun nodded and, pointing towards the shadows forward, indicated to the men that they should make their way there. He himself started quickly while the deck was level; the hands followed, making rushes to strategic points where they hung on before darting for the next. The water was only ankle deep now; most of it had poured down the ladderway below. Guy stepped inside over the coaming and turned to look at the scene of his recent encounter. A convenient flash of lightning lit it for him; he saw the loose gun on its side, its short barrel miraculously wedged between another 64-pounder barrel and slide. He turned quickly and yelled for the bo'sun to forget the net and bring a chain and line.

The light in the sky flickered off. As the thunder broke, almost overhead it seemed, the ship began another of her swoops to the valley floor, leaning this time to port. He held his breath, expecting to see the gun break loose and charge across to its proper side of the deck. The great breech appeared to swing – or it may have been an illusion caused by all the other movement – but it held, and the bow began to rise and the deck to level without the usual concussions.

The sky lit again. Staring through the flying scud in an effort to gauge whether the gun was still firmly wedged, Guy became aware of something missing on the other side of the deck; looking, he saw with a start that the port side of the bridge had gone, and the chart-house and binnacles and the rails all around. Only the conning tower survived before the funnel which was leaning at a drunken angle, swaying even as he watched. The port side ladder had disappeared, and the bulwarks where the bridge had rested were curved and split open, the hammock netting stanchions straightened inward like a row of pins. This was the tremendous crash and rending he had heard; it explained the gun breaking loose. As he stared he made out an empty space by the split in the bulwark where the piece should have been: number eight – Davis's gun!

It was suddenly dark again. He gripped the dogs inside the frame of the doorway as the bow dropped away beneath him – down, flinging him round, his back jarring against the flat bulkhead – she juddered at the bottom of the plunge and he bent his knees involuntarily, wondering how much more she could take, and where they were in relation to the centre of the storm. He pulled himself round again as the deck began to rise, and tried to make out if the gun were still there, but his pupils had adjusted to the light inside, and he could see nothing but glistening lines of driven spume.

He realized that his leg, where it had banged against something out there, was aching furiously. He hadn't felt it before. He was cold. His boots were half full of sea, every inch of clothing inside his oilskin saturated.

As his pupils adjusted he became aware of something moving on deck under the starboard bridge, and wondered if the gun were on its way again; it was a dark shape weaving or swaying – not the motion of a 64-pounder on the loose. He made out a figure, several figures, working their way along the lifeline towards him; he could see the pallor of their faces beneath the sou'westers. They hung at all angles as the ship, climbing another mountain, flattened almost on her beam ends at the top; they hung like crows until she came back, then scrambled upright and clawed along the line again, faces averted from the driving spray, oilskins standing out stiffly to leeward. He prayed the gun would not free itself; if it did they would be mown down like so many ninepins. There was nothing he could do but watch. No words could hasten them; they were coming as fast as they could. They wouldn't hear in any event.

He felt the deck begin to drop, and hardened his grip on the dogs, his eyes riveted to the little procession as it stopped and hung, sprawling away to port abreast of the gun. Whether they had noticed it or not, there was nothing they could do now but pray; he remembered his own helpless feelings out there as the deck slipped away and the ship plunged giddily into the abyss with the rock bottom. He felt the crash up his legs and spine as she hit; the noise echoed up through the enclosed small spaces of the forward compartments, and she staggered sickeningly before the climb. He heard water pouring across the deck above; a sheet of it cascaded down, cutting him from all view of the party on the lifeline.

As it shredded away, he saw them still there, struggling to their feet. The gun had not moved. The bow was swooping up again; they hauled themselves on; he willed them to move faster.

There was a metallic ringing behind him, and he turned, thankful to see one of the hands – he recognized him as Cox, known as Sandy – making a dash for the riding bitts, dragging the end of a chain – the messenger chain for the cable. There was another man behind him, hauling it from forward. He began to feel more confident; if the gun had not moved in that last swoop it was likely to remain wedged for a little while yet.

'*Idea . . . thing . . . loose. . . .*'

The voice was close in his ear. He turned; the leading figure on the lifeline was D'Arcy, now gripping the frame of the doorway next to him. He grinned and put a hand out to help him in. Just behind was the quartermaster, Smithson, and a young ordinary seaman named MacArthur. They bundled over the coaming, and slid down to wedge themselves between the bulkhead and the heads on the opposite side of the doorway.

Guy nodded to the hands bringing the messenger chain up,

more of them now, one with a luff tackle around his shoulder, and the bo'sun had joined them with a coil of inch line and a bunch of shackles loosely tied together with junk.

'64-pounder,' he yelled to D'Arcy, pointing towards it.

He stepped out over the coaming and took hold of the lifeline again; looking back for an instant to see the hands with the chain following, he stepped aft and, once out of the sheltered area, hauled himself towards the bridge pillar, feeling the line jerk as the others came on it behind. Abreast of the rogue gun, he waited his moment and, as the ship shuddered to starboard, he half ran, half dived for the breeching of the secure piece it had wedged itself beneath, pushing his arm between the rope and the metal of the breech, feeling a thrill of triumph as he locked his hands against the roll back. His blood ran high.

He looked over his shoulder and, seeing Sandy with the end of the chain, nodded to him to slide it towards him. The man gathered in slack from behind as the deck tilted to port, then as they came back threw the chain towards him; it hit the deck before his feet and snaked on in coils. He released an arm to gather it in and, while the ship lurched to starboard, dived for the loose tackle of the jammed gun, and drew himself over the upturned slide and carriage to the barrel itself, throwing the end of the chain over, quickly pushing more links after it. He clung on, waiting for the opposite heel to swing the chain back to him beneath the barrel, his muscles tensing as the movement began.

He wondered if his weight would upset the balance which kept the piece wedged; if so the consequences were unthinkable. He tried to concentrate on the chain but, as the momentum of the roll increased, he was horribly aware that he would have to draw himself up further between the two gun barrels to reach it. He heaved with both hands, prepared at the slightest sign of movement in the wedged piece to let go and hope to fall free before the barrels swung together; he ought to be able to catch the lifeline or the legs of the men as he slid down past.

The bight of chain arced towards him, the end caught somewhere. He stretched his right arm out; his fingers touched metal, touched again, eased through a link and drew it carefully towards him, his every sense keyed for any movement in the gun itself.

The ship hung, pounding on the port rail before beginning a

slow swing back; he realized he was holding his breath, and let it out with inexpressible relief, then snatched at the chain balanced over his fingers and grasped it fairly in his hand. As he came level once more he hauled it towards him, then more and more of it, hoping that Sandy would have the sense to keep on feeding it out. He felt someone beside him and heard D'Arcy's voice, although not what he was saying. He motioned to him to pull the slack towards the breech so that it could be made fast there. D'Arcy caught on at once, and grasping the links with one hand used the other to work back along the barrel, apparently careless of his own safety as the side dipped to starboard again, threatening to stand them both on their heads. Beyond him, Guy saw the bo'sun leaning flat back against the bulkhead as if on a couch, gripping an eye-bolt between his knees and using both hands to loose a shackle from the bunch he was carrying.

D'Arcy reached the breech. He was forced to wait while the vessel corkscrewed as if caught between waves advancing from several directions at once but, as the ship came out of it and the bow jerked upwards, he slid the slack of the chain towards the bo'sun, who caught it deftly between his feet and, bending, placed the shackle in the eye-bolt; holding on with one hand as the bow reached the apex of its dizzy climb, he drew the chain up on his foot to the shackle and over it, and secured the pin.

'Bravo!' Guy yelled. The sound was torn away downwind; he scarcely heard it himself.

D'Arcy looked round, questioning. He shook his head.

As they worked to shackle the chain to the breeching loop and thence to ring-bolts on deck the ship seemed to steady, almost as if she had spent her energy in the vain effort to shake them free. Guy had the impression the bow was yawing. She still staggered and shipped water deep over the fo'c's'le, which cascaded down and swirled about their legs as they bowsed the chain in bar tight; but there was a different feel to the pitch and roll and they spent less time hearing the sea swirl a few inches below them the other side of the bulwark. When the gun had been secured and he made a dash back for the lifeline, he realized the wind had changed. It pushed him bodily towards the line and he was nearly somersaulted over it as it caught him across the midriff. Saxmundham could not have contemplated going round in that mountainous confusion; in any case he would have been unable to do so. The wind itself must have shifted. They had passed the centre.

He looked round as he felt someone jerk the line behind him, and, seeing D'Arcy, pointed towards the new wind direction. His arm was forced back like a weather vane, but D'Arcy nodded, his teeth gleamed.

Light flickered over the sky. Beyond D'Arcy's streaming sou'wester, he saw a wall of sea standing above the quarter, its top lashed into white mist. He locked his arms around the line as he felt the stern swing and the deck slip away to port. His feet hung over a void; the rope burnt the skin inside his elbow as his weight came on it. The noise and the pressure had moved away somewhere, and he heard jarring sounds below, muffled as if from the depths of the ship and the roar of water falling on the stern and crashing thunder at the same time. His feet touched the deck, and he felt her trying to come up, but instead she was knocked down again. He heard the squeal of metal on metal from the starboard bulwark, and prayed the shackles would hold; at this angle he and D'Arcy were immediately below the piece. He wondered where the bo'sun was; the old man moved around like a monkey, using his knees instead of a tail! The young MacArthur had not looked too secure.

The ship came up at last. It was pitch black, but he sensed or saw a pale mist high above the fo'c's'le. Lightning revealed it as the white crest of a sea ahead. He clawed his feet beneath him and braced himself as the bow rose. The lightning flickered on closing images of water like a furious magic lantern show. Miraculously the mountain shrank, leaving a haze in the fore rigging. As it shredded away and the bow began to fall he had a brief glimpse over a chaos of ridges and peaks streaked white like a blizzard gleaming ahead and, amidst them, unbelievably, the masts and yards of a ship. Three masts with t'gallants struck, streaming spray or torn canvas, it was impossible to tell which, beneath them a white prow thrusting above the white sea, and a single funnel. He recognized the space between the masts and the proportions of the thin, raked funnel, and the lines of the bow as those of a gunboat.

The picture disappeared as the lightning flickered off. He turned quickly to D'Arcy to ask if he had seen her, but there was no chance of making himself heard and the man was hunched, pulling himself along the line towards him. He turned towards the fo'c's'le himself and worked forward, seeing the startling picture again in his mind and groping for detail. It wouldn't come. The image was sharp, but strangely toneless. The more he thought about it the less certain he became of anything. Had the small section of the forward hull he glimpsed been white, or was that an impression lent by the waste of spray around her? Try as he would, he could not give a colour to the funnel; it had shape but no shade. It might have been a trick of light – or even pure imagination. He had thought about the *Curlew* so much recently, perhaps he had imagined her features in the strange vessel.

He began to wonder if he had imagined the whole ship. His brain whirled with noise and continual movement and the effort of simply holding on against the contortions underfoot; he couldn't be certain of anything. He knew the gun was safe; it had been a real gun. Had it been a real ship? It had been exactly as he had imagined the *Curlew*. Had his mind placed her image in that brief glimpse of wilderness ahead?

As he reached the entrance to the fo'c's'le and pulled himself in, he saw the bo'sun watching him from inside; he was relieved the man was safe, but surprised that he had contrived to get there before him. The other hands were in there too – including MacArthur he was glad to see – but they had left the gun before him.

He slid down towards the old sailor and shouted in his ear, '*Did . . . you . . . see . . . her?*'

It was evident from the man's expression that he either hadn't heard, or didn't understand. He tried again. The veined old eyes still showed no sign of comprehension, and he turned to see if D'Arcy had arrived. He was just heaving himself inside the doorway. He clawed his way back and repeated the question in his ear.

D'Arcy grinned and yelled something. He caught the words '*Make . . . libation . . . tomorrow . . .*' and put his ear closer.

'*Preserved . . . say . . . absolute . . . cream . . .*' the high tones continued.

He examined his face for traces of hysteria. The green eyes were eager beneath brows now stiff with salt; beads of water glistened on a slight stubble above the thick upper lip, his mouth was parted in enjoyment of the wild scene and shared hazard.

Guy gave up the riddle, and clapped him across the back. '*Good work*!'

The smile broadened.

Guy looked round at the bo'sun and the rest of the men, and as the deck steadied put both hands to his mouth and yelled, '*Good . . . work*!'

Their tired eyes lit.

He pointed aft in the general direction of the quarter-deck, and mimed holding a glass and drinking. '*Sax . . . extra . . . tot*!'

They grinned, their shadows swaying as the ship heaved giddily over to port.

He heard D'Arcy's voice behind him, and looking round saw him hanging half out of the doorway, gesturing to something on the bulkhead just outside; he caught the words '*extra . . . tot. . . .*'

A tot for St Barbara! He understood the nonsense about libations. The goose! He thought of the way D'Arcy had clawed along the rogue gun careless of safety as the bulwark dipped down almost into the sea beneath them, and wished Saxmundham had been there to see it. He would tell him. He would have to choose his moment with care; perhaps it would come better from the bo'sun.

He wondered if the Old Man had seen the gunboat in that brief instant from the top of the crest, then wondered again if he had seen it himself. It was like one of those vivid waking dreams one tried vainly to recapture; he couldn't separate it from his mental picture of the *Curlew*.

The bruise on his leg throbbed painfully. His eyes smarted. The rain outside spun in the light.

'*Did* you see her, or did you not see her?' The skin beneath Saxmundham's eyes was shadowed and the usually clear whites were tinged with pink at the corners.

'Had anyone else seen her,' Guy replied, 'I would unhesitatingly say yes, sir.'

The Old Man growled, 'I wish to know whether *you* saw her sir!'

'Yes, sir, I did.'

'Why the devil couldn't you say that in the first place?'

'I thought it curious that no one else had seen her and,' he hurried on to forestall the eruption, 'because she was just as I had pictured the *Curlew* to myself. I thought I might have imagined her. It was a matter of a moment only, in a flash of lightning, then it was dark again and we were no longer on the crest.'

Stainton coughed. 'Caesar's ghost!'

Guy nodded. 'My conscience is clear though!'

'I'll not have philosophy,' Saxmundham thundered. 'You saw her – or you did not see her.'

'I'm sorry, sir. It was my distinct impression I saw her running before the storm – without a stitch on her that hadn't blown out of the gaskets.'

'Is that how you pictured the *Curlew* to yourself?'

'No, sir.'

'Well, then – ?'

'I'd say I did see her, sir.'

The Old Man snorted and paced away, then returned and stood with his hands clasped behind him, glowering at Stainton. 'Don't know where we are!'

'Not precisely, sir – near enough.'

'Supposin' Greville did see her, supposin' she was the *Curlew*, supposin' she'd run straight from Cherbaniani – ' Saxmundham's tone was heavy with irony. 'Where was she makin' for, near enough?'

Stainton grinned. 'My guess is she was making for a landfall at Cape Comorin, sir.'

The Old Man stared at him thoughtfully, then at Guy. 'We'll wait for her there.' He turned to Stainton. 'Unless you've another suggestion?'

'No, sir. I confess I had not looked forward to finding Kalpeni without a chart.'

'Can you find Comorin?'

'Head east until we sight the coast and follow it down, sir?'

'Anythin' in the way?'

'Not as I recall.'

'*Imray's* go as well?'

'Everything, sir. I've a number of charts under my bunk – none of this area though.'

The Old Man looked up the deck at the armourer's gang riveting a plate on the funnel, which had been hauled into a more or less upright position with purchases to the stays which had carried away. The noise was deafening. The carpenter's mates, aided by a number of ABs and boys, were clearing away the wreckage of the pinnaces and booms just aft of them. Of all the boats, only the jolly boat right at the stern had escaped total destruction. Beyond them the fore topsail and t'gallant swung against a sky still messy with cloud, but with the blue gaining every minute. Sunlight glared off yellow paintwork and glistening blocks. There was a fresh feel to the air.

'Do you go and fog out a compass course, pilot,' Saxmundham said abruptly and, as Stainton made off, turned to Guy. 'It appears the supernumerary was not at his station.' He nodded up at the missing wing of the bridge, a look in his eye which Guy could not interpret.

'He was securing the loose gun, sir. A capital job he made of it – in the most trying conditions.'

The blue gaze seemed to go right through him as though the Old Man were hearing with his ears, not with his mind. 'I'm pleased we did not lose the supernumerary, Greville.'

'So am I sir. A good hand – amazing pluck!'

'He'd need to have my boy. To greet his commandin' officer in that manner.'

Guy grinned.

'It would've bin on my conscience if we'd lost the scamp,' Saxmundham said after a moment.

Evidently his attitude was mellowing; 'scamp' was coming up the scale.

Suddenly he shot out, 'You fancy I've bin unreasonable towards him, Greville?'

Guy groped for alternatives; whatever he replied would inevitably be wrong. 'I've come to admire him tremendously.'

'So you keep sayin'!' Saxmundham's voice rose. 'I can fathom your game, you young pup! Now, look here, you tell him' – he jabbed a stubby finger towards Guy's midriff – 'you tell him if he fancies comin' to me with an apology, I'll be happy to – On my life! I'll ask him to brekker.'

'An apology, sir – '

'An apology sir!' The beard jutted.

'I'll speak to him.'

'Good! It don't do – bad blood in a small ship. It's a poison that spreads.' He turned him a suddenly keen glance. 'That fellow Davis – '

Guy looked at him.

'You know what I mean. It occurred to me, after James informed me of the circumstances, it might be the answer to the mischief in the *Curlew*.'

'The jacks taking the law into their own hands sir?'

'But this thing you found on the reef,' his eyes were puzzled. 'Can you see 'em carryin' it that far?'

'I've given it some thought, sir.' It was an understatement; apart from the delirious moments of action in the hurricane, he'd been able to think of little else. Saxmundham was gazing at him almost eagerly. 'I was hard put to it to stop myself dropping off last night – ' he started.

'Devil you were!'

He smiled. 'The noise and the movement in the fo'c's'le were stunning. I lost some blood,' he pointed down to his white trouser leg concealing the stitches the surgeon had put in his shin that morning. 'You know how it is when you're about to nod off, I had one of these amazing – ' he was about to say 'dreams', but changed it to 'visions'. 'A large man in a yellow robe, one shoulder bare, how they wear them, sitting on the floor in a cabin with stern windows, cross-legged, how one sees the Buddha.'

'On my life!' Saxmundham slapped his thigh impatiently, and started forward to view the work in progress on the shattered bulwark. 'Was your sightin' of the *Curlew* of the same character?'

Guy fell in beside him. 'No, sir, that was a good deal earlier. But the monk was so vivid I can see him now, I heard a voice – I believe it was Heighurst's voice, at all events he said the same thing to me the evening before – saying, "Reason don't serve – not between people," and the whole thing came to me in a flash. The monk was Commander Vaneyke and he had turned his back on his ship and applied himself to contemplation. As a result discipline had gone hang, and the MAA or the petty officers had been forced to take matters into their own hands – somewhat drastically. It seemed crystal clear at the time,' he finished.

'But it don't now!' Saxmundham contemplated the torn edge of the bulwark and gave a brief word of encouragement to the carpenter shoring it up. He continued on towards the fo'c's'le, passing some marines attempting to hammer a flattened ventilator cowl into a semblance of its former shape. The noise was worse, if anything, than by the funnel. 'All the officers wearin' the yellow robe too!' he shouted.

'That is the difficulty, sir.'

'You see a difficulty?' It was evidently the Old Man's morning for irony.

'But I should like to know who the officers are – particularly the first lieutenant, sir.'

Saxmundham stopped suddenly, his former interest recaptured. 'The first thing you've said this mornin' that makes sense.'

Guy grinned. 'It made a good deal of sense to me last night – early this morning,' he corrected himself.

The blue eyes lit with zest. 'How did she do?'

Guy realized he was referring to the ship. 'Famously!' he replied with enthusiasm. 'I'm certain I've not been in anything to equal it before.'

'Nor have many – and come through to tell the tale. She's got pluck, bless my soul!' He placed a hand on Guy's shoulder. 'Tell that fellow, a decent apology and we'll shuffle the cards – a fresh deal.' His brows rose. 'Although I could wish he had a few less rings on his fingers.' He turned to mount the fo'c's'le ladder to survey the damage up there, catching sight of St Barbara's baleful eye as he did so. He nodded towards her. 'The devil looks after his own!'

Guy laughed. 'D'Arcy fancies she saved our bacon last night – with the loose gun. He means to give her a tot at noon.'

Saxmundham stared for a moment. 'I don't object to that. But I trust you'll ensure the geese don't get the extra ration on this occasion.'

'I don't believe they deserve it, sir. They were in an awful funk.'

The Old Man laughed as he started up the ladder.

7

Guy was below, snatching some sleep in late afternoon, when the pad of feet and thudding of ropes on the deck above roused him; the ship lay over, and he heard the surge and gurgle of the sea close below his port. They must have brought the wind round on the beam unless it had changed direction since he came below, but not so suddenly – no, they must be heading away, southwest – away from the coast. He swung his legs down from the bunk and leant across to the chair, balancing as he pulled his trousers on. He poured cold water into his hands from the carafe – Basset! it was almost empty – and slapped the sleep from his face, then combed his hair in the mirror. His eyes were deeper than usual; there were distinct lines beneath, and the set of his face was severe. He smiled and noted thankfully that it wasn't a permanent condition. But he was thinner about the cheeks; his nose stood out more prominently than ever. Lord! he felt done up.

There was a knock on the door surround, and Fisher, the Old Man's doggie, poked his head around the curtain.

'Captain's compliments, sir, and he wishes to warn you we shall be clearing for action shortly.'

Guy stared at the lad for a moment. 'French fleet in sight?'

Fisher grinned. 'No, sir. It looks like the *Curlew*, sir.' His tone was excited.

'Well,' he went on as Guy continued to stare at him. 'She's a gunboat at all events.'

'How far off?'

'Still hull down from the deck, sir.'

'I'm on my way up.'

'Aye, aye, sir!' Fisher disappeared.

Saxmundham turned as Guy approached the wheel; the great face was alive with zest, the shadows beneath his eyes still apparent but cancelled out by the sparkling blue above.

'You were right!' he roared.

'Thank goodness.'

Saxmundham chuckled. 'He's easin' away. What does that suggest to you?'

Guy looked briefly at Stainton standing nearby with his glasses slung around his neck, brows raised and a conspiratorial gleam in his brown eyes, then back to Saxmundham.

'Not one of his "At Home" days,' he ventured.

The Old Man nodded, evidently pleased with the deduction. 'He came on as bold as you please until he was near enough to make us out – then he alters away. Why should he make an alteration here unless he don't wish to be seen?'

'I can't think of any reason. Unless the pilot knows of one.' He looked at Stainton.

'I thank you, kind sir, for your confidence.' Stainton's expression belied the words. 'All I can say is one hill looks rather like another.'

'We've sighted India?'

'There's a lot of it. I claim no credit.'

'No one would make an alteration on a sight of the Western ghats.'

'The Cardamons, I trust – '

'Where would they alter to?' Saxmundham rumbled. 'Hang it!' he looked at Stainton. 'There's nothin' out there.'

'The nine degree channel must be out there somewhere, but I wouldn't care to find it from a distant hill sight with only a couple of hours of daylight left.'

Saxmundham's brows drew together. 'That's the deuce of it.' He looked half up, eyes narrowed as though willing the sun to suspend its motion until they closed the stranger.

Guy saw Fisher pounding towards them from forward, and the chief engineer's plump figure appearing from the companionway. They converged on the wheel, Fisher arriving first, his face flushed, eyes starting.

'She's gone about, sir, she's taking in sail – all sail by the looks of it.'

'By thunder!' Saxmundham turned his attention to the chief and clapped an arm around his shoulder. 'All the steam you have Chief – spare no exertion!' His beard bristled by the engineer's round, balding head. 'The rascal thinks he'll escape upwind!' and drawing his head up, he roared at full lung, '*Hands about ship*!'

The chief's eyes closed involuntarily, and he leant away, disengaging as he saw there was more to come.

'*Ready all*!'

The watch on deck were already throwing the coils off the pins.

Saxmundham turned to the quartermaster, 'Ease the helm down!' then, looking aft and raising his voice again, 'Haul over the boom!'

The bow started coming up into the wind, lifting over a still confused swell; the jibs and fore staysails slapped as their sheets were loosed.

The chief made a large detour around Saxmundham to come up beside Guy, whom he usually regarded as an ally.

'He doesna reelize,' he started in a low voice, nodding towards Saxmundham, 'he canna do 't. F'r yeearrs he maks oot he's go' no ing'nes – noo it's purrpetual bluidy motion – fu' pressure – they're no' inanimate lumps o' bluidy iron.'

'What's wrong, Chief?'

The engineer looked up with sad, pale green eyes. 'It's the preencipal – '

Guy grinned at his expression. 'Well, if that's all!'

'It's mebbe all the noo – ' The implication in his tone was of impending dire disaster.

Complaint had become second nature to the poor fellow. 'I'd enjoy it, Chief.' Guy eyed the hands hauling up the clew garnets of the fore and mainsails. 'Lord, man! He canna do withoot ye the noo.'

'Aye, that's right.' There was a self-deprecating droop to the old chief's lips. 'He'd sup wi' th' de'il himsel' if he had the need, d'ye think I canna see the length o' *his* spuin?'

'Let go the t'gallant bowlines! Haul well taut the mainbrace!' Saxmundham roared. '*Mainsail haul*!'

The mainyard flew round, the hands gathering in the slack of the brace hand over hand. The canvas on the foreyards slapped and rattled the lines and blocks in a discordant medley, and spray rose over the fo'c's'le rail as the bow swinging through the wind dipped into a trough between rollers.

'*Head braces*!' Saxmundham cautioned and, as the bow fell off sweetly on the new tack, 'Of all *haul*!' and, turning to the quartermaster, 'Right the helm!'

'Right the hellum, sir!'

The groups on the headlines charged aft; the foreyards swung round, their canvas shivered, filled, and the little ship leaned away with a shudder as if shaking off the temporary check to her progress, the bow gliding up the swell.

Guy looked round at the chief. 'D'you blame him?'

'If it's a yacht he wants, le' him purrchase one, he wouldna feel it. Ah'm his *lackey* here – spare no exurrtion, Chief!'

Guy heard a crack from somewhere forward, then shouting, and above it a high cry, 'Man overboard!' He was already pacing down the deck to the lee side; he jumped up on a gun slide and looked over the hammock nettings as Saxmundham cautioned the watch. A tangle of jibs and head rigging flew out to leeward of the foresail and he saw the flying jib boom waving from amidst the loose canvas. There was a man in the water, eyes and one arm raised as he slid towards the quarter. On the rail-less half of the bridge above D'Arcy was tearing off his jacket; he threw it down and, stepping to the edge of the bridge, made a neat dive far out away from the side. As he entered the water, Guy heard the pipe shrilling for the sea boat's crew, and Saxmundham asking where the man was.

He turned, shouting, 'The head gear's carried away – we'll lose the topmast if we go about.' Perhaps the foremast and the main topmast as well, he thought, as he watched D'Arcy's head surfacing.

'*All hands! In fore-royals fore-t'gallants fore-topsails*! Up mainsail and spanker! Jib downhauls!' Saxmundham was moving to the side. He hopped up next to Guy.

The sailor in the water had passed the stern; D'Arcy was swimming strongly through the tumbling wash to reach him. A lifebuoy bobbed between the two.

Saxmundham jumped back down to the deck, and strode forward. Guy heard Stainton telling his midshipman to run aloft and keep his glasses on the men in the water. He jumped down and followed Saxmundham. There was feverish activity about the pin rail of the foremast; the topyard men were already in the rigging below the crosstrees waiting for the yards to come down. He seized the fo'c's'le ladder rail and doubled up, seeing the confused tangle of stays, booms and billowing canvas tugging away to leeward; everything had gone before the bowsprit; the dolphin striker, hanging from its martingales and stays, bounced over the waves.

'Haul taut! Shorten sail!' Saxmundham roared then, seeing Guy, 'Do you see to the boat, Greville. I'll bring her to directly they come down,' he nodded aloft. 'Send young Penfold away in her – they'll have a long pull. And attend to the after canvas!'

'Aye, aye, sir!' Guy returned the way he had come, calling up to the midshipman aloft to make sure he could still see the men in the water. The lad pointed astern, but whatever he said was lost as Saxmundham hurled out orders to back the main topsail.

He told off Hardy-Penfold to take the boat away, and accompanied him to the stern rail, where the jolly boat hung, the crew already sitting on the thwarts, hands standing by the falls. It would need nice judgement to get her away safely. If they lowered too soon while the ship was making way through the water, she would be jerked over on her side before they could release the falls – too late and the ship might make a sternboard on top of her. He cautioned Penfold to wait for his shout, then called to the quartermaster to fetch a leadline and, telling Stainton to look out for the after sails, climbed over the starboard nettings to the leadsman's stool. They were still sliding along, but much more gently; the water was not going much faster than tideways he'd seen; if they had a single boat at the side they would have been able to get her away by now. It was a miracle they had any boats at all.

The quartermaster handed him the coil of leadline. The ship's way was coming off visibly as the backed topsail took effect; it merely remained for the Old Man to bring her up a shade into the wind. He lowered the lead into the sea; it tended astern, and he pulled it out again, dipping it in and out until he was satisfied that they were dead in the water, then raised his head and shouted aft.

'Slip the gripes.' He heard the orders from the boat follow in rapid succession, 'Turns for lowering! Lower away!' Penfold appreciated the delicacy of his position. He climbed back inboard and strode aft. By the time he reached the davits the falls were hanging loose, and the boat was under oars heading for the smooth water in the lee before rounding away. He called to the midshipman aloft for a direction, and repeated it to Penfold with his arm. Penfold acknowledged cheerily.

He heard Heighurst beside him. 'I fancy we should have lost

her in any event.'

He looked round, remembering the *Curlew* again, and nodded. It would have been a miracle if they had been able to hold on to her through the hours of darkness.

'Was that the supernumerary went bathin'?'

'Yes.' He watched the boat turning with starboard oars backed.

Heighurst pulled the end of his moustache. 'Something of a poser for old Sax – do he recommend him for a medal, or charge him with bein' absent without leave!'

'Let's hope he has the choice.'

'You don't get rid of a fellow like that so easily.' Heighurst's tone was less assured than the words. The seas were high, the sun sinking fast.

Guy realized he had come to like D'Arcy a great deal; despite his damaging effect on the harmony aft, he was personally a tonic. The ship would not be the same now without him. 'I hope not' he replied. 'I hope he don't close with the fellow too quick.' An image came into his mind of D'Arcy hurling himself on the huge fish at the seining party. 'He's such a direct fellow.'

They were silent for a moment, watching the boat climb an unusually steep swell, oars glinting in the low sun, spray whipped across her starboard bow. She looked very small.

'They have a lifebuoy,' Heighurst said.

He nodded. The trouble was D'Arcy had been making for the man, not for the buoy to take to the man. He turned and made his way forward, meeting Saxmundham coming aft. The Old Man nodded briefly at his report, and told him to see to getting the wreckage inboard. He carried on forward.

By the time the jolly boat returned and hooked on to the falls the sun was just above the horizon and the strange gunboat little more than a wisp of smoke ahead. The wreckage of the jib-booms and dolphin striker had been hoisted aboard, the lines cleared, and the bo'sun's choice hands were rigging two replacement spars the carpenter had fashioned. Guy walked aft.

The hands pounded down the deck with the falls until brought to a halt with the blocks inches from the davit heads.

The officers waiting in groups moved expectantly. Saxmundham strode to the rail. Guy saw blond hair, damp and tangled above the nettings; he'd been overjoyed when the word had been passed that both men were in the boat. He stepped up as D'Arcy was assisted inboard; his upper half was bulky with several white jumpers the boat's crew must have contributed, his face was pale, his thick lips open, his teeth rattling involuntarily. Below the layers of jumpers his trousers were crinkled, the once elegant flares hanging loose about one bare, one stockinged ankle without shoes.

Saxmundham surveyed him as the rescued man, also bulky with jumpers, was heaved inboard after him; he was in far worse shape, apparently barely conscious; the surgeon stepped up quickly and with a couple of hands from the falls assisted him forward.

'Prompt work!' Saxmundham said in an unnaturally clipped voice.

D'Arcy stared back. 'Thank you, sir.' His shoulders were shaking.

'A rub down with brandy. I'll have my steward fetch a bottle down.'

'I'm obliged, sir.'

'Good!' Saxmundham turned to Guy, and raised his voice angrily. 'What's the position forward?'

'Another couple of hours work I'd say sir.'

The blue eyes stared, then moved to D'Arcy's retreating back. Finally he turned and called Fisher over, telling him to have his steward take a bottle of brandy to the supernumerary's cabin, and afterwards find the chief engineer and inform him steam was not required for the night.

'I must confess, I'm not sorry,' he said, starting to pace the deck, evidently expecting Guy to accompany him. 'The wee man's bin puffin' himself up, I fancy.' There was a questioning look in his eye.

Guy thought of the chief's lugubrious predictions, and smiled. 'I don't believe so, sir. I'd say he was finding it difficult to get used to the new fashion.'

Saxmundham looked at him suspiciously. After a while he said, 'It's all for the best. The beggar would have given us the slip durin' the night – depend on it.'

Guy agreed.

'We shall manage without his confounded airs – and clinkers.'

'What d'you intend, sir?'

'The fellow was bound south before he turned.' Saxmundham waved up the deck, taking in the twisted davits and bulwark, the missing bridge, boats and booms, sheep pens and hen coops, the patched funnel and crumpled-looking ventilator cowls, rust already discolouring the broken paintwork. 'So are we. So I intend makin' for Galle – between Galle and Dondra Head if the pilot can find his way. We'll haunt the point for a day or so in case he comes by. There are any number of fishermen who may assist. If he don't come' – he slapped a hand against his thigh – 'we'll steer for Trinky – report our findin's, and get her shipshape again.' He looked round as though expecting an opinion.

'If we were to make for Colombo first, sir, the pilot would be able to get some charts. We should also be able to cable the Admiral.'

'Cable! Cable! Bless my soul! Things were managed well enough before the cable! What d'you want with it?'

Guy smiled. 'I'm not certain what ships the Admiral has with him.'

'*We're* here, you're certain of that ain't you? We've seen the beggar. Put yourself in *his* shoes, m'boy!' The blue eyes were keen.

Guy thought for a moment. 'If I were Vaneyke, I'd alter course directly it came on dark, shut my steam off in case sparks gave me away, and set all sail and run like the devil downwind – hoping you would continue to chase north.'

Saxmundham nodded. 'If we make a diversion to Colombo, we may lose the beggar. Mark you, I'm not anxious to steer by the Basses without a chart – bless my soul! If the pilot takes us to Colombo in error, I'll not stand on my pride, m'boy – he can go inside and purchase as many charts as he pleases, and you can send your cable – much good may it do you!' He chuckled. 'But as I recall it, Colombo harbour's a good deal harder to find than the point of the land.'

'We might ask a fisherman!'

'It wouldn't be the first time that's been done.' He turned and started forward. 'To tell the truth, I'm pleased the head gear parted. It don't do to give the engineers the idea we rely on them, not this fellow here. You know what the scamp made a point of tellin' me the other mornin'? He wishes his sons to go to the University – at Glasgow. He never had the opportunity it seems. Bless my soul, d'you know Greville, I'm pleased I'm not your age. A man's supposed to wish not to grow old, but when I see the changes you're goin' to have to put up with, my boy, and the beastly smells and the new ships – on my life! I'm thankful my time's near enough done.' The look in his eyes suggested other thoughts, possibly even regrets.

They paced in silence for a while as the ship rolled idly and the canvas flushed with the splendours of sunset.

'The supernumerary has not brought me his apology yet, Greville.'

Guy's mind flashed to the scene in the ward-room when he had told D'Arcy of the Old Man's suggestion for patching up a truce – the green eyes had seemed about to pop from their sockets. 'I believe he's mad. Would you ask a fellow for an apology if you'd just whipped him? When he offers to paste my letter together – ' the letter figured prominently in any conversation with D'Arcy about the Old Man, 'I'll offer to apologize, but you'll have to inform me what it is I'm apologizin' for. Hang it – why don't you ask the old bugger – see if he can answer that!'

He looked round. Saxmundham was staring straight ahead as he paced.

'I dare say he needs time,' he replied.

The Old Man studied his face. 'Is that all you have to say?'

'He's aggrieved about his letter – the one you tore up.'

The Old Man's brows rose in surprise. 'What letter?'

'His letter of appointment – from their Lordships.'

'Does he say I tore it up?'

'You did. Sir.'

The gaze sharpened, then he chuckled. 'Must've mistaken it for one of those cravats. I'd not say no to tearin' up a few of those yellow rags I can tell you, Greville! How many does he have?'

Guy grinned. 'I'm not certain. I know he has six dozen shirts though, and another four dozen on their way home, P & O, to be laundered.'

'You don't say so! I never did trust an Indian dhobi myself.'

He grunted. 'See how the bo'sun's gettin' on, Greville, and ask the pilot to step up here.'

When Guy returned to report Stainton was with him; they looked round as he came up.

'They're getting on rather faster than I expected, sir. Another hour, the bo'sun says – he's making do with lashings – the heel chain and crupper went over – '

'Of course,' Saxmundham grunted, 'we'd be here all night otherwise.' He glanced at Stainton. 'The pilot is confident he can find Point de Galle.'

Stainton's look was anything but confident. 'I was fortunate in finding the chief has an atlas, which may be a shade more accurate than the imperial map in Hardy-Penfold's stamp album.' He gazed skywards. 'He is watching over us, I feel certain.'

'Latitude sailin',' Saxmundham said. 'We'll make south or near enough south through the night to keep well clear of the land, then haul round gradually south east until we hit the latitude of the point.'

'As ascertained from the chief's atlas,' Stainton put in.

'Then due east, and keep on till we sight the point. That's goin' back a few years – bless my soul!' He looked at Guy with his old zest. 'The fellow may beat us by makin' a more direct course, but we'll give him a run for his money.'

'He may not make a direct course for fear of meeting up with us again.'

'He may not. We may meet him on the great circle!'

'Third time lucky,' Stainton said.

'The beggar shan't get away next time!'

Stainton left after a few moments, and Guy was about to go with him when Saxmundham called him back. He started pacing again, evidently immersed in thought. 'He's got more to him than meets the eye straight off,' he said at last.

'A capital fellow,' Guy agreed.

Saxmundham looked round testily. 'So you keep tellin' me.'

Guy couldn't remember discussing Stainton with him before.

'Now, as regards this letter of his you say I tore up, it can't be mended now.' He grunted. 'In any event, in my experience it's the safest way with communications of that sort. I shall invite him to dinner.' He gazed at Guy for a moment. 'And do you come along too, Greville – or, bless my soul!' He shook his head, then looked round keenly. 'What does the supernumerary wear to dinner?'

Guy smiled. 'He's surprisingly conventional. Except – '

'Yes?'

'His trousers – the cut of them makes it difficult for him to sit for long.'

'I'll not begrudge him his hardships. No, I've bin keepin' a weather eye on the fellow. He's quick. And resourceful.'

Guy nodded. 'He was in the water in the time it took me to cross the deck.'

'It was prompt, I'll grant you. I'll write a letter to the Royal Humane Society. I'll do it right away – while the mood's on me. I'll give him ten minutes.'

Guy looked round, unable to follow the argument.

'He's prompt,' Saxmundham explained irritably. 'You said so yourself. On my life! If he can't come up with an apology in ten minutes – hang it, how long would you give him?'

'I dare say he's still recovering sir. I understood you were to invite him to dinner.'

'And so I shall.' Saxmundham's beard quivered dangerously, and he thumped a clenched fist in the air. 'I'll give the beggar ten minutes from the time he comes in the door. That's fair, ain't it?'

Guy wondered what would happen when the ultimatum expired, as it must, for he was certain D'Arcy would never apologize.

'Well – ain't it?'

'Is the invitation to be conditional, sir?'

'Bless my soul! No, of course it ain't! I'll not tell the beggar what's expected – no more shall you. If he knows how to behave, he'll come out with it without any promptin'. If not he'll go without his dinner. I say ten minutes is fair. What do you say?'

'I don't believe he'll know what's expected.'

Saxmundham stopped and faced him. The dusk was deepening rapidly. His eyes looked dark against the glow still in the western sky. 'Do you tell him, then Greville.' The tone was reluctant.

'I shall do that, sir.' Guy was suddenly determined to make D'Arcy seize the opportunity; Saxmundham had conceded more than he thought possible.

'Good, but Greville – '

'Sir.'

'No word of a time. Simply inform him he's to make his apology.'

'I'll not give him a time, sir.'

'And do you remain quiet when he comes in. We'll not queer his pitch. I'll not say a word.'

Guy smiled at the prospect. 'I dare say he'll out with it straight away!'

'Yes, of course he shall. I've had my eye on him. He's got the right stuff in him. If he does look as if he's off to a fancy ball.'

. . . the very queerest dinner I ever was at, Trojan. I'd told D'Arcy what was expected, and we'd fogged out the form of words to use, and I was positive we'd straighten the whole thing out over the old man's best cham, but when we arrive there was old Sax sitting saying not a word after a fairly civil "good evenin' – sit you down" etc., his mouth as taut as a bottle and his gold hunter laid out with the fish knives. Whether D'Arcy cottoned on to the fact he was being timed and thought he'd have some fun, or whether he grew obstinate at the Old Man obviously waiting for the little speech we'd cooked up – and that wasn't as easy as you might imagine – he started away furiously with the most fearful rodomontade, did Old Sax know Lord Eaglemount, he'd spent a famous weekend at Castle Eaglemount etc. etc. Old Sax just sipped his soup – turtle I may say – and kept glancing down at his hunter, and I could see him *bulge* with the effort of keeping himself in! I sat opposite D'Arcy trying to stare him down and get him to come out with the little speech we'd agreed before it was too late, and then suddenly old Sax can't contain himself a moment longer, and roars at D'Arcy as if he were in the fore top, "On my life, sir, I admire your cursed pluck!" or something of that sort, which at least succeeds in bringing D'Arcy to a halt. Then Sax picks up his hunter and glares at it, then at D'Arcy and for all his cool nerve I fancy D'Arcy's face turned a shade paler, then back at the hunter for a moment or two in the most *thumping* silence you ever heard! Then Sax says very calmly, "I trust you enjoyed your soup, Mr Green." "It was perfect," says D'Arcy at his most *suaviter in modo*. "I am glad," growls Sax, "for it's all you're gettin'!" D'Arcy's eyebrows which are almost colourless I may say, ascended unto the heavens and his eyeballs which are curiously round and clear green started right out of his head, and he was struck dumb for the second time. Round two to Old Sax, I thought, because there was no doubt D'Arcy had walked away with the first round. Then Sax taps the hunter and says, "Ten minutes, sir – ain't that long enough for you?" "Ah," says D'Arcy beginning to recover some colour, "I'd have tucked it away somewhat quicker if I'd known." "Tucked it away?" roars Sax. "A manner of speakin'" says D'Arcy. "I didn't know the form – I must apologize." At that the Old Man's eyes narrowed and he stole a glance at the hunter and said, "I'll grant you another minute – is that enough for you?" his beard quivering the way it does. D'Arcy looked nonplussed for a moment or two, then said he thought he could manage the fish course in a minute but he'd never timed himself so couldn't be certain. "*Apology*!" yells Sax. "I shall have an apology, sir, if it takes us all night," and he looked at me as though I'd mismanaged the whole thing and asked what in heaven's name I'd said to D'Arcy. Well, when D'Arcy saw I was in the rattle, as the jacks say, he promptly jumps to the rescue and comes out with the speech saying he has to apologize for taking over as first lieutenant in Sax's absence, sticking up carvings around Sax's ship, painting the funnel in Sax's colours without permission etc. etc. Old Sax sat there with a pleased expression coming over his face, and as soon as D'Arcy finished, he tucks the hunter away and calls out to his steward to bring the cham. In it comes clinking and beaded all over, and there's not another uncivil word; Old Sax is as charming as could be, and says he has just written about D'Arcy's gallant rescue to the Royal Humane Society etc. You would have thought they were the best of chums. And afterwards – by which time I may say D'Arcy was not altogether sure of his words for he'd taken in a quarter of a bottle of the Old Man's brandy before the meal, and had the rest rubbed in through his epidermic layer, as poor old Cameron would have said – we toasted a "Happy Ship!" and old Sax came out with a little speech about bad blood almost as if *he* were making an apology! And the next day D'Arcy appeared with only *one* ring on his finger and a *black* cravat! We asked him who had died, and he said he was mourning his lost integrity – whatever that meant. And he and Old Sax had a turn up and down the quarter-deck together as if to show everyone they'd made it up. It was really quite touching. The bo'sun came up to me afterwards and said, if ever I get in the Old Man's black book, he'll push someone over the side for me! For my part, I don't feel it was as simple as that. At all events *pray* it continues. The ship's completely different. I even plucked up the courage to go down and see Davis, you know the gun captain who was flogged by the hands, and we had a chat about the storm. He wasn't forthcoming but he didn't cut me dead – in fact I thought perhaps he was pleased to see me when I first looked in. He's mending fast, poor fellow.

We've been haunting the southern end of Ceylon the whole day tacking off and on – Stainton brought us here on an old school atlas belonging to the chief engineer, which didn't please Old Sax who's frightened of nothin' save engineers getting ideas above their station! To tell the truth I believe we smelt our way here, for we were met by the most amazing fragrance out at sea before we saw Adam's Peak; it's indescribable – the effect of land scents after being for some days at sea. The scent off Ceylon makes one realize what it must have been like in the Garden of Eden.

D'Arcy's been out in the jolly boat all day meeting returning fishermen in their catamarans to ask if they've seen a warship – he took one of the bumboatmen who came out to the ship and spoke tolerable English as an interpreter, but no luck. It's my guess if Vaneyke did pass this way he would have taken care to do so by night, for he might have expected us to be waiting for him. Despite all our setbacks I still have a curious feeling we are close to him – and I may say close to the terrible Mrs V! I find myself puzzled more and more by her now there's a chance I might meet her again, for we steer up for Trinco tomorrow at first light – even Old Sax don't care to navigate around the Basses reefs in the dark with a school atlas! I'm not certain *puzzled* is the right word for my feelings about the TMV!

He saw her steady grey eyes and asymmetric smile trembling slightly as though not quite under control, and heard her distinct accents, 'Do you have doubts, Mr Greville?' He longed to hear them again and to discuss things with her, and find out more about Vaneyke himself. Did she know what had taken place in the *Curlew*? Would she still be at Trincomalee? How long was it since they had left Bombay? They were so close now – a day's sailing with a fair wind. Thank the Lord Saxmundham had called for steam in the morning.

8

Third time lucky, Stainton had said, and so it had proved. There she lay motionless to a single anchor, yards squared and sails furled, white sides streaked here and there with rust and wearing a slightly battered look although the awnings spread overall hid much from view. No boats were visible; probably they were around the other side, and some away ashore. There was no smoke from the single, raked funnel and no activity about the deck; she might have been deserted.

There was the name standing out boldly on her counter – all that could be made out from this angle of approach was: RLEW. Whatever she did now, she could not escape them. She was doing nothing.

'Deuced queer!' Saxmundham said again. 'They must have seen us.'

Guy ran his glasses forward along the line of her bulwarks. There was not a sign of life.

'No one *to* see us so far as I can make out.'

'All ashore for a punishment party,' Stainton said brightly.

'Made up your mind where we are?' Saxmundham growled.

'Batticaloa, sir,' Stainton replied promptly.

Saxmundham gazed at him.

'It's not Trinco, it's not Vendeloos Bay, I trust? You can just make out a fort.' Stainton pointed. 'Looks like a river.'

'And you had the name from the chief's atlas?'

'It is mentioned.'

A cry floated down from forward, 'Shoal ahead!'

'*Ready all*!' Saxmundham roared and jumped down to the deck.

They listened for the leadsman's sing-song, ' – by the mark – ten –'

Saxmundham called up to the lookouts, 'How's the water to starboard?'

'Clear!' came the prompt reply.

' – and a half – nine – '

'Helm down!' Saxmundham said to the quartermaster and, turning to Guy, 'We'll have the canvas off her when she's round – feel our way in with the engines.'

Guy stepped down and made his way forward. The hands were casting the head sheets off the pins; the jibs shook. The bow was swinging rapidly in the smooth water, the freshly-planed jib-boom standing up above the greenery of the low shoreline. The hills beyond were blue with distance, capped with white cloud. He heard the sails on the foremast slap against the rigging as they were taken aback; the new flying jib-boom quivered like an alder, but held. The parrel of the main yard behind him groaned as the spar swung round.

The *Curlew* was right ahead of them now, the huge ensign at her gaff floating out lazily towards them. She was evidently riding to a strong southerly setting current as she was almost broadside on. He steadied himself against the rail and levelled his binoculars – still no sign of life beneath that white, stretched awning or on the little bridge, with its rails intact he noticed. It was decidely eerie to see one of Her Majesty's ships of war at anchor off a foreign coast in broad afternoon with her colours flying, gear taut, hammocks in the nettings and no lookout, no watch on deck, no boats, not a stir of movement – so far as he could see quite deserted.

He lowered his glasses and stepped forward to the cathead, looking over to check that the bower anchor was ready for letting go; the rail leant towards the water as the headyards were braced round. The links of the shank painter squealed as the anchor swayed away from the side. The stem below was still cleaving through at a fair speed; the water was very green and clear a long way down.

He heard the leadsman's chant, ' – by the deep – twelve – ' and Saxmundham's voice an octave lower, 'Brace up the mainyard!'

'Cable's ranged, sir.'

He turned. 'Thank you, bo'sun! We'll be shortening down presently.'

The old sailor nodded and ambled towards the break of the fo'c's'le to caution the hands. Guy stepped across the deck around the covered Nordenfelt to the port rail for another look at the *Curlew*. There could be small doubt about it; either the officer of the day and all hands were lying in a drunken stupor or she had been abandoned. Yet she was not aground, nor sinking – indeed she looked in better shape than the *Dulcinea*. He wondered how she had come through the hurricane with so little obvious damage. Then he wondered whether she had come through it. Against the solidity of the image in his glasses, the memory of that strangely *colourless* vessel glimpsed for a flash in wastes of salt took on an even more unreal aspect. He thought of the *Flying Dutchman*; the night played strange tricks if one were looking out for something – not that he'd been consciously looking.

Perhaps she had been here all the time. He felt intense disappointment as he realized what had happened. She was so near Trincomalee. The Admiral had learnt of her whereabouts – surely he must have done so – and come out and taken Vaneyke and his officers and men back to base for court martial proceedings. That was not the answer either. Another crew would have been placed aboard to bring her in; they could never have left her abandoned, riding to a single anchor off this exposed coast, in the north-east monsoon.

He scanned up her masts, noting the beautiful stow of the sails, the yards so square and level, the taut tresses of rigging – hall-marks of pride – and yet abandoned! They would soon find out.

He strode to the fo'c's'le ladder and down to see how much cable the bo'sun had ranged. When he came out again Saxmundham was cautioning the hands for taking in sail, and the next few minutes raced by in tumultuous activity: the yards slid down and the topyard men, slipped from their waiting crouch like sprinters, hurled themselves up the rigging and out along the footropes, looking for split seconds to beat their rival tops. Guy saw Saxmundham in his habitual timing position, eyes fixed on the hunter in his palm.

It was a faultless display but no eyes witnessed it save those in the *Dulcinea* herself; as Saxmundham brought her round through the wind to point directly at the anchored gunboat there was not a stir of movement from her.

They closed rapidly under the screw, smoke clouding over the quarter, the leadsman singing out the shallowing depths, ' – and a half – eight – and a quarter – eight – '

Guy had a sudden, wild thought that the crew of the gunboat

were waiting concealed behind the bulwarks ready to spring into action and blast them with shell as they drew into point blank. Lord! He'd chased too many dhows! Yet the scene was unreal –

' – and a half – seven – '

'Ease her!' Saxmundham called, and the midshipman doing duty for the wrecked engine-room telegraph held up a board with the words painted on it so that it could be seen through the skylights from below, where another lad was stationed.

'Stop her!'

The midshipman dropped his board and held up another.

Presently the thumping underfoot ceased; the waves could be heard splashing against the stem as she glided on, and Saxmundham's order to the quartermaster to port the helm carried clearly up the deck in the quiet. The gunboat was little more than four hundred yards ahead as the bow began to swing away to starboard. Guy turned and nodded to the bo'sun, who went to the open skylight and shouted down to caution the hands at the compressor while he stepped quickly across to the starboard side and looked down over the rail, hearing Saxmundham order the engines astern. There was a boil of water under the counter; the deck heaved underfoot. The water below him had the pale green translucence of a sand bottom with here and there dark patches rippling at the edges as the waves crossed. The turbulence from the screw widened, sliding forward along the side. He saw Saxmundham standing in the entrance port looking down as it approached.

'Stop her!'

The leadsman indicated that his line was up and down; Saxmundham looked forward and opened his lungs; Guy nodded to Purkiss at the release lever, and a moment afterwards the anchor hit the water and the familiar juddering thunder of the running cable filled the air.

When they had brought up and bitted the cable, Guy went aft. Saxmundham was waiting for him; he nodded in the direction of the gunboat.

'See what you can find!'

Guy's anticipation showed, and the Old Man growled, 'Take no chances. They may be in the boats ashore. If they're mutineers they'll not be pleased to see you.' He rubbed his beard. 'It's hard to see what else it could be,' and started towards the entrance port. 'Remember, you'll have no assistance if you're outnumbered. Mr Green is bringin' the jolly boat to the gangway. She's armed. He's already proved his pluck – don't allow him his head if it comes to a scrap with a number of 'em. Cut and run!'

'Aye, aye, sir!'

'I suggest you arm yourself.'

Guy went below, snatched his revolver belt and raced up again, buckling it on. The boat was waiting at the gangway when he arrived back at the entrance port, D'Arcy looking up, and he saw Heighurst in the sternsheets and a party of marines, rifles laid along the bottom boards.

'Take her away,' Saxmundham growled, and he went down.

He had the mast raised and the sail set after they had pushed off, not so much because of the distance to the *Curlew* but just in case they were met around the other side by the flotilla of boats Saxmundham's words conjured up. The fresh breeze moved them along at a lively pace.

'What does he think we'll find?' Heighurst gestured towards the rifles.

'*Mutineers*!' Guy grinned.

The marine studied the gunboat's bare side. 'They're amazin' quiet.'

'They could be ashore.'

'*All* of them?'

They gazed at the vessel as they began to open her stern. There was a strange fascination in seeing the name – CURLEW – so close and tangible, weeping rust marks after all the speculation about her. The davits above the name were empty.

Heighurst raised a hand to his moustache. 'I'd say they was sittin' up there, cross-legged, chewin' over the noble fourfold path' – He looked at Guy innocently – 'wouldn't you?'

'The four noble truths,' Guy corrected him, 'The eightfold path.'

'Four or eight, what's the difference?'

'They'll be in an ugly mood in that case,' D'Arcy said with feeling. 'It's not pleasant what comes into a man after a spell of contemplation.'

Heighurst's brow rose fractionally. 'You ain't addicted?'

'Hang it!' D'Arcy's eyes started out, 'My dear old chum, when I was pacin' that buggerin' bridge – '

'With an independent air – ' Heighurst sang softly.

'You should hear the girls declare,' Guy joined in, 'he must be a millionaire – you can hear them sigh – '

' – and wish to die – '

They rounded the stern. There were no boats on the port side, only davit falls and hanging lifelines and the waves lapping at the foot of the empty gangway – no one in the entrance port above, no friendly hail. From this quarter she was more obviously abandoned than had appeared from seaward. The mood in the boat changed.

'How long have they bin gone, I wonder,' Heighurst said.

D'Arcy called, 'Ready about!' The breeze would allow them to fetch the gangway comfortably. 'Shift over!'

They settled to the new heel and examined the empty ports along her quarter, the uneven surface of the plates, corrugated by years of buffeting about the oceans of the world, rows of outstanding rivets casting shadows on the white paint, flaked in places, rust marks down from the scuppers and in the way of the engine-room outflow. She presented an unusual mixture of smartness and neglect. Wondering about it, Guy realized that she would probably not have been able to procure paint when her stocks ran out. Yet the rigging was trim and shining, not a loose pennant or a rusty block to be seen; the brasswork of the gangway was clean and bright.

'They've not been away long,' he said, pointing.

Heighurst nodded.

As D'Arcy had the sail dropped and brought the boat's bows up level with the foot of the gangway, stemming the current some distance away, then nosed her in with effortless judgement, Heighurst cautioned the marines.

He looked at Guy. 'We'll cover you.'

The boat was heaved along until the stern fetched the gangway. Guy stepped out and made his way up quickly, aware of the rifles pointing towards the entrance port. It was a short climb to the top. He went in, turning instinctively to salute the quarter-deck. There was a movement behind him; it was so unexpected he swung, pulse racing. A brown hen eyed him stupidly from the wire of her coop and clucked.

Lor – ! He relaxed, wondering idly why she appeared to be the only one; the other coops were empty.

The air was still under the tarpaulin; silence and heat seemed to well up the skylights and companions from below. The deck was flush from stem to stern, dominated by a great 7-inch gun amidships, lined up precisely fore and aft, its dark bulk and toothed elevating wheels gleaming above the brass racers set in the deck. Forward of it was a 64-pounder of a pattern familiar from the *Dulcinea*, and before that the foremast, rigging coiled neatly on the pin rack around it. The skylights above the mess-deck in the bows were open. There was a sense of habitation; it came of the order and cleanliness of the deck and the distinctive warm ship smell of oil, tar, iron, hemp, timber, salt, cooking and many men and a few animals living in close confinement. There was also a feeling of emptiness, perhaps caused by the unusual quiet.

He turned back to the port where Heighurst had followed him. His marines were arriving at the top of the gangway; below them he saw D'Arcy watching as the crew dropped the boat aft.

He nodded towards the after companion. 'I'll take a look below.'

'I'll take the mess-deck,' Heighurst replied. 'I'll leave a couple of fellows here.'

It was dim at the foot of the ladder, and the atmosphere heavy with the smell of lubricating oil. A door to the engine-room was open, and he saw smooth steel gleaming in the light from the sky-lights above, and the shining handrails of the ladder leading down. He turned away towards the after flat. The first thing he noticed as he entered were the rifle and pistol racks empty. He saw the ladderway leading down to the ward-room stores open, and he peered in; he could make out little in the shadows, but it seemed very empty. To his right was the pantry; the dishes were in their racks, the glasses, mugs and cups in place in good order, the wooden serving tops scrubbed almost white, the gauze over the meat and butter safes clean, drawers and cupboard doors closed. He stepped over and opened one – cruets and bottles of vinegar and relish, two bottles of Harvey's sauce! They were nearly empty. He closed it again.

Footsteps sounded down the ladder, and he turned. It was D'Arcy, his eyes bulging with interest.

'Found any bodies yet?' His voice echoed from the low deck-head. 'I don't believe this is a mutiny; hang it, would *you* polish up the brass and wash decks if you'd just cast the owner adrift in a boat? You wouldn't catch me doin' it, I'm certain – hanged if you would!'

Guy waved to the empty arms racks.

D'Arcy gazed at them for a moment, and shrugged. 'They've taken 'em – sensible precaution I'd say.'

Guy moved to the door into the ward-room. There was a green baize over the centre table, bright from the open skylight above; heavy chairs were tucked in along the sides. Beyond, against the bulkhead partitioning off the captain's quarters in the stern was the buffet, its top covered with a clean, white linen; above it was a familiar framed picture of the Queen–Empress, practically the only decoration in the small compartment. The timber mouldings around the deckhead and over the beams were plain white. Along either side the louvred doors to the officers' cabins were closed.

'Oh, dear!' D'Arcy exclaimed. 'Here's your answer! If you cooped me in a dismal cell like this I'm certain *I'd* go native. Imagination, my dear – it's a quality nine out of ten of our fellows do not know *exists* – let alone exercise. The tenth is too ashamed to reveal his guilty secret – and *here* you have it –'

Guy left him to his soliloquy, and strode on through a door that had been left half open into the stern quarters. So close now to the puzzle that Vaneyke represented, he longed to see where he had lived, *breathe* the atmosphere, touch some trace of the real man behind the conflicting accounts he had heard. He entered a small lobby; there was a door into Vaneyke's cabin ahead, and to his right a pantry with sunlight streaming in through the port on to scrubbed surfaces and crockery stowed and shining. To his left was the mizzen mast disappearing up through the deckhead at a rakish angle, and just beyond it a chest of chart drawers with a single chart open on the top, held by weights at the corners, a parallel rule and dividers and pencil arranged along the upper border. A light with a frilled green shade was suspended above on what looked like a system of weights and pulleys; he thought of Mrs Vaneyke and the gadgets she had said filled her husband's ships.

He stepped over to the chart, curious to see if there was any indication as to where they were. The ship's track was marked in pencil with numerous cross-bearings and times; it stopped half a mile north-east of the entrance to the Batticaloa river.

Stainton would be delighted! Three anchor bearings were noted in a neat hand alongside the small 'cocked hat' of the fix. There was no indication of the date the ship had arrived – only times.

Beside the chest was another door leading aft, and he squeezed round and opened it, entering Vaneyke's stern cabin. It was remarkably light after the compartments he had come through, with gleaming brass-bound ports all round streaming sunlight. Right aft under the stern ports were shelves with a few books but chiefly filled with growing plants, some of whose trailing leaves overflowed to a floral chintz settee following round the curve of the stern just below. There was a table in front of the settee draped with a different heavy chintz, otherwise bare. To the right was Vaneyke's bunk, apparently made up and covered with a rich red counterpane, polished drawers beneath and more drawers fitted into the curve of the ship's side just abaft it. A mahogany washstand stood against the forward bulkhead by the head of the bunk with pipes leading into a cabinet above; as he looked more closely he saw another pipe leading from the stand itself apparently through the drawer surround beneath the bunk – another of Vaneyke's contrivances, running water – why not?

There were two unfamilar, cylindrical shapes poking down from the deckhead above the bunk and, stepping across to see what they were, he made out the nearer as a hanging compass of a design he'd never seen before; the points were marked around the outside of a drum which revolved in what looked like a glass bowl with a vertical lubber's line painted down the forward side. He smiled at the thought of Vaneyke lying in bed watching the course, and heard her accents again, 'Robby is an oak – an oak with imagination. That is his trouble.' The idea was so simple – not so simple to put into practice, he thought, as he peered at the other thing beside it. It was an angled mirror. He put his knee on the edge of the bunk and pulled himself nearer. Amazingly, he saw planking in the glass – seams of planking and red scuppers and the bulwarks of the upper deck. He moved his head and received a slightly different view. He lay down on the bunk with his head on the pillow and looked up again into the mirror – raised skylights and beyond them the wheel with a binnacle either side, and well forward of that he made out coils of rigging on the pin rack at the mainmast. An oak with imagination, indeed!

'I could do with forty winks meself! It's hot down here – hanged if it ain't!'

He jumped down and invited D'Arcy to have a look at the magic show. 'The exception to your rule, I fancy!'

There was a rich Persian carpet on the deck, no doubt bought in the course of Vaneyke's voyaging. On the forward bulkhead between the two doors hung a service sword, and above it a plaque with carved and painted armorial bearings; the motto was *Diu Delibera*: 'Think for a long time'! He smiled.

On the other side of the cabin were a narrow wardrobe, a chiffonier with nicely carved doors, a chest of very shallow drawers looking like his own specimen drawers at home for his butterfly collection, and against the forward bulkhead a solid oak desk. There had been pictures above it, a lot of them; the paintwork of the bulkhead showed a pattern of lighter rectangles, most of them rather small, probably photographs he thought. He stepped across, drawn to the specimen drawers and pulled the top one open, feeling a wave of guilt as if Vaneyke were at his elbow, watching him investigate without leave his private possessions. It was filled with shells, each held in place by pins sited at strategic intervals around the fluted circumference, and most of them labelled with Latin names; a few were grouped together under the same label – different markings and colours of the same type. They were beautiful, and beautifully arranged. He closed the drawer carefully and opened the next; it too was bright with the delicately shaped and patterned molluscs – and the next and the next all the way down. The writing on the labels was in the same neat hand as the anchor bearings on the chart.

D'Arcy was standing behind watching. Guy looked at him for a moment, then turned to the desk and pulled open the top right-hand drawer; already he was closer to Vaneyke – the impression of a restless analytical ordered brain was clear, touching off affinities in himself.

'Imagination perhaps,' D'Arcy said, 'but positively no refinement of taste! Can you hear that counterpane? My dear fellow, the *Turks* wouldn't have it in a room with these chintzes.'

There was a large and well-worn Bible upside down in the

drawer, nothing else. Guy picked it up, feeling again nagging guilt, and turned it the right way round.

'I'll see what the other cabins look like,' D'Arcy said. 'I fear the worst.'

Guy heard him leaving as he opened the Bible where its black silk marker was inserted. A photograph fell out and landed face up on the carpet; he saw at once that it was her – very much younger, but unmistakeably her – a defiant thrust to the fine chin and that smile slightly more mobile on one side than the other; he could almost see it quiver. He knelt and picked the picture up. She had been very young. Behind were the mullioned windows of a house, a large English house – Bickley Hall perhaps? He sat in the desk chair and placed the photograph down before him, staring at it while his mind raced with speculation – a favourite photograph? Yet it was in pristine condition, not a thumb print on it, not a corner turned, unlike the pages of the Bible itself which had been worn thin from working over. The picture had spent most of its life in an album or a frame – one of the frames which had left their imprint on the paintwork above the desk perhaps? Had Vaneyke removed it before he left the ship, placed it in the Bible, placed the Bible in the empty right hand drawer, closed the drawer? If so he had had a reason, this was not a man of impulse. What had she said? 'Imagination – thoroughness – arrogance'? It seemed there was some sentiment too.

He looked at the pages from which the picture had fallen – the 'Song of Songs' – and his eyes moved without conscious volition over the lines at the top:

Awake, O north wind; and come, thou south;
Blow upon my gentle garden, that the spices thereof may flow out
Let my beloved come into his garden,
And eat his precious fruits.
I am come into my garden, my sister, *my* bride:
I have gathered my myrrh with my spice.

A photograph of Vaneyke's young bride between the leaves of the most beautiful love song in the world in a Bible upside down in the centre of an empty drawer – he sensed complete despair. It was an uncanny physical feeling to be sitting in his chair at his desk seeing with his eyes almost as he made his last testament aboard. He replaced the photograph and shut the

Bible with an uncomfortable sense of having violated a shrine, and turned it upside down and placed it back in the drawer and shut the drawer gently.

He knew what he would find in the other drawers before he opened them – nothing. Every one was empty, swept clean of bric-a-brac and dust – bare, stained deals. There was nothing on the top of the desk either.

He rose and went to the drawers on the other side of the cabin and pulled them open, one after the other, rifling through shirts and underclothing and socks, seeing only the photograph and the Bible in the empty desk, wondering what circumstances could have brought Vaneyke to this mute statement – and whether he had been forced to leave the ship by mutiny. If so, it appeared a remarkably orderly one.

He heard Heighurst's voice from the ward-room, and his footsteps approaching the open door, and turned. D'Arcy was behind the marine.

'They've gone,' Heighurst said. 'Taken everythin' – there's not a ditty box or so much as a rag anywhere – not even the mess traps. They've packed their bags and left, every man jack. They made a tiddly job of clearin' up afterwards – Admiral's inspection! I've a couple of fellows goin' through the boiler rooms and stokeholes but, judgin' by the state of the decks, they'll not find much.'

'Hang it!' D'Arcy said. 'It don't make sense.'

'As to that' – Heighurst curled the end of his moustache, gazing at Guy with a strange expression – 'I'm not certain you weren't close to the mark.'

'Mutiny?'

'Not exactly. Come with me.'

He turned and they followed him back through the ward-room, up the ladder to the deck and along to a position just forward of the bridge. It was immediately apparent what he had brought them to see: a large timber plaque, beautifully carved and painted in glowing reds, blues and golds, had been fixed to the forward bridge rails. It was difficult to make it out because of the tarpaulin stretched beneath, but peering up in the space between the canvas and the rails Guy made out the startling legend:

THE EIGHTFOLD PATH

Right understanding, right thought, right speech, right action, right living, right effort, right awareness, right concentration.

He looked at Heighurst, astonished. 'You were right!'

The marine's lips lifted. 'To coin a phrase.'

'What do it mean?' D'Arcy asked.

'The eightfold path to Nirvana,' Guy replied, looking up again, scarcely able to believe his eyes. 'It's hard to explain. The way to the Buddhist paradise, if you like.' It wasn't his idea of paradise; he tried to recall exactly what it was. 'A state of nothingness – cravings put behind you – all pain is caused by desire.' He thought of the picture of her enclosed in the 'Song of Songs' in the empty desk.

Heighurst raised a brow at D'Arcy. 'No wenchin', d'you see.'

'An odd sort of paradise,' D'Arcy said. 'I shouldn't take to it.'

'The Curlews haven't either, by the look of it.'

Guy turned to D'Arcy, 'Did you find anything?'

'Uncommonly little. They ain't goin' to dress for dinner wherever it is they're goin', and they ain't goin' to take sights – nor play tennis, or racquets –'

'An orderly disembarkation?'

'Decidedly.'

'But they do anticipate a spot of shootin',' Heighurst said, nodding forward. 'They've taken both Nordenfelts and most of the ammunition for them. I sent a fellow down.'

'All the small arms too,' Guy said, starting back towards the companionway.

Heighurst peered at the plaque for a moment before following. 'Don't say anythin' about right shootin' up there!'

'Right concentration,' D'Arcy rejoined quickly.

Outdone at his own game, Heighurst remained silent.

'I wonder who it was played racquets,' Guy said.

'My dear fellow,' D'Arcy replied, 'Hardwicke. I can give you all the names. They left the pay book.'

Guy stopped at the entrance to the companion. 'That's useful.'

'They've left all the ship's books so far as I can make out – stores, indents, magazines, victualling –'

'The log?'

'That I have not seen. I'll take another dekko.'

They went below again. Leaving D'Arcy and Heighurst to search for the log book, Guy went through the ward-room to Vaneyke's cabin as if drawn by magnetic forces. There was only the chiffonier and the small wardrobe to examine now; he'd looked in all the drawers. He went across and pulled open the door of the wardrobe; it smelt of damp and mothballs and was packed with uniforms, mess dress, two tweed suits, heavy weather gear, and below them rows of shoes. He bent to look and found a covering of dust over the leather, which came off on his finger. There was an unused feel about the cupboard. He shut the door and turned to the chiffonier, but that too revealed little. There were glasses and cloths, decanters, mostly empty – nothing very personal.

Straightening, he looked around the cabin to see if there was anything he might have missed, but it was apparent that Vaneyke had removed practically all trace of himself from the compartment, leaving only the clothes he didn't need, and the collection of shells and plants which presumably he couldn't take – and the Bible and the single photograph. All other pictures had gone, and the ornaments and mementoes that sailors collected over the world like jackdaws, and letters, papers, even writing materials – all gone, either with him or dumped overboard. The empty drawers in the desk suggested to him that they had probably gone over the side, although he couldn't say why; perhaps it was the starkness of emotion revealed. His eye caught the few books on the after shelves and he went across to see what they were. The fact that there were so few was another pointer to a careful clearing up of personal belongings, a man apparently so immersed in eastern religions must surely have had more of a library than this.

The first book he picked up was another well-thumbed copy of the Bible, but there was nothing inside; the next was a prayer book, and the next two both hymnals, no markers and nothing inside them either; strange for a man with the Buddhist creed displayed on his forward bridge rail to have so much of the literature of the Church of England in his cabin! The last book was different, it had a green cloth binding and titling in plain black letters: *The Patient's Vade Mecum: How to get Most Benefit from Medical Advice*. There was a yellowed paper sticking from it; he opened the pages there, glancing over them:

Residence abroad, especially in the East, often has an effect on a person's constitution, so such points should not be overlooked as unimportant. If the patient is a heavy drinker he should not hide this information, though as a rule a heavy drinker shows signs of his weakness on his face. Anyone who has at any time suffered syphilis should say so without delay, as this knowledge may be of the utmost importance. It is not unusual for a patient to keep back information from the doctor from a false sense of modesty. Needless to say such a situation is not only unfair to the doctor. . . .

He stopped reading and looked back to the general heading – *The Nervous System*.

It appeared that Vaneyke had not opened the book for some time for the stiffened, yellowed edge of the paper that had been used as a marker corresponded to the area that had been sticking out from the book; most of the paper had been enclosed by the pages and was white and almost fresh-looking. He turned it over, seeing with a start of interest several lines in the neat hand he had come to recognize as Vaneyke's. It was the start of a letter to 'My dearest Harriet' – was that her name? He had no idea; it had been written off Hormuz some two and a half years previously.

The heat is simply frightful and it is only by reversing the Act of Creation (sic!) calling the light 'night' and the darkness 'day' that I am able to continue my studies, but Brewer is an excellent officer and the work of the ship has not suffered. I can only now realize the extent of the inconsistencies in the account of the Creation and subsequent references to it. We must not mistake irrationality for the 'Mystery'. The Holy Spirit before the flood spoke of the imagination of man's heart being 'only evil continually'.

The letter stopped, and below it in the same hand, but rather more unevenly and at a slight angle as if they had been written at some later date, were two lines:

'There is no fire like concupiscence, no seizure like hate.
There is no net like delusion, no river like desire.

An arrow joined this to the last sentence of the letter, and there was a neat number in brackets alongside, '(19)'. The passage sounded as if it might be something out of Ecclesiasticus or the Proverbs, but the metre was wrong.

He re-read the letter above it. The name, Brewer, had given him abrupt pause at the first reading. He had the most unpleasant image of a huge, pale-faced brute of a sub ruling the gun-room in his first ship with every device of barbarity that he considered he might perpetrate without being brought to book. J. R. L. de P. Brewer – the name, the boorish eyes and flaccid lips were carved indelibly in his memory. He had not suffered personally; his height and reputation as a sportsman had more than insured him from Brewer's attentions – the brute had even tried to toady up to him until he had learnt better – but the weaker members had gone through torture and the atmosphere of the gun-room in those first few months before Brewer left the ship had been enough to make him wonder why he had joined the service.

He strode to the door, calling, 'Where's the pay book? D'you remember who the number one was?'

D'Arcy's voice came back, 'They're all on the table.'

He went through the lobby into the ward-room, and saw the green baize piled with official-looking volumes.

D'Arcy came out of a cabin to his left at the same time. 'They've taken the log', he said, 'or ditched it.' He waved towards the table. 'That's all there are. Number one, you said –' he bent to look at the spines of the books and extracted a long, flat one. 'Here we are – I can't say the name meant anythin' to me' – he flipped over the pages – but I can assure you his sense of colour is execrable. Brewer, that's the name.'

'Initials?'

'My dear fellow –'

Guy realized he was glaring. He smiled. 'I'm sorry. My first nursemaid was called Brewer. I prefer not to remember.'

'An unpleasant customer?' D'Arcy looked at the book again. 'Well, this fellow's mater was not takin' any chances – J. R. L. de P.' He looked up again.

'That's him,' Guy said. 'I'm beginning to understand.'

9

Saxmundham's expression was rapt as Guy made his report; he didn't interject once.

'I see,' he said at last. 'It all takes some swallowin'! On my life!' He gazed at each of the others seated around his table, D'Arcy, Heighurst, Stainton. 'Anythin' else?'

They shook their heads.

'I see,' he repeated, and gazed down at the chart Guy had brought back from the gunboat as if it represented the one intelligible factor to come from their investigation. 'Bless my soul! Not fifty miles from Trinky!' He looked up at Stainton as if defying him to argue.

Stainton nodded his agreement.

'The audacity of the beggar!' Saxmundham started chuckling, then suddenly thumped the chart with his hand over the anchor bearings. 'It's him all right – I'll stake my life on it – brought her here himself.' He glared across the table at Guy. 'Can you see mutineers sailin' *towards* the commander-in-chief, Greville?'

It was a point Guy hadn't thought of in the excitement of his findings aboard. This was the old Saxmundham with his sure nose for the commonsense solution. 'Now you mention it, no sir – I can't.'

A suspicious look passed across the blue eyes. 'You had not considered it?'

'No sir.'

'D'you dispute it?'

'I can't dispute it sir.' As the Old Man continued to gaze at him, he went on, 'We all felt everything was left far too orderly for a mutiny.'

What did he or any of them know of mutiny?

Saxmundham sat back in his chair, still gazing at him. 'Out with it then!'

Guy gazed back.

'Your cursed theories! On my life! I don't profess to understand how you knew the fellow had taken the yellow robe, but since you did – what do you think?'

'I believe he's unbalanced, sir –'

'Unbalanced! Bless my soul! Beggar disappears for six months – brings his ship back within a deuce of the Admiral – then decamps with his entire complement – heaven knows where – he's as mad as a march hare!' He looked round the table, beard jutting. 'Always was if you ask my opinion!'

'*Ce monde est plein de fous*!' Stainton said quietly.

Saxmundham stared at him. 'I trust that is intended as a general observation, pilot.'

'Decidedly – extremely general, sir.'

'Oblige me by speakin' English.' He turned back to Guy, then had second thoughts. 'If you must use a foreign lingo, steer clear of that cursed froggy!'

'I'm sorry, sir.'

Saxmundham looked at Guy. 'Where was we?'

Guy had to recall himself. 'And from the letter – the unfinished letter, sir –' he pointed to the sheet he had taken from *The Patient's Vade Mecum*, now on the table by Saxmundham's right arm, 'he was at one time delegating a good deal of authority to his number one – Brewer.'

Saxmundham nodded, a thoughtful look in his eye.

'I know Brewer, sir. I had the experience of being a green snottie in a gun room he looked after – and did his level best to wreck.'

Saxmundham's brows rose at his expression. 'Unpleasant?'

'In those days, remarkably.'

'In my experience a rotten apple don't generally mend.'

'I don't like to black a fellow I haven't seen for years – but I can say if he ran the *Curlew* as he ran that gun-room – and without having to pay too much attention to his commanding officer – what's been happening does not seem so improbable.'

Saxmundham leaned forward. 'The floggin's – I can see that – but what 're the rascals doin' runnin' ashore here ' – he thumped the chart – 'right next door to the Admiral?'

Heighurst said, 'There was no coal in the bunkers.'

Saxmundham looked at him thoughtfully. 'All the more reason for stoppin' on the other side of the island – if they must come here.'

'I believe they must,' Guy said.

The Old Man grimaced. 'So! We return to the yellow robe.' He pulled the hunter from his pocket, 'it didn't take long. Out with it then!'

Guy grinned. 'I've been giving it a deal of thought, sir, and it occurs to me there are two possible reasons for him to come around this side of the island – one is that we frightened him off his original course for a departure from Cape Comorin, and he decided to make a detour well to seaward of us, so fetching up off the southern end of the island. The winds have been generally in the north-west or westerly quarter over the last few days – it would have been natural for him to carry on up the east coast rather than beat back – and perhaps run into us again.'

Saxmundham was gazing at the chart.

'Having committed himself to the east coast,' Guy went on, 'Batticaloa was the first good anchorage where he might expect to procure provisions for his expedition. There were virtually no provisions aboard,' he finished.

'And your second reason?'

'The alternative is simply that he intended making for Batticaloa all along because it was the most convenient anchorage for wherever it is he wants to go.'

Saxmundham gazed at him. 'I know the beggar, and I'd lay long odds it's your second reason.' He looked down at the chart again. 'So where's he headin' for?'

'I'd say that's anyone's guess, sir.'

The brows lifted over the blue eyes. 'Except – ?'

Guy grinned. 'It did occur to me – my father made something of a study of oriental religions – it's a hobby of his –'

'Does he pin the eightfold path over his pulpit in illuminated letters?'

'No sir. I understand he had his doubts at one time. Now he's very strong for the Church.'

'I'm pleased to hear it. Godalming ain't it? How long do he speak for?'

Guy smiled. 'He believes a sermon should on no account exceed eight minutes, sir.'

'On my life! I enjoy a sermon with meat. Do 'e fetch 'em in?'

Guy laughed. 'Indeed!' He thought of Helen's last letter. 'From the sick bed at times!'

'Bless my soul! Godalming –' He rubbed the hair on his cheek thoughtfully. 'Eight minutes, it ain't a long time.'

'He finds it difficult. He has been known to stop without finishing.'

Saxmundham chuckled. 'I dare say that wakes 'em up! I shall try it. D'you know it's an odd thing I've never been cursed with doubts.' He shot a glance at Stainton who was smiling. 'What about you, pilot?'

Stainton's amused expression fell away, and he looked round quickly. 'I'd say: "There's a divinity that shapes our ends, rough-hew them how we will." – Hamlet, sir,' he added in the silence.

'That's what I say,' D'Arcy put in feelingly, 'hanged if it ain't!'

Saxmundham turned to him with mild surprise. 'I'll attend to that in a moment or two, Mr Green.' He looked suspiciously at Heighurst's expression, then at Guy again. 'Where was we?'

'Godalming, sir. On my last time home father was very excited about a Ceylon Archaeological Commission Report he was reading – they come out annually. This one had pages of photographs of the ruins of one of the lost cities – I forget the name –'

'Lost cities?'

'There are two principal ones. They were formerly the capitals of the Sinhalese kings – centres of an incredible civilization that flourished from about the fourth century BC if I remember – based on tremendous schemes of interlocking canals and tanks – lakes – for irrigating the country. They had nothing to learn from the Romans on that score, judging by the descriptions. The photographs show the most marvellous pillars and stone carvings and baths –' he checked his enthusiasm. 'At all events, waves of invaders swarmed across from southern India – the Tamils – and succeeded eventually in taking these capitals and driving the unfortunate Sinhalese further into the hills, up to Kandy in fact. The irrigation works were allowed to go hang under the new regime, the system collapsed and the jungle crept over the cities and their temples and gardens and public buildings –' He caught Saxmundham's expression and hurried to finish. 'Until some ten or twenty years ago we, that is the Ceylon Civil Service, became interested in uncovering them –'

'I find it all most interestin',' Saxmundham said. 'Where's it leadin'?'

'These were not only royal capitals, but sacred cities – the Sinhalese were converted to Buddhism long before our Lord's time, and in one of them, I forget which, they planted the sacred bo-tree. I understand that in the eyes of Buddhists this is only preceded in importance as a shrine by the temple of the Worshipful Tooth at Kandy, said to be the actual tooth of the Buddha, and the Buddha's footprint at the summit of Adam's Peak.'

'You're not tellin' us you believe the beggar's set off on a pilgrimage to a sacred tree? Or a tooth?' The blue eyes were wide with disbelief.

'Not a pilgrimage, no sir. I just tried to put myself in his place – if I were seeking nirvana –' he shouldn't have said it; another explanation was necessary. 'The goal of Buddhism – a kind of detachment from the world.' Saxmundham's frown eased. Guy went on, 'What better place than one of the lost cities in the heart of the island where the old shrines still exist – and sufficient of the ruins and masonry to construct shelters of some kind without too much difficulty?'

'And where the Ceylon Civil Service is busy pokin' around – as I understand you to say. Is that the place you'd go?'

'The archaeological people are concentrating on the oldest, northernmost city, sir. The other's pretty well untouched so far. I don't suppose they'd find anyone there. I remember this because I remember thinking, if I ever got to Trinco, I'd like to visit this other place –'

'Near Trinky?' Saxmundham's gaze sharpened.

'Not too far. Off the road to Kandy.'

'What puzzles me a little,' Heighurst's brow expressed his usual cynicism, 'what would they be wantin' with Nordenfelts and all the trimmin's on the path to nirvana?'

Saxmundham thumped the chart, 'I was wonderin' that myself!'

'A kind of detachment,' Stainton murmured.

Guy laughed.

'Well – !' Saxmundham stared at him.

'The only suggestion I have, sir, is that we're dealing with two separate matters: one is Vaneyke hell-bent along the eightfold path, or words to that effect; the other is Brewer.'

'Hell-bent?'

'Precisely!' Guy nodded. 'He may be in too deep – he may have been given so much rein by Vaneyke he has no alternative now. He has to disappear into the hills, and he has to arm himself against capture by the search parties that are going to come after him directly the *Curlew*'s found – rather sooner than expected as it turns out.'

Saxmundham pulled at his beard, looking round at Heighurst. 'That satisfy you? The penalty for desertion is death as I recall.'

Heighurst's eyes were unusually serious. 'We'll be dealin' with some desperate fellows.'

'We?'

The marine brought a hand up to his moustache. 'Whoever it is has the good fortune to be sent after 'em.'

'You're applyin' are you?' Saxmundham turned back to Guy and gazed at him with a speculative expression. 'It all takes some swallowin'.' He was silent.

D'Arcy's voice broke in, 'I'd say we hadn't paid much attention to the other fellows – Hardwicke and the others.'

Saxmundham turned. 'Lord Hardwicke's boy?'

'And the other poor fellows. Caught between the devil and the deep sea, I'd say – hang it what do you do if the commandin' officer *and* number one are mad?'

Saxmundham's brows drew down a fraction. 'There's a lot in what you say,' he growled at last.

'There's another thing,' Guy came in to turn the subject. 'I couldn't help feeling before that Mrs Vaneyke knew something of her husband's intentions, and was making the journey to Ceylon to find him – not just to see the Admiral.'

'On my life!' Saxmundham thumped the table again. '*Cherchez la femme*! You young dog!'

Guy fought back a smile. 'Finding the *Curlew* here like this confirms that opinion.'

'It would!' Saxmundham noticed Stainton's eyes, and his brows drew together. 'There's an exception to every rule, you'll learn my boy!' and he thumped the table again, '*Cherchez la femme*!' He looked round as if challenging them to dispute his exception.

In the ensuing silence he growled, 'That's enough jawin'. It don't make much sense whichever way you look at it – though it's not the first commandin' officer lost his wits on this station.' He shot a glance at D'Arcy, and a reflective tone came into his voice. 'I've known more than one had to be relieved of his command, poor fellow, and sent home – and it wasn't always that cursed grog.' He shook his head, and raised both arms. 'It's the scope of it. You said, I fancy, Mr Green – it's the *others*. I know the Hardwicke boy – a first rate officer in my opinion.' His eyes were hard. 'Between the two of 'em, they've done for the poor fellow. And all the others.' He looked across at Guy, beard jutting, 'Do you go after them, Greville. Run 'em to ground. See if you can establish communication with Hardwicke or some of the others – they'll not want to go through with this madness. Then send a report of your findin's to the Admiral. We'll make our way to Trinky and prepare a brigade. Send your messengers back along the Kandy road. We'll march that way so we don't miss each other.'

He turned to Heighurst. 'Soldier – take a platoon of your fellows with Greville. But I want no skirmishin' mind, not if it can be avoided. Englishmen shootin' Englishmen ain't to my taste – I hope it's not to yours.' He stared at the marine. 'It's only two of the beggars we want – and I fancy that's best achieved with brains, not guns.' He looked at Guy again. 'You won't need the Gardner guns or rockets. Rifles only for self-defence. If they come at you – cut and run! Equip yourself for speed. If you start in the mornin' at first light you won't be far behind the rascals. They won't make such good speed as you can. Any questions?' He looked from one to the other.

Guy said, 'Shall I cable the Admiral, sir?'

Saxmundham stared doubtfully for a moment, then shrugged. 'Tell him we're on our way in with the *Curlew*.'

He looked around again but, seeing there were no questions, turned to D'Arcy, who had a disappointed expression. 'Mr Green, I'm promotin' you to actin' commander to take command of the *Curlew*. I'll recommend the Admiral leaves you there –' He held up a hand as D'Arcy, overcome with delight, tried to say something, and turned to Stainton. 'Take over as number one for the time bein' pilot. Release some hands to Mr Green for a scratch crew for the *Curlew*. And oblige me by havin' everythin' ready for weighin' in the mornin'.' A thought struck him, and he looked at Guy. 'We've only the one confounded boat. We'll wait until it comes back from takin' your party ashore. Don't delay!'

'We'll be away at first light,' Guy replied.

Saxmundham turned to D'Arcy. 'Let us know directly you're shortened up. When we've weighed, take station on our starn.'

'Aye, aye, sir!'

D'Arcy could not conceal his jubilation. Again he started to say something, and again Saxmundham held his hand up. 'And when we reach Trinky you may take St Barbara.'

An earnest expression came into D'Arcy's eyes. 'I'd be happy for you to keep her.'

'I'm obliged to you. I prefer to keep the Don – I fancy it was a good omen he survived the hurricane' – a mellower look came into the blue eyes – 'as we did ourselves. No, if I am to keep the Don, do you take St Barbara.' He gazed innocently across the table. 'That's fair ain't it?'

D'Arcy grinned. 'Done sir! Hang it – ain't she just –' Words failed him.

Saxmundham's brows rose; he said drily, 'It is most satisfactory, we are both pleased.'

The rollers lifted as they felt the shelving bottom, and broke, coursing on in seething ranks towards the low shoreline. Guy steered for the gap in the line of palms, wondering if he would be able to hold her against broaching to. He had expected difficulty in finding the entrance over the shifting sand bar, but that consideration paled before the unexpected height of the swell. In the grey half-light before dawn it looked murderous.

He had the sail lowered and the oars manned, unshipped the rudder and substituted a long steering oar, had the boxes of provisions stowed in the bow passed aft, and ordered the two bowmen into the stern sheets. He had the rest of the men on the oars turn to sit facing the bows, thwart by thwart from forward.

'Imagine you're facing the right way,' he yelled over the noise of the breakers ahead. 'When I say "Give way!" pull like the devil!'

He turned to the bowmen, 'We'll tow the yard and sail over the stern as a drogue. Lash the end of the stern painter to one end of the yard, the sheets to the other, and veer them out either side – Adams, port – McKay, starboard!'

The boat lifted as Adams scrambled forward over the thwarts to release the halliard and pass the yard aft. Guy leant his weight to the steering oar. The effects of the orders and the feel of the rough timber in his palms gave him a new confidence; he looked forward to the tussle.

When the two bowmen had the yard prepared, he ducked; they lifted it above his head and heaved it out over the stern. A balloon of canvas rose to the surface.

'Back together!' he shouted.

The boat moved forward up a retreating swell, and the two men veered out their lines until the yard was some distance astern, well out of range of his oar. He nodded and they took a turn around the cleats.

Another comber lifted them, and he felt the boat surge on for a moment, but they hadn't quite reached the breaking zone, and he didn't stop the hands on the oars. She felt the drag of the yard and canvas; the bow lifted.

A larger hillock rose up astern, its surface dark against the light creeping over the sky; the yard and its pale drag of canvas rose crazily; he tensed against the oar as he felt the boards rising beneath his feet; the stern veered to starboard; he fought it back. The boat swept on beneath him, locked just ahead of the wave, bows depressed and cleaving sheets of spray out either side. Suddenly the wave was passing and the bow lifting. He felt the thrill of triumph. Lord knew where they were headed, but it could be done! He flashed a grin at Helghurst, who looked as green as the water. Aimes, who was to take the boat out again afterwards – if there was an afterwards – had a set look on his face as if determined to endure without flinching.

Some smaller rollers passed, helping them in towards the danger zone as the hands pushed their chests against the looms of the oars, fighting the drag of the towed canvas. He saw a larger swell looming astern; they were too close to take any chances now.

'Give way!' he shouted.

The blades lifted in mid-stroke and the hands leant right forward, dipping them and heaving back with all the power they could muster. The boat quivered, then the stern began to rise and she climbed up towards the crest. The lines to the spar slacked, the steering oar moved between his hands like a live thing. He was conscious of a giddy rising and rushing which he was powerless to control. They were in the hands of the gods; he gave himself to the sensation, for a moment elevated to a wild godlike status himself, and careless of consequences. Then the boat levelled up; the lopping top of the roller passed on; he heard it curl over itself just ahead and saw spray rise as he felt the boat descending stern first towards the trough.

'*Oars*! Back together! *All you have*!'

This would be the one! '*For your lives*!' he yelled.

The boat started forward again; he shouted to Adams and McKay, 'Veer the lines!'

Released from the drag aft, and impelled by the crew hurling their weight on the oars, which bent like canes, the boat surged forward into the white water left by the breaking wave they had just ridden. Guy looked aft, seeing the next one building up, developing an angry hollow as it advanced, translucent sections of the top flipping over and falling down the slope. It approached like fate itself. He heard thunder closing from his left and felt spray blown against his face. The top showed clear, bright green as it began to collapse. The spar and sail rising up towards it were hidden in a flurry of pounding water; the lines snapped taut, jumping through the bowmen's hands. The air filled with noise and white foam. As the torrent reached them, he felt the stern lifted bodily to starboard, and shouted to Adams to heave in on his line as he put all his weight against the oar, fighting her back; they rocked in the boil of hissing salt, driving on for a moment like a surf-boat, but she kept her bows to the beach, and the seething water outpaced them ahead; the stern began to settle.

They had done it!

For the first time since starting the approach, he looked ahead for the river entrance; he saw they had been set southwards; instead of pointing for the middle of the gap between the palms they were heading perilously close to land on their port bow. He could see the beach clearly now, and the broken waves pounding up it. He started easing her to starboard in the aftermath of each wave, then round again to meet the next stern on before it reached them. It had little effect, but there was nothing else he could do; to allow the breakers to catch the stern and hurl them broadside on would be disastrous; better to allow them to carry her up the beach, whence they could take the provisions and arms out, and walk her bodily over the low land to the river. He shouted to the new bowmen to boat their oars and stand by to hop out with the boat rope, run it up the beach, and if possible take a turn on a tree.

As she was carried in nearer and nearer he felt it becoming easier to control her, and the ferocity of the lift and surge became less. Astonishingly, he saw sand close to port, and looking up found they had reached the line of the shore and were passing in through the river mouth extraordinarily close to a spur of the left bank. The lines of breakers extended far away on the quarter merging into the sky. The motion of the boat was suddenly different and, as another wave passed, sizzling ahead, they dropped on to sand bottom with a thud that jarred right up his body. He looked round, wondering whether to order the bowmen out, but as suddenly as she had grounded, she lifted and swept on. The water ahead was a calm sheet of grey shading under the trees to the darkness of night. The air held a moist fragrance. They were in a different world.

'Oars!' he called.

The hands lifted the blades from the water and rested, chests heaving; their hair was crinkled by the salt water, their jumpers clinging to their backs. Guy realized his tunic was soaked; he was not cold; his blood still raced. Heighurst looked up, his face pale, the ends of his moustaches drooping moistly, and for once he seemed at a loss for some desperate pun. Guy grinned at him with sheer delight.

As some of the oarsmen turned to look back at the seas they had defeated, he called out, 'Good work!' It had been. They would have to go back out again, but it should not be too difficult facing the breakers and pulling up them.

He had the yard and sail hauled alongside and up into the boat, and had it set. They slid up the river as light spread from astern and thickets of mangrove on either hand woke to bird song. The wind was heavy with a thousand scents of a botanical garden.

They opened the reach up to Batticaloa island as the sun rose. The walls of an old fort and the sails of scores of native fishing craft raised to dry in the wind were touched with gold; beyond the mountains were purple-grey in the distance, the clouds about their peaks layered with a golden glow. Guy's imagination stirred. He heard the sound of a bugle and saw the

Union Jack blowing out as it rose up the flagstaff.

'They're expectin' us!' Heighurst said. He had recovered his colour and re-set his moustaches.

By the time they beached the boat, it was broad light and the sun was warm. They were surrounded by a circle of onlookers, light brown boys with merry eyes, darker, turbanned fishermen wearing only a calico loincloth over thin corded bodies, Sinhalese combing out their lustrous black locks; further away along the water's edge women in coloured cottons looked up as they slapped washing, their eyes as brilliant as the morning.

At the top of the beach by himself was an Englishman wearing a light suit and a topee, who waved as he saw them looking at him, and started down towards them. Guy told Aimes to land the provision then take the boat back, Heighurst ordered the marines to guard them and together they walked up to meet the man.

'Dickinson,' he said smiling and thrusting out his hand as they exchanged introductions. 'You haven't come to arrange a game of cricket, by any chance?' He looked hopefully from one to the other. 'We have a decent team here – we managed a not inglorious draw with the Colts before the rains –' his enthusiasm melted as Guy shook his head. 'Oh dear! Well – come along to the bungalow!'

He started up the beach and they fell in beside him. 'Perhaps I can persuade you over breakfast. I was on my way home when you were reported. I look after the province by the way.' He looked keenly at Guy, 'Greville did you say? Not G. W. W. Greville by any chance?'

'Yes.'

Dickinson stopped and gazed at him. 'By Jove!' His brows, which were dark and very straight, lending an air of great seriousness to his expression, were raised slightly as if in puzzlement, but his eyes had regained all their former enthusiasm. 'Well, well!' He set off again with a longer stride, shaking his head. 'By Jove! I'm going to enjoy this!' He looked around smiling.

Guy returned the smile, wondering if he were some distant relation he should have heard about but, as Dickinson seemed content to stride on purposefully, he asked if he had seen anything of the Curlews.

'Yes, indeed! They would not play, said they couldn't raise a team – not enough men if you please!' He looked round again. 'I don't suppose you've played on one of our earth wickets out here? Made from anthills, a rather decent surface – the rain doesn't affect it. The outfield's not too hot, mark you – a case of hit 'igh 'ard and hoften!' He smiled. 'Not your game I should imagine?'

'Not on this occasion, we're after the Curlews,' Guy replied, trying again to direct the talk to the matter in hand.

Dickinson's dark brows rose. 'Some kind of an exercise? I thought their behaviour queer at the time. They bought us right out of milk biscuit and rusk – there's not one to be had anywhere now – and precious little in the way of tinned food. It was like the plague of locusts! The Moormen are well satisfied though!'

'Did they say where they were off to?'

'They were not forthcoming about anything. They appeared to have one object in view – to find the bazaar and expropriate anything edible!' He looked at them each in turn. 'Strictly between ourselves I have a crow to pluck with Lieutenant Brown –'

'Brown!' Guy exclaimed. It was a name that had not appeared among the officers listed in the *Curlew*'s pay book.

'I think that was what he said – yes, I'm certain it was. I invited him along for a peg before tiffin. The fellow never showed up – one object in view, you see. But he was that kind of a fellow, if you understand,' he had a meaning look in his eye.

Guy gazed back, wondering what he meant.

'Strictly *players*' dressing room,' Dickinson said.

'Something of a tarpaulin!'

'Very much so – rather a *coarse* weave!'

Guy looked at Heighurst.

'Here we are,' Dickinson said, waving to a bungalow ahead of them across an expanse of grass. They were inside the walls of the fort; to their left was a simple, square-looking church in the Dutch style, tombstones rising nearby, and to their right more bungalows with high-pitched roofs, tiled in red, their verandahs and gardens embowered in greenery and a profusion of flowers of every shape and brilliant colour, as Dickinson's was.

'Charming,' Heighurst said, sounding as if he meant it.

'It suits my wife,' Dickinson replied. 'To tell the truth, it's a decent berth. I'm my own man out here. There's only one half decent road from the west coast skirting the hills, and out there,' he waved a hand, 'nothing but jungle. We're reclaiming it slowly, restoring the old irrigation works of the Wijayos – the great dynasty – we've more than 30,000 acres under rice this year.'

'How far is the old capital?' Guy asked.

'Pollanarua? As the crow flies, fifty or sixty miles – but a good deal further on the ground.' Dickinson looked at him quizzically, but they were interrupted by two children, a boy and a girl of some six or seven years old bounding out towards them from the bungalow. He stooped and picked the girl up as he introduced them, 'George – and Beatrice,' and looking down at the boy, 'I've a surprise in store for you.' He turned to Guy again. 'I took him to Colombo last year to see Lord Hawke's team when they came on from India. He got all their autographs.'

'F. S. Jackson,' George piped up, 'C. W. Wright, A. J. L. Hill –'

'Well,' Dickinson interrupted the flow, 'this is G. W. W. Greville.'

George looked up, silenced but uncertain whether to be impressed.

'150 not out,' Dickinson said proudly, 'Navy versus the gentlemen of the MCC at Lords,' he looked at Guy.

'146 actually,' Guy said; the pang of that last wicket falling was only a memory now.

'And a midshipman at the time.'

Guy nodded. George gazed up with wide eyes, then turned and scampered back for the bungalow, where his mother had appeared, and was standing waiting on the verandah with a pleased smile on her face.

'Ah!' Dickinson beckoned and introduced them to her, 'My wife Elizabeth.'

'We *are* honoured,' she said, 'two ships in three days! Usually it takes us a whole year to reach that score. But however did you come in over the bar?' She had an attractive, wide mouth and her eyes looked as though she smiled a lot.

'We shut our eyes,' Heighurst said.

She laughed.

George tugged at her skirt, and said in a stage whisper, 'It's G. W. W. Greville.'

'Number three for the Navy,' Dickinson explained.

She looked at him with raised brows. 'We *shall* have an enjoyable breakfast! Do come in.' She turned and called to a native hovering in the shadows to fetch two towels for the visitors.

As they followed her, Guy caught sight of several words painted in gold above the trellis, now partially obscured by broad leaves and tendrils; he peered up.

KEEP YOUR PROMISE   KEEP YOUR TEMPER
KEEP YOUR WICKET UP

He saw it was bordered in red, black and gold. The I Zingari! He turned with a delighted smile.

Dickinson was watching him. 'I find it particularly appropriate out here.'

'I'd give anything for a game,' Guy said, yearning suddenly for the feel of a bat in his hands.

'Well –' Dickinson held an arm out.

'Impossible, I'm afraid.' Guy drew him to the side before they entered and told him as briefly and quickly as he could the essence of their commission. Dickinson listened intently.

During breakfast Elizabeth Dickinson managed to steer the conversation away from detailed descriptions of the varieties of wicket to be found in the up-country game, and George and Beatrice assisted by cross-examining them on facets of English life culled from the illustrated papers. Heighurst lied shamelessly about his close acquaintence with Princess May of Teck and Ellen Terry, and enthralled them all with an account of how he and Mr Gilbert and Mr Sullivan had devised the plot of the new opera, 'The Mountebanks', over a dozen bottles of Stone's ginger wine. Tears of laughter streamed from Elizabeth's eyes. Guy guessed other tears would follow in a few months time; George was to be sent 'home' in August to start his preparatory schooling. It was difficult to think of this charming family broken up; it would not be the same for any of them again, and from the way she looked at the boy from time to time it was evident the thought was never far from her mind. Dickinson would need all his cricket then.

Afterwards, when they had expressed their thanks for the

hospitality, and she had hoped – and obviously she meant it – that they would see them both again, Dickinson led them away.

'I've been thinking,' he said, 'I've just the man for you – one of our itinerant native clergy. Knows the district like the back of his hand. If he's willing to go along he'll be better than any map I can provide.' His tone was crisp; with work to be done, he was a different man.

'It sounds ideal,' Guy said.

'Good. We'll nose him out.' He turned. 'You're anxious to be off as soon as possible I take it? It will impress him if we call ourselves rather than send a boy. He's a decent fellow, very sincere – they tend to be if they give up the ancestral gods – comes from a strict Buddhist family, I imagine it must be lonely for him.' He smiled. 'He'll feel something of a dog when we pay our respects.'

Away on the beach Guy saw a colourful throng of Sinhalese women by their piled provisions and caught a glimpse of British beards and pith helmets amongst them. Two of the bluejackets in stained straw hats were galloping round, showing off a jig; there was a sound of clapping in time and laughter from the women. He wondered how Aimes had fared going out through the breakers, and remembered the wire he should be sending to the Admiral.

'Is the cable office on the way?' he asked.

Dickinson turned with his serious expression. 'No longer, I'm afraid. It was burnt down the day before yesterday. I thought it was one of our caste feuds but, since you've told me about your chums from the *Curlew*, it seems more likely to have been some of them. Perhaps Mr Brown himself!' He looked round again. 'D'you know I've been thinking about Brown in the light of what you've told me – he didn't strike me at the time as being the kind of fellow to hold a commission, now I'm certain of it. His uniform was rather large – *hung* somewhat – and 'e 'ardly 'ad an "H" to 'is naime. Obviously unsure of himself too – aggressive, no form – I thought he must have been appointed from the ranks. But now –' he left the sentence unfinished.

'Any other officers come ashore?'

'Not a soul. Brown's bazaar-raiding party was all we saw of them – not surprising, mark you. We don't expect visitors at this season!' He looked round keenly.

Guy laughed, but remembered the wild sensation as the comber had taken control. 'We'll remember next time!' He wondered whether Vaneyke had chosen the north-east monsoon for that reason; from what he'd heard of him, he was inclined to believe he had.

'Ah!' Dickinson exclaimed. 'He's in!'

They had come to a bungalow even more charming from the outside than Dickinson's, for the roof was thatched with palm leaves which blended with the luxuriant vegetation and flowers around the verandah rather better than the half-round, red tiles of the buildings within the fort. It was smaller and the grass before it was sparse and tufted, the coral path to the front steps overgrown.

A small man with mild features and shining black hair cut short and parted European style was looking at them with evident surprise from a chair on the verandah. He wore a loose white shirt, open at the neck and wide white trousers; as they approached, Guy saw an open book on his knees. His feet were bare.

When he realized they were coming to him, one hand flew to his shirt collar, catching the opening together, then he rose, smiling widely and came down the steps to meet them. His teeth were very white, his eyes as black as coals.

'The Reverend Neera!' Dickinson said in an imposing voice as he introduced them.

'Gentlemen,' Neera said, 'You have caught me at a ticklish moment –' and his hand went to his shirt front again.

'Nonsense!' Dickinson replied, and nodded at the volume left behind on the chair. 'Our Lord never wore a dog collar did he?'

The smile widened again as Dickinson turned to them. 'Very useful left arm round the wicket.'

'I was given a trial for the Colts,' Neera said, attempting a modest look.

Guy nodded approvingly.

'Would have made it too,' Dickinson put in, 'had he not spent so much time with the Good Book!'

Neera shook his head laughing.

'Another Kelaart,' Dickinson went on, 'if only he'd kept it up. Well,' he shrugged, looking at Guy, 'you're in much the same boat,' and explaining to Neera, 'plays for the Navy when his duties allow.'

It was Neera's turn to nod. 'I say!'

'What does a fellow do here if flannels don't suit him?' Heighurst asked with a puzzled look.

'He doesn't last long,' Dickinson replied crisply.

Neera laughed.

'These two officers are going up-country after renegades,' Dickinson went on. 'They believe they may be making for Pollanarua – their leader appears to have taken the saffron robe.'

Neera gazed at them in surprise. 'A renegade!'

'Strictly between ourselves,' Dickinson said, 'the commander of the gunboat that anchored off the other day,' and, as Neera's eyes widened further, 'not by any means the first naval captain to succumb to the East Indies station.'

Neera was smiling. 'Succumb? Because he has chosen to become a Buddhist?'

'Good Lord, no!'

'Caught and bowled!' Heighurst said.

'No you are quite correct,' Neera said. 'Buddhism is only tolerable here because we are happy by nature. In any case, in its strict sense not one in a hundred can perceive the inner meanings – no, they worship their gods as they have always done. But for a serious-minded Englishman to attempt to follow the path –' he shook his head. 'If he is not already mad, he should be!'

He had such a jolly look that they broke out laughing.

Dickinson pretended to fan his face with relief.

'You wish that I take the gentlemen to Pollanarua?' Neera said.

'I can't think of a better guide,' Dickinson replied.

'Very well.' He looked at them in turn with his kindly black eyes. 'It shall be my pleasure – if you do not object to a very short stay at Chandeville – there is a Christian community there – but it is on the way.'

'Of course not,' Guy said.

Dickinson nodded. 'Excellent. I am pleased. I only wish I could come with you.'

'Is there a wicket at Pollywhatsit?' Heighurst said.

'It wasn't *such* a great a dynasty!' Dickinson smiled. 'Now' – he looked from one to the other – 'I'll fix up for a boat to take you across, and some porters – anything else I can do?'

Guy looked at Heighurst. 'I believe we've brought everything.'

'Mosquito netting?'

'No.'

'Water filter?'

Guy shook his head, smiling.

'Right. I'll see what I can do.' Dickinson waved to Neera. 'While you're getting your traps together –' and, turning to Guy, 'Give me three quarters of an hour.'

They watched him stride away rapidly over the grass towards the fort.

'A good man,' Neera said. 'I have asked myself many times, did the English make cricket what it is, or did cricket make the English what they are?' He looked at them, his dark eyes twinkling.

'Not one in a hundred perceive the inner meaning!' Guy said.

Neera laughed. 'You are probably right,' then his face became serious. 'One day you will be gone – two hundred years from now – five hundred? It is certain I do not know, but it has always happened to the greatest empires. But don't forget this, you will have left behind you one of the finest philosophies invented by man. And it will not be overgrown and forgotten like Pollanarua is forgotten. It will be *played* – all over the world – in India, here in Ceylon, Australia, New Zealand, Jamaica, Cyprus – wherever you have been.' He smiled again. 'But you are waiting. How long must I be?'

'Three-quarters of an hour?' Guy said.

'I shall be on the beach with my bag.'

'Did he say *mosquito* nets?' Heighurst asked when they were out of earshot.

10

In something under an hour the twelve natives Dickinson had engaged for them as porters were loading their biscuit boxes of provisions into a flat-sided rice boat at the water's edge, chanting energetically. In addition to the mosquito nets and water filter he had promised – the water filter turned out to be three baskets one inside the other with sand packed between the outside and charcoal between the inside baskets – Dickinson had produced a box of ripe green oranges and pineapples, two large bags of rice for the porters, and talipot palm leaves for each of the members of the party for use as rain shelters, sun shades, and at night when arranged together extempore tents. They were huge leaves, naturally pleated like fans; folded they took up little space and were easy to carry. Every traveller in Ceylon carried one, Dickinson informed them.

'In ancient times they also served as badges of rank. The exact grade of a noble was shown by the number of leaves he was entitled to have carried before him!'

The Reverend Neera, now 'dressed' with dog collar, white linen jacket, neat shoes and equally neat umbrella stood by his gladstone bag smiling benignly, a slight and rounded figure beside the five marines with their thick shoulders and necks and hardened, brick-red faces. The sergeant of marines was in the water fixing the natives handing up the ammunition boxes with a terrifying stare, the upstanding ends of his moustaches glistening in the sun. Guy glanced at Basset, saturnine and impassive as ever; he wondered if the expedition would break down his reserve. He had been anxious to come – but who had not?

As the last of the boxes and the rice bags were taken inboard Heighurst nodded to the sergeant, who grated out an order, and the marines, taking their rifles, splashed into the water and up over the side of the boat. Guy saw Basset hand his shotgun in carefully before going aboard. The sergeant gestured at the porters on the beach and they too clambered aboard. The three bluejackets in the party, who had been concerning themselves with the circle of feminine admiration, now spread back some way, looked towards Guy; he nodded at Neera and, while one bearded fellow ducked across and took the Reverend Neera's bag, swinging it over to a marine in the boat, the other two trotted each to one side of the small man, placed their inside arm around his waist and lifting him suddenly off his feet, ran him into the water. The smile shrank to a gasp of surprise until he realized what was happening, then, with his legs lifted over the boat's side by the bluejackets, he looked back towards Dickinson, managing a 'Goodbye old man!'

Guy and Heighurst turned, laughing, to make their own farewells and thanks.

'Think nothing of it,' Dickinson replied, shaking their hands vigorously. 'I didn't like the fellow. Hope you get him.' He raised a hand in salutation. 'Good hunting!' His voice was unusually clipped.

They jumped for the flat, overhanging stern of the boat and swung themselves over. Guy nodded to the old man with oblique red and white lines on his forehead who appeared to be in charge of the crew of Tamil fishermen and, while they arranged themselves at their paddles, beginning a new chant, the old man pushed off with a steering pole. Guy looked at his watch – not yet ten o'clock. He turned and waved at Dickinson.

The Englishman waved back, his face dark under the brim of his huge topee. Guy made a resolution to ask Old Sax if they could repay him for his invaluable help by returning and getting up a ship's team. He looked forward to it himself.

'A stout fellow!' Heighurst said as he waved.

'I Zingari!'

The marine's brow lifted cynically. 'He kept his promise.'

The bearded sailor known on the mess-deck as 'Evan the Voice' began humming softly to the tune of 'The Girl I Left Behind Me'. Guy looked at him and nodded, and he broke into the words of the song, soon taken up by the other two bluejackets and the sergeant with his cracked base, and then the rest of the marines. The Tamil's chant was drowned; they stopped, grinning broadly. Guy and Heighurst came in; the water rang with the air, Evan's hauntingly stirring tenor clear above the rest. Arms waved from the shore, and the bright, multi-coloured cottons rippled with movement. Dickinson stood by himself, watching.

'You are fortunate,' Guy said to Neera after the singing had been stilled by the heat of the sun, and the men, experimenting with their palm leaves, had constructed a canopy over the bow, under which they were resting. He waved an arm to take in the shores on either hand, mangrove-infested bays alternating with shining white sand and coconut palms – palm fronds waving in every direction as far as the eye could reach under the clear sky. To the right they were passing a little basin of glassy water covered with white lilies, their petals tipped with lilac; in perfect contrast, from beyond the narrow strip separating them from the ocean came the ever present, steady rumble of the breakers.

Neera smiled. 'You know the old name for the island? Lanka. It means dazzling – resplendent. When the Arabs came they thought they had found the site of the garden of Eden.'

'It does not surprise me.'

'And out of the ground made the Lord God to grow every tree that is pleasant to the sight, and good for food,' Neera quoted in ministerial cadences.

'And the tree of the knowledge of good and evil.' Guy said.

'I am afraid that is very true,' Neera shook his head. 'We are an exceedingly violent people, you know.'

Guy smiled at the incongruity of such a suggestion from the little minister.

'Oh, yes, yes, you would be surprised at the great number of murders and riotous gatherings even in this quiet province.' He turned his head and thrust back the hair to reveal a long, white scar across the scalp. 'I was fortunate to escape myself.'

In answer to Guy's questioning look, he went on, 'You know of course of the caste system,' he nodded at the Tamils effortlessly plying the paddles, 'these are of the Fisher caste – to be correct I ought to say one sub-section of the Fisher section of the fourth great caste of menials born from the feet of Brahma, the Creator.' He smiled at Heighurst's look. 'Yes, there are many, many sub-sections of the Fishers – those who fish from the rocks, those who fish from boats, those who catch turtle, those who cast nets, and so on and so forth.'

'Our trade unions have something to learn.' Heighurst said.

'Oh, caste is very much more than trade unions.' Neera pointed to the scar, now hidden again by his lustrous, black hair. 'You cannot understand this without understanding that to these people caste is everything.' He waved his head from side to side and spread his arms to emphasize the point, frowning in his efforts to explain. 'You English, I think, play at religion – as you like to play at everything. I do not mean you are not serious about it, but it is not a *part* of you. It *is* a part of us. And caste, you see, is part of religion, for the castes were formed at the Creation, this is what these Tamil people believe. And the Sinhalese people believe it too in their hearts although as Buddhists who are not supposed to believe in a Creator, they are not supposed to entertain caste notions either. But caste is deeper and older even than Buddhism. That will give you an idea of the part it plays here.' He looked at Guy and Heighurst, anxious that they were following him.

They nodded.

'Each caste section has its life-task – these people are fishermen from boats, and their sons will be fishermen from boats, and their sons' sons – and each has its order in the scale, and its customs and privileges. These are of the essence of life itself, you must understand – it is a point many of your missionaries do not – not until they have stayed some time here. Some years ago, for reasons I will not go into or we should never reach the end of the story, a whole village near here who were toddy drawers, that is low in the caste order, decided to become Christians. This is exceedingly rare, you know. The bishop came over from Colombo to baptize them – those who were ready for it. Now, as Christians they refused to work on Sundays or perform services at the Hindu temples which they were supposed to do, and some took to carrying umbrellas, which is not permitted to toddy drawers. A neighbouring village of Fishers' – he pointed at the crew on the paddles – 'took an exceedingly vindictive opinion on these matters and, when the Christians were away at the coconut plantations drawing toddy, they burnt their huts and gave blows to their wives and children and so forth, and went on doing this sort of thing over and over until the poor Christians were frightened to come back. Mr Dickinson of course found out who were the leaders of the Fishers, and they were sent into prison. Then, thinking it would be safe for the Christians to return to their village – or where their village had stood, for the Fishers had not left a hut there – Mr Dickinson asked me to go and persuade the headman that it was safe for his people to go back. Unfortunately, instead of the headman, I was met by one of the Fishers, an exceedingly excitable, fierce gentleman waving a sword around his head. I naturally returned to my boat, but he began pelting the boatmen with stones threatening what he would do to them if they did not bring me back – and so, poor fellows, they did.' He pointed to his scar again, 'and this was the result, and another one here,' he pointed to his right forearm.

'This sort of thing is always happening between different categories of people,' he added. 'In one way the caste system makes for peace and order, for every person knows his rightful place, in another way it makes for riotous behaviour and all uncharitableness. Even an educated man cannot rise above his caste – not in the eyes of his fellows. There are some very surprising manifestations to Europeans. For example, we shall probably see some Veddas on our journey – these are descendants of the aboriginal inhabitants of the island. Maybe we shall not see the pure Veddas for they are exceedingly shy and live in caves in the foothills and run from people, but we shall most certainly see some Veddas who have maybe intermarried with the coastal peoples. The pure Veddas you cannot mistake if you see them; they are small and exceedingly hideous and dirty and truly naked – the only naked people you will see in Ceylon, do you know? And yet they are reverenced by our people as of exceedingly high caste, next only to the Vellalas, or cultivators, and anyone is proud to claim Veddah blood.'

'Curious.' Guy said.

'You will certainly think so if you see them. They never wash,' his dark eyes twinkled, 'their hair provides a home for many creatures – you know how we reverence all life! These fellows' – he waved towards the Tamils – 'they are low caste because their occupation obliges them to take life.'

It was uncomfortably hot in the boat as the sun climbed towards its zenith; Guy thought of the box of fruit Dickinson had provided, and called out to Basset to break out the oranges, one for each man, and toss three back to them. He caught them as they were lobbed over and distributed one each to Neera and Heighurst.

Neera smiled as he took his, left-handed, and arranged his

fingers as if holding a cricket ball, then flipped his hand over. 'This is one that goes the wrong way.'

'Ah – I'm determined we shall come back and give you a match when this is all over. Don't give your secrets away!'

Neera laughed. 'That will be exceedingly jolly.'

As they peeled the tough, green skin, he went on seriously, 'The poor fellow. Many of you English are attracted to Buddhism, I have often wondered why. It is a grim philosophy. Perhaps he was an unhappy man?'

Guy thought of Vaneyke's cabin in the *Curlew*, and the photograph in the upturned Bible, and the reputation Mrs Vaneyke appeared to have made for herself in Bombay, and he thought of what she had told him about Vaneyke's quarrels with the Admiralty, and what Old Sax had said about the man's once brilliant prospects, and nodded. 'I believe he was. I fancy he had reason to be.' He thought of the scrap of unfinished letter he had found. 'He also had doubts.'

'Oh, doubts.' Neera smiled. 'You English and your doubts!'

Guy bit into segments of orange and felt the delicious juice spread over his tongue. 'Are you the man to talk of doubt?' He fixed him with a quizzical stare.

Neera laughed. 'No, no, I did not have doubts. You must understand I went the other way – from a creed of pure disbelief to faith. I have no doubts. Doubting is simply lack of faith. Doubting is what I was born into, but I escaped.' He smiled again.

'How did it happen?' Heighurst asked, 'if that is not an impertinent question.'

'Of course it is not. I am exceedingly happy to explain it to you – in so far as miracles can be explained.' His teeth were very white as he smiled. 'But maybe it is not such a miracle – few of our people can achieve the faith in non-faith, if you understand me, demanded by our creed; nearly all have turned to the old gods and worship at the old shrines, while paying still their temple dues to the priests. Yes, I am afraid the majority are Hindus at heart, you know, despite the teachings of Gautama. The eightfold path is exceedingly narrow and too steep for most men.'

Seeing their eyes on him, he went on, 'My father sent me to St Thomas's College in Mutwal, a suburb of Colombo – not because it is a Christian establishment, but because it provides a first-class modern education, and that is something the Buddhist priesthood does not provide. One does not need an education to live in a cave attempting to distance oneself from the world. The monks are really very ignorant people you know. I was excited by what I learnt at the College – mathematics especially I liked – I was always top of my class. I loved it there. I loved the cricket too – the headmaster was such a splendid fellow, he hit the most boisterous sixes! And one day I got him out. He was LBW. When the umpire lifted his finger he just looked at me and smiled quickly and walked away at once swinging his bat. That was the moment I knew I was a Christian. The smile cost him so much you know. He was a mighty hitter. It had been coming on me for a long time before of course – I found myself attracted to the doctrine of God's love for the world. It is much more practical than our pessimism and withdrawal. I thought of my mother's love for me even when I had been exceedingly bad, and I saw God's love in those terms, and thought how much better, indeed how much more *practical* to spread love for each other than for each to withdraw into his own mind. I liked the doctrine of redemption also. I saw the headmaster as a Christ-like figure. He had come out to Ceylon for our sake and for our salvation – but that was my road to Damascus, watching him walk away swinging that mighty bat of his.'

Heighhurst nodded silently.

'Eton and Balliol,' Neera added. 'An exceedingly fine gentleman.'

There did not seem much to be said after that, and they lapsed into a hot and slumberous silence, Guy wondering idly what Heighurst had made of Neera's ingenuous sincerity. The sound of the water along the side and the rhythmic splash of the paddles and soft chant of the Tamils was very soothing.

He heard Neera's voice again as if from a distance. 'You must have been many times to the Long Room at Lords.'

'Only once.'

'That is enough. I should like to go there once – before I die.'

Guy smiled, eyes closed. He was glad Dickinson had suggested Neera – he was a very decent fellow. Queer that his chosen pilgrimage should be to London, Vaneyke's to Pollanarua! He thought of the photographs of the lost cities in the Archaeological Report – ranks of columns, many awry, many fallen, that had once supported palaces or temples, huge slabs of masonry covered with creeping plants, and carvings prized from the undergrowth, sinuous and lively even in reproduction, and always in the background great trees and jungle.

He was roused from reverie by a new note in the Tamil voices and, opening his eyes to look out, saw that they were coming in to land; the fronds of a coconut slid towards them across the bright sky; he felt the tremor as the flat bow grounded on sand.

'That is the easiest part of the journey, I am afraid,' Neera said. 'I thought it best to go as far as we could by boat. Now we shall have a little way to walk.'

The provisions were unloaded and they made a light lunch in the shade before starting the march along a deep sand track between palms. They walked in a long column, each with his talipot leaf extended overhead. Neera went in front with Guy and Heighurst, followed by four marines in pairs, followed by the three bluejackets, shambling like apes with their boots strung around their necks, continually shifting their rifles and palm leaves in their hands, then the twelve porters with the boxes of provisions and ammunition high on their heads, finally the sergeant and one other marine in the rear.

It was hard going in the shifting sand and, although the talipot leaves protected them from the direct rays of the sun, the heat and glare were reflected up at them from the path ahead. Talk was desultory, soon petering out altogether. All life seemed to be stilled; their own deadened footfalls and the rumble of the breakers from the distant shoreline and the rustle of the palm fronds were the only sounds. Perspiration coursed down their faces from beneath the pith helmets. Guy felt his spine pad uncomfortably damp. There was a salt taste on his lips; sharp grains of sand had somehow worked inside his boots and gaiters, intensely irritating about his ankles, and his socks were moist.

He wondered if the Curlews were also marching in the heat of the day; probably not – and his thoughts turned to Lieutenant Brown. Had a mutiny inspired by Brewer's unpleasant character replaced the officers with men from the lower deck? Was Vaneyke then a prisoner with Brewer and Hardwicke and the others? But why should they come here? Strange indeed, as Old Sax had said, for mutineers to bring their ship in so close to the commander-in-chief! No – Vaneyke was still in command. But that too posed problems; how could a Buddhist seeking the annihilation of 'self' along the path of virtue presume to command others? And how, under these circumstances, could he retain control of such a potentially violent crew as British bluejackets? Probably that was how it had all started. But how had it ended? How was it going to end?

He was about to order a halt for a spell when Neera pointed to trees ahead and said they were nearly there. The scenery was changing subtly. Palms still rose about them and the sun still glared from the white sand, but they were closing rice fields to their left, acre upon flat acre of intensely fresh green young plants on which it was a delight to rest the eye, and the foliage of the trees ahead suggested more fertile country, probably a river valley from the way they extended either side.

As they approached the trees, the sand with its straggly, convolvulus-like covering gave way to shrubs and plantations of Indian corn and cassava, and they made out the thatched huts of a village.

'I am hoping we shall be able to hire some boats here,' Neera said matter-of-factly, as if they were approaching the Wey at Guildford. 'This is the Moondim Aar,' he went on. 'You will see it soon. Providing we can find sufficient boats we shall reach Chandeville before sunset. There is a coconut plantation owned by Mr Brander, an exceedingly fine gentleman – you will like him. He will be delighted to put you up for the night, I am certain.'

'And you?'

Neera smiled. 'I have my flock to tend.'

The village awoke to life at their approach, seemingly deserted huts issuing women and naked children who gathered in groups to stare. Evan the Voice started singing 'Hearts of Oak', and the other bluejackets and marines took it up. Guy felt his step lifting as they strode on.

'I should like that man to assist with my service,' Neera said.

'You shall have him,' Guy smiled.

'No, no – it was only a joke.'

'No, you are helping us – the least we can do in return. I'm certain Evan will not object if his name is scrubbed from the watch list this evening!'

'It is a truly beautiful voice. He is a most fortunate fellow.'

The path, which had changed from sand to dry, beaten earth, led on between the village huts to what looked like an embankment for the river, beyond which they could see a luxuriant growth of trees on the far side. Neera suggested that the porters continue and deposit their loads by the bank while he tried to arrange for boats. He broke off and went towards a group of men in colourful loin cloths and enormous turbans; one was still winding his on.

The villagers were not so attractive as those they had seen at Batticaloa; they looked unkempt and poorer. Some of the women had broad faces and wide, flaring nostrils, and their men, many of whom sat cross-legged, indolently plaiting mats, were small fellows with masses of shaggy, uncombed hair making their heads appear unnaturally large. Red betel nut stains on their whiskers and gap-toothed gums contributed to a beggarly look.

Those whom Neera was addressing were altogether different; they were evidently Tamils. They had clean limbs and intelligent faces. Undoubtedly there were mixed races here, and some were the half-caste Veddas Neera had spoken of. The children were appealing, though, with their large, brown eyes and white teeth. A bluejacket broke off to approach one minute scrap who tottered out towards them, but she ran from him yelling, and was soon scooped up by a woman who turned, hurrying away.

Neera came towards them with the Tamil men. 'I am afraid you must take care not to admire anything belonging to these people – especially their children,' he smiled. 'It suggests to them that you are covetous – also there is danger of the "evil eye"!' He laughed.

'What luck?' Guy asked.

'Oh, they will help us. They say they have many boats. And we have plenty of rice, so that is all right.'

'Trade follows the flag,' Heighurst murmured. 'For my part I'd rather they had some ice.'

Neera smiled. 'The milk of the coconut is better than ice – of course it is better still in the early morning before the sun.' He saw Heighurst shaking his head, and went on in a different tone, 'But I have some news for you – a large party of English soldiers passed through a village further down the river two evenings ago.'

'Soldiers!'

'I am sure these people do not make any difference between soldiers and sailors. They must surely have been your men – there have been no soldiers in the district. They took all the boats and canoes from the village and went downstream.'

'The way you're taking us?' Guy asked.

Neera nodded. They came to the embankment and walked up the slope. There was the river, fallen it seemed from its highest level, but still a broad stream flowing between green banks overhung with luxuriant foliage. It was a breathtaking sight after the heat and dust of the march. 'They must have taken the more direct route over the land,' Neera went on. 'I do not believe they will have got far that night.' He clicked his teeth. 'But I think you have guessed their destination correctly, gentlemen.'

Several crows flew from the trees opposite, clamouring, and they saw movements among the foliage below, and heard deep, sobbing calls from the shadows. A small grey monkey swung into the sunlight for a moment and hung, staring at them with round eyes; it had a fringe of white hair on its head and a shaggy white beard, giving it the appearance of a wizened old village patriarch. From the movements in the branches beyond, it was evidently one of a troop of a score or more, and as the shaking foliage and calls moved down river it swung away, disappearing into deep green shadow.

'Wanderoos,' Neera smiled.

They walked down to the water over layered palm leaves laid by the villagers to cover the marshy parts, and cooled their faces and wrists while the Tamils brought up a craft formed of two dug-out canoes with a platform joining them, and began unloading bunches of plantains and passing them ashore. Neera intercepted one bunch and handed it to Heighurst.

'Maybe this will make up for the lack of ice!'

He watched as they each pulled one from the bunch and peeled it. They were small, almost red, and proved as delicious in their way as the green oranges.

'Marriage ain't for me,' Heighurst announced as they walked back to the top of the embankment and sat watching the porters making their way carefully in file with the boxes of provisions down to the water's edge. He looked round. 'I begin to fancy the life of single ease!'

Guy ignored him, and Neera looked puzzled.

He pressed on, 'They say a fellow can be more idle here than anywhere.'

'Oh, yes, that is true,' Neera nodded. He waved his arm towards the village. 'These people are exceedingly idle you know – '

As Neera launched into another of his local disquisitions, Guy caught sight of a group of butterflies fluttering over shadowed grass between the trees to their right, and turned to look; their wings were velvet-black, spotted crimson. He wondered about the species and wanted to go up for a closer look, but his will seemed numbed by the languorous heat and peace of the scene; he remained watching from a distance. Above the delicate creatures something like a bright autumn leaf quivered among the branches, soon joined by another; looking up, he saw they were butterflies too – huge ones. It was difficult to judge, but he thought their wings were probably five or six inches across.

He could have rested, watching the fairy glade and the butterflies and the river for a long time, but the provisions were soon loaded and Neera was beckoning up other craft to take the men; many were small, hollow-log canoes with an outrigger held by bamboos, and it required a flotilla of them before all the party was embarked. Guy ran his eye over them – five marines and the sergeant, three bluejackets, four porters with the provisions, eight in the canoes – and nodded to the Tamil at the bows of their own, larger catamaran. The man pushed off and leapt into the boat in the same motion, and they were off, caught in the current and moving downstream, away from the first spirals of smoke rising from the village fires begun for the evening meal. Villagers clustered on the bank watched impassively as they went. The sky was still bright above the trees, but the sun had lost the fierce heat of the earlier afternoon. Soon they were rounding a bend and the smoke and the villagers were lost to sight behind thick foliage.

A heron picked up its wings and rose lazily from a mud island as the leading canoes bore down in a cacophany of chanting. Further on, where the river broadened temporarily into marshy flats, a host of wading birds were clustered thick along the water's edge: egrets, white spoonbills sweeping their curiously bent necks from side to side, pale pink flamingoes prominent amongst them; the nearest rose as the armada approached, adding their cries to those of gulls wheeling above. A tern dropped straight into the water; Guy watched and saw it rise presently with a fish glittering in the sun.

He felt a tap on his arm. Neera was pointing to a reedy stretch of bank to the right; in the water before it were the unmistakable dark bubbles of crocodile eyes and snouts – far too many for comfort. He heard rippling movements further along and caught sight of a long, dark shape sliding beneath the surface.

'We shall see plenty more of those fellows,' the clergyman said happily. 'We have exceedingly large ones here, you know.' He sounded proud; he was evidently enjoying his role as guide. 'If these people did not make so much noise we should see some of them up on the banks – you could see for yourself how large they are.'

The water was very close beside him, dark below the surface with a muddy suspension. 'Do they take many people?' Guy asked.

'Oh, they do not care what they eat! One poor fisher fellow last year was caught in the shallows; his companions managed to pull him free, but he was in a terrible state – they brought me to see him but I could do nothing. He died before morning. Another fisher some years ago was swallowed whole – all except the head and one hand which had been bitten off first! The crocodile was a big fellow nearly twenty feet from head to tail; they caught him and found this poor fisherman inside. As a rule they drag the prey to the bottom and drown it – and eat it later perhaps when they are hungry. They will take anything – a small buffalo even, when it is drinking. But I think that more people are killed by snakes than by crocodiles.'

Guy laughed. 'Any particular one we should watch out for?'

'Oh, you will be all right. You have thick boots and gaiters. Besides there is a saying these people have: he only sees snakes who fears them. They are not brave creatures, you know.'

'Have you seen a snake?' Heighurst asked innocently.

Neera laughed. 'Oh, yes, yes, these people make pets of them, you know. In the roof space of their huts you may find rat snakes – they kill the rats, and some of these people feed their own snake so they will not lose him to a neighbour! Then there is the cobra – you have surely seen cobras? The snake charmers who go on board the ships have cobras in their baskets. It is our sacred snake, you know, you will find them still in some of our Buddhist temples. But the worship of snakes is older even than Buddhism. These people will not kill any snake. If they find a poisonous snake near their home sometimes they will coax it into a basket and then they will put the basket in the river so that it floats away – but they will not kill it.'

'Down to the next village!'

Neera smiled, wagging his head from side to side. 'You should never look inside a basket in the bullrushes in Ceylon, you know. But cobras also swim. Yes, they have been seen swimming right out to sea. Only the good Lord knows what they are doing it for!'

As Neera warmed to the snake theme – snake shrines in the jungle, the deadly ticpolonga, an eccentric merchant who kept his money in his house guarded by tame cobras gliding around like watchdogs, sea snakes, giant pythons – Guy's mind wandered in contemplation of the exquisite ferns and flowering shrubs and overhanging trees, some blazing scarlet, some shading to gold among the jungle greens and matted, bright emerald creepers which clothed the banks. The canoes they passed with fishermen watching from under wide, straw hats, only a coloured handkerchief as a loin cloth, blended into the scene as naturally as the water fowl and white cranes and smaller wading birds they raised in flocks at every bend. It was bewitching in its variety, a dazzling, truly resplendent panorama.

They joined, or were joined by, several other tributaries as they sped on, and passed inlets where the water was still and covered with lilies, white or pink. Even Neera, now running out of stories, could only point and study their faces happily as they followed the direction.

After one hauntingly tranquil scene, he said, 'Mr Dickinson has told me sometimes he longs for a real London 'pea-souper' or a drizzlingly cold autumn evening. There is just too much here that is beautiful – he gets tired of it, he says. I remind him of the disease and starvation in some of the villages, "That is surely ugly enough for anyone?" and he says, "Yes, that is very true," but I do not believe I am convincing him, you know.'

It was difficult here even to contemplate a London 'pea-souper'; it was a different world, inhabited by different beings.

It became cooler quickly after the sun disappeared below the level of the trees on their left, and long shadows spread across the water, climbing the far bank, and soon darkening the lower foliage and blossom, rendering the upper levels brilliant by contrast.

'We are nearly there now,' Neera said.

They reached the Branders' coconut plantation as a gentle pink began to creep over the sky above the trees. To the right were row upon row of palms, their tops touched with the last light from the west, and in a clearing not far from the river bank they saw the bungalow, a rougher build than the neat ones inside the fort at Batticaloa, and thatched with palm leaves, but with the same wide verandah all around, embowered with foliage and blossom, blue, crimson, flame, gold, white, which rose in floral festoons to a nearby acacia. Two crows were sitting on the topmost branches, sharp black against the sky.

Neera turned to Guy. 'You will like Mr and Mrs Brander, I am certain of it.'

One of the Tamils said something to him and he smiled, shaking his head. 'One of their silly nonsense superstitions, you know. They have only to see a crow and they prognosticate some pretty kettle of fish or other! On this occasion it is all right, though, they say your journey shall be a fortunate one and we shall find our heart's desire.' He smiled.

Guy had an image of Mrs Vaneyke. He looked up and saw the two crows had gone from the acacia.

Further on along the river, where the bank fell away into reeds, they saw several black cattle at the edge of the water; they were looking round at the sound of their approach.

'It is strange it is so quiet,' Neera said. 'After all, we are making enough noise, you would think someone should have heard us. There is no one about it seems.'

'You didn't advertise your service!' Heighurst said.

Neera laughed. 'Oh, yes – but there are usually many people about at this time. Well, perhaps something has happened somewhere else, this is an exceedingly large plantation, you know, perhaps one of the elephants has become frisky – we shall soon see!'

There was a proper landing stage built of mangrove poles

jutting into the water from the bank before the bungalow, and a small, clinker-built rowing boat tied up to it with a long painter. They came alongside, and the Tamil crew nudged the catamaran towards steps at the far side. They climbed out. It was good to feel the stage solid underfoot.

Neera said, 'Come along, we shall see what has happened, and I shall introduce you to Mr and Mrs Brander, then I shall come back and see to these people,' he turned and said something in rapid Tamil to the men, who replied in equally rapid voice, waving their arms. Neera's tone became sharper, and he began gesticulating himself, then turned and smiled, 'They are exceedingly queer fishes, you know.'

Guy had a sense of something very wrong. There was the bungalow only yards away, no sounds coming from it, no smoke rising. Surely, if the Branders were away, there should be servants at least to hear them. Some distance beyond the bungalow in a clearing was a heaped pile of broken husks of coconuts and coconut debris covered the area round about. Several of the black cattle they had seen by the water stared at them from the trees beyond, picking up their front legs nervously, shaking their heads and whisking their tails at swarming flies.

He pointed them out to Neera.

'Yes, they are loose,' Neera said, looking surprised. 'Usually they are picketed around fires about this time to protect them from the cheetahs.'

'There's no smoke,' Heighurst said. There was a sharp edge to his voice and his eyes were keen.

Guy turned to him. 'It would be best if I went on first.'

Heighurst nodded and said to Neera, 'Keep the boat at the steps,' and, turning to the sergeant, whose canoe was holding off until their catamaran could be manoeuvred out of the way, called urgently, 'Stop buggerin' about – and get up here, quick!'

The sergeant seized his rifle and, pointing it first at his Tamil paddler, gestured towards the landing stage with unmistakable intent.

Neera shouted to the boatmen, then looked from one to the other of them with round eyes.

Guy took his arm. 'Come on!'

In the shadows behind the luxuriant trellis of the verandah

he thought he caught sight of a man, evidently sitting in a low chair, and apparently gazing towards them. A mass of flame-coloured gloriosa shut out the view as he strode on. Surely the fellow must have heard them!

The steps up to the verandah were wide, and at either side were two enormous crocodile skulls, their upper jaws raised wide by some device, displaying the terrifying armoury of teeth. As he ran up the steps he saw more white skulls in the shadows within.

Mr and Mrs Brander were seated close together on long Bombay chairs her head resting on the back, chin pointing upwards, his head turned towards them as they reached the top, his open mouth writhing wordlessly, the shadows of his eye sockets alive with insects. The skin all over his face twitched with alien life. Guy stood fixed to the spot. The musky smell of death mixed with the scents from the blooms in the trellis. He heard Neera half sobbing words in a tongue he was not familiar with, and was aware of rapid movements of lizards or geckoes darting from beneath the chairs, and a rustling in the corner as some dark, coiled thing disappeared. From the river he heard the evening chorus of frogs, and a long way away jackals were crying and barking alternately. A bird was calling 'Did-ye-do-it – did-ye-do-it,' endlessly 'did-ye-do-it – ' He heard Neera's footsteps going down outside, and turned to follow him, unable for the moment to bear the sight.

Heighurst was standing by the landing stage with the sergeant. The other marines had spread themselves along the bank on their knees with rifles at the ready, and he heard others swearing from the canoes. He beckoned to Heighurst, and stood, drawing in deep draughts of air as he waited for him. The western sky was a dusky red, the mountains seen through the graceful trunks of the palms unusually sharp against it. Neera was on his knees, head down, repeating the Lord's Prayer in rapid, disjointed English as if a charm, ' – Thy kingdom come, thy will be done in earth as it is in heaven – '

Guy turned as Heighurst came up, gazing curiously at the kneeling clergyman, and they mounted the steps together.

The marine stood for a moment looking at the two bodies in silence, then he moved over to examine a stain on the planter's shirt front. His eyes were hard when he looked round. 'Fortunate we have someone to read the burial service.'

Guy said, 'I'm certain the bungalow's deserted. We'd better take a look though.' He stepped through the door from the verandah, breaking a web dotted with insects, hearing quick scraping sounds from the floor before him. There was a table to the left laid with a cloth and a teapot and cups, two plates with knives laid across them as if the Branders had finished a meal – breakfast it seemed – there was a toast rack and a dish of what might have been marmalade crawling with fat bugs. He was aware of movement from the side and turning his head saw beside a chair the distinctive shape of a cobra, head raised and hood extended, swaying gently. A frog on the chair was sitting mesmerized with terror.

'Don't move!' Heighurst snapped from behind him, and a moment afterwards Guy heard the report of his revolver.

The cobra was hurled against the chair leg, and slid to the floor, tail jerking and coiling. There was an ugly mash of blood where its head had been. The frog leaped off into space.

Heighurst looked down at his handiwork. 'A pity I didn't have a basket to coax him into!'

They heard Neera outside calling to the marines, 'Come up quickly – something terrible has happened.'

Heighurst went out. Guy caught sight of a large, blue book with gilt-edged leaves on a corner of the sideboard, and went over to it. It was a visitors' book. He opened the heavy cover and turned the pages until he came to the last entries, then took it to the door for more light. The first thing to catch his eye was 'HMS *Curlew*' in the address column; the last three entries were dittoed under it; he peered at the signatures – the top one in a very neat, heavy hand was obviously Vaneyke's, but the next beneath was an almost indecipherable swirl of curves and flourishes ending with two great dots. He stared, wondering if it could be Brewer. There was certainly what appeared to be a huge 'B' in the middle, and the ending could perhaps be a flat 'er'. He looked down at the last signature; it too was indecipherable, but for a different reason – whoever had made the marks was illiterate. It was a clumsy and meaningless scrawl, evidently copying the flourishes on the signature above. He thought of Lieutenant Brown.

Heighurst was coming back from the top of the steps, and he showed him the page.

'Most obligin' of them!' the marine said.

Neera, his face paler than Guy had seen it, mounted the steps behind him. 'Who can have done this terrible thing?'

'Our friends,' Heighurst said quietly.

'The captain of the *Curlew*?' Neera's eyes were wide with disbelief.

'I think not,' Guy said, pointing to the book. 'Would you sign your name to murder?'

'It would depend if I were mad or not,' Heighurst said icily.

The sergeant and another marine known as 'Lofty' appeared at the foot of the steps, and he turned to Neera. 'D'you know where we can find some spades and shovels?'

Neera gazed at him, then at the bodies in the long chairs, and looked as if he were about to break down, but after a moment he composed himself and turned. 'This way please.'

11

Neera watched, tears glistening in his eyes as the men shovelled earth back into the double grave in which they had lowered the Branders. His worn travelling Bible was clasped to his breast, and he stood quite still, seemingly oblivious of the hordes of attacking mosquitoes. Guy felt himself obliged to remain too until the task was complete; it was torture; he slapped his neck, wrists and shoulders as the pests found their way inside his tunic.

It was quite dark now outside the glow of light from the fires they had made for the burial service. Huge pale moths and diaphanously-winged dragonflies flickered around the flames; outside the circle fireflies moved up and down, back and forth with electric speed. The croak of frogs and singing sound of cicadas provided a continuous background to the scrape and thud of the shovels, and the patter of falling earth – sandy, tropical dust to English dust – 'And the Lord God formed man of the dust of the ground.' He thought of Vaneyke's concern for the 'inconsistencies in the account of the Creation.'

There was no doubt now: two separate factors were at work among the Curlews. One perhaps was Vaneyke and his turn to the teachings of Buddha, the other a more positive anti-Christ – Brewer? Lieutenant Brown? Or someone else who was using a breakdown of constitutional authority to impose his own Satanic order? Vaneyke would not shoot a couple in the back as the Branders had been shot while sitting in their verandah chairs after breakfast. And Brewer, for all his brutish habits, came from a gentlemanly background and held the Queen's commission; it was difficult to imagine him doing so. Lieutenant Brown?

All three had evidently been the Branders' guests; they had probably taken dinner with them, for the date in the visitors' book was two days back – the same date as the party of 'soldiers' had reportedly taken boats down the Moondim Aar;

they could not have arrived much before sunset according to Neera, and from the remains of the meal on the table it was evident that the Branders had been shot after breakfast. What reason could there have been for shooting them? No doubt the Curlews required porters; Neera had said they had taken few if any from Batticaloa. Now there was not a single man, woman or child to be found anywhere in this once thriving plantation community. They had taken them all. But shooting the owners in cold blood – to prevent them making their way down river to Vendeloos Bay and reporting the wholesale abduction of staff? He wondered if there was a telegraph station at Vendeloos Bay. The Curlews would not know. But they must know that word would find its way to Trinco sooner or later; if they had to have porters why had they not taken the Branders along as well? There were *two* unbalanced minds; one had chosen the eightfold path, the other the descent to hell.

Evan approached him. 'Cook of the mess, sir?'

He nodded. 'Of course!' He should have thought of it himself. Strangely, he was not feeling hungry, and the shock of finding the bodies had driven other considerations from his mind.

When all the earth had been replaced and patted firm, they placed a cross at the head. The sergeant had fashioned it from a beam found in the plantation workshop, and at Neera's bidding had cut in it a rough 'J and J B' – John and Jessica Brander – 'Ps. 25'.

They were very silent as some time afterwards, around another fire, they ate a hash of corned beef and peas and biscuit and chopped coconut that Evan had prepared.

'Whom the Lord loveth,' Neera said softly. 'he reproveth. I have sinned in his sight.'

'There is a greater sinner at large.'

Neera looked at him for a moment. 'The poor man.'

'We shall track him down,' Heighurst's voice was hard and dry. 'Make no mistake.'

The clergyman nodded. 'Yes, I hope so. Mr and Mrs Brander were fine people. But they have gone now – to a better world.' He stared into the fire. 'You know, we have a saying, if I can roughly translate – in the tank where there is no loolā, kannapaddi is the pundit.'

Noting their blank expressions, he explained, 'the kannapaddi is an exceedingly insignificant fish when compared with the loolā.'

Guy nodded. 'I'd been thinking along the same lines myself. Unfortunately our kannapaddi has learnt how to make himself quite significant.'

'If the commander was not always mad,' Neera shook his head sadly, 'I pray that he is by now. Oh, the poor fellow!'

They rose and made their way to the guest bungalow behind the main bungalow, where their bedding and mosquito nets had been laid out in the bedroom, the men's in the adjoining living room. Guy found Basset waiting for him.

'I've water on the boil, sir,' the marine gestured to a floral china washbasin he had found somewhere.

Guy wondered if it had come from the Branders' room, and hoped not. He found the attention surprising and touching. It was the kind of thing Figgy would have done. 'Thank you, Basset. You should not have troubled – it's been a long day.'

'Never too long if we catch 'im, sir – in the end.' The dark eyes were fierce.

'We shall.'

'I'd shoot him myself,' Basset lowered his voice, and looked briefly in the direction of the living room, 'there's not a man wouldn't do the same – like putting down a mad dog, the sarge said.'

Guy's brows rose. He wondered if Basset was again making sure he knew something he should. 'Who would you put down?'

Basset looked surprised. 'The commander –'

Guy shook his head, 'I don't think so.' He thought of the previous time the hands had been affected in this way after they had found the mutilated portion of body at Cherbaniani. 'I believe Commander Vaneyke lost control some time ago. This is someone else's work, Basset.'

Heighurst, nearby, cut in sharply, 'Vaneyke and the number one, and one other, were the only guests to sign in.'

Guy turned him a cool glance. 'They may be observing the *form* of authority – for the moment.'

'I'd say the sarn't is right,' Heighurst replied abruptly.

Guy controlled his rising blood; they were all done up; it was no time to have words, certainly not in front of Basset. He looked at his man and smiled briefly, 'The court is not agreed on its verdict!'

Basset looked doubtful.

'Everyone is innocent until proved guilty,' Guy went on. 'I'm certain the sarn't realizes that.'

Basset nodded. 'I'll fetch the water, sir.'

'Thank you no, Basset.'

The marine looked surprised.

'I'm dead beat!'

Guy went out to check the watch list with the sergeant and the sentry at his post, then back to the bungalow, and took off his boots and gaiters, his revolver belt and tunic, rolled himself in his blanket and arranged the small mosquito net around his head and neck, knowing that whatever he did some of the pests would find a way in.

Above him a scuffling and scratching from one end of the ceiling cloth to the other told him the inhabitants of the rafters were wide awake. From the sound of breathing it was evident that Heighurst and Neera were also awake. They said nothing.

He wondered if Heighurst were right, if Vaneyke were simply mad, but shooting in cold blood in the back – not a stubborn old English oak, not anyone she would marry. He wondered if she were at Trinco now – how long had they been away? Why *had* she come? If she had come because she knew 'Robbie' would be here was it guesswork or had she been told *exactly* where? His heart began to beat faster as he thought of her somewhere ahead of them at a jungle rendezvous. Yet a wife was difficult to square with the eightfold path – almost as difficult as murder. He wondered if Basset had been warning him about the sergeant's attitude, and his mind turned to Davis.

He heard the cattle sounding off from a long distance, and drumming hoofs stampeding back and forth for a long time, and the high, disjointed cries of the night.

When he was shaken from sleep at first light he wondered if he had dreamt them.

The sentry had cooked eggs found in the house, and toast, and they washed it down with tea and luxurious fresh milk from one of the cows; then, while Neera rounded up the fishermen and the porters were embarking, he shaved in steaming water that Basset poured into the china washbasin with its English glaze and red English roses in the enamel. Afterwards he felt twice the man.

'Well, Basset,' he said as the marine came back, 'what are the odds on us catching 'em up today?'

Basset's lips lifted for a moment. 'Do we know which way they've gone, sir?'

He slipped on his tunic. 'They must have gone downstream – no boats, only a small dinghy, left here – they must have taken whatever copra boats there were for their new hands.' He put on his revolver belt. 'The Reverend fancies he knows the path they'll be taking. We'll make better time than they can, depend on it!'

'I hope so, sir.' Basset's long face was serious. He picked up the washbasin. 'How do we carry on when we find them?'

'I've no doubt we shall be given a sign. Put yourself in their place, Basset – how would you feel now?'

'Scared daft.'

'Precisely!' Guy nodded. 'There won't be many with the stomach for it by now.'

'Bless us!' Heighurst said, rolling the end of his moustache and looking him up and down as he reached the landing stage. 'I'd forgotten it was Sunday.'

'So had I.' Guy looked at Neera, talking vehemently to the boatmen. 'But I'm certain the chaplain will oblige. *Auxilium ab alto*!'

'Oh, Lord!' Heighurst shouted angrily to the sergeant to get the troops aboard.

Neera looked pleased when it was put to him, and once the party was embarked and the flotilla was moving downstream, Guy suggested he direct the Tamils to drop the officers' catamaran back into the midst of the canoes. Heighurst beat the lid of a biscuit tin in slow time, the sergeant yelped, 'Off – caps!' and, in the streaky grey and gold just before dawn, Neera rose, swaying on bent knees to dedicate the day to the Lord. The fishermen hushed their chanting, and the men entered into the spirit of the novel church parade as the green banks slid past and light spread over the sky, and birds rose in myriads before the sound of their ringing responses.

'Exodus, chapter twenty-one,' Neera declaimed, and nearly lost his balance as they altered course around a bend fringed with reeds. He recovered, and his voice rose, 'He that smiteth a man, so that he die shall surely be put to death. And if a man lie not in wait, but God deliver him into his hand, then I shall appoint a place whither he shall flee. And if a man come presumptuously upon his neighbour to slay him with guile; thou shalt take him from mine altar, that he may die –'

Heighurst leant towards Guy. 'An old testament man! I'd placed him amongst the humble and meek.'

'He's rising to the occasion.'

'And he that stealeth a man, and selleth him, or if he be found in his hand, he shall surely be put to death –'

Guy glanced at the marines and bluejackets in the canoes. They were thoroughly enjoying it; whether it was the little clergyman's vehement accents or the spirit of retribution, or whether they simply wondered when he would keel over into the river was not certain. The sergeant's cold blue gaze was fixed on his back as the frog's on the cobra's hood. But Neera completed the list of transgressions without incident, and after a fervent prayer for the success of the expedition and the blessing he called on the 'gentleman with the splendid voice' to lead them in a final hymn. Evan chose 'Eternal Father'. All knew the words and by the final chorus the Tamils had picked up the tune and were adding their voices to the lusty roar – Evan as always soaring high above.

Neera clapped his hands enthusiastically. 'Oh, beautiful!'

'The collection will be for the Batticaloa cricket club,' Heighurst murmured.

Neera smiled, but did not respond. 'We shall be reaching the path shortly. It will be difficult to see. I think I had better be watching out.'

'I notice you omitted the fate of those found not watching,' Guy said.

Neera laughed. 'At any rate, I feel better now.'

'And so do we all,' Heighurst said. 'A capital service. But should we not see their boats? They must leave them.'

'I think they will not know the path I am taking you. It lies off the main river.'

He had scarcely finished speaking when the Tamil at the bows turned to him and said something, pointing to the left bank. Neera looked. It was full day by now; all Guy could see were some dozen still, log-like forms of crocodiles lying clustered together on the sloping bank of a spur or possibly a low island jutting into the river, and beyond them the dark green foliage and interlaced trunks of mangroves. Neera seemed to recognize the spot, though, and spoke excitedly to the fishermen, who inclined the bows towards the muddy bank.

The crocodiles watched torpidly as they approached. One was enormous.

'I fancy a shot at that brute,' Heighurst said.

As if in response it began padding sluggishly towards the river, its great tail flowing from side to side; the others followed its lead so that for a moment the bank was alive with swaying, reptilian movement; then all had splashed in and sunk; they drifted like dark logs under the water, only the eyes and noses and an occasional scale of the spine breaking the calm surface.

'More intelligent than I had imagined,' Heighurst said.

'He's marked you down!'

'I fancy there are enough for us all if they've not made a good breakfast.'

It was not a pleasant thought. An upset at this point was horrible to contemplate. Yet the beasts were sluggish as they passed the point; they might have been dismembered trunks of trees had it not been for the wickedly tapering snouts.

A narrow inlet opened to view between the point and the mangroves, and the Tamils nosed the catamaran towards it, helped by the back eddy from the current. There was a yellowish slick on the water here and intermixed branches and green leaves floating round in a slow circuit, then they had passed into the cleaner water of the stream flowing into the main river and were feeling the current against them. The Tamils plied their paddles strenuously, their chant intensifying.

They heard voices ahead and rounding a bend saw two outrigged canoes making towards them, laden with reddish plantains such as they had tasted the day before. The chanting gave way to an excited chattering and waving as they threaded past, and then quite suddenly they were at a village, two old men in large turbans squatting at the water's edge beside piled dhobi, staring as the boats headed in. Beyond were more of the low mud and reed and palm-thatch huts which they had seen at the former village, and women and children, alerted by the sounds of the flotilla, coming to the bank to gaze. The women had on colourful two-piece calicoes, and most wore metal earrings and nose-rings, bangles and anklets; even the children had ornaments of some kind, although no clothes. It was a bright scene in the early sun. The grass in the shade of the trees by the river was still dark with dew. Beyond the lush vegetation along the bank rose the inevitable palms.

They went ashore and, while the porters were unloading the boxes, and Neera was 'seeing to these fishermen', providing them with rice and other presents in return for their unusual services, Guy and Heighurst took his advice to taste the early morning *curumbu* from coconuts fallen in the night. It was cool and subtly refreshing, quite different from the milk they had tasted from nuts bought off bazaar stalls.

'And now, gentlemen,' Neera said when he had completed negotiations, 'we have a long walk I am afraid.'

The going was easy to begin with; the air was hot, but not over-heated and the path after leaving the coconut plantation was flat, bordering expanses of shining green paddy. They forded streams, swayed over bridges across irrigation canals and, entering riverside villages similar to those they had come from, were ferried across to the continuation of the path on the further bank. At midday, after crossing the largest of these, the Moondrai Aar, they made lunch in the shade of trees, well satisfied with their progress. They had left the coastal plantations now, and the rice fields; the rest of the way lay through jungle and beside jungle rivers.

Neera had been unable to learn anything of the Curlews from the villagers, but he was not surprised since they had taken a different route.

'It is perhaps a day's walking to the next large river,' he said. 'If we are fortunate. When we are across it is three or four hours only to Pollanarua.' He looked up. 'But I think we have used up our good fortune.'

The sky had been clouding for some time; now rain was beginning to patter on the leaves overhead. Guy had been wondering whether to press on again through the heat of the afternoon; it seemed the decision had been made for him. They arranged the talipot leaves into two tents, one encompassing most of the provisions and ammunition boxes, spread out their blanket rolls beneath the other, and lay down, listening to waves of water beating above them, and the tinkle and gurgle of pools and streamlets forming all around.

'A return of the monsoon,' Neera said. 'It happens often. If this continues for a long time we shall perhaps find some of the paths impassable.'

'Difficulties take time,' Heighurst said, 'the impassable a little longer. Ain't that so, Sar'nt!'

'Impassable!' the sergeant responded promptly. 'What's that mean, sir?'

Neera laughed politely. 'I pray, gentlemen, we do not have to test your sublime confidence.'

'And so say all of us. But if it's irksome for us, imagine what the Curlews will make of it.'

'They may already have reached the Mahaweli Ganga and gone over. It will be in full running after this – it is our largest river, you know.'

'One more river –' Heighurst began lightly.

'And that's the river of Jordan,' Evan came in, 'one more river.'

Even the torrential sounds overhead were drowned as the men joined in.

It was the most uncomfortable night Guy could remember. They were unable to make a fire as the rain was continuous and there was not a dry twig or fern from which they could have lit one; water seeping over the ground on which they had constructed the makeshift tents obliged them to fetch some of the boxes of provisions and make a floor of them on which to spread their blankets; as the space was restricted they slept, or attempted to sleep, by rota, while those whose turn it was to sit up consoled themselves with their clay pipes. Soon the atmosphere became thick with smoke and they were told to put them out. Guy could not remember sleeping, only turning over and over to find different areas of his body to torture with the edge of the boxes while lightning illumined confused visions of swollen rivers and crocodiles floating down like logs on the flood, and priests in yellow robes amidst roofless, leaning pillars of the ancient capital. Thunder rolled unceasing.

It was still raining at first light, although more moderately, and, deciding that anything was preferable to spending more time in their cramped tent, they made an early breakfast of dry biscuits and fruit, and set off along a path that had been turned into a ribbon of moist and slippery mud. Jungle trees arched overhead filtering out the pale light so that they appeared to be walking into ever deeper thickets, hanging lianas and creepers as thick as cables, barbed with thorns, ripped the talipot leaves from their hands as they passed, snatched off helmets, tore their tunics and drew long, bloody scars over their shoulders and arms. The porters with the boxes overhead were in continual trouble, and when Guy ordered the first break after some two hours, he wondered if they had made more than a mile. At this rate it would take a week to reach the great river.

As they rested they could feel the sun rising above the trees and cloud layer, drawing a thousand tangled scents from the vegetation, and lighting the green spaces between with a sepulchral glow. Sweat beaded their faces under the helmets and mixed with the damp of their tunics and jumpers. When they started again the air was loaded with heat and moisture; breathing became a conscious effort.

After a while the trees to their left thinned away, and they caught glimpses of the river they had crossed the day before; it was dark with mud and flowing faster than Guy remembered. A great tree with upstanding branches trailing a mass of creeper slid rapidly down on the current. He thought of the crocodiles they had seen, and those in his half-remembered visions during the night.

In places near the river the path disappeared into running streams or still lakes through which they had to wade, waist deep at times. Great drops of water released from the leaves overhead patterned the surface with circles. They forced their way through, not speaking, the men's rifles held high, each concerned only with his own balance and the next footfall in the slime. Their once white or grey trousers were dark with mud and their hands and what could be seen of their faces between helmet and beard or stubble, splashed and streaked dark brown. At other times the path bent back into the jungle and they had to use knives and bayonets to hack a way through creepers that had formed barriers across the track since the last men or heavy animals had used it. The thorns, the thick, intertwining cords of vegetation and the heat washed out other perceptions. Troops of monkeys chattered in the branches overhead, keeping them company for a while, staring curiously; but they paid no attention. When the river appeared again suddenly beside them, shining under a dark sky, they scarcely gave it a glance. Guy saw a flash of deep sapphire blue; some subconscious part of his mind turned up the image of a kingfisher, but it was immediately forgotten as he picked his way around an overgrown branch.

The hours merged into an effort of will; morning, afternoon, weariness, damp, the exhalations of the jungle, became as one; attention narrowed to the next step, the next creeper; there was nothing else, nothing to think of save the path and the jungle ahead. When the rain ceased it made no impact.

Soon after the rain stopped they found themselves entering a small village; it was just after four o'clock, and they decided to halt for the day; a fire and hot food were essential after the previous night and scratch meals on the march, and Neera said he would be able to procure kindling and shelter from the villagers – poorer people than they had come across yet, not a few with grossly swollen and diseased limbs and sightless eyes. The children were pathetic; in the mud before the nearest hut one little girl sat, apparently oblivious of their presence, flies swarming about her eyes, a hideously bloated belly distended over her knees and spindly legs. It seemed incredible in a land of such plenty where every tree appeared to bring forth abundance.

Guy left Neera and the sergeant to arrange shelter, and went with Heighurst after game for the evening pot, careful to note their course by pocket compass after leaving the huts. They raised a hare but failed to get a fair shot at it, alerted a herd of spotted deer too soon, and started back with only a pigeon and a pair of snipe. They were more exhausted than they had thought, their patience and concentration sapped by the sustained efforts of the day. Before they reached the village, Guy had flung the pigeon away into the undergrowth; Heighurst did the same with the snipe without a word.

They came to a shallow stream they had crossed on the way out; the sight of the water running clear gave Guy a sudden craving for a bathe and he left the path to follow it, coming almost at once to a bend where the bottom dropped into a rock basin some three feet deep and the water eddied fresh and inviting. He rested his shotgun carefully against a mound of matted creeper which had stifled a trunk or fallen branch, wearily unstrapped his revolver belt and hung it over the gun, and bent to unfasten his gaiters and boots. As he straightened again he saw Heighurst looking at him curiously.

'A quick tub,' he explained, hearing his voice rasp.

The water was as soft and cool and refreshing as it had looked. He sat back and rested his head against the rock, and closed his eyes and allowed the current to keel him slowly sideways; the stream closed over his head. Peace at last! He brought his hands up and washed his face and tangled hair before he surfaced.

They sat in the basin for some time, allowing the blisters and aches and scratches of the march to ease before thinking they ought to get back lest an alarm were raised.

'You forgot the towels,' Heighurst said, wiping water down from his legs with both hands.

'You forgot the soap!'

After they had eaten and while the men, comfortable beneath an extempore thatched shelter, and revived by hot food and drink, sang to the night, they returned to the stream and sat again in the delicious water in the rock basin, talking idly of Vaneyke and Brewer and Lieutenant Brown and the ancient, jungle-grown ruins of Pollanarua, and what the Curlews must be thinking, and what they might do to make secret contact with the other officers when they reached the encampment. Their brief quarrel at the guest bungalow was tacitly forgotten. They wondered how Saxmundham was faring at Trinco; if all their days were as slow as this one, the main expedition would reach Pollanarua before they did – if Saxmundham made for the ancient capital. Surely he would.

As the men's singing faded, and the pauses in their conversation lengthened and the cicadas and strange night cries took over, Guy found himself thinking of Mrs Vaneyke, wondering again if and where they would find her. Anything seemed possible; sitting up to their necks in a stream in the jungle night – the devil knew where – making for a lost city in pursuit of the company of a British man of war – nothing was impossible. Of course she knew where her husband was making for – of course she would be with him at the sacred city.

They reached the village of Periatorre, just short of the Mahaweli Ganga on the evening of the next day, and learnt through Neera that a party of English had camped at Pollanarua before the rain. The news, although anticipated, electrified the men; the weariness slipped away from their stained faces, and their eyes became keen again. Guy called them together.

'Our aim is simply reconnaissance,' he began. 'If we find a chance of making contact with men who may not like what has occurred' – he paused as a low growl rose around him – 'be certain we shall seize it. The difficulty is how do we recognize these men and how do we get them away from the others? Our best chance may be with an isolated picket – or at the latrines –' He smiled as a roar of perhaps nervous laughter broke around him. 'Do *not* underestimate the difficulties. Every one of those men may dislike what he's doing – most undoubtedly will – but the fact that they're here at all makes it certain they're under discipline. From what we've seen I believe we all know what that discipline is inspired by –' The growl of assent broke out again. 'I'd be willing to lay long odds they're frightened men, every one of them. They're caught both ways now – the 'cat', or worse, from whoever it is in command, or a court martial with the death penalty at the end if we take them back to Trinco.' He looked into their serious eyes, his gaze resting eventually on the sergeant, whom he addressed, 'Take no chances with frightened men – they'll pull you down with them. And if it comes to a scrap we're all dead men. They have two Nordenfelts and unlimited ammunition. They outnumber us by at least ten to one.'

The sergeant said, ''Oo is in command if it ain't the capting?'

It sounded more like an expression of disbelief than a question, but the sight of his square, red and mud-spattered face and fierce blue eyes reminded Guy of the man's cast-iron dependability; instead of snapping, he smiled. 'I haven't the least idea. There's only one thing more difficult than spotting men who'll help us, Sarn't, that's spotting the fellow in command.'

'He may have a separate latrine,' Heighurst said softly, and the laughter broke out again.

'We cannot be sure of anything,' Guy went on. 'The captain and officers may be prisoners, they may not be. Our task is to find out exactly what is happening and who is responsible so that when the main body comes up from Trinco we may avoid a shooting match.' He stared into the sergeant's glittering eye. 'Not to make judgement on insufficient information – assuredly not to risk the rest of the party by acting on those judgements.'

'Sir!' the sergeant said crisply.

'The rifles are for self defence – only if there is no alternative. Our orders are to cut and run at the first sign of a scrap.' He looked round their faces, then went on, 'We shall cross the river at first light tomorrow – the Reverend is attending to the boats – and march for an hour or so, until we find a suitable place to leave the porters and the remaining provisions. We'll need every man. The porters will have to look out for themselves – if we find on our return that they've made off,' he shrugged, 'it's not far to the Kandy–Trinco road. There's any amount of game about for the pot –' he caught the sergeant's expression and smiled wryly.

'We'll move forward in three sections under Lieutenant Heighurst, the sarn't and myself,' he went on. 'Leading section in skirmishing order, so far as possible, a hundred yards or so ahead of the other two – again according to the nature of the ground – halting every hour to change the lead. If the leading section comes upon an isolated picket or outpost and it appears possible to surprise the men without raising the alarm, endeavour to do so, but if there is the slightest doubt far better to halt and allow the party to concentrate before making an attempt. It may be decided to press on inside their lines or wait and observe until nightfall. Each man to take as much biscuit as he can conveniently carry – leave your packs with the porters.'

He looked at Heighurst.

The marine said, 'If the leading section is engaged by a number of the enemy I suggest they avoid fallin' back on the others – lead 'em off in another direction.'

Guy nodded. 'Yes, certainly. It's up to the other sections to decide whether they can take advantage of the diversion provided!'

'Rendezvous, sir?' the sergeant asked.

Guy looked at Heighurst again. 'Wherever we leave the porters?'

'I'd say so,' Heighurst nodded. 'And after twenty-four hours, if no one shows up, make for the Trinco road where the main body will be comin' and tell 'em all you know.'

Guy looked at the faces, keen still, but calmer now that the full hazards of the enterprise were clear, and smiled encouragingly. 'We have the advantage of surprise. They'll not expect us to be on to them so quick, and they won't know how many we are.' He had an idea. 'We'll have whistle signals for use if any section is spotted – morse C's and D's – anything you fancy. It will tell the other sections you've been seen – if they don't know already – and suggest several divisions behind you. They won't care to dash out too quick after you.'

Heighurst nodded.

'Any questions?'

'If we do 'appen to see the capting –' the enormous fair-haired marine known as 'Shorty' began.

'The poor fellow will probably be contemplating his navel,' Guy cut in. 'The eightfold path specifically excludes murder, I can assure you. In my opinion the fellow's more to be pitied. At all events, your orders are absolutely clear – no shooting except as a last resort in self defence. These are your own fellows, for heaven's sake!' He looked at the sergeant; his moustaches were drooping after the day's march, but they seemed quite as belligerent as when upraised. He clapped a hand on his arm. 'Not such a tall order Sarn't!'

The blue eyes were clear and cold. 'You can't never tell with madmen, sir.'

'Well, don't worry,' Heighurst said easily. 'The moon's not full for some days.'

They made a hearty cooked breakfast before they started across the river the next morning, then set off by their sections in three craft that Neera had produced. It took longer than expected as the great river was coursing down, carrying the boats well below the landing place, and they had to be punted laboriously upstream along the far bank. Neera insisted on accompanying the party, although they tried to dissuade him, and he took the village headman with him as he seemed not to have visited the lost city himself.

They waited while the boats returned for the porters and provisions and the sergeant, who had stayed with them, then set off behind the loping headman along a path between great trees and luxuriant ferns and flowering shrubs. Guy, looking at his watch, was astonished to see that it was well after ten o'clock. The sky, glimpsed through the foliage, was clear again, the air already fiercely hot.

The path wound back and forth and was crossed by several other wider and evidently more frequented tracks, and Guy was thankful for the headman's sure stride. After an hour and a half he called a rest in the shade of a spreading tree like an English oak with a red tint to the young leaves, and there after a spell they left the porters and provisions and separated into their sections for the final approach. Guy took the lead for the first stage, walking with Neera and Basset behind the headman while two bluejackets spread out either side wherever animal tracks or grass permitted. The rest of the party followed a long way behind. He wondered if the precautions were necessary yet; the morning was bright and peaceful; there was not a sign of a soul.

When he called a halt to allow Heighurst's section to the front the bluejackets who had taken off their boots again and strung them around their necks came up to show him leeches clinging to their ankles, some well over an inch long and obscenely gorged with blood. A number of bloody smears around about marked where others had been forcibly removed, leaving their jaws behind in the flesh.

Neera laughed, 'Oh, if you have a lime or salt or a match we shall soon get rid of those fellows!'

Guy handed him a box of lucifers. He lit one and applied it to the largest of the bloated bodies, which shortly curled up and dropped off.

'Fortunate they're only leeches,' Guy said with a hard stare, 'if you'd run into a snake with bare feet –'

'Oh yes,' Neera nodded, 'numbers of our people are killed by snake bite every year, but exceedingly few Englishmen – I have not heard of one Englishman dying from snake bite, this is because they wear boots, you see.'

The bluejackets unslung their boots from their necks and began untying the laces.

The next hour passed uneventfully, and shortly after the sergeant's section took the lead they entered an area of obviously cultivated although overgrown fields. In the more open landscape they saw forested slopes to the left and a long way beyond the mountains, sharp and purple, capped with cloud. Presently they reached the huts of a village. The sergeant waited while the other sections caught up and Neera spoke to a group of villagers about the party at Pollanarua. He learnt little more than they knew already.

'They have many porters, and they have built their huts on the bund which runs beside the great lake, Topa Wewa.' He shrugged.

Guy looked at Heighurst. 'They're bound to have an outpost covering the path,' and turning to Neera again, 'Can you find someone to guide us to the encampment – preferably off the main track?'

Neera shook his head. 'I have asked them. They are not interested. They say there is nothing in the old city except for bears and snakes and monkeys, and if we wish to see them all we have to do is to follow the path, we do not need any guide,' he pointed straight on through more fields at the other side of the village towards jungle-clad rising ground. 'I think perhaps they are frightened of the spirits of the place, you know.'

Heighurst pulled out his watch, glanced at it and looked up at the sergeant. 'You've half an hour to go, Sarn't!'

The sergeant turned to Guy. 'You didn't say nothing about spirits, sir.' There was an accusing edge to his voice.

'I didn't like to frighten you,' Guy laughed.

A glimmer of doubt appeared in the blue gaze, then the man turned abruptly and yelped at his section.

'Go carefully,' Guy called out after him. 'We're close now!' He looked at his watch. Half past three already – the day had sped by. They had wasted too much time crossing the Mahaweli Ganga. Perhaps they ought to have left the porters to look after themselves – that would have been an invitation to desertion.

He felt intense relief when they had crossed the fields and entered the jungle again. There was no sound from the sergeant's party ahead, nor sight of them. He was surprised the Curlews had not stationed a lookout at the edge of the trees, but perhaps there was still some way to go; the native idea of distance was somewhat elastic.

As they went forward in the shade, every sense alert, he realized suddenly that they were in the city. They had passed a number of raised, creeper-clad mounds, but he had thought nothing of them after the similar natural formations they had seen amongst the trees below the Mahaweli Ganga; now he realized that a mound ahead to the left was too steeply-sided and regular to be anything but the remains of a building. He saw what looked like a low entrance through the matted vegetation and approaching discovered a path had been beaten to it. He pointed it out to Heighurst and they were squatting, trying to peer into the darkness within when low grumbling sounds warned of an animal there.

Neera came up and pulled at their shoulders, whispering, 'A bear – exceedingly dangerous –'

They backed away and waited tensely, Guy's hand resting on his revolver; if it came at them they would have to shoot; if they did so they would raise every Curlew for miles; there was no solution.

He became aware of movement to his left among the circle of watching men, and heard the rattle of a bayonet scabbard. Glancing round briefly, he saw Basset approaching, fixing his bayonet. He measured the distance, wondering if he would be in time before the beast appeared.

The muttering stopped; they picked their steps carefully away. He nodded at Basset in acknowledgement of his quick thinking.

'They always go for the face,' Neera whispered, when they had put some distance between them and the beast's lair. 'It is terrible what they do to a man's face, they tear his eyes out for no reason other than bad temper – oh, they are evil-tempered animals – we have been exceedingly fortunate.'

The evidence that they had reached the city became clearer with every step. The mounds covered with vegetation became more frequent and there were glimpses of brick and stonework behind the tangled creepers; at one point they came across a stone pillar with square, carved top evidently only recently fallen as its upper portion was but lightly twined with growth.

Soon afterwards they came to a mass of tumbled blocks that might have been a natural landslip had they not been so regular. A stream ran through and beneath them, while the path rose above, leading to what appeared a vast area of ruins; some were covered with vegetation and had trees and shrubs growing out of them, but others had evidently been excavated by the Archaeological Survey; red-brick walls glowed against the green shadows of the forest and there were flashes of white stone blocks and carved dwarf pillars with square tops like the one they had seen before. As they approached they saw that the walls and mounds outlined a warren of chambers and passageways like the ruins of a medieval monastery and, unable to resist a closer inspection, they made a diversion to one huge section of wall which had been partially cleared. It was fully ten feet thick with a row of cavities for floor beams high above their heads, suggesting a hall of spectacular dimensions. Chaffinch-like birds with crested heads and white wings showing a flash of red flew from its crevices; huge butterflies, velvety black and white and red, flickered in and out of blossom where once, in Guy's excited imagination, saffron-robed priests passed on sandalled feet.

The sergeant appeared surprisingly from behind a tall plant with striped maroon and orange leaves. The headman was with him; they had evidently been looking for them. 'The lake's that way, sir,' he said, pointing beyond the path from which they had come.

'Any sign of them?'

'Not just 'ere, sir.'

Neera said, 'That is not surprising. This is an exceedingly large city, you know – I have been told that it covers a greater area than London. Some of the palaces were seven storeys high,' he added with evident pride. 'It was laid out with magnificent pleasure gardens and ornamental lakes, fountains and bathing places as well as temples and palaces and music halls and libraries – it was a truly *wonderful* city, it is all written in our ancient texts. I am exceedingly grateful to you for bringing me here – I can see it all as it was.'

Guy smiled at his enthusiasm, and bowed his head briefly. 'We are exceedingly grateful to *you*!' He looked round for his section and, raising a hand at Heighurst, led off with the headman in the direction the sergeant had indicated towards the lake.

A troop of monkeys who had been calling and chattering amongst themselves whilst feeding on the seeds of a huge banyan tree to the right, swung across into a mass of shaking branches and festooned lianas ahead, and watched them with round, bright eyes for a moment before showing off more of their aerial mastery. Some were females with young clinging to tufts of hair on their necks, or even to their tails, delighting in the fun. A flock of green birds circled noisily above; below, amongst rows of dwarf stone pillars that opened to view, around an overgrown ruin a score of peacocks in radiant plumage picked their way over grass, fluttering their wings as they became aware of strangers. It was an entrancing scene in the late afternoon sun; Guy wanted to stop at almost every step to gaze at some strange bird or butterfly or lizard, or examine the carving on one of the pillars scraped clean by the archaeologists, and had to remind himself continually of danger: any of these mounds spread about them might conceal an outpost, a Nordenfelt party even. It was doubtful since they had left the main track now, but if they *had* been spotted it was ideal ground for an ambush.

He nearly tripped over a tortoise feeding quietly on the grass; it lumbered off with surprising speed towards others of its kind, some as large as footballs. He caught sight of one of his bluejackets darting from behind a wall to his left, rifle at the hip in excellent imitation of the skirmishing tactics of the marines; he became lost to sight behind a bush. Then the headman beside him was pointing, and he saw through a gap in the vegetation an expanse of water with the sun flashing off it full in their faces, and the far mountains, hazy against the sky.

Some minutes later they reached the edge of the lake. He saw that they were on a section of the retaining bank which jutted out from the more or less straight shoreline elsewhere. The ground fell sharply before their feet to broken rocks and bushes and reeds, beyond which the surface of the water was covered with giant lotus flowers nestling on their floating beds of leaves in a profusion and splendour of colour he thought he had not seen equalled. Other parts of the lake were covered with blue and white lilies, while reed-fringed islets and the far shores were alive with water birds of every description and spectacular shape, but it was the reds of the lotus which drew his eye and held him for a moment spellbound. Neera's words returned – Lanka – resplendent –

'Why, it's Mr Greville!'

It was her voice; he looked quickly down the bank to the left, and saw her sitting on one of the tumbled boulders, her pale dress merging perfectly into the colours of the rocks, her face shadowed beneath a wide straw hat tilted to one side. Her knees were drawn up, and one slim arm was raised to her hat, the other down by her side, her fingers toying with what appeared to be a stone. He stared at the vision for a second, whispering to his section to drop, then searched the area with his eyes.

She would not be alone – yet she seemed to be. He wondered if it were a trap. Why should they bother? There were a hundred or more of them to a dozen. If they had spotted them entering the jungle-grown area of ruins they could have brought up a party to surround them whenever they wished. He wondered whether to blow his whistle to alert Heighurst, but that would certainly alert them too. He drew his revolver and ran down the slope towards her.

She gazed up, surprised by the gun; then her face broke into the provokingly irregular smile. 'Whatever are you doing with that thing? They're only babies –'

He followed a movement of her hand towards a muddy stretch further down the bank where a number of lizard-like creatures were disporting themselves in the sun; their jaws showed them to be young crocodiles.

'Mrs Vaneyke,' he said sternly. 'Where is your husband?'

Her eyes shadowed. 'I wish I knew.'

'He is not with them?'

'With whom?'

'With the Curlews?'

'Yes, I'm sure he is.' Her voice sounded resigned. 'I suppose you are looking for him too.'

He knelt beside her, puzzled. 'Are you not allowed to see him?'

'We have not found him yet,' she replied, looking equally puzzled. 'Did I not say that?'

He stared. 'You're *looking* for him?'

'Gracious me! Whatever do you imagine I'd be doing out here if I were not looking for him?' She turned to gaze out over the water. 'But I do love it. It is so beautiful, do you not think so?'

'They're dangerous men,' he said urgently. 'Where are they?'

She looked startled. 'I have already told you we have not found them.' Frowning slightly, she rose. 'You do not look well,' and, resting a hand on his torn and stained sleeve as he rose beside her, 'you must come back with me.'

He was beginning to realize his mistake. 'You're not with the Curlews?'

'Mr Greville, I have no idea where the Curlews are – nor do I care. We are looking for my husband. We expected that he would come here,' she shrugged, 'but to the best of my knowledge he has not put in an appearance. But that's Robbie – he's a perverse devil!'

'And you are camped on the bund?'

She nodded. 'I'll take you there.' Her eyes were playing over his uniform. 'I imagine you have come a long way.'

He nodded. *Lord*! What an idiot! He had jumped to conclusions fitting in with his pre-conceived notions. He banged his helmet in disgust with the butt of his revolver – too hard for comfort – before slipping the gun back into its holster, and pulling out his whistle; he blew it long and loud to bring Heighurst and the others to the scene.

'Are you arresting me, Mr Greville?' Her brows rose. 'I think in that case we had better be introduced properly – we never were introduced you know –' her eyes were alive with shared merriment at the thought of their escapade in Bombay, and she held out her hand very formally.

He took it and raised it to his lips holding it rather longer than necessary. 'Guy Greville, lieutenant, Royal Navy – ma'am!'

'I am delighted to make your acquaintance, Mr Greville. I am Harriet Vaneyke – *adoring* wife of Robert Fairlie Vaneyke, Commander, Royal Navy.' She smiled, her eyes wide with devilry.

Vaneyke's unfinished letter had been to her.

When they reached the top of the bank, Heighurst was waiting, standing before the rest of the men. He raised his helmet, 'Good day to you, ma'am,' and, after she had smiled a reply, fell in beside Guy, saying softly, '*Cherchez la femme*! Are we to follow into her parlour?'

'We made a mistake,' Guy replied. 'It's not the Curlews. They must have gone somewhere else.'

The marine eyed him coldly. '*We*?'

12

'Are you two decent?' she called in.

'I am,' Guy replied. 'Heighurst can't manage it.'

'Come on out, then,' she laughed, and, as he appeared at the entrance to the hut, looked him up and down with approval. 'If it were not for the uniform – ! I'll get it to the dhobi-man tomorrow, I'm sure we'll be able to fix you up with something in the meantime' – she cocked her head to one side – 'but then you are *rather* tall,' and, catching sight of Heighurst appearing behind him, smiled widely, 'Mr Heighurst *come* – I'll introduce you. Everyone has returned by now from the digging,' she raised her brows expressively. 'I'm sure you'll like *most* of them!'

'Your slaves?' Guy asked smiling.

'Count us among them,' Heighurst said, falling in beside them.

Guy glanced at him; he had not seen the marine so taken before. While tubbing in the hut to which she had led them – vacated recently by two members of the party who had left – Heighurst's mask of indifference to the world, its pains and pleasures had slipped, and he had plied questions about Guy's first meeting with her, and why he had kept her so dark, interjecting every so often in wonder, 'By Jupiter! She's a nailer!'

Even more so out here, he thought. The wildness of the place matched an untamed quality in her, the ravishing colours transformed now in a sunset glow over the lake to a soft and haunting serenity perfectly set off her northern coolness, that exquisite composure which he thought at times even mocked itself, hinting at depths unplumbed by convention. The feeling he had from the overgrown ruins and the peacocks and the lotus-covered lake that they were visitors out of time to scenes of splendour and pleasure undreamed of in Babylon touched off fantastical visions of her in his mind.

'I have two new recruits for you,' she said as they came up to a rather short, stocky man standing outside a thatched structure somewhat like a bandstand; from inside came a buzz of conversation from many people. 'Lieutenant Greville – Lieutenant Heighurst – this is Mr Charles Harding, Ceylon's first archaeological commissioner – ' she smiled, 'and a very good friend.'

Guy shook the firm hand. 'My father takes your annual survey report.'

Harding's blonde brows rose with mixed surprise and pleasure. His face was broad and open, more the popular conception of a farmer than an academic.

'There!' she said. 'It's *such* a small world. But, I declare – Greville and I were affinities in a previous existence, Charles – I felt it the first time we met – met *again*!' she corrected herself with a little laugh.

Harding looked at Guy, then back to her, his eyes glinting. 'I'd always understood you to be sceptical of the doctrine of *bhavanga*.'

'I rather think I am sceptical of most doctrine,' she replied. 'Sometimes one simply knows!'

They laughed.

'I fancy Greville simply knew you were to be found here,' Heighurst said. He looked at Harding. 'Pretended he was takin' us direct to the Curlews – forced marches day and night, monsoons, wild bears, muggers, didn't worry him, not in the least. Straight to the lake – seventh boulder from the flowerin' mango – *there* she is!'

In the ensuing laughter he went on, 'Mind you, I don't blame him.'

'Come on,' she said, 'I'll introduce you to the others – *shameless* flatterer!'

'About the Curlews,' Harding said as they left, 'we'll have a jaw – after dinner.' He waved a square hand.

Immediately inside the enclosure they came up to a robust man in a Norfolk jacket who was standing together with a tall, thin man in faultless dark suiting and stiff shirt-front; he was as serious of countenance as the other was large and jovial. 'Mr Forbes-Robinson,' she said and, turning to the thin one, 'Lord ffort – the great *shikaris*!' She smiled.

Robinson guffawed.

'They go *anywhere* for an unusual head,' she went on. 'Yes, you know very well that is so.' She turned back to Guy and

Heighurst, 'They have just come back from – where was it?'

'Komodo,' Robinson replied, smiling hugely. 'The dragons of Komodo, have you come across them? A species of iguana I rather think – at all events we thought we ought to pot one.' He laughed.

'With a lance, I trust,' she said.

'A Remington Express,' Robinson chortled. 'We move with the times my dear!'

Lord ffort said drily, 'But what are our heads compared to your *scalps*, Mrs Vaneyke?' He raised arched brows.

Robinson laughed again.

'The difference is,' Lord ffort continued to Guy and Heighurst, 'we have to seek out our trophies, but see' – he waved a languid arm at the company assembled – 'they flock to her!'

She laughed. 'You know very well it is the ancient city which has drawn you all,' and, evidently determined to allow no rejoinder, she turned to Guy and Heighurst, 'come on, you must meet some of the others.'

They followed, nodding to the hunters, and were introduced to a succession of army officers, planters attracted by a change of routine, assistants in the Public Works Department assessing the chances of restoring the tanks and sluices and irrigation canals of the old civilization, friends of Harding's who shared his interest in the ancient cities of the island, others who had come for the shooting.

'So this is not an expedition got up to find your husband?' Guy said when he was able to get a word to her at the call for dinner.

She looked up at him enigmatically. 'Charles Harding knows Robbie very well. They have corresponded for a long time. I'm sure he will tell you all about it after dinner.' She took his arm impetuously, and Heighurst's on her other side. 'I'm *so* pleased you came. You must *both* take me in. No one minds about that sort of thing up here – thank heavens.'

Guy suddenly remembered Neera, and looked down at her. 'Where did you put our guide?'

'The reverend gentleman? We found another hut for him.'

'Shouldn't he – ?' he nodded towards the succession of camp tables which had been arranged together to form a long dining table.

She stared for a moment, then laughed. 'Of course we must – if he brought you two here. Come on! Let's find him.'

They returned with a smiling Neera who insisted that this was the happiest day of his life. 'When I see all these good gentlemen who have come here to rediscover the glories of my ancestors, it makes me exceedingly proud that I too am a Christian. You will please introduce me to Mr Harding, I have heard so much about his digging.'

'Of course,' she smiled, 'and *you* must take me in,' she flashed a glance up at the other two.

After grace, for which Harding called on Neera, Guy looking at her realized that she had lost the nervous little mannerisms he had noticed at his uncle's dinner table. She was relaxed and her brightness was not assumed, or so it seemed to him; of course she was queen amongst a positive swarm of drones, but he thought there was more to it; she would assume that to be the case wherever she was.

They drew up chairs around the small table in Harding's hut. The oil lamp hanging from the central beam above cast gently swaying shadows into the corners, which were piled with books and papers; even the low camp bed was wholly covered with survey sheets. Guy felt her gaze on him, and glancing across saw her eyes grey and sparkling with reflections from the lamp. A pale pink chiffon scarf flowed around her neck; a white gloved hand moved restlessly against mosquitoes before her face. His heart beat a little faster. What a picture! Her eyes warmed in recognition of his look.

A servant placed tumblers of brandy and soda on the table. Neera waved his away, smiling, and Harding nodded to the man, who left.

'Would you object if we smoked?' Heighurst asked.

She shook her head, while Harding, rising suddenly, went across to an upturned packing case that was doing duty as a bedside table. 'Forgive me – ' He slid a carved wooden box from beneath two volumes balanced above it and, opening the lid, came back and offered it round. After Heighurst and Guy had each taken a cigar, Neera again declining, he placed the box on the table and, pulling a pipe from his pocket, started filling it from a leather pouch. 'One of the only things these mozzies understand,' he grunted.

There was silence for a while as they lit up, and Harding sucked away at the pipe until almost lost behind clouds of smoke.

'That's better,' he said at last. 'Now, gentlemen – I understand that you, too, are after Robert Vaneyke?'

'You mean to say – ' Guy shot her a swift glance, then back to Harding. 'All this' – he swept a hand at the survey sheets on the bed and the piled volumes – 'and you're actually looking for Commander Vaneyke?'

'No, no – we *are* working here,' he replied. 'Shall I put it like this – if it were not for Robbie I should be working still at Anuradhapura. I can't answer for the volunteers of course, but I hardly think they would be here.' He laughed shortly.

'You are at peril of your lives,' Heighurst said quietly. 'These are desperate men facing the long drop for two separate crimes at the very least.'

Harding took the pipe from his mouth. 'Robbie?'

Guy looked across at her; she was staring at Heighurst, eyes wider than before. He wondered if it were possible she had not heard of the floggings – but probably she would not have done so out here in the jungle. He wondered how much to say in front of her. Evidently Heighurst was thinking the same thing for he had turned and was looking at him with a quizzical expression.

'We believe the Curlews have mutinied,' Guy said shortly. 'At all events they've abandoned the ship and started up country. We thought they were headed here. That's why we've come.'

'I see.' Harding replaced his pipe and pulled at it furiously. 'The whole ship's company! That does put things in rather a different light. Our reception committee would not stand much chance?'

'None at all.'

'They have two Nordenfelts,' Heighurst said.

'Well! Thank heavens you've arrived!'

'I'm afraid we cannot protect you if they do turn up,' Guy said. 'But tell me, why do you think they might?'

Harding gazed at him with a speculative look, then at Harriet Vaneyke, who nodded silently; he bent towards an attaché case by the side of his chair, pulled it up and placing it on the table before him flicked the catches up. 'No one else has seen these,' he said, opening the lid and pulling out a bundle of letters. 'We had some words, Harriet and I, after she told me of your arrival.' He pulled another bundle out, then piles of loose letters, arranging them on the table, and finally shut the case, returned it to the floor and looked up. 'Harriet assured me she would answer for your silence – and, of course, now that I have met you – ' he made a dismissive gesture. 'In my opinion, gentlemen – Well, I can only say this,' he waved towards the table, 'this is the most singular collection of letters I have come across in all my life. I'm not without experience in these matters.' He sorted through them. 'Some are addressed to me, some to Harriet, together they provide the most remarkable record of a man's search for truth. And not by any means an ordinary man, you must understand – a remarkably gifted man,' he shook his head, 'superior brains, imagination, *ruthless* determination, even a gift for languages. When his search brought him here to Ceylon he taught himself the old priestly language so that he could go to the original texts of the Pāli canon. That is how he and I became acquainted, almost two years ago now, and how we began our correspondence. We have kept it up ever since. There are gaps. I suspect some letters went astray – for example, we do not have an account of his first successful journey from his body,' he smiled at their expressions, and nodded, 'yes, that *is* what I meant, gentlemen,' and looking at Neera, 'you, of course do not find it surprising.'

'Certainly not,' Neera replied, 'if he has this determination you speak of – oh yes, this is nothing out of the ordinary for my people.' He turned to Guy. 'It is, after all, the aim of asceticism – to escape from the prison of the flesh.'

Harding nodded. 'The earlier letters will not interest you so much.' He pulled a few from their envelopes and glanced over them quickly. 'They describe his furious sifting through the Bible for better explanations of the Creation than are provided in the first chapter of Genesis, particularly for some explanation of the inferior role allotted to the whole of the animal kingdom – in complete contrast of course to the main eastern religions which recognize all creation as interdependent.'

'He idolized his dogs,' Harriet Vaneyke came in. 'He used to say they were far more intelligent than ninety-nine per cent of the people he had to deal with, and I really believe it was separation from his beloved Jason and Antigone that started him off on all this. He only left them behind because he felt he could not confine them to a small ship, in the heat, away from the walks and smells they loved so. It was really a frightful wrench.'

Harding laughed. 'Well – it may have had something to do with it certainly, but I assure you, my dear, this was an *intellectual* quest.' He looked at Guy and Heighurst. 'I'm convinced that, had he only been given positions equal to his extraordinary abilities – Perhaps they could not have been found within the service, but no, I'm certain it could have been done. There are surely immense technical challenges to face?'

Guy nodded. 'Everything is changing furiously. There's never been a more exciting time – in a technical sense.'

'That's how I imagine it to be. Yet they send him out here' – Harding spread his arms in disbelief – 'in command of a gunboat launched at the time of the Crimea! I ask you. What was the poor fellow to do? Well' – he placed a hand on a pile of letters – 'this is what he did. I imagine he found it exciting enough – and dangerous, devilish dangerous!'

'Oh yes,' Neera shook his head vehemently. 'It is exceedingly dangerous for such a man. This does not surprise me now I have heard what you say – I can see it. It is very, very sad. The Pāli canon – !'

'Chiefly the *Dhammapada*,' Harding nodded. 'Well – to be brief, Robbie could find no satisfactory explanation of the Creation even in the New Testament. By comparison the Buddhist conception of a universe in which everything is, always was, transitory and dependent on a multitude of preconditions' – he spread his arms – 'in effect a cosmic law of cause and effect, this appealed to his intellect. It is certainly easier to reconcile with Darwin and other modern theories than our Biblical doctrines – at all events he placed a great deal of emphasis on the point for it seemed to him to shed light on the central tenet of Christianity – that is to say, if Christ held this, to Vaneyke, unsatisfactory, even arrogant, idea of man's place in Creation, could *He* have been the son of God?' He stopped. 'I'm sorry, this part is not really necessary for you.'

'Please go on,' Guy said.

Harding bowed his head briefly. 'I won't bore you with all the points he took for comparison between Christian and Buddhist doctrine during the course of what he liked to call his cosmic studies.' He smiled, 'But one crucial point was the agreement in the teachings of both Jesus Christ and Gautama of the dual nature of man – that is to say, spirit and flesh. He noted, by the by, that both men – and indeed Mahomet – retreated from the world for a time before commencing their mission. He perceived that both, in fasting and solitude, had gained insights into men and the universe which were strikingly similar in many ways – particularly, as I say, in the separation of what we call the spirit from the flesh – but strikingly different in others. Well – you can perhaps guess at the next stage?'

'To retire and fast,' Guy said.

'Exactly! The scientific spirit. And where better, he said, than in the after cabin of a cruising man of war, where the commander is condemned by his station practically to the existence of a hermit in any case.'

'How long ago was this?' Heighurst asked.

Harding rifled through some letters, and picking one up, skimmed over the pages with his eyes. 'Here we are, this will give you an idea – it was dated some eight months ago.' He started reading: 'the death of Christ was much much more than atonement although, heaven knows, we need that particular message every day of our lives. But I am more than ever convinced the crucifixion was the symbolic death of the flesh, that He might perfectly live in the spirit. The flesh corrodes the spiritual body, and this however so many times we strike away the scales, for the flesh is born of the devil, the spirit only of God, this surely is the message.'

Harding looked up. 'And then he quotes, "And they that are of Christ Jesus have crucified the flesh with the passions and lusts thereof" – Galatians 5:25 – and again, "Love not the world, neither the things that are in the world. If any man love the world, the love of the father is not *in* him." He underscores "in" heavily. "For all that is in the world, the lust of the flesh and the lust of the eyes and the vainglory of life, is not of the Father, but is of the world. And the world passeth away, and the lust thereof; but he that doeth the will of God abideth for ever" – I John 2:15–17.'

Harding turned the page, and they saw him skipping several lines. 'And then, of course, comes his inevitable comparison with Buddhism – verse 62 of the *Dhammapada*, "Sons I have, estates I have. So is the fool concerned, truly he is not his own. Whence sons? Whence estates?" And verse 75, "Decidedly the path that leads to worldly advantage is one, and the path that leads to Nibbana" – that is Pāli for Nirvana,' Harding explained – '"is another."' He skipped some more lines, condensing them for their benefit, 'He points to the opposing conclusions drawn from this hypothesis of the world and the flesh as corruption,' and he started quoting again from the letter, '"Christ gives the fruit of the spirit as love, joy, peace, long-suffering, kindness, goodness, faithfulness, which are all qualities of the world and the flesh, and whereas Gautama gives occasionally similar counsel the burden of his message drives the spiritual argument to its inescapable conclusion, which is the need to strive for complete *other-worldliness*, or utter separation from the world and the flesh, in a word for Nibbana, an alone and very private state –"'

Neera was shaking his head, muttering something. Harding looked up and he said, 'I am sorry, please do not mind me.'

Harding continued reading, ' – the only escape from the soul's weary journey through an infinite series of fleshly reincarnations. "Sorrowful is birth again and again." Now, here is the point, for Gautama the destruction of the flesh and its lusts and sorrows brings release from the cosmic law.' Harding looked up briefly, 'And he quotes from his own translation, 'For the enlightened, whose view is the void and the signless liberation, like birds through the air, these ones leave no trace."' And he continues, "But for Christ, on the other hand, the enlightened, who live in the Word inherit *Eternal Life*, and they only; the others are consumed in the fires. 'He will gather his wheat into the garner, but the chaff he will burn up with unquenchable fire' – Matthew, 3:12. I have been struck, my dear Charles, throughout this investigation, by the absolute impossibility of interpreting words which attempt to describe spiritual matters in worldly equivalents. It appears to me that while Buddhists insist that there is no *alpha* nor *omega*, it may nevertheless be true that Gautama's and Christ's visions were identical! Can we not read for 'the unquenchable fire' the passions of this world, hence the Buddhist's eternal reincarnation in flesh? And can we not read for 'Eternal Life' or the 'Kingdom of God,' complete separation from the flesh and the devil by stepping outside the cosmic laws into Nibbana? Can we not, I say! In truth, I intend to put it to the test, Charles, I shall not tell Harriet for I fear for her, and for myself, if it turns out as I believe it might.'

Harding stopped reading, and folding the pages, replaced them in the envelope. 'That is when he starts describing his intentions in more detail.' He looked at Guy, 'As you surmised, it was to retire from the world, and fast and meditate – with the help of some hints on posture and breathing exercises he had learned from a Brahman in Bombay.'

'Khandala,' Guy said quietly, remembering the cave temple. 'We had words with him. I should have guessed.'

'You got *here*,' Harding replied, brows raised.

'Robbie so loves an argument,' Harriet Vaneyke said, 'Those interminable arguments! He simply cannot abide the ordinary talk. I really don't know how I put up with it. We could not go anywhere without some poor unfortunate being picked up for some inconsequential remark he might have made – and Robbie was never content until he had driven the fellow completely into a corner and holed him up. Really he is insufferable, but he is not like that beneath – it's only reaction.' She placed a gloved hand gently on the letters almost as if caressing them. 'It was simple perversity, that is what this is d'you see? I have to find him before *they* do.'

Harding was looking at her steadily. Guy wondered if there was more than ordinary compassion in his gaze – yes, of course there was. He felt a stab of jealousy as he thought the man was in love with her – who would not be? He recalled the phrases at the end of the half-finished letter of Vaneyke's, 'There is no fire like concupiscence, no river like desire.' No doubt they were from the Pāli canon, and how true!

'I'm sure we shall,' Harding said, and turned to Guy and Heighurst. 'Unless you two gentlemen come into the category of "them"!'

'Rather the unquenchable fires.' Heighurst muttered.

Harding smiled, then started sorting through the envelopes in front of him. 'After that letter there was, as you might imagine, a considerable gap – '

'That would be about the time the *Curlew* went missing,'

Heighurst said.

Harding looked up. 'Yes, I suppose so. And I'm sure, as I said before, at least one subsequent letter went astray. But then' – he glanced quickly at Harriet – 'we have a rather different style. If we label his earlier letters "enquiry", then these subsequent ones might be called the "elucidation of the mystery",' his eyes as he looked at Guy were deep with meaning.

'He had found what he was looking for?'

Harding did not reply, but handed him a letter instead. 'See what you make of that.' He picked others from the same pile and handed them to Heighurst and Neera.

There was silence as they began to read.

Guy was struck by the abrupt opening of his letter. There was no concession to convention or reciprocity; it was a stark tract that might have been a leaf of a personal diary – that, in effect, was what it was.

Today Brewer came into the cabin and said he was mortally afraid, the ship's police were taking matters into their own hands and were not consulting him. There was nothing he could do, I must come out and speak to them. I told him they knew they could come aft at any time, indeed all the ship's company might come aft, it was entirely unnecessary for me to go 'out' as he put it. He began to shake and a white froth appeared at the corners of his lips, which I have noticed trembling loosely on many occasions recently. I told him it was not surprising if they adhered to the world and sought to oppress others, even him, for they were not receiving the correct example from those who should be their instructors. Brewer himself, I know, has been drunk for three days together this week. I told him that he should practise restraint and concentrate on the higher consciousness, and his fears would fall into perspective. I showed him some translations I had made and besought him to turn his mind to the four noble truths, pain and the cause of pain, the overcoming of pain and the noble eightfold path leading to the extinction of pain. He fell on his knees and began muttering and crying incoherently. I smiled and began my breathing exercises. When he had gone I thought over the interview and was very conscious that I have not yet broken the bonds, for when he spoke of the ship's police placing themselves above him, the first lieutenant, I had felt my passions rising as they used to, and I had to suppress them with every device of concentration. When I saw the state to which he had been reduced by his recent debaucheries and had to listen to his foul vapourings, it took me all my strength in restraint. Oh, my strength, Harriet, I do not believe I could have thrown him out if I had tried. I am seized with fits of trembling, uncontrollable fits, but my spiritual strength is growing in inverse proportion. My gums are painful, my knees and groin swelling. There are times I long for your touch but believe I am being truthful in saying these moments are becoming fewer, indeed I trust they are. I have a formula to keep them and other affections at bay – no to cut them off at the root. My senses are like knives.

I am not without disciples, Harriet. I know you will be surprised, but many come, and we read from my translations or meditate in silence. There is a young ord. called James, who is a ready learner and spends several hours each day with me, and I suppose I have seen practically all the ship's company at one time or another, except for the ship's police. I do not recall having seen one of them. Nor do I see the officers except for Brewer, and he is a sorry man, I have seen him blubbering like a child. Despite this the work of the ship goes along in the most perfect order, and I am left entirely free, for which I am thankful.

It was not long after Brewer came to see me that I found myself somewhere up by the mizzen truck again and looking down through the deck into my cabin saw myself as before on my bunk; indeed I not only *saw* myself, I was in a sense *attached* to myself by a gleaming silvery thread from my forehead, and I saw Brewer approaching the lobby and enter, blundering in like an enraged bull, and I knew he was intent on harming the me that was lying down there, but it seemed to matter not at all; I preferred to remain outside, a spectator at a distance. It was not a physical distance, but the distance between time and no time, bodily consciousness and spiritual consciousness, I can put it no better. It was as if I were floating most comfortably and happily in another sphere, as indeed I believe I was, in the trackless signless zone. It was exceptionally bright, radiant with a light I cannot attempt to describe, nor could I at one time have conceived it. I was aware of everything so that even while I was watching Brewer and seeing my physical body in the utmost danger, I knew that nothing would happen to it, for its time had not yet come. It was a strangely peaceful feeling.

Sure enough I saw the master-at-arms and two of his creatures rushing towards the lobby, and Brewer, when he heard them coming, uttered an extraordinary sound and dodged back out of the starboard door half slipping on the carpet in his hurry. The ship's police followed him round, and it was at this point that I caught sight of your photograph on the bulkhead, the one Harry took on that first afternoon you came down to Bickley. I could see the photograph as if it were a few feet only from my face, although from my position, where

I appeared to be high over the deckhead I should not have been able to see it; but there it was, as plain and square-on as if I were sitting at my desk staring up at it, and all the old longing for you and Bickley and Jason and Antigone and Harry and all the others flooded me, and I realized I was still chained to it all and had so much still to do to break the chains. That was the last I remember from that my second journey. Almost in the same instant I realized I had so much to do I found myself back on my bunk looking up at my anglescope, and there was the upper deck and the back of the quartermaster and the AB at the wheel, and the sheet lifting. The first thing I did when I got to my feet was to go to the desk and take down all the photographs above it and throw them one by one out of a port, wondering why on earth I had not done it before. But when I came to yours, last of all, something seemed to grip my arm. I tried to throw it after the others, tried as hard as I could but my arm was paralyzed, and it was not until I had decided not to throw it away that I was able to move at all. I put it in one of the drawers. Its time will come. "Look on this fair body, a festering mass, an infirm lump, much admired, in which nothing lasts, nothing is eternal – "

Guy looked up in mid-page to see what she was doing. Her seat was empty. He looked at Harding.

'She felt it rather oppressive in here.'

He thrust the sheets of the letter to the table and, rising, stepped quickly to the door and out. There was no sign of her. He wondered which of the huts clustered round about was hers; several had lights showing still, and he heard the murmur of talk. She would not be there. The lake gleamed under a half-moon to his left and, remembering where he had found her earlier, he started towards it. As he reached the bank and looked along it he saw her a long way away, a wraith with a pale scarf and white forearms slipping away across white-dappled shadow to the darkness of the jungle. He started after her and, as she disappeared beneath arching trees, quickened his pace to a run.

She was waiting for him, half smiling as he pounded up. A shaft of moonlight illumined her hair and one side of her face, tracing the fine structure of her nose and chin, leaving pools of shadow around her eyes.

'Mr Greville!'

'Where are you going?' he asked sharply, annoyed at her composure.

She turned away and started off again. 'I couldn't sit there and watch you all.'

He caught up and walked beside her. Odd shapes of overgrown pillars and pieces of wall reared up from the darkness to the right, twining stems and leaves and tricks of the moon turning them briefly into witches or little hobgoblins or sinister, unidentifiable groups lurking beneath the branches. Creepers looped and coiled like cables between the trees provided a fantastic backdrop. On every hand the sounds of the night were loud, the grunt and croaking of innumerable frogs, cicadas singing, an owl hooting somewhere, the scream of birds, and far away the harsh howl of jackals – the haunted forest was alive.

'I was feeling' – she paused, choosing her words – 'very happy before you came. We were here. I felt we had only to wait, and Robbie would be bound to come with a few of his disciples.' She looked up. 'And then – oh, but I don't know.' She seemed to quicken her pace. 'What do you think?'

'About what?'

'Now you have seen the letters.'

'I've seen only a part of one.'

'You think Robbie is mad?' she interrupted.

'What does Harding think?'

'Charles? He's a nice man. I don't know what I would have done without him. Robbie likes him too – and respects his intellect. Oh,' she laughed, 'that's quite an achievement! I thought between us we might do something – *would* do something. And Charles knows the Admiral.'

'Does the Admiral know of the letters?'

'No. We thought we must find Robbie first. Afterwards, it might not be necessary – '

'Why did you come here particularly?'

'Some time ago Robbie asked Charles for copies of his surveys of this region – Pollanarua and other ancient sites he had found in this area. Charles thought at the time it was connected with his studies, but then when I wrote to him about the *Curlew* being missing, and my fears for Robbie's – ' she hesitated. 'At the time I thought the heat in the Gulf and his frustration and loneliness and his studies, working all night and sleeping by day – But until this last time he seemed not to have been affected when he came back to Bombay; he was tired and thinner, much thinner, but happy – not happy, excited, on the quest – that was Robbie of course, he was only happy if he had his teeth into a problem, or some poor man.' She laughed briefly. 'It was only this last time after he decided on these dreadful experiments – ' Guy felt her arm slip through his and felt her shiver.

He had an absurd longing to put his arm around her shoulders, she was so light and he felt she was lost again as she had been when he had met her first. He thought of the letter he had read and marvelled that she could have been so composed then, after receiving that and others like it. For the first time he felt anger.

'Charles does not believe Robbie is insane,' she said softly. 'Sometimes I wish he were. I could understand it then.'

'He married you.' Guy heard his voice hard and dry as if from a long way off. 'He has no right to leave you in search of his own private salvation.'

She looked up at his tone and gripped his hand with her gloved fingers, then suddenly started shaking with sobs – deep, gasping cries that rasped up uncontrollably – and he felt her fingers tighten over his like a vice. Uncertain what to do, he stopped and, half turning, placed his other hand lightly on her shoulder, feeling her body torn by spasms of grief beneath his fingers. She leant her head forward and rested it, jerking, on his chest. He stood, tense and uncomfortable, helpless. From somewhere above them to the right came an unearthly, long-drawn, gurgling shriek as if from a soul in torment. It was answered mockingly by other birds, but they failed to match the agonized quality of the original. The moon went behind a cloud.

'I'll take you back,' he said, exerting gentle pressure on her shoulder to turn her. He felt her resist.

She looked up, her eyes dark as pools. 'It is – not – so simple you – see.' She tried to control herself. 'I'm – sorry – very sorry.'

'I should not have said – '

'It must – seem – like that.'

He remained silent, not wishing to repeat his mistake.

She took her hand from his and brought the end of her scarf up to her eyes. He searched about in his pocket for a handkerchief; he could not find one.

'Stupid – ' she said, turning away, and starting to walk slowly up the path, her chest heaving every so often, but little sound coming up.

He went to her. 'We should go back.'

She looked round but said nothing, merely continuing to walk on. The moon had come out again and as she passed into a patch of light he saw the thrust of her chin and the strength in her finely-formed nose, and wondered again how any man could seek detachment from a life that held such a noble and exquisite creature. Surely he must be insane.

She walked on in silence, her breathing becoming steadier, and her stride lengthening; she had a loose, graceful walk; everything she did had an unconscious grace. He wondered where on earth she thought they were going and realized that he had not been keeping track of their progress; they had passed several intersecting paths, and the great lake which had been to their left had disappeared long since. They were in the heart of the jungle.

'I hope you know the way back,' he said.

She looked round and her lips parted in that slightly crooked smile. 'Are you worried, Guy?'

Guy! She had never called him that before. There was no trace of tears now; her eyes were clear.

'To tell the truth – yes!'

She laughed. 'Don't worry, I've been along this path many, many times.' She had an enigmatic, half-amused expression as she looked at him. She was a different person from that stricken creature of a few moments ago. He wasn't sure that he liked the sudden change.

He reflected how easily the mind was diverted; under normal circumstances he would never have entered the jungle without noting his track by pocket compass and marking key turnings, yet here he was without the least idea of where they had been or how many turnings they had taken; he had been conscious only of her. He thought of Vaneyke turning the full focus of his consciousness inwards, and tried to visualize him floating, disembodied, above the *Curlew*'s poop, seeing himself through the deck below, and Brewer charging in. He remembered Helen had told him of a peculiar experience she had had once at the dinner table; her mind had seemed to move away out of the tide of conversation and she had seen herself from behind, seated eating with the others as if she had been one of them – someone else or somewhere else for an instant, quite removed. With fasting and seclusion, who knew what the mind might achieve? Harding did not think Vaneyke insane – or had he just said that to reassure her?

'Now, do you believe me?' she said.

They had emerged from the trees, and she was looking to the left to where a great, tree- and vegetation-covered dome rose, huge against the night and the stars, with a pinnacle shining in the moonlight above tangled shrubs at the top, fully two hundred feet high, he thought, stunned by the sight of it rising, as it were, from nothing.

'The Rankot *dagaba*,' she murmured. 'I prefer the other name for it: *Ruanwelle-saye*, the place of golden dust.'

Guy gazed, wondering at the immense energy and architectural skill of the race that had erected it, and its aching emptiness now in the grip of the jungle. Ozymandias, king of kings –

'It was a shrine,' she said. '*Dagabas* are shrines for the reception of relics. This is the largest in Pollanarua. It was built for the second wife of King Parakrama. I'll show you his statue tomorrow, if you are interested.'

'Of course,' he said quickly.

'Look – ' she pointed up the track across more or less open ground to where a mile or so away another dome, and huge columns, reared silvery and dark-seamed above a spread of ruins. 'Does it make you feel rather queer?'

'Decidedly.'

'You have imagination.'

'One could not fail to have – here.'

'Charles thinks she was the one known as "Rupavati", the fairest of beings,' she appeared to be quoting, 'who, like the moon, drew upon her the eyes of the world,' she started walking towards the far ruins. 'Among many hundreds of women in the inner chambers of the palace, she was beloved the most and, save her own husband, she regarded not as much even as a blade of grass, any other.' She turned her head to gaze at him with wide eyes. 'Do you believe in reincarnation?'

He smiled. 'I have not given it much thought. But I don't,' he added.

'Of course – with your background.'

He gazed at her, wondering what she knew of his background; he couldn't remember saying anything to her about it.

She sensed his puzzlement and smiled. 'One of your marines – the one who looks after you – '

'Basset!'

'He must be devoted to you – is he?'

'He gives little sign of it.' But he thought of the warning about Davis that Basset had tried to give him.

'No,' she went on, 'I don't suppose you would know how to talk to him.'

'I'm obliged!' He bowed his head.

She laughed and slipped her arm into his again. His pulse beat a little faster, and a curious suspicion stole over him. Why was she leading him out here? He had accompanied her out of sympathy, but now he thought about it her step had been sure all the way, she had been determined to go on, she had known where she was taking him. Surely she could not imagine she was the Queen Rupavati, 'fairest of beings', returned to her pleasant haunts? Why had the thought flashed upon him?

'I love it here,' she said. 'From the moment I saw it,' she gestured with her free arm to take in the ruins ahead and the jungle-grown remains and the lake they had left far behind. 'I felt an affinity at once,' she smiled, looking up, and gave his arm a squeeze which sent his pulse racing away again, 'just as I did with you! And then when Charles read to me from the *Mahawansa* bits describing how splendid it was' – she waved her arm ahead – 'laid out with ornamental lakes and islands with pavilions from which to view them, and roads wide enough for elephants lined with shops and halls for music and dancing, bathing places and fountains and groves and gardens – ' she laughed. 'But I mustn't spoil it for you. I'll get Charles to show you around tomorrow. He's a wizard at bringing it all back – he's already identified dozens of the buildings. Do you know there are twenty-nine chapters of the *Mahawansa* devoted to just one of the kings here – Parakrama, Rupavati's husband.'

He smiled at her enthusiasm. 'I can't imagine a better guide than I have.'

'False flatterer!'

'I shall never see it like this again,' he said seriously, 'however many chapters Charles Harding reads to me.'

She took his hand again. 'Nor shall I. It's always the first time, isn't it?'

He looked down at her. He didn't know what it was, but something about the way she said it released a flow of memories: Uncle Jack at the head of the table, teasing, 'sittin' you next to her, the devil of a risk I said!' – and the gleaming eye of Colonel Case as he had left the whist tables that night, 'Your luck *has* turned, young fella!' – Lord ffort's arching brows, 'What are our heads compared to your *scalps*, Mrs Vaneyke?'

His nerves tingled unnaturally; if he were being led to the scalping – no, it couldn't be. Yet she had him already and undoubtedly she knew it. Lord! What a devil of a way to march a fellow to his doom!

She was as much of an enigma as ever, her moods changing as suddenly as the clouds passing across the moon. How could she think of such a thing with Vaneyke in the condition he was? He thought of her anguished crying and the way she had looked up at him, 'It is – not – so simple – '

It was not so simple of course; she herself was one of the pressures which had acted on Vaneyke's mind, and of course she knew it. Vaneyke loved her. While at sea he would have thought of her in Bombay society or in the hot weather at Simla or Poona or one of the other hill stations where 'fast' and would-be 'fast' young officers toasted absent husbands; he would have imagined them drawn to her as so many moths to the flame. Whether she had encouraged them or not, he would have had the image and the possibility always before him in his hot cabin. It was what the Brahman at Khandala had inferred, surely, when he had likened the ladies to lamps burning along the path to hell. She had acquired a reputation in Bombay, even here apparently in the short time the camp had existed. He wondered whether it had always been thus, or whether it had been Vaneyke's doubts and inward-circling search for truth that had precipitated her search for sensation. He would never know; probably she didn't know herself, but undoubtedly the two had reacted on one another, driving each other to excess; they were both imperious characters. And undoubtedly she felt her responsibility; it has been the cause of her anguish.

As they neared the ruins looming ahead, the shadows before them moved, and they made out a herd of spotted deer rippling away; soon they had disappeared into the night. Guy remembered the bear they had disturbed in the overgrown building on the way in to the city, and moved his right hand in hers to touch his revolver holster, resolving to free his arm directly they approached the buildings. She looked up quizzically.

'Would you have come all this way if I hadn't come after you?' he asked, smiling.

She looked down and he thought for a moment she was not going to reply. At last she said, 'That is an absurd question.'

He grinned; probably it was. All things were conditional; out here in the moonlight approaching the wreckage of time they were peculiarly so; he wondered for an instant if this journey were really any different from that Vaneyke had described in his letter. The sensation passed in an instant; there was absolutely no doubt that she was there in the flesh.

The path led on past the first substantial ruin, and she eased him off it to the left, skirting thorny scrub directly towards a stair entrance to the crumbling building. The steps gleamed white; they had evidently been cleared or excavated in contrast to the rest of the pile which was quite overgrown; several thin, vertical windows could be made out among the foliage and twisting roots and stems. Bats swooped above uttering high-pitched squeaks.

She released his hand as they picked their way over the uneven ground, and arriving at the bottom of the flight stood gazing down at a great semi-circular stone which formed the lowest step. It was carved with bands of different design concentric to the outside curve. The outer band was of floral pattern, then came a row of geese, following each other beak to tail, then rather fat lions similarly chasing each other's tails, then a band of elephants, marvellously lifelike as they paced one after the other in stately procession, then horses with curiously depressed bodies and ornamental collars, and finally a broad, stylized scroll enclosing a lotus at the centre. In the clear white light the carving was etched as sharply as if it had just been made. The workmanship and sense of form and movement were exquisite; it reminded him of a tapestry in stone.

She was looking at him.

'It's beautiful,' he said.

'A moonstone – not the kind I used to think of. They are found nowhere but Ceylon. Charles is particularly pleased with this one,' she knelt and pointed. 'It is the only one at Pollanarua with lions – the only one he has found. All the moonstones at Anuradhapura have lions – and bulls as well, although bulls do not appear here at all.'

'Curious.'

She rose. 'Everyone makes such a fuss of Egyptian ruins, but really – ' she shook her head, looking down. 'I think this must be how moonstones were meant to be seen, don't you?'

'I'm certain of it.'

She gazed at him, head slightly to one side. 'Come on! I'll show you something to pierce that stony heart.'

'You have already.'

Her brows rose in recognition of the compliment as she swept past. 'Basset said you weren't much of a one for words!'

He followed her around the wall of the building wondering what that remark signified. 'I could say the same of him. You appear to have been very chummy with Basset.'

'I knew I wouldn't find out much from you.'

He wondered what his man had told her, and if he had mentioned the murders of the Branders; he doubted it, but she was bound to learn sooner or later.

Rounding the building he saw the mighty walls of what might have been a cathedral they were so long and high, although they were broken at the top and roofless with the inevitable shrubs growing from ledges and crannies in the brickwork. At the right hand end the walls terminated in the two huge polygonal columns he had seen from the distance, much of their lower halves still coated with white plaster and fluted and in one place carved, their upper sections crumbling red brick sprouting branches, the leaves shining against black shadow. At the foot of these gigantic columns amidst a jumble of hummocks and thick undergrowth were a number of standing white stone blocks, and further away raised on a platform whose carved stonework could just be made out behind the scrub were ranks of upstanding pillars with intricate designs worked on their square bases and capitals. Several were leaning at different angles.

As they made a circuitous course towards them, the outline of a dome similar to the huge dome they had passed at the edge of the forest rose into view beyond the columns. It too was covered with bushes and trees, some of whose snaking roots were outlined in the moonlight; at the summit the same kind of pinnacle was visible between the branches although the top of this one had broken off.

'The milk-white *dagaba*,' she said, seeing the direction of his gaze. 'The whole of it was coated with chunam which gleamed like white marble. It was topped by a golden spire.'

'It must have been very impressive,' he said. It was graceful still, even with its rough coating of foliage.

As they picked their way towards the group of standing pillars, there opened the view of a long aisle between the columns at the end of the walls of the cathedral-like building. It was choked with fallen debris and vegetation growing from it, but as the far wall came in sight a long way beyond the nearer column they saw clearly illumined in moonlight the head, shoulders and chest of a giant statue perhaps fifty feet high; the lower body was in shadow and the legs obscured by branches and foliage, but this only seemed to accentuate the immense scale of the figure. Guy moved towards it, drawn by the unexpectedness and shining quality of the sight. The plaster which must have covered the statue, as it had once covered the awesome columns flanking the open end of the aisle, was all gone, and the brickwork was worn by the elements, but there was still a recognizable face, perhaps more impressive, he thought, for showing the ravages of time.

The approach to the entrance was rough with mounds and fallen masonry, amongst which were the upstanding white stone blocks he had noticed earlier. They were like large tombstones with rounded tops and had evidently been scraped clean by Harding's men. Each had a figure carved on the side towards him in intricate and sinuous relief, swaying as if in a dance; the effect of life and movement was marvellous. He stopped by one and ran his finger over the beautiful work.

'A guardian stone,' she said, coming up. 'Aren't they lovely?'

'Superb. This one must have been buried face down. It's as sharp as the day it was cut.'

She stood gazing up the aisle. 'Charles believes they must have had a concealed window in the roof lighting up just the head and shoulders of the Buddha,' she nodded towards the statue. 'It faces due east. They have that system in a pagoda on the Irrawaddy river. In Burma,' she added.

He smiled at the geography lesson. 'We're being granted a view of it much as it was.'

'Isn't it strange?'

He felt she was very close as they stood in the presence of the vanished worshippers. The shadows and the night were black and soft and velvet, the stars very bright around, the air warm and languorous.

'Robbie thinks he is the Buddha,' she said quietly.

He looked down at her startled.

Her eyes were serious as she met his look. 'I simply couldn't bear it in there with all of you reading those letters. I had to come out.' She sank down and smoothed her dress out before sitting on the ground, then smiled up. 'But I'm so glad you're here.'

He bent his knees and crouched in front of her. 'He surely cannot believe he is the Buddha?'

'Charles has been very careful not to tell me what he thinks, but I know he thinks so too.'

He stared at her.

'He explains things to his disciples,' she said, looking down, toying with the tendrils of a ground plant. 'He has all his sayings written down always by a clerk in the cabin with him. He has even explained Nibbana – of course he has only made it more incomprehensible, but he believes he has explained it. All these sayings of his are meticulously recorded and sent to poor Charles. You would have seen them had you waited.'

He wondered if her anxiety had made her read more into the letters than was there. She sensed his disbelief. 'Ask Charles,' she said.

He nodded. 'I shall.'

'I should have known it would come to this. Robbie is so thorough. And so certain – '

He laughed.

'No, it is true. It would be nothing very marvellous to him – becoming Buddha. I really think it would mean no more than a promotion – spiritual commander-in-chief. Buddha does not have to be the son of God or anything like that – in fact he is definitely *not* the son of God. He is a man who has succeeded at last in breaking all the shackles of the flesh.'

'But he hasn't – ' He stopped suddenly, wishing he'd not said it. He couldn't tell her about her photograph in the upturned Bible.

She looked at him curiously.

'He hadn't at the time of the letter I was reading,' he said.

'No, but you have not seen his later effusions.' She gazed out beyond him. 'Having discovered how to move out of himself, if that is what he discovered – and Charles says there is nothing really very peculiar about that, not out here – he went on to what he called control techniques.' She made a little grimace. 'It made me quite dizzy just to read about it. This way, that way, up, down, he seems to have been able to move out in which ever direction he chose!'

He gazed at her, wondering what exactly she felt for Vaneyke; the way she spoke of him he might have been an exasperating little boy playing with toy trains.

She moved her head nearer and said with great significance. 'He does not even have to come back!'

He smiled. 'It's hard to believe.'

'Charles does not find it difficult to believe, not to a man of Robbie's calibre, not out here. He says we must get him home or we shall lose him. Robbie finds it so *pleasant* out there you see, and he's so weak, weak in his body – he must be. Charles thinks probably he has the beginnings of scurvy. But he must be all right now if he's ashore. You are *sure* he's come ashore?' She had an anxious expression.

'I could not be more positive.'

'Well,' she said, leaning back until she was lying full length, stretching her arms out, 'he'll be here somewhere. He only came back so that he could start a community and spread his message. Like Gautama. We know it must be somewhere near because of the surveys he asked for.' She looked up at the sky. 'Besides, where else? Anuradhapura is simply teeming with people, there's even a native village and a bazaar. But I thought it would be here, it seemed so fitting.' She stretched an arm languorously towards him like a cat in the sun. 'I'm so pleased you came instead.'

His chest thumped. The time had come! As in a pagan rite, she lay in view of the great shining Buddha statue, her scarf, washed almost white by the moon trailing over a clump of creeper towards the sinuous legs of the guardian figure in the white stone, her eyes grey and steady on his.

'Which came first?' he asked, hearing a catch in his voice as he took her gloved fingers in his. Had *he* said it?

Her eyes opened wider.

'His journeys or yours?' he plunged on. Hanged if he was going to be used for a priest at her sacrificial altar.

She stared for a moment, then snatched her hand away. 'I despise them. Charles was right. *They* have done this to Robbie.' She rose to a sitting position and clasped her knees. 'I'm being eaten alive. How can you just *sit* there?'

He laughed helplessly.

She rose to her feet and started walking away. 'Don't follow me this time.'

He watched her picking her way around the hillocks, the way they had come, wondering what on earth she was up to; as she continued on, disappearing eventually behind the line of a creeper-clad wall, he began to feel anxious. The thought of her walking back alone and unarmed through the jungle was alarming; if he let her gain too much of a start he might never find her – certainly he would never find his own way back! But he wanted her; the night which had been filled with excitement only a moment ago was strangely dead. The exquisite guardian in the stone was dead without her to share the delight. He turned and looked at the Buddha; the brow had been worn down so that there was only the faintest declivity for the eyes which seemed to gaze out blindly past the despoliation of the walls into the night.

He rose and started back the way he had seen her take towards the long mound which had once been a wall. As he reached it, he heard her call. He threaded his way towards the voice, unable to see her despite the fact that the sound had seemed quite close and there was little high enough to hide behind. He began to feel annoyed.

He climbed a slanting block of masonry to get a better view over the ground, and heard her again, a musical drawing in of her breath and half laugh, somewhere just ahead and below. There was a movement and he saw her head and shoulders in the middle of a sheet of water which stretched between more tumbled blocks and thick bushes. Her dress and scarf hung over the branches. She was looking up at him. He couldn't see her face, only the silhouette of her hair and neck and the white outline of her shoulders above the surface. She rose slightly and spread her arms. 'It's gorgeous!'

'I hope there are no muggers!'

'Of course not. This is an old *pokuna* – a real bathing place. Charles had it cleared for me. I always bathe here. Come on!'

He imagined the amused look in her eyes, and wondered if Harding had bathed here with her.

She laughed. 'I'll close my eyes.'

He picked his way down the masonry and skirted the edge of the pool until he was at the far end with the moon behind him, and sat down and started unfastening his boots.

She had turned, and he could see her face now when he looked up. Her eyes had that composed look which had struck him at their first meeting, clear and penetrating but not in any way presumptuous – the most outward, yet marvellously self-contained, gaze he had ever seen. The hint of a smile played about her lips, the shadow beneath her chin was sharp, her shoulders smooth white, and beneath them the shape of her body rippled through the surface water disturbed by her arms wafting lazily across before her. He was reminded of John Dollman's pictures at the Royal Academy, milk-white naiads – a girl disturbed while bathing. She had the knack, whatever she did, of presenting herself as if for a picture.

He pulled off a boot and placed it beside him, then the other. 'Is this certified for mixed bathing?' he asked unsteadily, knowing he would get a provocative answer or none at all.

'Only on *special* nights.'

'And this is one?'

'Do you not think so?'

He unstrapped his revolver belt, and placed it very carefully over his boots so that the butt of the gun was towards the pool. 'It is the most *singular* one I can remember.' He wondered if she had picked up the unevenness in his voice.

'I shall always remember it,' she said.

He smiled wryly. 'I fancy I shan't forget it,' and, unfastening his tunic, took it off.

'What splendid shoulders!'

'You said you would shut your eyes!'

She laughed. 'I forgot,' and brought her arms out of the water and clasped her hands over her eyes. The ripples stilled. He saw clearly the shape of her breasts and the shadows below, and the slim waist – She was keeping her part of the bargain and he was not reciprocating, but he couldn't help himself – an instant only, and then he had jumped up and, half turning, removed the rest of his clothes.

The water was warm as the night. He half slipped on some treacherous growth on the masonry, and felt the scar left by the storm wound strike painfully against a boulder. He put a hand down to steady himself.

'Take care,' she said and, moving her hands from her eyes, stretched one out towards him.

He went cautiously forward and down over successive inclined stone blocks towards her. 'I think Charles might have put in some steps!'

'Charles is very careful to preserve *exact* authenticity. Besides, you have chosen the most difficult way!'

He heard the amusement in her voice at his care to get the light behind him. Then he half slipped on some vegetation down to what seemed to be the bottom of the pool and very close to her. He took her outstretched hand. 'Harriet Vaneyke – I presume?' It sounded banal.

'Guy – Greville,' she said softly, her eyes steady and shining. 'I said I would not compliment you, but I think really you look better out of uniform than in it!'

'You cheated!' he said, pulling her slowly towards him.

'All the way!' she smiled.

'I've thought of you. Ever since that first evening – did you see me looking at you across the whist tables?'

'You were a little obvious!'

As he pulled her closer, she ducked suddenly away beneath the water. He leapt after her.

After breakfast, as Guy stood gazing out over the lotus on Topa Wewa hearing the clear, early morning cry of the jungle fowl and cooing of pigeons, and thinking he had never felt fresher and more in tune with any scene, Harding came up and said sharply, 'We've found 'em.'

He turned. Harding had been frostily correct when he had seen him briefly at breakfast. He looked into the pale eyes; there was no flicker of any warmer mood. He couldn't blame him. He would have felt the same himself had the positions been reversed.

'They're at Sigiriya,' Harding went on in the same clipped tone.

Guy realized he was referring to the Curlews, and returned abruptly to the present. 'Splendid!'

Harding turned away. 'Come with me! I don't think you'll find it such good news.'

He followed and they walked in silence to Harding's hut and went inside. A map was spread out on the table where Vaneyke's letters had been piled the night before; he saw the case in which they were kept thrust carelessly on top of a pile of books in the corner. Harding leant over the map and placed his finger on it. 'There it is. Had you not disappeared last night – ' He stopped and went on in flat tones, 'I suspected he might be making for Sigiriya. I sent two boys up there. They've just returned.'

Guy nodded as he studied the map. There was a fair-sized river to cross which ever way they went. He estimated the distance – fifteen miles perhaps, due west – not far short of a day's march across this kind of country; there were contours sketched in showing hills across the direct route, a huge lake if they went between the hills. The place was very close to the Trinco road. He wondered if the naval brigade had started yet, or if they would wait for his report.

'I suppose we had better leave it to you now,' Harding said, turning without expression, then added reluctantly, 'we'll help, of course – if you need any.'

Guy gazed at him. 'Why d'you doubt the good news?'

Harding turned back to the map. 'Sigiriya is a natural fortress. Absolutely impregnable.' He eyed Guy again. 'A dozen men could hold it against an army. You say they have machine guns – ' He shrugged, 'Slaughter!'

'In that case we had better go on by ourselves. Our orders are merely to seek intelligence – we have no need of extra hands.'

'So Lieutenant Heighurst said.'

'I'll send a couple of our fellows to Trinco to report. I suppose they're *all* at Sigiriya?'

'No doubt of it. My boys reported a party of two hundred. That's an exaggeration, of course. They would never have gone close. The natives are certain it's haunted.'

Guy attempted a light tone. 'So it is – now!'

Harding did not respond. 'I heard about the Branders last night, Harriet has no idea.' He paused, staring hard at Guy, 'She is devoted to Robbie. I imagine you may find that difficult to believe.'

'I can believe it.' He thought of her in the pool. 'She is – remarkable.'

Harding turned back to the map and started rolling it up. 'You had better take this.'

'Have you a plan of Sigiriya itself?'

'No, it has not been properly surveyed or excavated.' He handed him the rolled map. 'All you need to know is that the rock is impregnable. The upper portion is sheer on every side – overhanging in places – four hundred feet high. There is only one way up, on the western face, and that demands certain mountaineering skills. I dare say Robbie has brought ropes, though.' He gazed at Guy. 'You'll not get up except by invitation – or as a prisoner.'

'You've been there?'

'My dear fellow!' Harding turned angrily away and went to the entrance, stopping as he was about to leave. 'Harriet will want to go with you of course.'

Guy thought for a moment. 'It hardly sounds a ladies' picnic.'

A sceptical look came across the square face.

'On the other hand,' Guy went on, 'you say we have no chance of getting up – '

Harding stepped back towards him, his mouth setting in a tight line, a vein throbbing at his temple. 'You won't send Harriet up!'

'I was thinking we might perhaps entice *him* down,' Guy replied stiffly.

Harding's look was contemptuous. 'I wasn't aware the Royal Navy was in the habit of using female agents on its more dangerous assignments.'

Guy's blood flared. 'You will retract!'

Harding stood his ground, his fingers clenched, pale eyes glaring.

Guy swung away and strode out of the hut with the map. He heard Harding call after him and turned.

'He'll not come down,' Harding said after a brief pause. All traces of anger seemed to have gone, replaced by sad acceptance. 'You see, Robbie is convinced he is the Buddha. He has cut all ties. He would as soon come down for you as for Harriet. But he won't. Not for either of you.'

Guy bowed his head briefly. 'I am obliged.'

'She'll try to come,' Harding went on, 'I know her.'

Guy knew he was right. He nodded. 'I'll see she doesn't.'

'Thank God!' Harding came out of the hut towards him. 'It's a ghastly business. I had no idea – or I should, of course, have been in touch with the Admiral at once.'

'It wouldn't have saved the Branders.'

'Would it not? If Bousfield had known Robbie was making for the east coast?'

Guy gazed at him. Of course he should have told the Admiral what he knew; equally certainly he had been bewitched. 'None of us knew how serious it was,' he said.

Harding looked doubtful. 'I'm working at the Jetawaranama temple today – if you don't need me. I dare say you'll be gone before we get back.'

Guy nodded.

'Well – I wish you luck. I advise you to take no chances.' His look was strained. 'I should not like your party on my conscience as well.'

'Stuff! You couldn't possibly have known.'

Harding thrust out his hand. 'Goodbye. I did not exaggerate Sigiriya. I believe the natives are right. It's an accursed place.'

13

Guy stared at the rock towering sheer above the jungle. In the light from the western sun the granite shone red between dark lines of erosion which curved round the overhang at the top, enhancing an extraordinary mushroom-like bulge. It was like a great, bare boulder tumbled down by a giant from the mountains. Harding had not exaggerated: apart from a set of rough steps that appeared from this angle to disappear into the rock face itself, there was no possible way up without alpine equipment. On the plateau at the very top a few trees were visible; from below they appeared no larger than shrubs.

He looked round at Heighurst.

The marine gave an ironic bow. 'After you!'

Neera's voice came from beside them, 'You can feel it is evil.' He was gazing up, wide-eyed as a child, his head shaking from side to side. 'What it is to see it at last! Oh, I am so awfully happy you gentlemen brought me here with you.'

'Perhaps you would like to mount first,' Heighurst said politely.

Neera turned his head, brows rising, 'Oh, no thank you – thank you, but I do not care to go up inside that place at all.'

The marine fixed him with a cold stare. 'You understand of course that as a member of this expedition you have the acting rank of chaplain, Royal Navy.'

Neera turned to Guy.

'A tradition of the service,' Guy said, 'chaplains share the common danger.'

'A peerage or Westminster Abbey!' Heighurst added. 'The last words of one of our more celebrated chaplains.'

'It was,' Guy nodded sadly, 'the latter.'

'Oh, no, no, no, no' Neera waved his head about, 'no, no, no – '

'I dare say we could make it the Long Room at Lords instead,' Guy ventured, looking at Heighurst.

Neera eyed them suspiciously, and an uncertain smile spread across his round face. 'You gentlemen are humbugging me – yes, yes, I am certain of it.'

Heighurst raised his brows. 'Taken like a Christian martyr!'

'Oh, indeed!' The little clergyman laughed his relief. 'Sigiriya – it means lion's rock, you know – it would have been throwing me to the lion indeed!' He shook with chuckles. 'No, no, you say what you like I do not care to go up whether the *Curlew* people are there or not.' He looked from one to the other. 'You have not heard of King Kaasyapa? He was an exceedingly violent man – oh, many of our kings were, you know, exceedingly cruel and violent. His father was King Dhatu Sen. He was also a violent man. He had a poor monk who was meditating by a tank he was causing to be built – the Kalu Wewa at Anuradhapura, a marvellous lake exceeding in beauty even the Topa Wewa you have seen at Pollanarua – Dhatu Sen had the engineer who was building the bund heap earth upon this poor man while he was lost in his meditation, and he was buried alive.' He shook his head. 'Kaasyapa, his son, later perpetrated a similar act on him. He caused him to be stripped naked and bound with chains so that he was unable to move, and had a wall built around him, most slowly and carefully so that it took some time and the father could watch it rising until at last he was entombed alive.'

'Here?'

'No, no, that was at Anuradhapura, but you see, after he had murdered his father and taken his throne, he tried to have his younger brother Moggalana killed, but he failed, and Moggalana escaped across the water to India. Kaasyapa was afraid of Moggalana coming back with an army of Tamils, also he was haunted by his guilt, I think, and his people, I should say, made it apparent to him that the manner in which he had disposed of his father, Dhatu Sen, was an abomination. So he fled here to Sigiriya.'

'Uneasy lies the head – '

'Oh, that is most true about our kings, I should say so,' Neera waved his head vigorously. 'Kaasyapa was so afraid that he built his palace on the summit here, an exceedingly fine palace, with tanks and bathing places and houses for his servants and his guard – and his wives,' Neera smiled. 'There is a cave in the rock near the summit, and on the roof Kaasyapa had his wives and their serving ladies painted – exceedingly voluptuous ladies they were.'

'But you have not been here?' Heighurst said.

'No, no, that is correct, but Mr Murray, one of your engineers, a fine, brave gentleman, copied them a few years ago; he lay on his back on a platform he had built beneath the roof of the cave.'

'There are tanks at the top?' Guy said.

'Oh, I do not know if they are there still, but there is also a spring, they will not be short of water after the monsoon.'

'Providing they have enough food with them, they'll be able to withstand a long siege.'

'Oh, most certainly. Kaasyapa ruled eighteen years from here, and when his brother Moggalana came at last with an army from India he could have remained another eighteen had he wished. Moggalana's men found it impossible to surmount even the lower wall that Kaasyapa had built at the foot of the rock.' He nodded towards their right. 'That tank we passed was the moat for the lower wall.'

'But he didn't manage another eighteen?' Heighurst said.

'Oh, no, Kaasyapa came down for some reason, the *Mahawansa* does not tell us why, and he met his brother in battle on the plains – it is recorded that the two armies came together like two seas that had burst their bounds. But Kaasyapa's elephant feared to go forward into marshy ground, and tried to find a way around – as elephants will, you know – and Kaasyapa's army, believing him to be retreating, fled – whereupon Kaasyapa, rather than fall into the hands of his brother, cut his own throat.'

'I don't blame him,' Heighurst murmured.

Guy gazed up to the summit of the rock. 'I wonder why he came down.

'He was a most unhappy man, you know,' Neera replied. 'I believe it was bad conscience. All the time he was here he did penance and practised abstinence and self-flagellation, he lived the life of an ascetic, giving all the time to the temples, and building parks and hospitals for the people.'

'Purchasing salvation?'

'Attempting to do so. I believe that is why he came down, you know?'

'Our friend has found his salvation,' Heighurst said, looking up towards the flat summit.

'Oh, yes I am afraid so,' Neera clicked his teeth. 'He must be a remarkable man. I hope to meet him.'

'I'll second that,' Guy said. 'But it's the kannapaddi we need on this occasion.'

Neera's teeth flashed very white. 'You have remembered our proverb.' Then his expression darkened. 'But I think this kannapaddi has no conscience.'

'His chums will have,' Heighurst said.

Shadows crept upwards over the rock as the sun sank, leaving the extraordinary bulging top glowing like a platform in the sky.

'Yes,' Guy nodded, 'one of them will tell us who it is. My money's on Lieutenant Brown.' He turned to Heighurst. 'They're bound to send parties down from time to time. I suggest we keep the steps under observation. When one does come down – see if we can surprise a straggler.'

Heighurst's brow lifted cynically. 'I made certain you'd wish to see the ruins at the top.'

Neera cut in, 'I think I see someone, yes, look over there.'

They followed the direction of his arm, and saw shadows of movement in the bushes on the slope to the beginning of the steps up the rock. It was a sizeable party. As they watched, the heads of the leaders emerged above the foliage; they were natives carrying piles of greenish fruit or vegetables. Neera drew in his breath sharply.

'Your flock!' Guy said.

'Yes, they are my people,' he nodded. 'From the Branders' plantation.'

Guy looked at Heighurst. 'They'll have guards.'

The marine bent away under the branches and they heard him making to where the sergeant waited. Guy beckoned to Neera and they followed. The sergeant's eyes were fierce with anticipation as he gathered the rest of the party, very small since two marines had been sent down the Trincomalee road.

'We'll nab the last man up,' Heighurst said. 'He's certain to be a Curlew. Don't worry about the nig – ' He glanced quickly at Neera, correcting himself, 'natives,' then stared at the sergeant. 'Alive!'

The sergeant nodded.

'Darken hands, faces, bayonets, fix bayonets before we

Mstart.' Heighurst looked at Guy as the men crouched and pulled at the vegetation to get at the earth below. 'The overhang of the cliff will give us cover once we're close.'

'I could wish it were later,' Guy said, looking up at the sky, still blue behind the rock. 'We'll need to wait until the last moment. We may have to rush the last fellow as he goes up – they'll not be looking back. I suggest we split up, one party to act as decoy to draw them off the scent when we've bagged our man.'

Heighurst nodded and turned to the sergeant, who told off the two bluejackets and Basset for the decoy party.

Guy looked at Neera. 'We shall have to fix a rendezvous.'

'Let me go with your decoys,' the little clergyman said earnestly.

Guy heard the click of bayonets; there was no time to lose. He nodded. 'Very well. We shall need a rendezvous all the same – the south shore of the tank if we're parted.'

Neera nodded, smiling happily. 'I shall pray for your success.'

'You're the one who'll need the prayers,' Heighurst said, staring at his dog collar and white jacket and trousers.

Neera looked down. 'Oh, dear – '

Evan came up with a handful of earth and thrust it roughly over his shirt-front and collar, while the other bluejacket seized his coat, pulled it from his shoulders and, throwing it to the ground, dug his boots in with evident relish.

Guy grinned, nodding at Heighurst.

'Let's go!'

The marines in the assault party started, rifles at the hip, bayonets still glinting in places despite the mess of leaf-moistened earth smeared over them. Their eyes showed very white from their mud-plastered faces as they looked round briefly at the officers, then spread out either side, ducking under creepers as they jogged through green shade. Guy struck out diagonally from the path, feeling his feet sink into debris from centuries of growth, and slowed to a walk, picking his way carefully over firmer ground and around overgrown mounds reminiscent of the ruins at Pollanarua. The sergeant closed on his left; Heighurst moved ahead to the right.

A bugle sounded above the evening cries of the birds, causing him a start of alarm until he realized it came from high up the rock and was playing sunset.

'Damn them!' Heighurst muttered savagely as the long-drawn notes faded.

They pressed on, guided more by the sounds from the porters' party and occasional barked orders from the Curlews overseeing them than from their original line of direction as they negotiated what appeared to be the remains of an immense wall; boulders or stones from the ruin were jumbled about in the undergrowth making it more of a scramble than a walk.

As Guy leant his way around one tall mound he became aware of movement on the far side. He stopped and drew his hand up carefully to his revolver, every sense at full stretch. Whatever it was moved again – stealthy sounds – a man, he felt certain. A jungle animal would not make little pausing noises; it would remain still or move away quickly. Heighurst was going ahead some distance to his right; he looked round on the other side and saw the sergeant staring at him. He waved his left arm in a wide circling motion; the man nodded and started off cautiously that way. He listened. There was no sound from behind the mound. Whoever or whatever it was remained absolutely still.

He gave the sergeant a few moments to make his way to the left, then crouched and slowly eased himself around the dark, laurel-like leaves and stems near the base of the mound. Two men, from their dress evidently bluejackets, were crouched nervously back to back against matted vegetation with rifles at the ready. In the instant he made them out something gave way under his right foot and both turned quickly, bringing their rifles round. He stayed quite still.

The nearer of the two was a young lad with dark shadows under his eyes which were a curious mottled green colour beneath high brows giving him a wild look; his lips were parted, his cheeks and jawline cadaverous. He stared for a moment, apparently astonished at the sight of Guy, his gun barrel waving dangerously; then he said in a hoarse whisper, 'Where you from?'

Guy let his revolver drop to the soft ground and rose carefully before replying. 'I might ask the same of you.'

The other man was also young with a square face, thick-necked, his hair cropped close. He appeared to look to his companion for a lead as they both stared uncertainly. Guy caught sight of a movement to their right, and said, 'Be good enough to point those guns away.' Anxious to hold their attention as he saw the sergeant moving slowly out from cover, he went on, 'What are you doing out after sunset? Why aren't you with the rest of your division? Where are – '

The sergeant's growl broke in, 'Now put them toys down – ' The point of his bayonet touched the bull-necked one beneath the ear and, as the cadaverous youth swung on him, Guy threw himself to the ground, picking up his revolver and rolling away in one motion. The acrobatics were unnecessary. The two remained motionless after their first violent reaction, gazing up into the sergeant's face, apparently paralyzed, their knuckles white around their guns.

The sergeant jerked his bayonet and the bull-necked lad gave a little yelp.

The blue eyes glistened. 'Didn't you 'ear me? I said put 'em down *them guns*!' he barked, as they continued gazing up at him.

They lowered their rifles suddenly and let them fall at their feet.

The sergeant stepped back. 'Now – *git up*!'

They rose silently.

Guy saw Heighurst crouching some distance away to the right, watching with his revolver pointed, and just beyond him one of the marines, his gun at the ready. He stepped up to the two men and kicked their rifles away. 'Now perhaps you'll answer – where are the rest of your party?'

The two turned. He realized they were terrified; the cadaverous one's jaw hung, quivering; the eyes which had seemed wild at first were indeed wide and staring, and his face had drained of blood, giving him an unhealthy, drawn look; two high spots burned on his cheeks. He shook his head, trying to say something, but only managed to jabber unintelligibly.

The sergeant jabbed the bayonet between his shoulder blades, and he collapsed with a shrill cry and lay on the ground, staring up.

Guy looked down at him, startled. 'That's enough, Sarn't,' he said and jerked his pistol as an indication to the man to get up. He beckoned to Heighurst, and waited while all the party assembled again, joined by Neera and the decoy group coming up behind. 'We have our birds! Time we retired.'

Heighurst looked at them. 'Names?'

'Long, sir,' the cadaverous one replied.

'Dickins, sir,' the other one said quickly after him.

'Ship?'

'*Curlew*, sir.'

'At last!' The marine's eyes glinted, and he looked round at Guy. 'I look forward to this!'

They started back, cutting away to the left to regain the path they had left, the prisoners hurrying and stumbling before the marines' bayonets as the dusk closed in. Mosquitoes and winged tormenters of every description swarmed about them, attacking arms, faces and necks; the mud with which they had plastered themselves became spotted with blood as they slapped at them, swearing softly. It would be an uncomfortable night without even a fire for fear of giving themselves away.

By the time they judged themselves out of earshot of any sentries at the foot of the rock, it was quite dark. They halted by a stream and bathed their faces and necks, then separated the Curlews, sending Dickins away with the sergeant and Basset while they interrogated Long on his own.

The youth's voice was unsteady as he answered Guy's preliminary questions: his home was near Chichester, he was an ordinary seaman in the fo'c's'le division, his divisional officer had been Lieutenant Hardwicke, but now he didn't think he had one –

'You don't *think* so?'

'No, sir.'

'What has become of Lieutenant Hardwicke?'

Long looked from Guy to Heighurst and back, his lips slightly open, dark against the pale hollows of his face, his eyes wide still under their curiously high brows. 'I dunno, sir.'

'Has he left the ship?'

'He's dead, sir.' The youth's glance moved quickly from one to the other again, then the words started tumbling out, 'We was told 'e'd gorn a-swimmin', sir, in the night. There was a line, sir, with a bight 'angin' from the chains – in the water, sir, that's all. We all knew 'e wouldn' a done nothin' so daft, not 'ardo, not Lieutenant 'ardwicke, sir – '

'How long ago was this?'

Long paused, evidently thinking.

'It doesn't matter now. What were you and Dickins doing

out there on your own?'

'Runnin', sir.'

'Running away?'

Long nodded 'E's my raggie, sir – Dick is. We were on freedom duty, sir.'

'Freedom duty?'

Long seemed to shiver and drew in an unsteady breath. 'To make them niggers work, sir. If they work – them as works best, they let their wives and chil'ren go free. They'll be let go free theirselves when the works done – that's what they *say* – '

'Who's the "they" you keep mentioning?'

'The commi'ee, sir – the jaundy commi'ee.'

'Committee!' Heighurst exclaimed. 'The master-at-arms has a *committee*!'

'The commi'ee runs the ship, sir.'

'What's become of Commander Vaneyke and the first lieutenant?'

'The Old Man, 'e's not with us no more – well, 'e's *with* us, but 'e ain't in a manner of speakin' – 'e spends most of all 'is time in Nibbanar. When 'e comes back 'e's a right gen'leman as ever 'e was. Me and Dick, we go aft for a yarn with 'im an' 'e tells us where 'e's a-goin' to next time or where 'e's a-come back from – a right palmy 'ole an' all.'

'And the first lieutenant?' Guy cut in.

'Lieutenant Brewer, sir – ' Long shrugged. 'We don't pay 'im much 'eed.'

'Where is he?'

''e's *'ere* all right, but 'e ain't. If you know my meanin'.'

'We don't. Best start from the beginning, Long.'

'Beginin', sir?' The lad looked uncomprehending.

'The first time the "cat" was used, then,' Heighurst prompted.

'Oh, that, sir, I'll not forget it. It were the fust time I seen a man flogged; it were the fust time mos' of us seen it I reckon. Dusty it were – down on the mess-deck, for'ard. It were diff'ren' then; the Old Man – well we didn' see 'm 'cept on Sundays, but we knew 'e were there, an' Lieutenant Brewer, 'e were the jimmy all right, a proper – ' He hesitated, ''e 'ad the ship on a split yarn, sir; in them days, you dursn't look twice at the stropper – that's what we called 'im – 'e wasn't never pleased with nothing, not unless 'e seen a boy gittin' a canin' –

we reckoned 'e liked that. With Dusty it were diff'ren' – a big feller, Dusty, 'e started arguin' wi' the stropper – well, this were after the blacklist were done away with.'

'Done away with? Altogether?'

'It were in the nature of a trial run, that's what the Old Man says when 'e comes out an' tells us. ' "A trial run," 'e says, "you're all reasonable men," 'e says, "an' I've decided it's 'igh time we gave reason a chance. These 'ere punishments," 'e says, "number ten an' suchlike, they're all right for boys as don't know what's what an' what's right an' what's wrong, but," 'e says, "now you, 'awkins there, if you swear at your orficer," 'e says, "is that right or wrong?" "Wrong, sir!" says 'awkins smartish. "Very good, my man," 'e says, "you're quite right." 'e 'ad a way of jokin', sir, the Old Man, leastways 'e used to. "So," 'e says, "you all of you know what's right and what's wrong an,' if any of you don't know, you jus' come aft an' 'ave a yarn wi' me. Now," 'e says, "their lordships in their wisdom 've scrapped floggin' and suchlike, but I'm a-goin' to take it to its logical occasion," 'e says, "I'm scrappin' *all* punishments. For a week for starters," 'e says, an' 'e stares at the jaundy as 'e says that, "I'm a-scrappin' all punishments for a week, an' we'll give reason a chance. If any of you fellas fancies the MAA or the bo'sun's mates are unreasonable in what they expect, don' you swear at 'em, *reason* with 'em, give it a fair ol' run," 'e says, "and Lieutenant Brewer will settle any arguments if reason don't an', if *'e* can't, you bring it along to me." 'e 'ad a great sign painted and stuck up on the bridge rail, "You are all reasoning men" – the word "Reasoning" tricked out all in gold leaf – that were afore the eightfold path, sir.'

'Lord bless us!' Heighurst said.

'Well – that's what we said, sir, in a manner of speakin'. We didn' know 'ow to carry on, not that first day – it were very quiet, and the jaundy and crusher was very quiet an' mos' of us kep' our 'eads down – it were even quiet after grog – unna'ural quiet like at a vicar's par'y, sir – '

'Go on.'

'Well, sir – next thing, we find the jaundy's givin' us what 'e calls "pos'poned number ten A", pos'poned stoppage of leave an' suchlike, an' Dusty says 'e'll go an' see the jimmy, 'e'll reason wi' the stropper 'cause it's clean agin what the Old Man said – we all thought the world of the Old Man in them days, sir, despite we didn' see 'm 'ardly at all, 'ceptin' Sundays. Well, ol' Dusty goes along to see the stropper an' gets a right ol' bottle from 'im, an' next day Nobby Clarke's workin' overside – we're at anchor off Hormuz – an' 'e 'ears the stropper and the jaundy together, an' the stropper's sayin', "This 'ere can't go on like this," and the jaundy's a-sayin', "No, sir, that it can't, sir, three bags full," an' such like, an' the stropper says, "These 'ere crossin' sweepers 'aven't as much reason in their 'eads as I 'ave in my arse," and the jaundy says, "They 'aven't that much sir." "'Ow do 'e know?" Nobby says. "Leastways, we'll 'ave an example," says the stropper, "sommat to make 'em see reason," 'e says. "'Ow about Dusty? I'd fancy a-fixin' 'im good an' proper." 'e says it all gen'lemanlike an' proper, but that's what it comes down to. Well, a couple a days after this Dusty's 'avin' a caulk on a tarpaulin on the fo'c's'le an' 'e don't 'ear the pipe – out to the world 'e is – an' one of the corps sees 'im an' picks up the corner of the tarpaulin an' yanks it out from under. Ol' Dusty gets straight up off the deck a-rubbing 'is eyes an' lands the corp one right on the nose. Well, after what Nobby tol' us about what 'e'd 'eard –! Sure enough, after tea there's the pipe, "All 'ands to the fo'ard mess-deck!" We stayed up on the foc's'le in the Gulf an', when we gets down, the jaundy's there a-tellin' us it's "'ands to witness punishment," an' the corps 're draggin' Dusty out an' lashin' 'm to a stanchion – ' Long's voice faltered and his eyes seemed to waver somewhere out beyond them in the darkness.

'The stropper's there with a kind of look in 'is eyes,' he went on slowly, 'an' 'is lips all wet and pink, jus' starin' at Dusty as they puts the gag in 'is mouth. Then, "Lay it on, my man!" 'e says, "Lay it on my man!"' He shivered and the words dried up altogether.

'How many did they give him?' Heighurst asked grimly.

'It were four dozen, sir. To start with. Then the stropper goes up to 'im while 'e's still lashed up an' pulls the gag out an' says, "I trust that'll learn you reason, my man!" and Dusty turns 'is 'ead all slow-like as if 'e's pushin' a weight roun', an' 'e looks at the stropper for a minute, an' then 'e jus' spits in 'is eye - leastways 'e tries to spit in 'is eye, but it plops out an' lands in the blood on 'is own shoulder. The stropper belts 'im across the face with 'is gloves, an' calls out, "Give 'im another two dozen!" an' when the crusher come up to put the gag in 'is mouth agin, 'e says, "That'll not be necessary, Tomkins, I want to 'ear 'im!" Oh Christ, sir! 'e didn' 'ear 'im, so 'e says, "Give 'im another two dozen, I will 'ear 'im.' Then 'ardwicke come out – 'ardo we called 'im, the mos' popular orficer in the ship, 'e were, an' a smart 'and too. 'e says to the stropper, "The surgeon wishes to see the prisoner." Well, the surgeon's a good way away from 'ardo, sir, so we knows that's a proper lie, an' so does the stropper, but it makes 'im stop an' think, an' 'e says, "Cut 'im down!" and marches straight off, an' 'ardo jus' stands there as white as a ghost, an' then 'e goes too, an' the other orficers after 'im like a funeral parade.'

'Did Commander Vaneyke know about this?'

'Oh, no, sir, that's why they 'as it down on the mess-deck, no, if 'e'd ever known, sir – '

'Why did someone not inform him?'

Long gave a short, mirthless laugh. 'The jaundy tol' us what 'ld 'appen to the fust man to let out a word. "Dusty's an example," 'e says. "The jimmy wants to give you an example so's you won't fancy reason 'as any place on the mess decks. From 'ere on you'll forget that word's in the dictionary", 'e says. "An' any man what goes to the Old Man about it, 'e'll find 'isself triced up to that there same stanchion as Dusty." There was lines of blood on the stanchion, sir, an' spots of it on the deck.'

'What about the officers?'

'We reckon 'ardo tried to tell the Old Man. 'e tol' a frien' of 'is when we meets our chummy ship in Muscat – but it weren't long after 'e went for 'is swim.'

'And the others?'

'The pilot, we reckoned 'e were properly scared, leastways 'e used to attend punishment parade afterwards wi' the stropper.'

'There were other floggings?'

Long nodded lifelessly and, half turning, started pulling up his jumper at the back. They saw dark weals against the flesh.

'It's proper 'ell, sir – it's the only way I can put it. The wust of it is, sir, you can't tell 'oo your mates are, an' 'oo'll go straight to the jaundy or the commi'ee – that's 'ow I got mine, I were a-goin' jump off afore – but someone told 'em.'

'When did the committee come into being?'

'It didn' take the jaundy an' 'is long to fathom out they 'ad the stropper by 'is knockers, if you'll pardon the expression, sir – illegal punishments an' such-like – they 'ad 'im just where they wanted 'im, over a barrel, an' they didn' like 'im any more'n what we did. The other orficers seen it too, an' it didn' take us long to catch on they seen it. I reckon the stropper were the last one in the ship. Then when 'e seen it 'e jus' crumples up. Like an empty bag.'

'And the committee?'

'At fust it weren't a commi'ee, it were the jaundy an' the chief buffer – leastways that's what we thought – an' them two seemed in mortal fear of the Old Man findin' out what was a-goin' on, an' there was punishment parades mos' every day – some of us wanted to tell 'im you see.'

'But you didn't?'

'Well – I dunno, sir. One or two – well, it come to it you couldn' 'ardly b'lieve anyone 'cause you knew they were a-thinkin' you might go straight to the jaundy or one of 'is, if you foller me.'

'We follow you very well,' Guy said angrily.

'Then we caught on there's this commi'ee, a secret commi'ee, an' the jaundy don' do nothin' without 'e ask the commi'ee fust – that's what I 'eard an' I b'lieved it too. Them that didn't toe the line – well, we didn' see 'em no more.'

'What d'you mean?'

'They went, sir.'

'Disappeared?'

'Yes, sir. Dusty went, sir, an' the chief buffer, 'e disappeared, so then we knew there must be a commi'ee.'

'And Commander Vaneyke had no notion of what was taking place?'

'Well, sir, all this 'appened about the time 'e started a-goin' up to Nibbanar. Well, as I learned it from 'im, from the Old Man 'isself, sir, when we used to go aft to see 'im – that was after all this I'm a-tellin' you of now, sir – 'e fust started to run the ship by reason when 'e come to b'lieve in the Buddha. 'e couldn' be a proper Buddhist an' oppress 'is fellow man, that's what 'e says, an' 'e asks me what I thinks of it, an' 'ow I thinks it's goin', an' weren' the discipline jus' as tight, but we was never allowed in there by ourselves, sir, an' we never knows 'oo might be lis'enin' an' goin to the commi'ee straight after.'

'So you didn't tell him?'

'Well, sir, *I* didn' – but I dunno – '

'What?'

Before Long could answer they heard sounds of a struggle, grunts and muffled oaths from the direction towards the rock where they had posted the lookout. They pulled out their revolvers and, while Guy pointed his at Long, and waved him down, Heighurst disappeared into the trees towards the sounds. They heard stealthy noises as other marines also made towards the struggle.

They lay waiting in silence.

Presently the crashing and grunting ceased and Guy heard them coming back. He looked up.

Heighurst was leading. 'It's the mighty hunter,' he said.

Behind him, in the glow of the moon just risen, his arms pinioned by Evan and Basset, Guy recognized the lean, immaculately tailored figure of Lord ffort. He slid his revolver back into the holster and rose, smiling.

'What the devil's the meanin' of this?' ffort said, trying to shake himself free.

Heighurst nodded to Basset and the two released their grip. Lord ffort moved his arm round slowly in an exploratory way.

'Whose head are you after this evening, sir?' Guy asked pleasantly.

'It's that cursed woman,' ffort said, rounding on him. 'I've lorst her. Then your blasted bears jumped me!'

Guy's brows rose.

'Harriet!' ffort said, his brows arching in annoyance.

'What's she doing here?' Guy snapped.

'Ain't that rather obvious?'

Guy stared at him.

ffort shrugged. 'It's my own damnable fault. For heaven's sake!'

'Sigiriya?'

'She thought we might induce Robbie down. At least that's what she told me.' He paused and said simply, 'She's given me the slip.'

'How long ago?'

'Before sunset.'

'If she means to see Vaneyke – ' Guy left the sentence unfinished.

ffort nodded. 'I fear she's up there by now.'

Guy looked at Heighurst, then at Long, who had stood when he rose. 'Where are the guards posted?'

'There's two sentries at the bottom of the steps, sir, an' the guard with one of the Nordenfelts on what we calls the crosstrees, sir, below the upper steps – we call 'em the t'gallants an' royals.'

'How many in the guard?'

Long thought for a moment. 'Eight I reckon, sir, eight or nine – all turkeys, sir,' he looked at Heighurst, 'a-beggin' your pardon, sir.'

Heighurst looked at Guy. 'You're mad.'

'I shall take Long and Dickins,' Guy said, returning the look.

'No, sir' There was a hysterical note to Long's voice, and he clutched at Guy's sleeve.

Guy jerked his arm away. 'If you wish to earn a pardon, you'll be wise to come.'

'Is that fair?' Neera started. Guy had not heard him come up.

'Of course it ain't,' Heighurst said, 'it ain't sense either. How d'you propose gettin' her down again once we get inside – if we do get in alive?'

'I said nothing about "we".'

Heighurst laughed. 'Don Quixote!'

'She has that effect,' Lord ffort said ruefully, and looked at Guy. 'He's right.'

'What do *you* suggest?' Guy asked.

'That' – ffort rubbed his chin – 'is a question to which at present I see no answer. Perhaps if we address ourselves to it in the mornin' –

'The morning?' Guy heard his voice unnaturally loud.

They gazed at him. He had to take a grip on his nerves; all he could think of was Harriet mounting the steps, assisted by one of the sentries, taken to the corporal of the guard, by the corporal to the committee – and Vaneyke way above it all, cut off from everything, and the officers, whoever was left now, powerless.

He knew he had to get to her whether or not it made sense to Heighurst and Lord ffort.

'Best to wait, sir,' Long was saying, 'they'll send 'er down mos' likely with a freedom par'y, sir.'

Guy swung on him.

'A freedom par'y, sir, tomorrow evenin'. I'll show you where they takes 'em – '

'Take them?'

Long's eyes were wide and pale in the moonlight. 'They takes 'em to the tank – for the crocodiles, sir.'

There was absolute silence as they stared at the youth, who stood with his lips trembling half open.'

'Dick'll tell you, sir,' he added shakily.

Guy turned to Heighurst. 'I fancy that clinches it.'

Heighurst returned the glance; Guy saw from his expression that he had accepted it.

'I shall go alone,' he said and, pulling out his revolver, handed it to the marine, 'unarmed.'

Basset stepped forward without expression. 'Volunteer, sir.'

Guy was startled for a moment before he replied, 'Thank you, no, Basset. I'm most grateful. But it's not guns or numbers we'll need on this occasion.'

Heighurst grinned suddenly as he took the revolver. 'Damn cheek, that's all. We'll wait for you – with the muggers.'

'It ain't the jaundy, sir,' Long said urgently, ' 'e's as scared as anyone. It's the commi'ee.'

'And who is in charge of the committee?'

'I dunno, sir.'

14

'Ahoy there!' Guy shouted some time before he estimated he was near the steps; he wished to leave the sentries in no doubt that he was not hostile. Bluff was the only tactic. There was no reply. He began to wonder if he were going in the right direction. The moon was bright now, where it found a way in through the leaves above, but everything looked different. The ruins of the wall they had negotiated earlier seemed as thick as a house with huge roots twisting out; they shone in a patch of clear, blue-white light. The thorns of a creeper that he had failed to notice seized the flesh down his cheek in a painful grip. He stopped and eased them away, and ducked around.

It was surely somewhere here that he had come upon Long and Dickins. He clambered over mounds in the way of a part of the wall that had fallen, and started pushing his way through bushes and softer, fernlike leaves that rose waist- and sometimes shoulder-high over tumbled stones. The branches above thinned away, but it remained dark ahead; he realized he was climbing towards the base of a rock face. Away to the right he saw the night and the stars, and below a white and black fairyland of delicate ferns and taller bushes with glistening leaves.

He stopped and yelled, 'Ahoy there! Curlews!'

His voice bounced back from the cliff ahead, and several birds answered him, sounding remarkably like rooks at home in the spring.

He was about to push on when a sharp voice came from the right, ''Oo's there?'

His pulse raced; the man was close. 'Lieutenant Greville – to see Commander Vaneyke.'

There was silence. He remained motionless, trying to make out vague features he could discern in the wall of darkness ahead.

''Oo's with yer?'

'I'm alone.'

'Come on by yersel'!'

He made his way towards the sound.

After a while he was able to make out the dark shape of a gully in the cliff face and, remembering his daylight view of the steps, guessed that he had reached them. He half turned to head that way.

'Mr Greville, sir –' a whisper came from close behind. He swung round and found a bluejacket with a rifle pointing at his chest. 'Farrow, sir – d'yer remember, sir?'

Of course he remembered that square face and huge black beard; he searched for associations – 'Whaley!'

The face lit delightedly. 'We took the shine off Lieutenant Collard – on the field guns, sir.'

Guy grinned. 'I don't believe there was a smarter team.'

'There weren't, sir –' Farrow looked towards the gully; his eyes were unnaturally sunk and dark. 'Don't you come up, sir, they'll do for yer like they done for our orficers. Run, sir, tell the Admiral we're jus' a-waitin' for 'im – we can't do nothin' without 'elp. Go, sir, quick! I'll wait a tick an' fire in the air.'

'Has a lady gone aboard Farrow?'

'Gawd help us – Commander's wife, sir.'

'Then I'm afraid I shall have to go up.'

The man jerked his rifle towards him in his anxiety. 'You *can't*, sir, you can't do nothin', not by yersel', sir, git *'elp*!' The whisper rose in pitch, 'I can't stand 'ere yarnin', sir, you must go for the Admiral, 'e must 'elp us!'

'Who's "us"?'

'There's a few I knows of, and a lot more, but they dursn't say nothin'.'

'The Admiral's on his way, Farrow. Now, if you will take me up!'

The man stood, undecided, when they heard a shout.

'Comin' corp!' Farrow replied, and, looking at Guy, 'Don't give me none o' that lip!' Then he whispered, '*Run*, sir!'

'Thank you Farrow,' Guy smiled. He started walking towards the gully where the shout had come from, hearing the bluejacket follow.

'What kep' yer?' A corporal of marines with bayonet fixed stared suspiciously at Farrow after eyeing Guy's empty revolver holster.

'We were at Whaley together,' Guy said easily. 'Now, if

you'd be good enough to put up that rifle, corporal, I'd like to see the commander.'

The man stiffened at his tone, and seemed about to say something; instead he jerked his head at Farrow, 'Take 'im up!'

Guy continued to look at him. 'Name?'

The man's eyes dropped for a moment, and he hesitated, conflicting habits of discipline seeming to battle within before he said, 'Farrow'll take you up,' he added grudgingly, 'sir.'

'And I shall make certain you lose your rating,' Guy said quietly.

The steps built in the gully were worn and broken in places, and it was necessary to climb cautiously; an assault party would be decimated he thought, before they were halfway up.

At the top was an area of rising ground impinging on another steep climb; it was strewn with boulders, around which rose a profusion of ferns and bushes, even trees, some clinging to the tops of seemingly bare rock, thrusting a network of roots down the sides to find the earth below. Farrow led him silently along a path through the foliage to another set of steps, more broken and rubble-strewn than the first. A rope had been fixed from somewhere above, however, and with its aid he scrambled up, Farrow close behind, and eventually reached a small platform where he was able to turn and survey the tops of the trees and a broad expanse of lake shining below. He felt a chill as he thought of Long's 'freedom party'. Neera was right: there was a sense of unease about this rock brooding above the forest; he imagined the tormented King Kaasyapa gazing down year after year for a sight of his brother's arrival and, when Moggalana came, recognizing his own conscience.

'This way, sir,' Farrow said.

He followed the bluejacket into a horizontal gallery apparently constructed out of the face of the rock, with a wall high above their heads along the outer side. As at Pollanarua, he was struck by the sheer skill of the ancient builders. In places the wall had broken and there was little to prevent them falling into the darkness below, in others even the floor of the gallery had crumbled away; here the gaps were spanned with flimsy bamboo ladders which swung alarmingly as they stepped across them. Bats swooped, disappearing and emerging from impenetrable blackness in the cliff above.

Eventually the gallery ceased, in its place an iron bridge, evidently constructed by Harding's men; the supports were driven into the sheer face. They leant their way along to the end of the west cliff, where broken ground, covered with shrubs, rose up the north side to what appeared to be a brow or small plateau about halfway to the summit.

Farrow glanced back at him and pointed up, 'The crosstrees, sir. I 'ave to leave you at the guard'ouse.'

'Is this where you left Mrs Vaneyke?' Guy asked as they started scrambling up.

'Yes, sir.'

'D'you know where she went after?'

'No, sir.'

Some half a dozen marines were waiting, staring at them as they reached the brow; they were in darkness for the vast, overhanging upper section of the rock reared above, shutting out the light from the moon. To their right, among the tumbled debris Guy had become accustomed to at the base of a cliff, he made out the shape of a hut, no doubt the guardhouse, with faint glimmers of light showing through gaps in the structure. He saw the harder lines of a Nordenfelt gun mounted before it. Beyond, a group of men were working at what looked like the framework of a second hut.

Someone stepped forward; he wore officer's uniform.

'Lieutenant Greville, sir,' Farrow said, saluting, 'To see the commander.'

The officer stood looking at Guy. 'You'll be fortunate!' It was intended as an exaggerated quarter-deck voice; he turned to the men behind for approval. They growled.

'Where 're you from?' he went on, reverting to what was evidently his usual accent.

Guy thought of Dickinson's description of Lieutenant Brown; this brute fitted it perfectly. 'HMS *Dulcinea* at Trincomalee,' he replied crisply.

' 'avin' a dekko 'ow you can all git up 'ere, that's your game! I dessay you seen 'ow easy it is?' He laughed.

'My business is with Commander Vaneyke.'

The officer stepped closer and thrust a shoulder forward so that Guy could see the epaulette.

'In't that good enough?'

Guy gazed at him in silence. The eyes moved quickly away,

then as quickly looked up again. 'Come from the Admiral! 'aven't seen enough yet 'ave you?' He jerked his head towards the rock towering above. 'Commander's up top. Want to see what it's like up there?' His teeth showed for an instant. 'Providin' you don't fall outta the futtocks you cin git back an' tell the Admiral jus' 'ow easy it is!' He laughed. He had a wide, flat face with a straggling, light-coloured beard and whiskers; his eyes moved as he talked, never quite holding Guy's for more than an instant. 'We cin show you sommat else afore you go,' the eyes shifted up craftily before sliding away again, 'but then, mebbe you knows about 'er?'

'Her?'

''*er* – Mrs Vaneyke 'erself.' He laughed again.

'I don't believe it.'

The first lieutenant turned away to bring the others into the joke. 'Don't believe it!' They chuckled.

'Mrs Vaneyke is in Bombay,' Guy said crisply.

'She's like 'er ol' man then,' he turned again, 'in two places at once.'

The men roared dutifully.

The lieutenant swung back, 'You tell the Admiral 'e can't git up 'ere – not till every last one of us 'as slipped 'is moorin's. 'e can't starve us out – we got provisions. If 'e tries to starve us, 'e'll starve 'er fust – *an'* all of them niggers.' He laughed, and the crafty look came over his face again. 'We'll let 'er go when we gits a pardon. Signed by 'er Majesty – mind, we in't done nothin' – it's *'im* as brought us 'ere.' He nodded up towards the summit of the rock towering above.

'You won't need a pardon in that case.'

'Ah, but you officers –' he stopped abruptly, realizing his mistake. 'Come on!' he said roughly, and walked away past the watching group towards the hut. Guy followed.

It was a makeshift affair in the shape of a long tent, open at both ends and thatched in the native fashion almost to the ground. Inside was a crude table with a single candle on it providing the only illumination, and two benches either side fashioned roughly from split tree trunks. A man rose from the right hand bench as they appeared. Guy saw the crown of a corporal in the ship's police on his arm. From the opposite side of the table, he saw Harriet looking up at him.

'We do meet in the strangest places,' she said.

The light from the candle threw shadows up her cheeks, accentuating the line of her chin, and touched the steady, grey eyes with points of fire. Looking at her, he felt an unaccountable accession of optimism. Even in this dim cave, she had a quality to lift the spirit. He bowed his head. 'I do *follow* you to the strangest places!'

'It is so nice to see you.' Her eyes gave added meaning to the words.

'May I ask what you are doing here?' he said.

She flashed a glance at the lieutenant beside him. 'Apparently, Robbie is away on one of his journeys. Lieutenant Brown suggested I await his return here.'

Guy looked round. He had been right. He wondered if Brown were the leader of the committee Long had spoken of. He doubted it. He looked a strong enough brute, but he lacked edge, some quality of sharpness and decision he would expect in a man wielding such illegal power and evident terror.

Brown was nodding in the direction of the rock face above. 'You wouldn' want to go a-climbin', not in the dark, mum.' His tone was strangely respectful.

She flashed him a smile. 'Of course not,' and turned again to Guy. 'But really! Do you not think we might try it together? I am so *tired* of sitting.'

Guy looked at Brown again, wondering how he would react; it seemed from Harriet's attitude that she was not aware she was a prisoner. Brown was looking at the corporal standing opposite her; studying the corporal's face for the first time, Guy saw dark eyes set very close, a long, slightly curving nose overhanging a tight upper lip, a bulging jaw seemingly wider than the face above; with the hard line of the mouth it gave an impression of implacable will; it was a disturbing face – one would expect no charity there. Seeing Brown eyeing the man a suspicion began to form – why could he not make up his own mind?

As Brown's glance slid back to Harriet for an instant, and as quickly dropped away to the table, they heard a disturbance outside – whistles and shouted comments, followed by laughter, and shortly afterwards a figure appeared in the entrance behind them; it came straight in, bumping Brown on the way, but scarcely seeming to notice, a heavy man puffing with effort; long straggly hair and an unkempt beard hid much of his face, but what could be seen in the candlelight was not pleasant; the eyes were almost lost in puffy folds of flesh. He wore what was evidently a sari, draped somewhat in the manner of a Roman toga, leaving one gross white shoulder bare; on the other, pinned to the sari, was a lieutenant's epaulette.

Extraordinary as the figure appeared, Brown and the corporal registered little interest and no surprise.

The man went straight to Harriet and holding out a thick hand said, 'Mrs Vaneyke, I'm delighted you could come.' The voice was soft and unmistakeably that of a gentleman. 'My apologies for taking so long. It's not their fault, they never know where I'm to be found.' He laughed, a high-pitched neighing sound. His lips, visible for a moment from behind the unkempt beard, shone pink and wet.

Seeing them, Guy was reminded suddenly of Brewer; he stared, wondering and horrified.

Harriet was looking up with a puzzled expression; she had not taken the outstretched hand, which the man let drop, faltering to his side.

'Lieutenant Brewer, mum,' Brown said flatly.

Her eyes opened wider. 'I'm sorry, I didn't recognize you, Brewer, with your beard.'

Brewer neighed again. 'They never know where to find me.' He leant closer. 'There's so much to do. I'm the only one left.' He looked at Brown, then back again to Harriet and started laughing showing her the shoulder with the epaulette and patting it with his hand. He stopped abruptly and straightened, turning towards Guy, 'You have brought the mail!'

Guy thought he saw a start of recognition as the small eyes met his, then the expression became blank. He thrust out his hand. 'Greville, sir, you may remember – in the old *Colossus*?'

'*Colossus*?' Brewer moved his head slowly to the side, his gaze holding Guy's suspiciously.

Brown gave a short laugh. 'Can't remember what 'appened yesterday!'

Brewer turned on him, his brows drawing down and his lips working as though he were trying to say something but couldn't find the words, when they heard from a long way off the sound of a man's voice; it was small but distinct in the still night. After a moment it became apparent that he was singing, and with a thrill of recognition Guy realized it was Evan. The words were indistinguishable at this distance, but he knew the tune, 'Lead kindly light . . .' It was coming from somewhere way below at the base of the rock. He wondered whether Neera or Heighurst had thought of it – or Evan himself. It was like a hand stretched up to them.

Another voice took up the strain, but this one was from *above*; he remembered Neera's flock.

'Lead thou me on . . .'

Brown had turned with a startled expression. More voices joined in from above until Evan's beautiful but distant tenor was lost in a swelling chorus from the summit.

'. . . the night is dark, and I am far from home. . . .'

'The niggers!' the corporal exclaimed. He had moved towards the door, and Guy had an impression of his eyes like burning needles as he turned his head briefly to look at Brown. The earlier suspicion crystallized. This was the kannapaddi – this blazing, tight-lipped corporal whom Brown had looked at when Harriet had suggested climbing to the summit was the real leader of the secret committee; as he stared into the close eyes, he felt the force and intellect and some wild, uncontrollable quality there; he was certain he was right.

He joined in the hymn, 'Lead thou me on. . . .'

'Stow it!' the corporal hissed, turning and taking a step towards him, as though about to strike, but Brown's bulky figure was in the way.

Harriet's voice, high and clear, joined in from his left, 'Keep thou my feet. . . .' and from outside the hut from the direction of the group of working men, first one, then several other voices took up the strain until the night seemed to fill far and near with male voices, Harriet's soprano sweet and high over them. Guy's nerves tingled; the sheer unexpectedness and defiance of the singing plucked at his deepest chords.

The corporal swung on Brown, his quick anger equally quickly controlled. 'Best to stop 'em, sir.' His voice was low and hoarse. He nodded towards Guy and Harriet. 'I'll see to them.'

Brown looked round for an instant, then blundered out, and Guy heard him shouting as the corporal, who had backed away and reached for a rifle against the side of the hut, brought the barrel up to point at Guy's midriff.

Brewer started laughing, and leant over the table towards

Harriet, pointing at Guy, 'They don't last long –'

She had stopped singing and was staring at the corporal in astonishment.

' – not in uniform,' Brewer continued, his mouth hanging open loosely.

A shot sounded from somewhere high above them, and the hymn gave way to confused sounds of shouting. The corporal's attention was momentarily diverted; Guy estimated the distance for a standing leap at the rifle, but discarded the idea, and the next instant the man was staring at him again, his lips stretched and the corners turned down in an attempted smile, as if he had guessed what had been in his mind. 'I'd be careful if I was you *sir*.' He nodded at Brewer. ''e's right – for once.'

Harriet was staring up. 'What is this idiot doing, Guy?'

The corporal's expression sharpened and the smile disappeared. 'You two knows each uvver!'

Harriet stood abruptly. 'This is intolerable.'

The rifle swung towards her. 'Sit down, lady!'

Brewer started neighing again, and slumped on the bench, his elbows wide on the table, staring up at her with a peculiar gleam in the small eyes, apparently still helpless with mirth. She shot him a glance of the most withering scorn before turning again to Guy. 'Does he know what he's doing?' She nodded towards the corporal.

Guy looked at the man. 'I fancy he does.' He held the gaze, seeing hatred mixed with curiosity, knowing he had to feed the curiosity, 'He is afraid.'

The thin lips twisted down again.

Guy looked round at her. 'You're from the real world – something the men up there haven't been allowed to see for some time. He looked back at the corporal, continuing to address her. 'He was afraid of the effect you'd have once you got up there amongst them, but now it's too late for him – the hymn has done it instead. Listen – they're rebelling against the tyranny of the committee –'

'The committee?' she said.

'We should have told you – when Brewer proved unequal to the command –' glancing down at Brewer, he thought he detected a brief flash of intelligence, but the eyes dulled almost immediately and the man started his neighing laugh again.

'Do be quiet!' she flashed.

'The ship passed into the hands of a committee,' he went on, gazing at the corporal. 'The committee imposed itself with flogging and every imaginable device of barbarism including murder – not one but several.' He heard her breath drawn in. 'All the officers were killed – with the exception of our chum here,' he nodded at Brewer, still shaking with mirth, 'and the ship's company sank beneath this bestial tyranny. Now, they're breaking loose.' He stared at the corporal. 'Heaven help the committee!'

The man's eyes were dark with passion. 'So we taken lessons from the orficers – so *you* don't 'ev to flog men no more – you got us – ship's police,' he waved the rifle ominously, 'we're your kep' dogs. We sets under your table a-keepin' the other dogs in their proper place so's they won't chaw your legs off of you. So you c'n 'ev it you don't know 'ow we carries on – so you c'n set up aft wi' your white linen 'n' your china dishes 'n' your fancy lip-o –' He took a step towards Guy, his hand on the rifle quivering. ''n' don't fency we didn' see the stropper,' he nodded towards Brewer, now quiet but observing with eager expectancy, 'watchin' 'em a-git their stripy, dribblin' down 'is fet chops, 'ands all of a twitch – 'e liked it, oh, 'e couldn' 'ev enough of it, not 'im – but it's *our* tails they chawed off after, *ours* not 'is.'

Brewer started laughing again. The corporal swung the butt of the rifle at his face, catching him on the upper arm as he raised it involuntarily to protect himself. He was knocked half across the table, and the bench he was sitting on flew from under his legs. He raised both arms to ward off another blow, uttering little moaning grunts.

The suddenness and savagery of the demonstration left Guy momentarily shocked. Harriet had her hand to her mouth, looking down at Brewer as he started jerking and sliding himself away towards the far end of the table.

The corporal lost interest in him immediately. He stared at Guy again, his thin lips twisting downwards. Guy had a startling impression that his finger was within an ace of the hairbreadth increase in pressure necessary to fire the rifle; so vivid and frightening was the moment that his muscles braced against the impact, his pulse raced, and he felt a sick, empty sensation in his stomach.

A shot sounded from the top of the rock; he sensed the crisis had passed: the corporal's attention was divided by a renewed tumult of voices from high above. Another shot sounded. He heard steps approaching rapidly, and Brown burst into view in the entrance.

'They got guns.'

The corporal's glance was withering. He said in the low, hoarse voice he had used earlier, 'I dessay the MAA c'n look arter 'issel', sir. I reckon thet's 'is gun we 'eard – or John-o's. Best to send –'

The hut suddenly went black. Guy had caught a glimpse of Harriet's gloved hand over the candle the instant before, and he was already hurling himself at Brown, head towards the pit of his stomach, arms around him in a driving tackle, pulling him round on top as they fell together. He heard the corporal's rifle going off, and felt Brown jerk and utter a thin, high cry like a child. He held him as he struggled, coughing and choking for breath. From the other end of the hut he heard Harriet give a little gasp. Another explosion sounded close above, ringing in his ears as he felt Brown quiver and go limp. He slid away from the still legs towards the table to back away under it, but knocked into the bench instead. Another shot sounded and he heard the bullet plug into timber very close. He continued backing past the bench, expecting to come up against Harriet's legs – but there was no one. He heard movements from the other side of the table and guessed the corporal was following the sounds he was making. He stopped. He could hear men gathering around the entrance where Brown's body lay. Carefully he arched his back and raised himself on his arms and knees until he could feel the underside of the table; he tested the weight, then heaved up and sideways towards where he imagined the corporal to be. He heard a grunt of pain and felt something collapsing against the side of the hut and timber poles cracking. He leapt for the opening, and when outside ran towards bushes which showed black against the sky.

Diving behind the nearest, he felt the sleeve of his tunic rip, and hard stems scraped up his arm. He lay, trying to control his breathing, wondering if they had seen him. He could hear voices and movements from about the hut, but it was too dark in the shadow of the great cliff face to make out any details. From the summit the confused shouting was interspersed now by savage roars in unison, and cries of women – the native women from the Branders' plantation, he thought – it was impossible to imagine what was taking place up there.

Where was Harriet? That little gasp she had given, he had thought because of the shooting, but Brewer had been near her then, and by the time he had worked his way under the table Brewer too had gone. As he thought of Harriet and Brewer together all other considerations vanished. An image of wet, pink lips and unkempt hair filled his mind, the brutish fingers over her mouth, that absurd sari draping gross flesh. They could not be far away; they must be somewhere in these bushes – there was no other cover near. She would put up a fight; surely he must hear them. He held his breath.

A rustling and cracking of twigs sounded some way to his right, then a smothered gasp, followed by a male cry of surprise, an oath and a sudden eruption of scuffling. He rose on bent knees, his heart pounding, and scrambled and ran towards the sounds, which increased in frenzy as he neared. He heard a falsetto cry of pain, and saw something large and pale tumbling away down a slight slope until brought up in the darkness at the base of a bush. He made out an arm and the sheen of a sari from amongst the foliage, and leapt, seeing too late that Brewer was doubled up as if in agony with his knees and shins towards him. He struck bone with his right shoulder, hearing a crack, feeling searing pain and knowing it was his collar-bone – he had cracked it before playing rugger. Strangled sounds were coming from the sari, which he realized now was wrapped around Brewer's head; the man was scrabbling at it with his hands and thrashing his legs about. Guy felt a blow in his side causing him to twist, and he almost yelled with the agony in his shoulder; he heard himself gasping with the pain as he rolled away on to his left side.

'Guy –' She was bending over him, one hand on his arm. Her hair was loose, wisps of it falling over her pale face; her gown was torn and hanging loosely down one side. Behind her, he could hear shouts and the sound of men approaching.

'*Run*!' he whispered urgently.

'You're hurt!' She was leaning closer, her hair tickling his neck, her eyes were anxious.

'Go – *go* – now!' He heard the desperation in his voice, but knew it was already too late. The men were practically on them.

'Oh, my darling' – her hand moved softly, probing up his arm – 'Where?'

Footsteps crashed about them. He saw faces looking down and, just over her shoulder, where the dress had been ripped, the corporal standing staring at him. There was no mistaking the expression; this time there would be no reprieve. Had there been any doubt in his mind before, the manic light in the man's eyes would have expunged it – this was the kannapaddi. Below the long nose was a smear, dark against the pallor of his face, spreading over his lips and down his chin.

'Help me up!' he said to Harriet, giving her his good arm, and clenched his teeth against shooting agony as he hauled himself somehow to his feet. He heard movements in the undergrowth where Brewer had been lying.

The corporal's eyes shifted briefly in that direction. 'Well done, sir!' he said cynically, and his gaze returned to Guy, 'we'll 'ev to report you to the commi'ee. Sir.' The menace in the low tone left Guy with hollow limbs; his heart thumped unnaturally.

'He's hurt,' Harriet exclaimed. 'Can't you see?'

The corporal shifted his rifle and raised a hand deliberately to the mess of blood above his lip, gazing at the fingers as he brought them away. 'I am sorry – lady.'

She looked up at Guy.

He attempted a smile, feeling despair and futility closing in. What could he do for her in this condition? She looked so vulnerable with her loose hair and torn and crumpled dress.

'You *does* know each uvver!' The corporal's lips were drawn down at the corners. Suddenly he jerked his rifle. 'Move on!'

Guy looked down at her again, then started slowly back through the bushes towards the cliff face and the guard hut. She took his arm.

'Fetch the stropper!' the corporal called to one of the guard and, as Guy passed him, said softly, 'jes' a small commi'ee this time, sir – Lieutenant Brown, 'e's dead and Jaundy and John-o, they're up top. Jes' me and the stropper, sir – beggin' your pardon Lieutenant Brewer, jes' us two.' He paused. 'I dessay we'll manage some'ow!'

'You know the penalty for mutiny?' Guy said.

'Mu'ny, sir! Commander Vaneyke it were – *'e* brought us 'ere, 'im and Lieutenant Brewer.'

'Where is the Commander?'

'Didn' Lieutenant Brown tell you? 'e's payin' a call at Nibbarna. P'raps you'll meet 'im, sir – in Nibbarna.'

Guy felt Harriet's grip tighten; he started to look round at the corporal, now just behind them, but felt the pain searing through his shoulder.

'A tidy berth, sir. The skipper, 'e like it well enough – can't keep away, that's the truth.'

They were nearing the guard hut again; Guy saw two men beside the dark shape of the Nordenfelt, which had been pointed towards the cliff. The men of the working group by the framework of the second hut were standing still before the levelled rifle of one of the guard.

'There's lots a diff'ren' ways a gettin' there, sir.'

The corporal stopped as they heard a yell from above on the cliff face.

'John-o!' someone exclaimed.

'What's 'e comin darn for?'

There was another shout, this time with a drawn, despairing pitch to it, ending in a high quaver of despair. Guy thought he saw shadows of movement about a third of the way down the face, and a moment afterwards a shape detached itself from the wall of rock, taking form in the air above, sprouting arms and legs and somersaulting towards them; it landed with a horrifying crack on beaten earth and stone before Guy's feet, the skull splitting like a ripe fig; something fizzed out and plopped some distance away. He heard Harriet gasp, and felt her finger-nails biting into his arm. It had been so sudden, the man might have landed on top of them almost before they could have moved. There was not a sound from the men round about. He moved away to the side.

Another shout came from the rock face above, joined soon by others, so that it was difficult to make out what was being said; it was an angry, savage discord, repeating the same noises over and over; Guy thought he caught the words 'Brown' and 'You're next!' and 'Comin' dahn'

'Let 'em come!' the corporal said behind him, then roared up, 'come on then – Bessie's a-witin' for you!'

Another yell sounded from the summit to the right of the voices on the cliff, and they saw another figure hurtling out, dark against the light sky, turning over and over as it fell; it disappeared into the trees at the bottom of the slope below them without a sound. There was a brief pause, then a distant noise of cheering from the summit, and a shot. One of the voices from the cliff called, 'That's Jaundy – you're next Brown-o,' and the others took up the chorus, 'Brown – o – Brown – o –' exultantly.

Guy shivered. He looked down at Harriet and said with an assurance he was far from feeling, 'An interesting situation.'

She had moved closer; he could feel the curve of her hip, firm and warm against his thigh. 'Whatever are they doing?'

'Turning on the committee! They know we're here.' He nodded to the group under guard to their left. 'Word will have been passed up. When they heard Evan from below they must have been convinced of the Admiral's arrival. That's what they were waiting for – it was all they needed.' He saw the corporal coming back towards him, and felt the malevolence and will radiating from him. 'Unfortunately, the game's not over for our friend here.' He looked round painfully at the faces of the marines about them, wondering if he could detach them to his side. They were tense but their rifles were steady and they were glancing at the corporal who still held most of the cards on this halfway plateau. With the Nordenfelt he could prevent anyone coming down the cliff face, or up from below. He wondered whether he, too, thought that the force from Trinco had arrived down there.

'Pity sir' – the corporal's thin mouth was stretched in that aggressive, humourless leer – 'we seems to 'ev lost Lieutenant Brewer.'

'The committee does seem to be falling apart!'

The lips tightened. 'Don' you worry, sir. We'll manage some'ow.' His eyes moved to Harriet. 'And don' you 'ev no fears for 'er, sir. *I'll* look arter 'er.'

Guy felt her nails digging into his arm again. 'You realize the Admiral is below with a naval brigade,' he said. 'For all I know he may already be on his way up.'

'I 'ope not, sir,' the corporal nodded towards the Nordenfelt. 'Bessie wouldn' like thet!' He lowered his tone. 'No – you 'n' me 'n' 'er – we're a-goin' below to see the Admiral, leastways you'll see 'im sir, 'n' tell 'im we don't want no one follerin' 'n' shootin'.' He looked at Harriet. 'She might get 'urt else.'

Guy felt the sudden, empty sensation he had experienced at the same tone a few moments before. He made a guess, and nodded towards the marines of the guard. 'I wonder how they'll feel when they learn you intend running and leaving them to face the music.'

The corporal moved suddenly closer, dropping his rifle to his right hand, and gripping her arm with his left. 'You tell 'em that, sir' – his voice was a hoarse whisper – ''n' she's *dead*. Thet's a promise. Sir!'

Looking into the dark and wild abyss behind his eyes, Guy knew the promise would be kept, kept with relish, and his own turn would follow quickly.

The man released his grip on her arm, and drew his bayonet, swinging the point very deliberately close across her breasts as he brought it to the barrel of the rifle, and fixed it. Then he turned his head and called out sharply, 'Legs – take over the guard!' and, looking at the other men, 'me and the lieutenant 'ere, we're a-going' below to parley with the Admiral.' He brought the rifle up so that the bayonet was touching Harriet's arm, 'We'll tell 'em we got *'er* – see?'

'Corp –'

'We're dead else – all on us,' the corporal went on without pause. 'Them bastards up there, they'll want to save their necks. They'll say *we* done it all.'

Grunts of assent rose from the men.

He went on vehemently, 'We're the ones what kep' the ship's comp'ny togevver when the skipper goes aloft 'n' stropper parts 'is preventers – we're the ones what brought 'em 'ere.'

A deep chorus of agreement rose around him.

'We won't get no gra'itude. Look what they done to Jaundy and John-o. They'll say it's us as mu'nied to save theirselves.' He lowered his voice and went on seriously, 'They'll 'ev to string someone up for this li'le picnic. It won't be the skipper – they don't string up orficers, not them – it'll be us for the air walk, that's the truth – you 'n' me togevver. I say we 'ev to parley now, afore it's Bessie's turn.'

'Aye – we'll take 'er.'

The corporal held up a hand. 'No, I'll leave 'er whiles I go below. Look arter 'er now – she's a smart un. She done for the stropper 'n' all.'

A shout of nervous laughter went up.

'Yes, you'll 'ev to watch 'er.' The corporal paused, seemingly deep in thought. 'But then, the Admiral – 'e'll mebbe need to see she's all right. 'e don' know what she jes' done for the stropper – with 'is sari!' he added to another outburst of laughter. 'Mebbe 't is best if I takes 'er below – stands 'er on the lower gangway so 'e c'n see 'er for 'isself'.'

'You show 'er to 'im, Corp!'

The corporal appeared to make up his mind. 'Yes, I'll take 'er – and the lieutenant 'ere. Neither one 'll run if they knows the uvver 'll cetch it – they're main friendly, 'ev you noticed?'

Another shout of laughter went up.

Guy felt the blood pounding in his head; the pressure of her fingers around his arm increased.

'You take 'em,' one of the men said and, gesturing towards the summit, 'we cin see to it they doesn't git down!'

'Bessie 'll see to it!' the corporal replied and, turning to Harriet, he jerked his rifle, 'You first, lady,' and to Guy, 'then you – sir. I'll be jes' be'ind.' He looked at Harriet again, 'Don' try nothin', lady, or I'll 'ev to poke 'im –' He thrust the bayonet deliberately forward, barely missing Guy's arm, then pulled it back with a jerk. 'You won't try nothin' now, will you lady?'

Harriet stared at him icily.

The corners of his lips drew down again. 'All right then, lady. 'ard a-starboard!' He pointed the rifle towards the slope down to their right. She released her grip on Guy's arm, held up the trailing hem of her dress and, looking at the ground, started picking her way towards the slope. Guy followed. She stepped very slowly, making elaborate pauses at every boulder and bush – to save his shoulder he thought, knowing how swiftly she could move if she wished. He could feel the point of the bayonet in his back, coming and going and sliding over different areas as the corporal walked; it urged him forward faster than Harriet was going and, as they started down a steeper section of the slope, he came up beside her.

'You'll 'ev to go quicker'n that!' the Corporal called to her.

'Come and show me!' she flashed back.

The pressure of the bayonet increased suddenly; he felt the point breaking through his flesh and instinctively arched his back.

She saw it and swung round, almost screaming, 'What have

you done?'

'*Sorry* – lady!'

She looked anxiously at Guy as she increased her pace to take the lead again.

'That's right, lady! You cetches on quick, thet's the truth!'

The cut from the bayonet was as nothing compared with the pain in his shoulder every time his weight moved. He struggled against waves of pain to think constructively; two against one, and the brief incident when the order of march had nearly changed reminded him of a prank he had played as a child with his sister against unwary newcomers. He wondered how to explain it to her without telling the corporal as well, and how they might contrive to re-arrange the order.

He saw her stumble slightly on loose shale. '*Zut*!' she exclaimed.

She was establishing the means of communication! He increased his pace to come up with her, and said rapidly, '*Plus tard – si tu vas derrière lui – le m'agenouillerais – tu le pousseras, fort*!'

'*Compris*.' she replied.

He heard the corporal's boots close behind and felt the bayonet again painfully near the wound it had made before. 'Stow it!' The voice was vibrant with suppressed ferocity.

'I simply asked her not to go so fast,' he said, affecting a grunt of pain, 'I have a broken collar-bone.'

'You'll 'ev an 'ole through it too if there's any more jebber-in'.'

They approached the iron bridge running around the western rock face where the ancient galleries had crumbled, and the corporal directed her curtly towards it. She mounted the bridge carefully, looked back for a moment, then set out around the cliff. They followed. To the right the ground fell away until they were balancing over a sheer drop to the base of the rock. Ahead in the darkness was the darker entrance to the end of the gallery system; bats flitted and wheeled above, appearing and disappearing into declivities or caves in the rock.

She paused as she reached the end of the ironwork before entering the gallery, and looked back, 'I'd rather not go in there first.'

'You came up this way, lady.'

'I followed the sentry – please don't make me go in there first.'

'It's *please* now, is it?'

Guy felt the point of the bayonet pressing; he moved forward against her.

She realized what was happening and turned quickly into the gallery. Their footsteps echoed between the high wall and the rock face to their left. Two bats appeared very suddenly, swooping low, causing them a start of surprise.

'Very quiet, the Admiral,' the corporal said after a moment.

'I don't suppose he wants to alarm you,' Guy replied.

'P'raps 'e 'esn't got 'ere yet.' There was a meaning edge to the tone.

Guy had a feeling that the man knew there was no naval brigade waiting below. 'We shall see!' He reflected on the consequences: Harriet the man needed, but not himself. Once they were down and away from the lower sentries, his own chances were slim indeed.

They came to the first of the bamboo ladders connecting the gaps where the gallery floor had fallen away. It was a long one. Harriet was gathering in her dress, about to extend her foot to the first rung when the corporal snapped, 'Wait!'

She looked round.

There was a pause as the man seemed to calculate the chances. It was evident the ladder would not take more than one person at a time, and beyond it the rock wall made a slight curve inwards where it might just be possible to shelter from a rifle shot – particularly a shot made from the middle of a swaying ladder.

'Come back 'ere, lady!' the corporal said and, as Guy turned sideways to let her squeeze past, he did the same, his back to the rock face, his rifle pointing to his left so that the bayonet nudged Guy's ribs still. 'Don't try nothin' now,' he went on as she attempted to move by without touching him. 'You foller us this time!'

'All right,' she said stonily.

Guy felt the bayonet urging him on. As he turned, he saw that she had reached a position in the rear of the corporal; the order was right – it was now or never! His heart thumped. He stepped forward to the edge of the gallery floor, feeling the pressure of the bayonet ease, bracing himself for the torture he must inflict on his shoulder.

'*Maintenant*!' he said softly and, moving forward in a pretence of stepping on to the ladder, dropped instead sideways to his hands and knees, gasping with pain as his right arm gave way beneath him. From black vortices of nausea he heard the rifle go off very close, and felt the corporal's shins hard against his side. He was already off balance, and he fell towards the ladder, hearing the snap of breaking bamboo, and Harriet scream.

She had one arm around his waist and was tugging at his left shoulder with her other hand, trying to draw him out of the abyss of pain, but every time she pulled, he sank in deeper. She sobbed with the effort.

He heard Heighurst's voice as if in a dream, 'Hold on – I'm coming!' and her reply from very close, '*No*! The other pole will go!'

Guys upper body was lying across something thin and hard and none too steady; he wished he could roll off it on to a less painful couch.

'Guy,' she sobbed, 'you must help me. I can't hold you, Guy – '

He must try and help, but what did she want? Every time she moved waves of nausea enveloped him; why would she not leave him?

'You must try –'

He must try. She wanted him to shift towards her. Perhaps she would leave him alone then. He attempted to roll her way, feeling her tug at his arm as he did so.

'That's it! Once more now!'

He jerked over on to his left side, feeling a solid surface beneath his ribs at last, and hearing Heighurst shout, 'Bravo!' She started crying. He wondered suddenly where the corporal was.

'Where is he?' he called.

No one answered, but he heard voices and a stir of movement, and a rope thudding down near him. He turned his head, and saw a figure teetering above. It came closer and bent down, and he recognized Heighurst's moustaches.

'How are you, old chum?'

'I fancy I've broken my collar-bone,' Guy replied, trying to keep his voice steady and to remember what on earth was happening.

'Let's get him away from the edge,' the marine said, and eased his hands down gently under Guy's chest and back.

'Where is he?' Guy repeated.

'Your escort – where he belongs I fancy by now.'

'He went over so easily,' Harriet said, helping Heighurst to slide him towards her. 'He didn't make a sound.'

He remembered the bamboo ladder and the crack as it had given way.

'He looked round as I pushed,' she went on, the words tumbling out in a way he had not heard from her before. 'I was terrified. Oh, his eyes! But it was too late – he had lost his balance – his gun went off as he fell. I think he didn't cry out because he was not going to give us that satisfaction. He just disappeared without a sound – it was uncanny – with that foul look. I heard a stone bouncing away down the rock, that was all.' She half laughed, half sobbed. 'I thought you would follow. You broke one side of the ladder, you were lying half off the edge on the other side. I just caught you – you fainted.'

'He was the kannapaddi,' he said.

Her eyes widened.

'Are you certain?' Heighurst asked, straightening.

'Perfectly. I don't know his name, but I could not be more certain.' He drew his knees up, and eased his back against the rock face. 'Give me a hand.'

'Are you all right?'

'Lord, no! Just help me up!'

He pulled himself to his feet with Heighurst's arm, clenching his teeth against searing pain, but thankful that the vortex had receded. 'How on earth did you get here?' He saw Basset and Neera and Evan and Farrow watching from the other side of the gap.

'We walked!' The marine brought a hand up to his moustache. 'We heard the most frightful bobbery up there and thought you might need a helping hand. The johnny at the foot assisted by blowing out the brains of his chum down there. He's with us here.' He stooped to the rope which had been thrown across the gap and took a turn with it around a spur of rock to let the others balance across the single bamboo to join them. 'And now – for the loolā!'

'I've no idea what you mean,' Harriet said, turning from him to Guy, 'but first we must get a sling on that arm.'

Basset evidently had the same thought, for he had already removed his shirt and was standing on it with one foot, ripping it up from an existing tear.

When she had tied the strips together and arranged it around his neck and arm to her satisfaction they started along the gallery back towards the plateau.

Realizing suddenly which way they were heading, she stopped. 'You're not going up there again, surely?'

Guy smiled. 'I fancy it may be rather different this time.' He nodded towards Heighurst and the men behind. 'Part of the Admiral's force. And besides, you've just pushed their chief overboard!'

She stared. 'Was he – ? Not Brewer – ?' She started walking again. 'What a perfectly odious little man he was.'

He grinned. 'It's not the pleasantest of tasks – ship's police –'

'*He* was well suited!'

'– spending their lives between the devil and the deep blue sea.'

'We know which he chose. But where d'you suppose he was taking us?'

'You were his passport to escape.' He wondered. 'On the other hand, perhaps he didn't really know, perhaps it was his conscience that made him lose his head – like the old king here, Kaasyapa.'

'Kaasyapa?'

He smiled. 'Remind me to read you the *Mahawansa* some day.'

Neera's voice came from behind, 'I suspect it was the demons of this place, you know.'

'There'll be a few more after tonight,' Guy replied.

'Oh, yes, I dare say you are right.'

They stepped on to the iron ladder at the end of the gallery and balanced round in silence. From way above on the summit they heard discordant voices punctuated by screams, and suddenly from the plateau ahead the rattle of the Nordenfelt very close and loud, followed by yelling.

The eruption was sudden and brief. By the time they had reached the end of the bridge and were working their way up the slope towards the plateau, all sounds from there had ceased. It was ominously quiet. Guy, helped by Harriet, and trailing behind the others, watched Heighurst with drawn revolver spread the men behind cover along the line of the top of the slope, then rise and walk forward. He waited with drawn breath for the burst from the machine gun. It didn't come. Instead, he heard Heighurst's calm accents, 'Lay down your guns! Move away from the Nordenfelt! There's a platoon in the bushes!'

Not a sound greeted the words. Guy saw Basset and Farrow and Evan rise from their positions behind cover and move forward with levelled rifles. Neera followed. By the time he and Harriet arrived, the guard had been disarmed, and lined up against their hut, while the men of the working party, white and brown, were crowding around, beginning to yell abuse at their former masters. Heighurst silenced them with the threat of his revolver, and ordered them off the plateau to the summit. Telling off Evan to watch the guard, he followed with Basset and Farrow towards the cliff face.

'We're coming too,' Guy shouted.

Heighurst looked back, then up at the towering rock above. 'You'll never make it.'

'Of course we shall,' Harriet called back from beside him, and turning said grimly, 'what does he think I came up here for.'

Thinking of her re-united with Vaneyke, Guy felt a sudden reluctance to go on. She was so close, he didn't want to let her go. The feeling passed, replaced by insistent, nostalgic regret: he remembered the promise of their first meeting – so long ago now it seemed – and the timeless stroll through the ruins of Pollanarua, and their bathe, and knew it was coming to an end. It was as though he were walking her towards a huge, dark liner about to sail and take her out of his life.

She nudged closer against his arm and looked up, 'After all, I did come to see Robbie.' Her tone was almost apologetic. He wondered if she had read his thoughts, and wondered how she felt.

He smiled. 'And so did I.'

'Poor Guy! What a dance we have led you!'

'I have enjoyed every minute.'

'And so have I.'

She knew too.

They came to where Heighurst and the others were waiting

for the last of the working party to start up the rubble below what appeared from the way the men were swarming up to be ladders set into the cliff. At the edge of the rubble, which he saw now was composed chiefly of old brickwork, the body of a man lay sprawled, his legs twisted up at an unnatural angle over a boulder.

There was a glint in Heighurst's eye. 'You'll never make it.' He gestured towards the climbing men. 'It's a smart scramble up the bricks – after that the ladders are vertical. Shall you use your teeth?'

'I'll get up,' Guy replied, brute obstinacy replacing reason. Damned if Heighurst was going to tell him what he could do – and damned if Harriet were going up without him.

Harriet was looking anxiously into his face but, seeing his expression, her lips broke into that imperfect and seductive smile. 'Of course we'll manage it.'

Heighurst bowed. 'You will forgive me, if I do not wait.'

Neera came up. 'I shall wait for you. I shall go up last of all and push if you need me!'

Guy remembered the little clergyman's extreme reluctance to go anywhere near the rock when they had seen it first that afternoon in the rays of the westering sun, and wondered what had brought him even this far. 'I'm obliged,' he smiled. It was his flock, no doubt. He tried not to think of what they might find up there but, reminded of the singing that had started the rebellion, he wondered if more might not help to calm the uproar they could still hear from way above. He looked round for Evan, and called to him, 'How about another hymn?'

Heighurst was beginning to scramble up the rubble; he looked back briefly, nodding.

Evan paused for a moment, then threw back his dark head and started, 'Rock of ages, cleft for me. . . .'

Others came in after a moment from the cliff face and, by the time Farrow and Basset were scrambling after Heighurst, answering voices were sounding from the summit. Following over the loose bricks and boulders, and hearing the chorus through waves of pain, Guy had a sensation of forces greater than himself, drawing him on. The pain ran in counterpoint to his determination. Harriet, her dress gathered in one hand, scrambled up to one side of him; Neera was somewhere behind.

It was not so difficult as it had looked from below; steps of a kind had been fashioned in the rubble and he found he could claw himself up with his left hand without undue strain.

Arriving at the foot of the first vertical ladder, which he was glad to see was made of iron, he paused to take breath and replenish his resources.

'It's not necessary,' she said quietly. 'Robbie will come down, I'm sure I'll persuade him.'

He stretched high and seized a rung with his left hand, and started climbing. When he had risen sufficiently to bring the hand to eye level he paused and, releasing his grip, clutched up for the next rung and took another step, repeating the laborious process again and again, uncomfortably aware as he mounted of the drop behind to the heaped rubble where the body lay.

By the time he reached the top of the ladder his left biceps was aching; he tried to wedge himself against a spur of rock for a moment to ease it, but felt himself slipping, and had to clutch at the iron again. The next ladder was a short distance to the right; he wondered how he could possibly heave himself that way when he felt Harriet's hand in the small of his back. The pressure was firm and reassuring. He paused, then released his grip and, finding her support sufficient, began leaning towards the right until he could turn himself enough to catch hold of a rung; he heard her draw in her breath, and wanted to look round and nod, but it was all he could do to hold on with his one hand and slide his legs towards the foot of the ladder. Fortunately, there was a sloping projection of the rock face on which he found he could rest for a while to relieve his muscles. He started up again in the same way as he had climbed the first rungs, beginning to wonder if Heighurst had not been right; if his one good arm gave out before the summit, or if he blacked out again as he had in the gallery, the prospect did not bear thinking of.

He concentrated on each rung as he ascended, his awareness narrowing to the rough, corroded iron and the cold rock, and the singing which had become a part of the night, and Harriet just below.

'. . . while I draw this fleeting breath, when mine eyes are closed in death. . . .'

As he was beginning to feel he could pull himself up no

further unless he found somewhere to rest and ease the breaking muscles in his left hand and arm, he saw through a haze over his eyes that he was at the end of the ladder system, and that the cliff face, which had been vertical or overhanging, was beginning to slope in towards the summit. The next part of the way was by steps cut into the rock itself, leading across the brow and tending upwards. Thankfully, he steadied his feet in the lowest of these and leant in against the slope of the rock, grateful that there was no wind, but not caring to look down.

'Are you all right?' she shouted up.

'Capital!' he replied. No – mad, he thought, undeniably, perfectly mad.

The hymn had stopped and it was strangely quiet. He wondered if Heighurst had reached the top. The sky was very bright, but the cliff against which he was resting shut him off from the moon. He wondered for an instant whether he were suspended in some silent, pain-induced delirium; the next moment he heard cheering from above, roar after roar, and reality returned: Heighurst had reached the top. He pushed himself cautiously upright and started out along the path of incised steps. It was a relief not to have to grasp and heave any more, but he would have been happier had there been something to clutch if he lost balance; there was nothing above or below except the smooth rock.

As he searched before his feet for each step, he could not help being aware of the vista stretching away beyond and far below the slope of the face – an endless panorama of moonlit foliage relieved here and there by the sheen of water or dark areas where rising ground or taller trees intervened; it was a sparkling scene, as resplendent in its clarity and velvet-black shadow as he knew the colours would be by daylight. He thought again of Kaasyapa gazing down on just such a still, warm night over the extent of his domains, and seeing in their tranquility images of his own guilt. Everything came down to imagination – of the past or of the future. He thought of Harriet; he could hear her every now and again as she followed. It was difficult to imagine his own future without even the prospect of seeing her.

He wanted to look round to gauge how she was coping with her long, torn dress and the height, but he couldn't turn; every movement had to be examined for the least strain on his shoulder; it would have been difficult even to look down, but that was the last thing he intended. He knew what was there: the slope to the line of the rock overhang below this mushroom-like top, then nothing until the half-way plateau and the body of the man who had somersaulted down to them from about where they were now. He heard again that frightful sound as the man's brains were expelled from their split cage, and thought of Vaneyke leaving his body and his head and brains behind as he travelled to another plane. Where was the real man if not in his head and imagination? Was everything on the human plane a product of the imagination of the brain, and was three another, more real, *timeless* plane that could only be reached by deliberately undermining the brain's control? Another sense perhaps – one that was normally dormant, but could be awakened if the other senses were damped, to enable one to 'see' the eternal harmonies and resolve the 'mystery' created by the brain, therefore insoluble by the brain?

He realized that the cut steps were coming to an end, and made out another of the vertical iron ladders set in the rock; looking up, he saw foliage and tufts of grass.

He heard Harriet's voice, 'The last lap!'

'I look forward to seeing Heighurst's face,' he called back.

'The impossible takes a little longer,' Neera called from behind her. 'By Jove, I shall always remember Lieutenant Heighurst saying so. I thought he was boasting you know, but now I see it is true – at any rate as far as the Royal Navy is concerned!'

'Hoist on his own petard!' Harriet said.

Guy stretched up for the highest rung, and started climbing.

Heighurst was waiting for him at the top, the moonlight around his hair leaving his face in deep shadow; one hand was stretched down to help him. 'Our wounded hero gains the summit,' he breathed, 'to tell the truth, you may be of some assistance – flag lieutenant suit –!'

Guy hauled himself up the last rungs and on to the grass gasping with pain. Now that he had reached the top – or what appeared to be the lowest of several grass-grown slopes ascending to the uppermost level – he wondered how on earth he had managed it. He was giddy with pain, and the sustained effort of fighting it.

Beyond Heighurst he saw and heard a cheering, roaring wall

of people; as the marine thrust out his other hand to steady him, they began jostling closer. It was like a transformation scene – one moment alone in the shadow of the cliff, the next in brilliant moonlight surrounded by shouting men and women, white and brown, wearing a fantastic variety of costumes, the moon high over their backs painting lights on their hair and shoulders and arms, and making patterns in the tall spear grass. The trees which had looked so small from below, reared up overhead black and silver, and beyond on the higher plateaux he could see the overgrown ruins of walls and other buildings such as they had found at the base of the rock.

Heighurst turned and held up his arm in an attempt to keep the crowd back, then swung round quickly as Harriet came up. The noise stilled as the crowd became aware of her; everyone was staring or shoving and craning their necks to get a better view. She smiled. Despite her torn dress and flowing hair, she looked regal, Guy thought; her bearing and the fine structure of her face and her slim figure gave an impression of quality which no creases or rock dust could remove.

In the silence Heighurst started to address the crowd, 'Here is the flag lieutenant to Admiral Bousfield' – gesturing towards Guy – 'he will be able to tell you better than I –'

His voice was drowned by shouts of 'the Admiral!' and ''e's 'ere!' and from the Sinhalese excited yells in their own tongue as they saw Neera arriving from the ladder. Again they swarmed closer. For a moment of alarm Guy thought that he and Harriet, Neera and Heighurst would be crowded off the edge of the cliff they had ascended so laboriously, but he realized the faces and the calls were friendly. His left arm was seized, and he felt other hands and arms about his legs, lifting him bodily. He ground his teeth and stilled a cry of pain as he was raised to the shoulders of two bluejackets; he put his left hand down on a head to steady himself.

'For he's a jolly good fellow!' the crowd roared.

He felt himself being carried through them towards the centre of the plateau. Looking round to see what had become of Harriet, he found she was perched on the shoulders of a rival group, which was yelling, 'For *she*'s a jolly good fellow!' The din was tremendous.

Directly the first chorus ceased, he pulled the ear of his left-side steed and, as the man looked up, called to him, 'the commander?'

'The commander –' the man repeated, and the cry was taken up by several of those around, then by Harriet's adherents. He felt the pace of progress increase, and closed his eyes against waves of agony through his right side. It was no good trying to tell them, they wouldn't understand in their present mood – or even hear him. He could only hope they would soon reach wherever it was Vaneyke had made his quarters.

Their pace slowed as they came to a steeper slope up to another level; his bearers leant forward and grabbed at clumps of the tall grass to haul themselves up with.

He took the opportunity to shout, 'I can walk!'

They paid no heed, but hauled themselves on doggedly, amidst chanting that began to sound hysterical. 'The Ad-miral – the Ad-miral –!'

Nearing the top of the slope, he saw another level before rising terraces of grass and ruined walls; shrubs grew thickly around both sides, shutting out any view of the cliff edge, but giving glimpses of other levels and ruins to the left. The space between was more or less open except for a pair of trees close together in the centre; his attention was drawn and held to the exclusion of all else by two figures against their lower trunks; they were hanging from their wrists, one quite naked, his skin gleaming white, patterned with shadows from the branches above, the other all in shadow, naked above the waist but wearing a pair of dark serge trousers. Their heads lolled against the bark, their knees were bent, their lower legs askew in the grass; they were as still as death.

As he was borne nearer, he saw the naked one move faintly, attempting to raise his head; it lolled back again almost at once; his body twitched. The small movements, like the last, feeble struggle of a moth in water, were more horrifying than his first thought that they were dead. He rapped on the head below him; as the man looked up, he shouted, 'Cut them down!'

The eyes widened.

He pointed. 'Cut them down at once!'

One of the throng about him broke off and ran towards the two trees, he thought to carry out his instructions; instead, he stopped over the naked one and spat at him several times. There was a roar of applause. Out of the corner of his eye, Guy saw two figures darting from a clump of bushes to the left; turning briefly, he saw a Sinhalese girl, her dark hair streaming, clutching some torn material over her breasts as she ran from a thick-set sailor; she was screaming, whether in terror or make-believe he couldn't tell. They disappeared down a slope behind more bushes.

He rapped on his bearer's head again, and jerked his legs about violently to make it plain he intended to dismount. Looking up in some surprise, they lowered him. Immediately he started towards the two trees, soon followed by the throng, quieter now, and evidently wondering at the turn events had taken. Nearing the naked body, he saw that the skin which had shone so white from the side was dark at the back, streaked and blotched with weals and smeared blood; as he closed he saw whole areas about the shoulder as raw and moist as underdone beef; the man had been ropes-ended brutally. He was quite still; he wondered if the feeble movements had been a final spasm. Great fat flies had settled on the blood and others were homing in.

He turned back, sickened, to the group about him, and asked who had a knife. There was no response. 'Very well – you'll have to unlash him!' He stared at the nearest two, bearded men with square, but sunken, faces.

Their gaze dropped and they shambled forward. He saw Heighurst pushing his way through from the back, followed by Basset, and beyond them Harriet, borne by her jostling group like some ancient Saxon queen towards the slope to the upper level.

When he looked back at the naked man, he saw that he had half turned his head as if trying to see who it was that had ordered his release; the one eye visible was almost closed, the line of the cheek drawn and drained of blood; he couldn't see the mouth; the flayed, fly-hung meat of the shoulder was in the way. The head dropped back again.

A voice near him said, 'A snooper sir – for the commi'ee.'

Guy swung round. 'Have you proof?'

Whoever it was that had spoken remained silent.

Heighurst came up and, affecting to study the beaten man as one wrist was released from the lashings, breathed, 'We'll need to tread handsomely. It'll not take much for them to cut loose again.'

'Settling old scores,' Guy said.

'They're in a queer mood – I don't care for it.'

As if to illustrate the point, they heard from the other side of the rock the agonized screaming of a woman, shriek after shriek until suddenly it stopped leaving a profound silence.

Guy thought of Harriet and looked round, but shc and all her group had disappeared up to the next level. He turned to Heighurst. 'Look after these fellows, will you – this one's alive – I'd like to keep an eye on Harriet.'

The marine raised a brow at the Christian name. 'I would!'

Guy turned away, past the group who had been cheering him, now unnaturally hushed, and strode as fast as he could towards the slope to the higher level. Reaching it, he saw the grass trampled flat where they had ascended; he started up.

As he neared the top he saw a few yards beyond him the low, overgrown ruins of a wall such as he was becoming used to, and just the other side of it the men who had been with Harriet standing silently, their backs towards him. There was a gap in the wall to his left, and he made for it, able to pull himself up the last few steps with thc branches of a bush there. On the other side of the wall, which had evidently formed a square at one time, the grass had been cropped, and in the centre a narrow platform had been constructed out of the old bricks some three feet high. Lying on this was the still figure of a man clothed in a single robe washed white by the moon. He knew at once that it was Vaneyke. Harriet was standing by his head, one hand on his brow, gazing down. It was like a tableau, so motionless were both figures.

He stood watching for a moment, not wishing to intrude, then he saw Harrict turn her head slightly as if looking for someone, or not quite certain of herself, and he stepped forward, slowly at first, still feeling that he was imposing on a private scene. There was no light of recognition in her eyes as she watched him approach, only anxiety.

He stepped to her side and looked down at Vaneyke, appalled by the sight; he was so emaciated. It was evident he had once been large, the bones of his arms and legs below the long robe, and the great broad cage of his ribs suggested more than ordinary size and power, but the flesh and muscle had withered, leaving hollows emphasized by the shadows cast by the moon. The skin of the face was discoloured with blotches, and stretched, taut and hollowed over the cheekbones; the eyes stared skywards from dark, sunken sockets. But despite, or perhaps in part because of, the collapse of the flesh it was the most powerful face Guy thought he had ever seen. The forehead was broad and high, the brows Mephistophelean over the deep eyes. The nose was arrogantly Roman, and below, the thin, determined line of the mouth and a massive crag of a chin, clean-shaven but darkening, suggested implacable resolution. Vaneyke was even more than he had been led to expect; he could believe everything he had heard about him.

'He's awfully cold,' Harriet said softly.

He looked at her.

'D'you think he's breathing?' she went on.

'If he's in a trance –' he started and, moving, turned so that he could take the attenuated wrist with his left hand. The arm was extraordinarily light. He tried to locate the pulse with his fingers, but could feel nothing; the skin was dry and cold.

She gazed at him anxiously.

He lowered the wrist, and turned to the silent, watching men. 'Is the surgeon here?'

They stared for a moment, then someone said, ''e went sir – next arter 'ardo.'

'Do any of you know – when the commander goes, when he meditates – can you feel his pulse?' He knew it was an absurd question as he asked it; he was out of his depth.

An old sailor with a petty officer's badge stepped forward slowly. 'I don't know 'bout 'is pulse, sir, but when 'e go aloft 'e don't breathe much – not so's you'd notice.'

Guy put his head on the great, upstanding chest, feeling the line of rib hard against his cheek; it was uncomfortably like mere skin and bone. He waited. He could feel no movement at all, no heartbeat, no breathing. He straightened and looked at the petty officer, who had moved opposite Harriet and was leaning over Vaneyke's face, his head cocked to one side as if listening.

After a moment the man straightened and looked at him, his eyes serious and rather wider, 'I reckon 'e's a-gorn this time, sir. There was times we thought we'd a-lorst 'im – this time I reckon we 'ave.'

Guy looked at Harriet. He thought he saw a tear glistening, then she had fallen over her husband's shoulders, her arms around him, shaking him, 'Robbie – Robbie – oh, Robbie – you *can't* –'

Guy had a sudden, certain knowledge he could not help her. He had accompanied her to the quay and seen her aboard; now she had gone. She had been so close. The strains of the hymn ringing about them as they ascended sounded again in his head '. . . when I soar through tracts unknown. . . .'

He had an image of Vaneyke hovering somewhere high above the rock, seeing them all down here around his still body, seeing Harriet heaving with sobs as she tried to shake him back to her. What did he feel for her now? Had he broken all the chains?

He remembered the words of the letter read in Harding's tent, 'It was not a physical distance, but the distance between time and no time, bodily consciousness and spiritual consciousness . . . it was as if I were floating most comfortably and happily in another sphere, as indeed I believe I was, in the trackless, signless zone. It was exceptionally bright, radiant with a light I cannot attempt to describe. . . .'

He looked up, so compulsive was the image. The moon was sharp and bright and cold as death.

. . . the extraordinary thing was, Trojan, they venerated him. Despite what his dereliction of duty caused them in suffering – suffering is not an adequate word, in fear and degradation and mutual suspicion and the loss of some of their best men, and practically all the officers – despite it all they could see something in him which enabled them to forgive, not simply forgive, but *look up to*. He still directed the course of the ship, and the whole expedition to Sigiriya was his idea, to found his own priesthood there – although no doubt it suited the committee! The question that bothers me is how he continued in ignorance of their barbarous practices. All the Curlews we have spoken to are assured he knew nothing of what was taking place and yet all his officers had been disposed of in one way or another – with the single exception of the obscene Brewer – while an ignorant blackguard of a disrated PO, Brown, had been appointed by the committee as number one. It's curious how they sought to preserve the forms and trappings of authority. Perhaps they did succeed in hoodwinking him. But I've a nasty idea there are as many roads to Nibbana as there are to hell, and the smartest with the blinkers on!

At all events he had a number of disciples, mostly young ords and other youngsters, it seems. I fancy they'll be allowed their discharge and not too many questions asked. The Admiral's setting up an enquiry out here; between you and me they're anxious to dispose of it quick before any reporters or MPs come out. They'll not make much of it. The only surviving officer is Brewer. They found him the next morning in a cave above the galleries which he shared with swarms of wasps and bats and murals of old King Kaasyapa's favourites! I'd not call him a survivor, he laughs and clowns all the time and pretends he don't know anything or anyone and wears whatever he fancies most outrageous – but he always had a streak of low cunning, now I think back, and I've more than a suspicion it's an act. I mean, what else could the fellow do? He's nowhere else to go, it's his only way out. I've tried to get him to recognize me, but he always goes into fits and calls me 'Admiral'. Some of the others didn't get off so lightly – although when you think about it perhaps they did. Theirs was quick at least. We found the MAA's body on the rocks below some days after, and his injuries were not all caused by his fall. There were two others near him also horribly mutilated. We buried them and all the other committee men and informers – if you had heard some of the diabolical acts they were responsible for!

Enough of that, I must try and forget. I never shall. It's strange how everything seemed to fit into place as I told you, as if *meant*. The final link was Neera. It was he who suggested Evan singing the hymn that started the revolt – a favourite with him apparently. Heighurst never believed the sound would carry, but Neera persisted – thank heavens – and fortunately it was a beautifully calm night. There must be something about sound over rock for they heard him better from the top than we did from halfway. We had rather a touching little ceremony when we parted with the splendid fellow. We, that is Heighurst and the sergeant and I, and Harriet and Lord ffort and all, presented him with an illuminated scroll raising him to Knight Commander of the CCG – for your elucidation the Order of Christian and Cricketing Gentlemen! He was tickled pink – or perhaps I should say a darker shade of brown – and looked as if he were about to shed the uncricketing tear, but pulled himself up in time and made a long speech about the marvellous cities of his ancestors. They *are* marvellous, too, Trojan, it's difficult to imagine why more is not known of them in England – for my money Pollanarua, even in ruin, beats the pyramids hands down –

He paused as he thought of the great illuminated Buddha figure at the Jetawaranama temple, and Harriet's eyes from the water.

As for Harriet, I fear she'll take a long time to find herself again. She was fearfully cut up, and seemed to blame herself. I tried to tell her there was nothing she could have done. 'Before', she kept on saying, 'you idiot!' I fancy we've lost a good man in a scrap in Vaneyke. He was halfstarved when we found him, more than half starved, but what presence! Even in death. He was too good a man for our peacetime Admiralty, born a century too late, I'd say. I can't help wondering where he is now.

Apropos of the fearful results of the complete turnover in authority he wished on the ship, I asked Basset 'how much for your socialist ideas now?' He said something of the kind is bound to happen in any revolution, which was why he personally was a Fabian socialist. I ask you! I don't think he would have admitted it before our little picnic at Sigiriya. 'A what?' I asked. He was most surprised – 'you an edicated gentleman', and so on! Anyhow it turns out that Bernard Shaw and a number of other brainy men are socialists who call themselves after an old Roman General called Fabius who achieved victory by delaying tactics. I promised Basset not to let out so much as a whisper about his guilty secret if on his part instead of attempting to wear away my brass port surround he spent some time explaining his credo to me. What with Buddhism and Fabianism I might turn out an edicated gentleman one way or another after all! But I fancy I've had the odd lesson already.

You'll see me in the despatches, by the by, but *you* need not believe them – Old Sax showed me what he had written; he came on the scene the next morning you see with a pukka naval brigade. What he says is all untrue! It was *her* I was after, only her, I never would have gone up else!

He thought of her again as she had been in the moonlight at the bathing place. He knew her so well, yet hardly at all. And he would never see her again. Where would she go? Not India. It was India that had done this to her. He thought of how he had prized the tight grip of her arms from Vaneyke's still form the next morning, and how she had walked away, numbed.

Sigiriya is a dreadful place, Trojan. The locals are absolutely right when they declare it haunted. It is – and by many more spirits now.

He looked up and gazed for a moment over Trincomalee Bay and the *Curlew* shining white and gold against the brilliant greens of the opposite shore; already she was looking a perfect little yacht. He was going to miss D'Arcy too, when they sailed.

I must now do my duty to Sober Island, Trojan, so shall close this description – it's a truer account than you'll find in the papers – or than will ever be allowed into the history books I dare say. I am halfway through painting the verandah here – with my left hand. Everyone who comes has a little duty, to open a new vista through the trees or build a bench for his successors, but this is all I'm good for at present, that and writing and thinking. Painting is a fine relaxation, one does not have to think.

I thank heaven this commission must be near its close now, I hope to see you before very many weeks have passed. Until then, *write* to me Trojan – of England and *fogs* and *ice* and *snow*!

He heard footsteps on the boards behind: Heighurst.

'Reasoned it all out?' The marine leant against the door-post gazing with his usual cynicism at the scribbled pages on the table.

'Go to the devil!'

The marine brought a hand up to twist the end of his moustaches. 'I believe I've seen enough of him for one commission.'

Images of flayed flesh rose in Guy's mind, and the still white form of Vaneyke staring upwards, and he turned away, overcome suddenly by thoughts of Harriet and her lonely journey, the Lord only knew where. Blindly he shuffled the pages of his letter together – 'Do you have doubts Mr Greville? Yes, you have imagination have you not? My husband has imagination.' – How many times must his mind return to their first evening? The ache was like a pit he kept falling into – a pit that he cherished, for when it filled there would be nothing of her left for him.

There was a long-drawn groan.

Was it him?

He heard Heighurst moving softly away.